FRONTIER DOCTOR TRILOGY

BOOK TWO

*B*ELOVED

PHYSICIAN

AL & JOANNA

LACY

Multnomah® Publishers

Sisters, Oregon

BELOVED PHYSICIAN
published by Multnomah Publishers, Inc.

© 2004 by ALJO PRODUCTIONS, INC.
International Standard Book Number: 1-59052-313-X

Cover design by Kirk DouPonce/UDG DesignWorks
Cover images by Robert Papp/Shannon Associates

Unless otherwise indicated, Scripture quotations are from:
The Holy Bible, King James Version

Multnomah is a trademark of Multnomah Publishers, Inc.,
and is registered in the U.S. Patent and Trademark Office.
The colophon is a trademark of Multnomah publishers, Inc.

Printed in the United States of America

For information:
Multnomah Publishers, Inc. • Post Office Box 1720 • Sisters, Oregon 97759

Library of Congress Cataloging-in-Publication Data

Lacy, Al.
    Beloved physician / by Al and JoAnna Lacy.
        p. cm. — (Frontier doctor trilogy ; bk. 2)
    ISBN 1-59052-313-X (pbk.)
    1. Denver (Colo.)—Fiction. 2. Married people—Fiction. 3. Physicians—
Fiction. 4. Nurses—Fiction. I. Lacy, JoAnna. II. Title.

    PS3562.A256B46 2004
    813'.54—dc22

                                            2003022088

04 05 06 07 08 09 10 — 10 9 8 7 6 5 4 3 2 1 0

We wish to dedicate this book to our good friend
and family physician, Dr. Terry Wade.
We also wish to express our heartfelt appreciation for the expert
medical advice he furnished for this book.
He is indeed our own beloved physician.

3 John 2

PROLOGUE

When the challenge of the Western frontier began luring men and women westward from the eastern, northern, southern, and midwestern states in the middle of the nineteenth century, they found a land that was beyond what they had imagined. From the wide Missouri River to the white-foamed shore of the Pacific Ocean, wherever they settled, they clung to the hope of a bright new beginning for their lives.

Often their hopes were dashed by fierce opposition from the Indians who had inhabited the land long before them. At times there was also struggle for survival against the hard winters and the loneliness of the vast frontier.

Those determined pioneers who braved the elements, the loneliness, and the attacks of the Indians, proved themselves to be a hardy lot and were unknowingly entering upon a struggle that would ultimately give their descendants control of half a continent.

In his book *The Winning of the West*, Theodore Roosevelt said, "The borderers who thronged across the mountains, the restless hunters, the hard, dogged frontier ranchers and farmers, were led by no one commander. They were not carrying out the plans of any far-sighted leader. In obedience to the instincts working half-blindly within their hearts, they made in the wilderness homes for their children."

These commendable accomplishments, however, were not without tremendous cost of life. Of all the perils confronting the settlers of the Wild West, serious illness, injuries from mishaps of countless number, and wounds from battles with Indians and outlaws were the most dreaded. The lack of proper medical care resulted in thousands of deaths.

The scarcity of medical doctors on the Frontier in those early years made life extremely difficult and sometimes unbearable. As towns were being established in the West, little by little, medical practitioners east of the wide Missouri caught the challenge of the Frontier and headed that direction.

Communities that grew around army posts and forts had the military doctors to care for them. But many towns had no doctors at all. However, as time passed, this improved. By the mid-1870s, towns of any size at all had at least one doctor. The larger towns had clinics, and a few even had hospitals.

Often the frontier doctor had to travel long distances at any hour—by day or night—in all kinds of weather. Time and again the doctor's own life was in jeopardy. He might ride on horseback or drive his buggy thirty miles or more to a distant home in the mountains, to a home in a small settlement on the prairie, or to a ranch or farm where he would care for a patient. He would perform surgery when needed, set broken bones, deliver a baby, or administer necessary medicines. Most of the time, he would sit with his patient for hours before leaving his or her side, then sleep on the return trip while his horse found the way home.

Quite often the frontier doctor's only remuneration consisted of fresh vegetables from a garden, maybe a jar or two of canned corn or beans, a plucked chicken, or a chunk of beef cut from a recently slaughtered steer. The successful frontier doctor was not only a hardy man, but was obviously dedicated to his profession.

In our third book of the Orphan Trains Trilogy, *Whispers in the Wind*, we introduced teenagers Dane Weston and Tharyn Myers, who were orphans living on the streets of New York City in the spring of 1871. After a period of separation, Dane and Tharyn eventually find each other again and decide to marry, and the story of the extraordinary events leading up to their wedding is told in *One More Sunrise*, book one of the Frontier Doctor trilogy.

"Luke, the beloved physician, and Demas, greet you."

COLOSSIANS 4:14

ONE

*I*n Denver, Colorado, the sun shone down from a crystal blue sky on Saturday, June 25, 1881. It was two o'clock in the afternoon.

To the west stood the magnificent Rocky Mountains with their snowcapped peaks and the restful green of pine and fir trees amid the cool gray of their stony crags. These mountain features seemed distant, yet were companionably close.

Puffy white clouds drifted on the summer breeze, and birds chirped in the branches of the tall cottonwoods and evergreens outside the white frame church building.

Inside, the pump organ was playing softly in accompaniment to Dottie Carroll as she sang a special wedding song. Dottie was the wife of Dr. Matthew Carroll, chief administrator of Denver's Mile High Hospital, and sister to Breanna Brockman, a longtime nurse at the hospital and wife of the best man.

Pastor Nathan Blandford stood on the platform, Bible in hand, and smiled at the happy faces in the packed sanctuary. He then looked down at Dr. Dane Logan, who stood on the floor to his left, sided by his best man, Chief United States Marshal John Brockman.

The pastor saw the nervousness in Dane Logan that grooms

always experienced when the bridal procession was about to appear.

Dane's heart was pounding in his chest as he fixed his gaze on those closed doors, and suddenly his mind flashed back just thirty-six days, to Saturday, May 21, when he stood on that very spot, expecting to see the bridal procession come through the doors any second.

His mouth went dry as he envisioned that awful moment when suddenly Tharyn's father, David Tabor, burst through the doors and ran into the auditorium, announcing that Tharyn had been abducted by four outlaws who left the message behind that they were going to kill her. Dane thought of how Tharyn had escaped the outlaws' hideout by the hand of God, and recalled the sweet reunion with her in Denver.

Suddenly, Dane was brought back to the present as the organist began playing the wedding march. He closed his eyes, took a deep breath, squared his shoulders, and focused once again on the doors at the rear of the auditorium, just as they were coming open.

He watched, a slight smile on his handsome face, as the wedding party wended its way forward, and told himself one would hardly guess that the first bridesmaid, Leanne Ross, was blind. Her eyes were fixed straight ahead and her hand was placed in the crook of the groomsman's arm. Her serene face was a joy to behold. The groomsman was Kenny Ross, her adoptive brother. They had both been adopted by the Ross family in Denver, who had also adopted other handicapped children. Kenny limped slightly on his wooden leg, but carefully guided his sister slowly down the aisle.

Leanne's dress was powder blue organza that dipped and swayed with each step. It had a square neck, trimmed with a satin ribbon that was a shade darker than the dress.

A few steps behind Leanne and Kenny were the second bridesmaid, Melinda Scott Kenyon, and her fiancé and second groomsman, Dr. Tim Braden. Melinda's dress was a copy of Leanne's, and a smile of delight was on the lips of both young women.

Standing close to the groom, the tall, dark John Brockman uttered a small gasp when his wife stepped through the doorway a few steps behind Tim and Melinda. She was even more beautiful than the day he had married her in that same church building ten years ago.

Breanna Brockman was Tharyn's matron of honor. Her organza dress was a light periwinkle blue with satin trim a shade darker around the neckline. Her blond hair was a shining halo on top of her head, and John's heart skipped a beat as he watched her move down the aisle, smiling at him.

Walking very carefully several steps behind Breanna were her two children. Eight-year-old Paul gingerly held a white satin pillow with the bride's ring tied securely to it with blue ribbons. He had been tutored many times over about his duty as ring bearer. His six-year-old sister, Ginny, walked at his side, strewing pink rose petals down the aisle.

Ginny was a small version of her lovely mother, both in looks and the dress she was wearing. When Breanna drew up to her place before the altar, she turned and looked at Paul and Ginny. She and John both smiled as they observed their precious children. A small sigh escaped Breanna's lips when both children reached the front without any mishaps.

When each person in the procession was in place, the organist raised the volume to announce the presence of the bride.

In the second row of pews, Kitty Tabor rose from her seat and looked back up the aisle. The crowd followed.

Tharyn and her father moved into the doorway, silhouetted against the bright sunlight that flowed through the vestibule windows.

In the bride's left hand was a bouquet of spring cut flowers.

She held onto her father's arm with the other hand and gave it a gentle squeeze. David Tabor looked at his beloved daughter, bent down, and placed a soft kiss on her cheek through her veil. "I love you, sweetheart. Thank you for coming into our home. From the moment we chose you off that orphan train, you have always been a source of joy to your mother and me."

Tharyn's eyes brimmed with tears. She smiled. "I love you too, Papa. You and Mama have given me such a special life. I will never forget what the two of you have done for me."

Father and daughter turned with nervous smiles gracing their faces and began their slow walk down the aisle.

Standing at the foot of the platform, Dane Logan was struck anew with Tharyn's beauty: both her outward physical beauty and, even more important, her inward spiritual beauty.

Tharyn was radiant in her white gown of organza over taffeta. A wide band of lace cupped her chin and edged the long, elegant sleeves. Her delicate veil of the same exquisite lace fell gracefully over her shoulders and down her slender back, ending in a small train.

Kitty was blinking at her tears and it was quite evident that her husband was also having a difficult time with his emotions.

With the sound of the organ filling the auditorium, Tharyn looked down the aisle and riveted her gaze on the young man she had loved for so long.

Dane's heart was pounding when his eyes met Tharyn's. He had come so close to losing his bride in the hands of the outlaws on what was supposed to be their wedding day, but this time nothing would prevent the marriage from taking place.

As Tharyn and her father drew closer, Dane breathed a prayer of thanks to the Lord for protecting her and delivering her from the outlaws.

When the bride and her father drew up, the organ stopped.

Pastor Nathan Blandford smiled down at father and daughter.

"Who gives this woman to be married to this man?"

David's throat was a bit constricted with emotion, but he managed to say, "Her mother and I."

Tharyn lifted the veil with her free hand and planted a tender kiss on his cheek.

David then placed Tharyn's hand in that of the groom. He gave a loving look to both of them, turned, and made his way toward Kitty.

Dane squeezed his bride's hand, let go of it, and offered her his arm. As they moved toward the platform steps, they smiled at each other, each knowing the other's thoughts: *At last, we are about to become husband and wife!*

TWO

At the reception in the church's fellowship hall, the bride and groom cut their wedding cake in front of the smiling crowd, fed each other a piece; then the guests began filing by slowly.

First in line were the groom's parents from Cheyenne, Dr. and Mrs. Jacob Logan, who exchanged hugs and kisses with Dane and Tharyn.

The well wishers took their time, speaking to the bride and groom as they came by.

Dane and Tharyn were pleased to see Pastor Mark Shane and his wife, Peggy. Shane pastored the church in Central City. He and Peggy knew that Dr. Dane and Tharyn would be transferring their membership to their church as soon as they returned from their honeymoon in Colorado Springs.

When everyone else had passed by, elderly Dr. Robert Fraser stepped up, his wife Esther at his side. With them was Nadine Wahl, the widow who had worked for Dr. Fraser for many years as his nurse and receptionist.

Nadine talked to them about her retirement when Tharyn would take over in her place after the Logans returned to Central City. Both Dr. Fraser and Nadine assured the newlyweds that they would fill in for them when they were needed, just as Dr. Fraser had done for Dr. Dane since he took over the practice.

The Frasers and Nadine also talked to the newlyweds about the house Dr. Dane had bought in Central City prior to the first wedding attempt, without Tharyn knowing it. They discussed how even though Dr. Dane wanted to surprise her, after her abduction and return to Denver, he felt he should tell her about it.

When Tharyn heard about the house, she immediately wanted to see it, so Dane took her to Central City and showed it to her, as well as introduced her to the Frasers and Nadine.

Soon the newlyweds changed clothes in separate Sunday school rooms, then in a hail of rice drove away in Dane's buggy—which had been all fixed up by some of the people with bright-colored paper streamers and a sign on the rear that said JUST MARRIED—and headed for the railroad station.

On Thursday, June 30, Dr. Dane Logan and his bride rode to Denver from Colorado Springs by train, then hopped in his buggy at the stable where horse and vehicle had been kept and headed west toward Central City.

As the buggy bounced along the road that climbed into higher country, Tharyn held onto her husband's arm and thought about her beautiful house in Central City. Suddenly time rolled back in her mind, and she was reliving that day she first saw the house...

When Dane turned off Main onto Spruce Street, she glanced at the sign and said, "Is this the street the house is on, or will we turn onto another one?"

Dane smiled at her. "This is the street, sweetheart. When we become husband and wife, we'll be living at 212 Spruce Street."

Tharyn watched the numbers on the houses, and when she spotted 212 up ahead, her heart picked up pace. When he pulled the buggy to a halt in the driveway, she sat speechless, just staring at the awesome house.

Seeing her eyes open wide but not hearing a comment, Dane was afraid he had made the wrong choice. Dropping the reins, he looked at her questioningly. "Wh-what's the matter, honey? Don't you like the house?"

His bride-to-be turned to him with tears in her eyes.

Dane swallowed hard. "What is it? What's wrong?"

She laid a hand on his arm. "Oh, darling, there's nothing wrong! I—I'm just in awe of it! What a beautiful house you have provided for us! I never dreamed it was anything like this!" She sniffed and shook her head. "See these? These are happy, happy tears!"

Dane let out a big sigh of relief. "Boy, you had me worried, little lady. I sure didn't want to do anything to disappoint you!"

Tharyn cupped his face in her hands and kissed him soundly. "You, my dear, are wonderful! I already love this house. Take me inside. I want to see it."

When Dane lifted his bride-to-be out of the buggy, she stood gazing at the house, memorizing each detail. "It isn't very old, is it?"

"No. Just five years old. As you can see, the people who owned it previously took very good care of it."

"That's for sure," she said, still running her gaze from side to side and top to bottom.

The frame house was painted a soft gray with brilliant white trim. The many mullioned windows sparkled in the late spring sunshine.

Tharyn noticed that there were no curtains adorning the windows and made a mental note that this would be one of the first decorating chores she would attend to. Her happy heart looked forward to making this fine house into a warm and cozy home. Already she was planning a flowing garden beside the wide front porch as they ascended the stairs leading to the front door.

Seconds later, standing in the parlor, Tharyn stared around her in amazement then smiled at the love of her life. "You just never cease to astonish me, darling. This house is so lovely."

"Well as you can see, the previous owners took their furniture, curtains, drapes, and decorations, and I haven't purchased any of these things because I knew that was something you would want a hand in doing."

She embraced him and they kissed. Tharyn smiled. "It will be my joy and pleasure, Doctor, to fill this house with whatever will make *both* of us happy."

Dane chuckled joyfully and placed a kiss on the tip of her nose. "When we get back to Denver, we'll go to all three furniture stores and both department stores. You can pick out everything you want, and we'll have it delivered between now and the wedding. Two weeks should be long enough to get most everything delivered here from Denver. When we get back from our honeymoon, you can enjoy turning this house into *our* home."

"Oh, Dane, I will love doing that. Thank you, sweetheart." She paused. "Of course, I'll have to do it on my off hours from working at the office, since Nadine is retiring right away."

Dane grinned. "I have an idea you'll get it done pretty fast, anyhow."

"I sure will. Well, I want to see the rest of the house."

Dane slipped his arm around her waist and led her into all the other rooms in the spacious two-story house.

Suddenly back to the present, Tharyn saw that they were pulling into Central City on Main Street. She squeezed Dane's arm. "Oh, darling, I just love this town already! I'm going to love living here as Mrs. Dane Logan, and as the nurse-receptionist for that handsome young doctor!"

Dane chuckled. "I know we're going to be very happy, sweetheart. And it's going to be great having you working with me at the office."

She looked into his eyes. "May I remind you, Doctor, that we agreed I would work as your nurse and receptionist for two to three years; then we would start our family. Of course at that time, you will have to find someone else to take my place."

Dane took hold of her hand and squeezed it gently. "Sure. Two to three years will be enough. I most certainly want to have children. I at least want a girl who looks like you and a boy who looks like me."

Tharyn laughed, then looked up ahead at Dane's office. "Darling, could we go to the house first, so I can freshen up before we see Dr. Fraser and Nadine?"

Dane nodded. "Certainly."

"Thank you, darling. And besides, I haven't seen our house since all the furniture and other things we ordered have been delivered."

Moments later, as they approached 212 Spruce Street, Tharyn could hardly sit still on the seat. "Oh, I'm so excited!"

"Me too," said Dane, smiling broadly. "But remember, honey, everything is sort of piled in the rooms. It'll take some time to sort it all out and put it where you want it. The furniture has been placed in the proper rooms, if they did as I left instructions, but you are going to be one busy lady getting it all organized."

"I will absolutely love setting everything in order, darling. Nothing could make me happier!"

"Good girl! You should be superbly happy. Just keep in mind that anything you need help with, you save until I'm home, okay?"

"Yes, Dr. Logan, sir," she said, her eyes sparkling with delight.

Some thirty minutes later, Dane guided the buggy up to the hitch rail in front of the office and hopped out. Somebody in a passing wagon called out to him and waved. He smiled and waved back, then dashed around to the other side and helped Tharyn down.

She paused and looked up at the sign next to the door: *Dane Logan, M.D.*

She sighed. "Oh, it's so wonderful that you have your own practice, just like you dreamed when we lived as street waifs in the alley in Manhattan so long ago."

Dane grinned. "It sure is wonderful, sweetheart. The Lord has been so good to me. Just think! I've got my own practice, and I'm married to the most beautiful woman He ever created. What more could I ask for?"

Tharyn laughed. "There are a lot of husbands who would argue with you on that 'most beautiful woman' bit."

Dane clipped her playfully on the chin. "Can I help it if those husbands are fooled?"

Laughing together, they entered the office and found Nadine Wahl at her desk, doing some paperwork. She looked up and smiled. "Well, if it isn't the newlyweds! Welcome home, boss and boss's wife!"

They both greeted her warmly. She said she hoped they had a wonderful honeymoon and told them that Dr. Fraser was with a patient in the examining room at the moment. He should be finished in a few minutes.

While they were talking about Tharyn taking over Nadine's job, Dr. Fraser came out of the examining room with his patient, a middle-aged man. Dr. Fraser introduced the man to Dr. Dane and Tharyn. The man shook hands with Dr. Dane and told him that Dr. Fraser was just telling him a lot about the new doctor. He said he was glad to meet Dr. Logan and his wife, then went on his way.

As Dr. Dane was thanking Dr. Fraser for filling in for him, a wagon thundered to a halt outside. A young man in his early twenties hopped down from the driver's seat and dashed toward the door. A second man on his knees in the wagon bed bent over what would seem to be another person. A sign on the side of the wagon read: *HOLTON COAL MINE—CENTRAL CITY, COLORADO.*

"Something's happened at the mine!" exclaimed the older physician and rushed to the open door as the young man bounded onto the boardwalk, his face coated with coal dust and his eyes wide.

As he approached the older doctor, he said, "Dr. Fraser! Ben Frye fell down one of the mine shafts! He's hurt bad!"

Dr. Dane was quickly at Fraser's side, and the elderly doctor said, "Greg, this is Dr. Dane Logan. He owns the practice now. Dr. Logan, this is Greg Holton, the son of Kirby Holton, who owns the mine. Ben Frye is the mine's foreman."

"Glad to meet you, Greg," said Dr. Dane. "Let's see about Mr. Frye." As he spoke, he rushed out the door to the wagon with young Holton on his heels. Dr. Fraser followed as hastily as he could.

The two women looked on from the open office door as Dr. Dane bounded over the tailgate, told the kneeling man who he was, and began examining the mine foreman, a man in his midfifties.

At the side of the wagon, Greg Holton said, "Dr. Logan, this man next to Ben is Art Berman, the assistant foreman."

Dr. Dane looked up briefly, nodded at Berman, then went back to his examination.

Greg said, "Art, I'm gonna run home and tell Dad about Ben's fall. He will want to come and see him."

"Sure," said Art. "He'd want to know as soon as possible about this."

Greg hurried away.

After looking a moaning Ben Frye over and asking him questions about his pain, Dr. Dane said, "Mr. Berman, we have a stretcher in the office. I'll get it, and I'll need you to help me carry him inside."

Berman nodded. "Certainly, Doctor."

Just as Dr. Dane hopped out of the wagon bed, Nadine Wahl came out the door, carrying the stretcher. Dr. Dane thanked her, took it, and as Greg Holton opened the tailgate, he laid the stretcher at the rear of the wagon bed.

Tharyn told Nadine she would help her husband with the injured mine foreman, and asked if she could get an apron. Nadine guided her to the examining room behind the office and soon had her clad in a starched full-length apron with shoulder straps, which she wore over her dress.

A few minutes later, while Dr. Dane and Art Berman were carrying the stretcher bearing the mine foreman into the examining room, Tharyn and Nadine were finishing their task of placing a clean sheet on the nearest examination table.

Dr. Fraser came in behind the two men carrying the stretcher. When they laid the stretcher on the table, they carefully lifted Ben Frye enough for the elderly physician to slip the stretcher out from under him. Dr. Dane caught sight of Tharyn wheeling a medicine cart up beside the table.

Nadine commented that since Tharyn was there to help, she would go back to her paperwork in the office.

Art Berman asked Dr. Dane if he could stay as long as he stood back from the table. Dr. Dane agreed.

Tharyn caught Dane's eye as he began removing Ben's shirt. He gave her a little smile and nodded his head to tell her he knew she would have everything ready and waiting for him to work on his patient.

Dr. Fraser moved up and stood at the foot of the table, indicating that he was there if needed, but would not get in Dr. Dane's way.

Tharyn stepped to the far side of the table and waited for her husband to tell her what to do next. A thrill of pure satisfaction reached her heart. *Well, here we are,* she thought. *Dane and I working together. This is exactly where God wants us to be, and I couldn't be happier. What a wonderful—*

"Tharyn," came Dane's voice, "would you please wash the coal dust off of Mr. Frye's face and clean the cuts on his temple and his neck? I'll go wash my hands and be right back."

Tharyn quickly began washing the injured man's face. *Thank You, Lord,* she prayed in her heart, *for letting me be here at Dane's side. Please give him wisdom as he tends to this patient.*

While washing off the coal dust, Tharyn spoke softly to the mine foreman, explaining that when she had removed the coal dust, she would be using pure alcohol to clean his cuts. She warned that it would burn some. At the same instant, Dr. Dane drew up to his position on the opposite side of the table.

Ben Frye nodded and closed his eyes, putting himself in their care. He winced and a small groan escaped his lips when she applied the alcohol to the first cut on his temple.

Dr. Dane began making a thorough examination of the injured mine foreman from the waist up, where the pain was centered. At the same time, he asked Art Berman how the fall happened and how far the foreman had fallen.

Berman explained that Ben was standing at the edge of one of the mine shafts, talking to a miner. The cage in that shaft was on its way down into the mine, carrying two miners and an empty rail car. The cage was about forty feet below the earth's surface when a strong gust of wind came down off the high peaks, causing Ben to lose his balance and fall into the shaft. He landed on the top of the cage, which made his fall right at forty feet.

"Forty feet, eh?" said Dr. Dane. "That's like falling from the fourth story of a building. Enough to do some serious damage."

Dr. Dane asked Dr. Fraser to move up beside him as he continued the examination, wanting the older physician's experienced eyes and hands nearby if needed.

Knowing how far the foreman had fallen, the doctors worked carefully to ascertain just how badly he was injured. Tharyn stood by to help.

THREE

*N*adine Wahl was just entering the office from the examination and surgical room when she saw Greg Holton and his father coming in from the boardwalk.

Kirby Holton, who was in his late forties, was obviously very much concerned for his foreman as he stepped ahead of Greg and said, "Nadine, how's Ben doing? How bad is he hurt?"

Nadine smiled. "I'm glad to tell you that his life is not in danger, Mr. Holton."

Kirby sighed and put an arm around his son, who was now standing at his side. "Oh, Nadine, I'm so glad to know Ben's not going to die."

"We all are, Mr. Holton. As soon as Dr. Logan advised Art Berman that Ben would live, he went back to the mine."

"Good. Since Ben's not there, Art sure needs to be. What are Ben's injuries and how serious are they?"

"It's best that I let Dr. Logan explain the injuries, Mr. Holton. Why don't you and Greg sit down over there in the waiting area? I'll advise Dr. Logan that you're here. I'm sure he will come and talk to you as soon as he and Dr. Fraser are finished getting Ben all bandaged up."

Kirby thanked her, and as he and Greg were heading for the

nearby waiting area, Nadine hurried through the door that led to the examination room.

As she moved up to the table, Tharyn was standing by with a three-inch-wide roll of heavy cloth in hand while the two doctors were wrapping Ben Frye's upper body with a length of it. Ben's eyes were closed, and he was gritting his teeth, obviously in pain.

"Dr. Logan," said Nadine, "Kirby Holton is here with Greg. I told him that Ben's injuries are not life threatening, but he wants to hear about them from you. He and Greg will wait till you can talk to them."

"All right, Nadine. Tell them it will be about half an hour."

"I'll tell them." With that, she turned and moved out the door.

While the doctors continued to work on Ben, Dr. Dane said, "I've worked on Greg for some minor injuries a couple of times since taking over the practice. As I recall, he said his mother died of consumption nine years ago."

Dr. Fraser nodded, keeping his attention on what they were doing. "Yes."

"I've only met Kirby one time. It was on the street shortly after I had taken care of Greg's second injury. He seems to be a nice guy."

"He is. Pastor Shane has made many a call at the Holton mansion, but both Kirby and Greg show no interest in the Lord. But knowing my pastor, he will keep trying to win them to Christ."

"We can't give up on people. It's our job to give them the gospel, and the Lord is able to bring just the right circumstances into their lives that will turn them to Him."

Kirby and Greg had been sitting in the waiting area about twenty-five minutes when the door of the examining room opened and Dr. Dane Logan came out. Sitting at her desk, Nadine smiled at him as he walked past her, and he smiled back.

Kirby jumped off his chair and headed toward the doctor, and Greg followed.

As Kirby drew up, he said, "Dr. Logan, I really appreciate the work you and Dr. Fraser are doing on Ben. Nadine told Greg and me that Ben's injuries are not life threatening."

"Ben will live, Mr. Holton, but he's got a lot of healing to do. His right arm is broken and he has four cracked ribs, along with a deep cut on his left temple and two lacerations on his neck. The arm is in a sling, and his ribs are wrapped tightly with heavy cloth. I'm estimating that it'll be some six to eight weeks before he can return to work."

Kirby nodded. "Well, at least he'll be returning to work. That fall could have killed him."

"For sure. Ben can go home in a couple of hours. I'll need to check on him three times a week so the bandages can be changed and I can be sure the ribs stay wrapped securely."

Kirby smiled. "I appreciate your taking such good care of him, Doctor. And will you send the bill to me? I'll pay it."

"Whatever you say. My wife is taking over for Nadine. I'll advise her to send the bill to you."

"Fine. I'll send Greg and another man back in a couple of hours to take Ben home. Could—could I see Ben before we go?"

"Of course. But only for a few minutes."

"I'll wait here, Dad," said Greg.

Kirby had been with Ben less than five minutes when he returned to the office. He told Nadine she would be missed, but that he was glad she could retire.

The father and son climbed into their wagon, and Greg guided the team up the street.

Kirby said, "Son, as long as we're going right by the hardware store, I need to run in for a minute. I broke my pocketknife this morning, and I need to get a new one."

"Sure, Dad," said Greg, angling the wagon toward the hardware store which was a few doors away. "I'll just wait out here for you."

Greg halted the wagon at an open space parallel with the boardwalk, and just as Kirby entered the hardware store, Greg noticed two young women coming his way. He recognized blond and lovely Rosemary Snyder, but not the striking brunette with her. Greg had known Rosemary ever since his family had come to Central City when they were both in school together. He was in the ninth grade at the time, and she was in the seventh.

Greg hopped down from the wagon as the two young women drew up. "Hello, Rosemary. Who's your friend?"

Rosemary smiled. "This is Cassandra Wheatley. Cassandra, this is Greg Holton. His father is Kirby Holton, who owns the Holton Coal Mine just west of town. Greg is employed at the mine."

Greg figured Cassandra was about the same age as Rosemary, who was twenty. Cassandra flashed him a winsome smile. "I'm very glad to meet you, Greg." She offered her hand.

Greg gently took the hand, clicked his heels, and did a slight bow. "Since I've still got some coal dust on my face, Miss Cassandra, I won't kiss your hand."

Cassandra giggled and said warmly, "I understand, Greg, and I appreciate that."

"Cassandra is from Aurora, Illinois," said Rosemary. "She has come to Central City to live with her Aunt Mabel Downing, who lives next door to us. She just arrived three days ago, and already the two of us have become good friends."

"Well, I'm glad," said Greg, a questioning look in his eyes.

Observing the look, Cassandra said, "I came to live with Aunt Mabel because both of my parents recently died. I have no other family. Aunt Mabel is my mother's sister."

"I'm sorry about your parents. If you ever need anything, please let me know."

She smiled. "Why, thank you, Greg."

Greg pointed up to the huge white mansion that stood on the

high side of town to the northwest. Behind it was a towering pine-covered mountain. "That's where I live, Cassandra. I would count it an honor if I could ever be of service to you."

Cassandra had noticed the huge three-story house when she first arrived in Central City on a stagecoach three days previously. She knew it had to belong to someone with plenty of money. *Certainly,* she thought, *the man who owns the coal mine has to be rich. And of course, that makes his son rich, too.*

She smiled warmly. "Thank you, Greg. I'll find a reason soon to take advantage of your offer."

Greg looked at her dreamily. "You do that."

Rosemary laughed. "I think you can count on it!"

Cassandra and Greg were both laughing at Rosemary's quip when Kirby came out of the hardware store and headed for the wagon.

Greg's laugh faded. "Miss Cassandra, I'll be waiting with great anticipation." He then turned his attention to Rosemary. "How's Phil doing?"

"Just fine. He loves his job at the post office in Idaho Springs, and I'm certain he's going to propose to me real soon."

"I sure hope so. The two of you make a handsome couple, and I'm sure you'll be very happy together."

Kirby climbed up onto the wagon seat.

Greg said, "Come with me, Cassandra. I want to introduce you to my dad."

Kirby heard it. He looked toward Rosemary, greeted her, then set his eyes on his son and the lovely brunette.

Greg introduced Cassandra to him. After Kirby said he was glad to meet her, Greg told her he would look forward to seeing her again, bid Rosemary good-bye, and climbed up onto the wagon seat. He took the reins in hand and trotted the team up the street.

As the wagon slipped into the traffic, Cassandra turned to

Rosemary. "That is one fine handsome young man. I hope he isn't attached."

"He isn't, honey. Greg has dated several young women here in town, and quite a few who live on surrounding ranches, but so far he hasn't gotten serious with any of them."

Cassandra looked up at the splendid mansion at the foot of the lofty mountain. "Rosemary, the Holtons must be very rich."

"Yes. Mrs. Holton died several years ago, and Mr. Holton has never remarried. He *is* quite wealthy, for sure. The coal mine has made him a multimillionaire."

Cassandra frowned. "Well, since Greg's father is so rich, why does he work in the mine? Certainly he doesn't have to."

Rosemary shook her head. "He doesn't have to in the sense that he needs a paycheck, for he is paid quite generously by the mine. But his father insists he work in the mine because he wants his son to learn what it is to work hard and shoulder responsibility. Greg is not a lazy person, and he understands what his father is trying to teach him. After all, one day when his father dies, Greg will own the mine and have full control of it. Mr. Holton is trying to prepare him for that day."

Cassandra's eyes brightened. "My, my! Then Greg will have all those millions to himself!"

At Dr. Dane Logan's office, Nadine and Tharyn were at the front desk where Nadine was showing her the office files and the financial books.

In the examining room, Dr. Dane and the elderly physician were standing over the table looking down at Ben Frye, who was asking questions about his injuries. When Dr. Dane had satisfied him that he would be back to work in a couple of months or so, Ben relaxed.

Dr. Dane listened to Ben's heart with his stethoscope for the fifth or sixth time since beginning the work on his injuries, then said, "Sounds good in there, Ben. I'm certain that even though you cracked up your ribs, there was no damage to your heart."

Ben managed a weak smile and raised his free hand to the bandage on his temple. "I'm glad for that, Doctor. And I'm glad this cut wasn't any worse."

"Me too. Now, Ben, I'll have to come to the house three times a week, check you over, change your bandages, and rewrap your ribs. Mr. Holton told me to send the entire bill to him. Knowing that ought to help you to get better faster."

Ben's eyes lit up. "He did?"

"He did."

"Well, it sure will help. Kirby is such a fine man. And he's so generous. I love working for him."

Dr. Dane rubbed his angular chin. "Young Greg seems to be a fine man, too. What little time I've been around him, he has impressed me."

Ben nodded. "Greg is indeed a fine young man, Doctor, especially for one who has such a rich father. I've seen sons and daughters of wealthy parents who are so spoiled, they're rotten. But not Greg. He's made out of good stuff."

"That's for sure," put in Dr. Fraser. "He was only thirteen when his mother died. A lot of boys that age would have rebelled and made life difficult around the house. But not Greg. He was a real help to Kirby in it all. Fine young man."

"Has to be," said Dr. Dane. "I'm amazed to see that he works in the mine. Most sons of wealthy parents don't want to work. They want to live it up and play a lot, since they don't have to work to make a living."

Ben adjusted the arm in the sling with his free hand. "Greg would work in the mine even if Kirby didn't wish him to do so. There's not a lazy bone in his body."

A smile creased Dr. Dane's face. "Good for him." Then he said to Dr. Fraser, "I need to take Tharyn home so we can unpack. You can be a man of leisure tomorrow and stay home."

Fraser laughed. "That really sounds good! But today, I'll see the rest of the patients who come in."

"And to me, that sounds good. See you gentlemen later."

When Dr. Dane entered the office, he said, "Well, Nadine, I hate to take Tharyn from you, but we've got to go home and unpack."

"That's all right, Doctor," Nadine said. "We've already made plans for me to help Tharyn get properly adapted to her new job."

Dr. Dane's eyebrows arched. "Oh, really?"

A sly grin curved her lips. "Mm-hmm. I will be here at the office every day for the next week to train her to work for that slave driver, Dr. Dane Logan."

The three of them had a good laugh together; then the Logans left the office and headed for home.

FOUR

$\mathcal{A}$s Dane and Tharyn Logan were driving toward home, she said, "Darling, ever since I saw the house when I came here with you before we were married, I've been thinking about some decorating I'd like to do both inside and outside. I love the house, but the lady who lived in it before didn't have the same tastes I have in decorating."

"Well, that's no surprise, honey. People always have their own ideas about things like that."

"True. In the ten years I lived with the Tabors as their adopted daughter, I learned a lot about decorating from Mama. I've pretty much developed the same tastes as hers."

Dane transferred the reins to his other hand and took her hand in his. "Sweetheart, you can decorate the house inside and out any way you want to."

She smiled at him. "I'll try not to be extravagant."

Dane chuckled. "I'm not worried about that."

When they pulled up in front of the house, Tharyn ran her gaze over the porch and the part of the yard that surrounded it. "Oh, I'm so excited! Let me tell you what I have in mind for outside the house before we go in."

Dane stepped down from the buggy, helped her out, then held her hand. "Okay, I'm all ears!"

Hand in hand they walked up close to the front porch.

Gesturing with her free hand, Tharyn said, "Right here on each side of the porch steps, I want to plant lots of bright, colorful flowers. They will say welcome to anyone who approaches our door."

"Sounds good to me."

She pointed up to the framework just above the railing that ran across the front of the porch. "I'd like to have some hanging baskets of geraniums up there, and if we could get a swing and maybe four comfortable chairs so we can relax with company when they come. How does that sound?"

"Sounds good to me, sweetheart. We'll do it. Do you want help planting all of the flowers?"

"Oh no. I'll enjoy getting my hands in the warm earth. It'll be fun for me."

"Well, okay, if you're sure."

"I'm quite sure, sweetheart. Now let's go to the backyard."

They walked around to the rear of the house where a green carpet of grass gleamed in the sunshine.

Tharyn bent down and put her hand in the grass. "It will be wonderful to walk barefoot in this on hot summer days."

A white picket fence surrounded the ample backyard. She had noticed the small barn behind the fence where Dane kept his horse and buggy, but this time, she spotted a plot of ground next to it.

Letting go of his hand, she hurried to the fence and said excitedly, "Oh, Dane! What a perfect spot for a garden! We can grow our own vegetables. That'll be all right, won't it?"

Dane drew up behind her. "Sure it's all right—but with our busy schedules, do you really think we'll have the time?"

"Sure we will. We won't make it too big. It'll be a great way to unwind at the end of a busy day."

"Okay, my love. It's worth a try. But I'll do the spading and raking of the ground."

"Fine. And I'll do the planting and watering." She turned and ran her gaze over the entire backyard. "The trees and plants out here are great. Maybe we can put a bench under that big cottonwood tree over there, so we can enjoy the backyard as well. And I'll put a few flower pots on the back porch. Okay?"

"Whatever you say, honey. Sounds good to me."

"Well, let's go inside. When we were here a little while ago for me to freshen up, all I saw was the kitchen. I love how wonderful the table and chairs we bought for the kitchen look in there. I'm eager to see the furniture in the rest of the house, as well as the curtains and drapes that are still packed."

They moved onto the back porch and entered the kitchen. As they walked from room to room, she explained in detail how she wanted to decorate each one and arrange its furniture. "The lady who lived here before us must have really loved this house. She took special care of it, and I want to do the same thing."

When they were in the last room—which was the master bedroom on the second floor—Tharyn finished describing how she wanted it, then said, "Now, honey, I realize we may not have the money to get the additional things I've mentioned all at once. Even if it takes a couple of years, that's all right."

Dane smiled at her. "I did well enough as Dad's partner in Cheyenne to put some money in the bank. It has helped me especially because Dr. Fraser is letting me pay for the purchase of the practice over a period of time. You can have the money to do your decorating whenever you want it."

Tharyn squealed joyfully, wrapped her arms around him, and kissed him. "Oh, darling, thank you!"

"Hey, it's your money now, too. Which makes me think. I need to take you to the bank tomorrow and put you on the business checking account, and both the personal checking account and the savings account."

She giggled and bowed. "At your service, sir!"

Later that night, long after Dane had gone to sleep, Tharyn lay awake thinking about her new home. In her mind, she could picture each room completed, even down to the small bedroom next to the master bedroom, which would be the nursery. She thought of the children that God would give them, and a contented sigh escaped her lips. A tiny smile worked its way across her face.

She whispered into the quiet moonlit room, "Thank You, Lord, for doing 'all things well.'"

It was a warm early July Sunday morning in Colorado's Rocky Mountains.

Tharyn had been up since she first heard a rooster crow from afar off. Clad in her robe, she worked at preparing breakfast. While she moved about the kitchen, she was excited and a bit nervous about attending the new church for the first time. She persuaded herself that being somewhat nervous was only natural.

She was at the stove pouring scrambled eggs from the skillet into a bowl when Dane entered the kitchen. She saw him from the corner of her eye and gave him a loving smile. He moved up behind her, slid his arms around her in a gentle hug, and kissed the nape of her neck.

She giggled at the tickle she felt, set the skillet down, turned about in his arms, and gave him a good-morning kiss.

Later, when they were finished eating and enjoying a second cup of fragrant coffee, Dane noticed Tharyn staring out the kitchen window, her thoughts seemingly diverted. One of her hands lay on the tulip-printed tablecloth.

He laid his hand over hers.

Startled by his touch, she turned and looked at him.

Dane squeezed her hand. "Is something wrong, honey? You seem like your thoughts are miles away."

She shook her head. "No, sweetheart. Nothing is wrong. My life is so wonderful. I'm married to the most marvelous man in all the world, and we're about to embark on a great career together, finally realizing the dreams of a lifetime. What could possibly be wrong?"

"Well, you seem to be distracted today. Anything you want to talk about?"

She looked down for a moment, then raised her eyes to meet his. "I—I'm just a little nervous about going to a new church. You know how long I've been a member of the one in Denver where I knew everyone. I so dearly love Pastor Blandford and Nellie. So…I'm a bit out of place. I really like Pastor and Mrs. Shane, but it's all so new. I know everything will be fine. You have told me how much you have enjoyed attending here when you couldn't make it to Denver."

"Very much so."

"There's nothing wrong at all, sweetheart. It's just that my life has taken on such a change. Please understand. I'm superbly happy being married to you and doing what God has planned for us. It's just that everything is a little different now."

Dane stood up, took hold of Tharyn's hand, and raised her to her feet. Taking both of her hands in his, he looked into her blue eyes. "I know that you have left everything that is familiar to you, but believe me, the people here are very kind and warm, especially the members of the church. You are going to fit in perfectly. The people of the church will welcome you with open arms. You have absolutely nothing to worry about."

She smiled. "Of course, darling. You're right. I guess I'm just a little jittery. But I know with you at my side, everything will be fine."

Dane embraced her, and Tharyn felt a special security in his arms.

Later that morning, the Logans entered the church building a few minutes before Sunday school was to start. Dane took his wife around to introduce her to his new friends. Tharyn was warmly welcomed by all. When they met up with Pastor Mark Shane and Peggy, the pastor welcomed her with a friendly smile and a handshake, and Peggy welcomed her with a big hug. The Shanes talked for a moment about what a beautiful wedding the Logans' had been.

Dr. Fraser and Esther arrived with Nadine Wahl, and after greeting the Logans, asked them to sit beside them.

When Sunday school was over, Tharyn turned to Dane. "Honey, I really enjoyed Pastor Shane's lesson. He's really a good teacher."

Dane grinned. "Tell you what. You'll like his preaching even better than his teaching. He really gets wound up when he preaches."

Dr. Fraser leaned close. "He's right, Tharyn. You'll like the preaching even better."

Tharyn thoroughly enjoyed the congregational singing, and when offering and announcement time came, the pastor walked to the pulpit and told the crowd that Dr. Dane Logan's new bride was with him. He asked the couple to stand up so Dr. Logan could introduce her.

When the doctor did so, telling the crowd that her name was Tharyn, she was surprised to hear them applaud.

When the pastor saw the stunned look on her face, he looked

down from the pulpit. "Tharyn, these people are welcoming you like this because they all love your husband and are happy that you are now a resident of Central City."

Tharyn nodded that she understood.

There was another congregational song. When the crowd was seated, three young ladies were introduced by the pastor and sang a heart-touching gospel song.

During the sermon, when Pastor Shane had just finished eloquently picturing Jesus dying on the cross for sinners, Tharyn leaned close to Dane and whispered, "You're right, honey. His teaching is excellent, but his preaching is really great!"

Nadine Wahl heard her words, smiled, and patted her hand.

When the sermon was over and the invitation was given, Dane and Tharyn walked down the aisle to present themselves for membership in the church, along with two adults and a child who had come to receive the Lord Jesus Christ as Saviour.

When the pastor presented the Logans to the people, the crowd was enthusiastic in accepting them as members.

The three who had come for salvation were baptized, and after the service, Pastor Shane had them—along with the Logans—stand in the vestibule so the people could pass by and greet them.

Pastor and Mrs. Shane were standing at the end of the line next to Dane and Tharyn, shaking hands with people as they were leaving the building.

A diminutive lady paused before Dane and Tharyn and smiled. "Hello. I'm Mabel Downing. Welcome into our church."

Mabel was immaculately dressed. Every hair was tucked into place under her white straw hat, which was trimmed with daisies and yellow ribbons. Her white straw reticule was clasped tightly in her tiny hands, which were clad with white lace gloves.

Dane and Tharyn both thanked her; then she said, "Dr. Fraser has long been my doctor, and I love him. But I am sure, Dr. Logan, that I will love you every bit as much. Already people in

Central City who have been treated by you have told me what a good doctor you are."

The young physician smiled from ear to ear. "I'm glad to hear this, ma'am. Thank you for telling me."

The pastor offered his hand. "Mabel, didn't your niece feel like coming to church with you today?"

Mabel's face pinched, and tears filmed her dark brown eyes. She tried to blink them away without success.

The Logans and Peggy looked on as the pastor asked, "Mabel, what's wrong?"

Mabel sniffed. "Cassandra refused to come to church, Pastor. She said she doesn't like churches, and doesn't want anything to do with the Bible because God is just in the imagination of people's minds."

Shane looked stunned. "She's an atheist?"

Mabel nodded and wiped tears from her cheeks. "That's exactly what she called herself, Pastor. I haven't seen Cassandra since she was a little girl. I wasn't aware of this at all. Her parents are not Christians and have never taken her to church, but they are not atheists. I wasn't aware that Cassandra felt this way until yesterday when I told her we needed to be at church today for Sunday school at ten o'clock. That's when she came out with this atheist business."

Peggy Shane said, "Mabel, when Pastor came home after seeing you at the general store on Tuesday, he told me you had informed him that your niece surprised you by knocking on your door that morning, saying she had come to live with you."

Mabel nodded. "That's right. I had no idea she was coming."

Peggy's brow furrowed. "Did something happen to Cassandra's parents?"

Mabel shook her head, working hard to keep her self-control. "No. Like I said, I haven't seen Cassandra since she was small, but I knew from my sister's letters that she had become somewhat of a problem about the time she turned fourteen.

"Myrtle and I exchanged letters often, and by the time Cassandra was eighteen, Myrtle said the girl made life positively miserable for her and her husband. As she grew into adulthood, matters just escalated. Cassandra has absolutely no ambition and refuses to get a job.

"Myrtle's husband is very ill and unable to work. Myrtle told Cassandra she was going to have to get a job and help out with the expenses. Cassandra threw a royal fit, saying she wasn't going to do it, so Myrtle told her to leave. This fact came to me in a letter just over a week ago. I had no idea Cassandra would show up on my doorstep, and neither did Myrtle."

Peggy shook her head. "Why do you suppose she came to you?"

"She must have found out from her parents that I received a substantial amount of money from a life insurance policy with a New York insurance company when my husband, Walter, was killed in that work accident four years ago."

"Oh."

"It looks to me like Cassandra figures her aunt will take care of her." Once again, Mabel wiped tears. "More than anything, I want to bring Cassandra out of her atheism, and to see her open her heart to Jesus. I want her to be saved."

Pastor Shane bit his lower lip and slowly shook his head. "Of course, Mabel. But what a shame that she calls herself an atheist. It is going to make your life miserable, having her in your home. Peggy and I will be praying for her, and for *you*. We'll ask God to give you grace in it all, and we'll be praying for her salvation. One day soon, I'll happen by the house and try to talk to her. As you heard me preach not long ago, there is no such thing as an honest atheist. Romans 1:19 and 20 declares plainly that that which may be known of God by men is manifest in them, for God has shown it unto them. Man's very conscience and his very nature tells him God exists. It also says that the invisible things of God from the creation of the world are clearly seen, being understood by the things He has made. His creation even shows His eternal power and His Godhead. So people who call themselves atheists are without excuse before Him.

"When a person says there is no God, they are being dishonest. They know He exists because God has put in them to know it. What they really mean, is they *wish* there was no God. Both Psalm 14 and Psalm 53 call the person who says there is no God a *fool*. We'll be praying earnestly for Cassandra."

"Yes, we will," said Peggy.

"And Tharyn and I will too, Mrs. Downing," said Dr. Dane, "and we'll ask our Father in heaven to give you strength as well."

Mabel ran her teary gaze over all four faces, thanked them, and walked away.

When Mabel Downing arrived home and stepped into the house, she saw no sign of her niece on the first floor. She climbed the stairs to the second floor and heard soft sounds coming from the bedroom that she had assigned to Cassandra. The door was open, and when Mabel reached it, she found Cassandra pawing through drawers in the dresser, removing their contents and placing them in a cardboard box.

Cassandra looked up at her aunt. "Back from church, huh?"

"Yes. What are you doing?"

"I'm making room for my own things that you are going to buy me from time to time. I'll carry this box up to the attic and store these things up there."

Mabel felt a touch of indignation at her niece's bold assumption. "I'll buy you the necessary things you need until you get a job of your own and you can buy them."

Cassandra gave her a smug look. "What kind of job would I find in this small town, Aunt Mabel?"

"There are stores and shops that employ women as clerks, and there are cafés and restaurants that employ them as waitresses."

Cassandra's brow wrinkled and her cheeks tinted with ire. "Clerks? Waitresses?"

Mabel ignored the reaction. "Yes. You should put your application all over town right away, so if there are no openings at present, you'll be given the first job that comes open."

Cassandra masked the revulsion she felt at the thought of being a lowly clerk or waitress and decided to change the subject. She lifted a slender wooden instrument out of one of the drawers. It was some eighteen inches in length with a carved handle at the bottom of the pole, and a carved head at its top with four wooden prongs extending outward like curved fingers with narrow tips about half an inch apart.

"What is this, Aunt Mabel?"

"It's an old Chinese backscratcher, Cassandra. The Chinese invented this implement to make it easy to scratch any itching spot. Your Uncle Walter bought it for me as a keepsake when we were in San Francisco's Chinatown on our honeymoon many years ago."

Cassandra looked at the wooden instrument. "It was nice of Uncle Walter to buy it for his bride. I'm sure it means a lot to you."

"That it does."

Cassandra placed the instrument back in the drawer, then looked at her aunt and smiled again. "I'll keep it safe for you."

"Well, dear, let's go down to the kitchen and get Sunday dinner cooking."

Cassandra reluctantly followed her aunt downstairs to the kitchen, but simply sat down at the table and watched Mabel prepare the dinner.

After a few minutes, Mabel stood at the stove and looked

toward her niece. "Cassandra, why don't you set the table while I'm cooking?"

The pretty brunette raised her eyebrows. "Set the table?"

"Yes. You know. Silverware. Plates. Coffee cups and saucers. You can do that, can't you?"

Disguising the loathing she felt at being prodded to do her part, Cassandra rose to her feet laboriously. "Mm-hmm. I can do that."

FIVE

*A*s the days passed, Dr. Dane Logan cared for the patients who came to the office, and also those who were ill at home and needed his attention. House calls in town and in the rural areas were a part of the daily routine.

Between patients in the office who needed Tharyn's care—sometimes alone, and at other times with the doctor—Nadine Wahl worked at training her in the keeping of the financial books and in knowing how to handle the job as receptionist. Nadine, of course, knew Tharyn's reputation as a nurse at Denver's Mile High Hospital, and that she needed no training in that area of responsibility.

Tharyn was delighted with her job, especially working alongside Dane with the patients. To her, it was a dream come true.

The Logans were up and about with the first light of dawn each day and worked many long hours. But Tharyn cheerfully performed each task, taking great pleasure in being a helper to her husband.

She had learned quickly that Dr. Dane Logan was the typical frontier doctor. He took care of people whether they could pay him or not. He often had to accept canned goods, garden vegetables, eggs, or other edibles from his patients who had little money.

It seemed that some days, Dane was making house calls at closing time, so Tharyn hurried home to prepare supper and make their home a haven for her tired man.

Sometimes after supper, Tharyn went out back to attend to her small vegetable garden. Since it was planted quite late in the season, she knew her crop would be small, but she loved getting her hands in the soil. She pulled weeds joyfully.

On Thursday evening after supper, Dane had been called away to deliver a baby in a mountain cabin some five miles from Central City. Tharyn went to her garden, pulled a few weeds, and stood gazing at the rows where seeds had been planted. Soon she would see the tiny plants peeping up out of the soil.

Standing with her hands clasped behind her back, she turned in a slow circle, taking in the charming house and yard. A cool breeze had sprung up as the last rays of the sun sank behind the mountain peaks to the west and a burst of orange light seemed to glow over the whole world.

She drew a deep breath. "Thank You, my Father, for this magnificent view and for sight with which to behold it."

By Friday, Nadine had Tharyn thoroughly trained in the care of the financial books and in the duties as receptionist. When it came time to close the office, Dr. Dane was at the local saw mill, tending to a person who had been injured.

As the two women were heading for the door, Nadine smiled. "Now, Tharyn, I want to remind you that you can call on me for help whenever you and Dr. Logan have to be out of town, or even if you need me when you are here at the office."

Tharyn hugged her. "Thank you, Nadine. And thank you for your patience in teaching me how to run the office."

Nadine kissed her cheek. "You're an easy student to teach, honey. It's been my pleasure."

On Saturday morning at the Downing house, Mabel was washing the inside of the parlor window while Cassandra was dusting the mantel, wishing she was living in some luxurious mansion as the wife of a wealthy man and had servants to do tedious tasks like she was being forced to do at the moment.

Cassandra's aunt was humming some unfamiliar tune while washing the large window. Cassandra paused in her dusting, looked at Mabel, and told herself it must be one of those church songs that were so meaningless and boring.

Mabel happened to look her niece's direction and saw that Cassandra was watching her. She stopped scrubbing and smiled. "Are you finished dusting the mantel already?"

Cassandra looked at the dust cloth in her hand and shook her head. "No. I was just wondering what song you're humming."

Mabel got a blank look on her face. "Well, I—uh—I don't know. I was just humming and praising the Lord in my heart. Whatever it was, it was a song about Jesus, I'm sure. When I received Him as my Saviour, He washed my sins away with His precious blood and put sweet music in my heart."

A dull look came into Cassandra's eyes. "Oh. Sweet music, eh?"

"Mm-hmm. He will do the same thing for you, dear, if you will put your faith and trust in Him. Jesus loves you. He went to the cross and—"

"That's all right, Aunt Mabel," cut in Cassandra, and started dusting again. "You don't need to preach to me. That gospel business just isn't my cup of tea."

Mabel started to say something else, but her attention was drawn outside as she heard hoofbeats and the sound of a buggy pulling into the driveway. She looked out the window and saw Pastor and Mrs. Shane in the buggy.

Cassandra had heard the sound too, but from where she stood

she could see the horse but not the occupants of the buggy. "Who's that, Aunt Mabel?"

Waving out the window with a smile on her face, Mabel said, "It's Pastor and Mrs. Shane, honey. They've been wanting to meet you."

Cassandra felt a cold antagonism well up inside her, but said nothing.

Mabel dropped the washcloth into the bucket of water, hurried out the door, and into the hall. As she headed toward the front door, she said in a whisper, "Please, dear Lord, let them get somewhere with Cassandra."

On Sunday, the Logans fully enjoyed the teaching and preaching and the fellowship of the solid Christians in the church. That evening after the service, they had Pastor and Mrs. Shane to their home for a light snack.

While they were sitting together at the dining room table and enjoying the food Tharyn had prepared, Dr. Dane said, "I noticed that Mabel Downing was alone in both services today. She must be having a hard time with her niece, trying to get her to come to church."

Pastor Shane and Peggy exchanged glances; then the pastor nodded and looked at the doctor. "Yes, she is. *Quite* a hard time. Peggy and I went to the Downing house yesterday morning and talked to Cassandra."

"Oh, you did?"

"Yes, but that girl's heart is hard when it comes to the things of the Lord. She was not impolite at that point, but she made it clear that she wants nothing to do with our church or the Bible, and she flat told us she is an atheist."

"Oh, I see," said Dr. Dane.

"This has to be very difficult for Mabel," put in Tharyn.

Peggy nodded. "That it is, Tharyn. We've known that Mabel was having a hard time with Cassandra ever since she came to live with her. Mabel winced with pain when Cassandra told us that she believes when people die, they simply pass out of existence; there is no heaven and there is no hell."

Pastor Shane sipped his coffee and placed the cup in its saucer. "We both gave her a lot of Scripture concerning God's existence and used common sense to go with it, but the girl refused to pay any heed to either. I went ahead and preached the gospel to her, wanting to plant the seed of the Word in her heart and mind. She would not respond at all. When we were about to leave, she did get somewhat impolite and told us she didn't want us talking about it to her ever again."

"Poor Mabel was so embarrassed," said Peggy. "My heart really went out to her."

Dr. Dane sighed. "Well, Tharyn and I will be praying for Cassandra, that the Lord will use the Scriptures the two of you gave her to open her eyes to the truth. I'm sure Mabel has been planting the seed of the Word in the girl's heart, too."

The pastor nodded. "Without a doubt. She's obviously very burdened for her. And please pray for Mabel. This situation is indeed extremely hard for her."

"We certainly will hold Mabel before the Lord, too, Pastor," said Dr. Dane.

On Monday afternoon, Mabel had Cassandra in the sewing room with her. She was doing some necessary sewing and was attempting to teach her niece how to sew at the same time.

Though Cassandra was not the least bit interested, she acted as if she was.

In between comments about sewing, Mabel talked about Jesus Christ, His virgin birth, what He did for sinners in His crucifixion, and His resurrection after He had died on the cross. When Mabel had brought up Jesus and His crucifixion for the fifth or sixth time, Cassandra said, "Aunt Mabel, I very much appreciate your taking me into your home, and am deeply grateful, but please don't talk to me about your religion."

Mabel's eyebrows arched. "Religion? Have I mentioned religion?"

"Well, yes. You keep talking about God and Jesus and that kind of thing."

"Honey, I've been talking to you about salvation. You don't need religion, but you need salvation, and that salvation comes only by repenting of your sin, believing on Jesus, and receiving Him into your heart as your own personal Saviour."

Cassandra drew a breath of air through her nose and let it out the same way. "Aunt Mabel, I don't believe in God, so I certainly don't believe in the Son of God. When somebody dies, they don't come back from the dead. I do not believe Jesus Christ rose from the dead. It is all a fairy tale."

Knowing the Word of God can penetrate the most stubborn mind and heart, Mabel went back to sewing, but as they worked together, she quoted Scripture after Scripture, doing her best to sow the seed of the Word in Cassandra's heart.

They had lunch together, at which time Cassandra did not bow her head when her aunt prayed over the food.

At one o'clock, they went back into the sewing room.

At one-thirty, Mabel was showing Cassandra a particular type of stitching to do when there was a knock at the front door of the house.

Cassandra sprang off her chair and hurried into the hall, saying she would get it. When she reached the front door, she opened it and found Rosemary Snyder standing there with a pained look in her eyes.

"Hello, neighbor. What can I do for you?"

Rosemary asked, "Can we talk?"

Cassandra stepped back and opened the door wider. "Why, of course. Please come in. We'll go into the parlor." As they were heading down the hall toward the parlor door, they saw Mabel coming toward them from the sewing room.

Mabel smiled. "Hello, Rosemary. It's nice to see you."

"It's nice to see you too, Mrs. Downing."

As her aunt drew near, Cassandra said, "Rosemary came over to talk to me about something. We're going to talk in the parlor."

"Oh, I see. Well, I'll go on back to the sewing room."

Rosemary shook her head. "Please, Mrs. Downing, I'd like for you to be in on the conversation too, if you don't mind."

"Well, all right, dear. I'll be back in a moment. I just want to go to the kitchen and get each of us a glass of lemonade. You two go on into the parlor."

Mabel bustled down the hall, and Cassandra led Rosemary into the parlor.

When they were heading for the spot where two overstuffed chairs, Mabel's favorite rocker, and the sofa were positioned in a circle, Cassandra looked at her friend. "What's this all about?"

"I'll tell both of you when your aunt gets back," said Rosemary, a tiny frown forming between her pretty green eyes.

Moments later, when Mabel returned carrying a tray with three full glasses of lemonade and a plate of sugar cookies, the young women were sitting side by side on the flowered sofa.

After giving the refreshments to Rosemary and Cassandra, Mabel placed the tray on an end table by the sofa, took the remaining glass and a couple of cookies, and lowered herself into her soft rocking chair. She took a small sip of the lemonade. "Now, dear, what is this all about?"

Rosemary shifted sideways on the sofa so she could look at Cassandra, glanced at Mabel, and said, "Mother and I were at the general store early this morning, and we got to talking to a couple of ladies from Mrs. Downing's church, Beulah Franks and Opal

Domire. The subject went to you, Cassandra."

Cassandra's brow furrowed. "Me?"

"Mm-hmm. The ladies informed Mother and me that Mrs. Downing had told them Cassandra had come to live with her because her parents had put her out of their home."

Cassandra's features reddened. She looked at her aunt, then turned to face Rosemary.

"Why did you tell me that your parents had died?" said Rosemary.

Flustered, Cassandra sent another hot glance toward her aunt, then silently looked at the floor for a few seconds. She nervously ran her tongue over her lips, cleared her throat, looked up at Rosemary, and said, "Well, in a way, my parents are dead to me, since they want nothing to do with me. I told you they were dead, Rosemary, because I didn't want you or anyone else to know that my parents had put me out."

Mabel's head bobbed. "Cassandra! That's a terrible thing to do! How would your parents feel if they knew you were telling people they were dead?"

Cassandra burst into tears and threw her hands to her face.

She sobbed hard for a minute, while Rosemary and Mabel looked at each other in consternation, then left the sofa and knelt in front of her aunt. "I'm sorry, Aunt Mabel! Please forgive me!"

Mabel's lower lip quivered as she reached out and patted her niece's cheek. "I forgive you, dear."

Cassandra turned her tear-filled eyes on Rosemary. "Will you forgive me, too?"

"Of course I will."

Secretly, Cassandra could not have cared less whether her aunt or Rosemary forgave her, but in order to stay in her aunt's good graces, she told herself she must play the penitent part.

Mabel set steady eyes on her niece. "Who else have you told this lie to?"

Cassandra blinked. "I—I told it to Greg Holton."

"Anyone else?" pressed Mabel.

"No. Just Rosemary and Greg."

Rosemary rose from the sofa and moved to Cassandra, who was now standing. She laid a hand on Cassandra's arm. "You should tell Greg the truth about this next time you talk to him. It is best to clear it up right away so he doesn't hear it from someone else like Mother and I did from Mrs. Franks and Mrs. Domire at the general store."

Cassandra wiped tears. "Yes. You're right. I'll tell Greg next time I see him." In her heart, she dreaded having to come clean with Greg about the lie, but because she most certainly wanted to get to know him better, she would do it.

Rosemary embraced Cassandra. "Well, I need to get back over to the house. Mother and I have a lot of washing and ironing to do."

Both Mabel and Cassandra knew that since Rosemary's father drove a freight wagon between Central City and Denver, and his income was sometimes sporadic, she and her mother took in washing and ironing from many of the single men who worked in the Holton Coal Mine.

Mabel left her rocker and moved up to Rosemary. "Thank you, dear, for forgiving Cassandra. I know it hurt you to learn that she had lied to you."

Rosemary bit down on her lower lip, looked at Cassandra, then back to Mabel. "It did, Mrs. Downing, but if I remember correctly, your Bible says that a friend loves at all times. I have come to love Cassandra in this short time, and even though she lied to me, I still love her."

Cassandra smiled. "Thank you, Rosemary."

Mabel stepped closer to Rosemary. "The verse you're referring to is Proverbs 17:17. In the very next chapter, it says, 'There is a friend that sticketh closer than a brother.' You know who that is?"

Rosemary grinned. "I'm sure it must be Jesus Christ."

"You're so right, and—"

"I really do have to go, Mrs. Downing," Rosemary cut in, heading for the parlor door. "Thanks for the lemonade and the cookies."

Mabel and Cassandra walked Rosemary to the front door, and when she had gone, Cassandra said, "Aunt Mabel, why is it you bring up Jesus so often?"

"Because He is my Saviour, dear. He is my everything. If only you would give Him a chance to be *your* Saviour."

Cassandra only looked at her, but did not reply.

Mabel said, "Well, dear, we need to go to the general store and buy some groceries."

"All right."

"I've made a list. It's in the kitchen. Anything special you want? I'll add it to the list."

Cassandra made a smile. "Whatever you cook is good, Aunt Mabel. You fix it, I'll eat it."

"Well, that makes me feel good. Let's go."

Together, the aunt and the niece headed for Main Street with Mabel pushing the small cart she used for shopping.

When they reached Main and headed toward the business district, Cassandra looked up at the big white mansion on the hill. *I hope Greg will come and see me soon. I'm not looking forward to admitting that I lied to him, but I sure want to get closer to him. If I could only think of some reason to ask his help for something, I would do it. So far, I haven't been able to come up with something that sounds reasonable. I need to concentrate on this.*

Meanwhile, at the Holton Coal Mine just west of town, assistant foreman Art Berman had written a list of articles to be purchased in town at Central City Hardware. He left his desk in the outer office and moved to the open door of Kirby Holton's office. "Boss, I've got the list all made up that you wanted. Think of anything else since we talked?"

Kirby looked up from the paperwork on his desk. "Nope. That oughtta do it. You're sending Greg, aren't you?"

"Yes, sir. I've got to get down into the mine and give instructions to those new men at level three. Greg's at the water pump washing up right now."

"Good. See you later."

Art left the office and made his way down the slope to the water pump where Greg was washing coal dust from his face and hands. He noted that Greg had already hitched a team of horses to a nearby wagon.

As he drew up, Greg took towel in hand and smiled at him with water dripping from his face.

While Greg was drying his face and hands, Art said, "Here's the list."

Greg took it. "Be back in a little while."

Art headed back for the office and when he was about to open the door, he looked over his shoulder to see Greg snapping the reins, putting the team into motion.

SIX

*M*abel Downing and her niece were within a half-block of the general store when suddenly Cassandra pointed up the street. "Aunt Mabel, look!"

Mabel turned to her, then followed the direction of her finger with her eyes and saw only the busy traffic moving both ways on the broad, dusty street. "What, honey?"

"Up there at the nearest intersection. It's Greg Holton in one of the mine's wagons! He's right behind that stagecoach. See him?"

Mabel squinted, moved a step closer to her niece, and focused her attention just behind the stagecoach. "Oh. Yes. Now I see him."

Cassandra stopped quickly and turned toward the large window of a boot and shoe store. She looked at her reflection and dabbed at her hair, trying to make herself look presentable. Then turning back toward her aunt who had stopped and backed up with the shopping cart, she looked down at the dress she was wearing and tried to brush out the wrinkles in the skirt. "Oh, Aunt Mabel," she said, doing what she could to smooth the fabric over her slim hips, "Greg's going to see me in this awful dress! It's so old. Can't we do something soon so I can have some decent clothes? This is embarrassing."

Mabel looked her up and down. "My dear, you look lovely. After all, clothes don't make the person."

Cassandra frowned. "Well, they may not, but it sure doesn't hurt to look one's best. Especially when the son of the richest man in town is coming our way."

Mabel chuckled. "I'm sure Greg won't even notice that your dress is old, child. And besides that, there is absolutely nothing wrong with what you're wearing."

"You just don't understand." Cassandra put on a smile while she waved to get Greg's attention.

A smile spread over Greg's face when he spotted the lovely brunette waving at him. He waved in return.

Greg quickly guided the wagon up to the side of the street, set the brake, and hopped out. "Hello, Mrs. Downing. Nice to see you."

Mabel warmed him with a smile. "Hello, Greg. Nice to see you, too."

Greg set adoring eyes on Cassandra. "And hello to you, young lady. My, don't you look gorgeous!"

Cassandra's face tinted. "Thank you, Greg."

Mabel ran her gaze between them. "Tell you what, children, I'm sure you'd like to chat for a few minutes. I'll go on to the general store and start shopping. Cassandra, you can come when you and Greg have had a few moments to get better acquainted."

Cassandra nodded and smiled.

"Thank you, ma'am," said Greg. "I do want to get better acquainted with her."

Mabel pushed the cart down the boardwalk, weaving among the people who were coming her way.

Greg looked at Cassandra. "I've been waiting to hear from you about something I could do for you, but so far you haven't contacted me."

"Well, I haven't thought of some particular thing you could do for me, but tell you what. I would sure like to have some time with you. Maybe dinner at one of the restaurants and a buggy ride in the moonlight."

A smile broke over his face. "Hey, I'd like that! Dad's cook and housekeeper already has supper planned for this evening, but could I take you to dinner tomorrow evening?"

Cassandra's features brightened. "Of course!"

"All right. Dad has two buggies at the house, so I could come and pick you up in one of them."

"Oh, I'd love it!"

"Do you have to get your aunt's permission to go out with me?"

She giggled. "Greg, I'm nineteen years old. I can do as I please. I'll tell Aunt Mabel that I'm going out with you tomorrow evening."

Greg's heart was pounding and his eyes were dancing. "All right! I'll pick you up at your aunt's house at six o'clock tomorrow evening."

"It's a date!"

"It's a date!" Greg echoed with exhilaration, his face beaming. "See you then."

He returned to the wagon and climbed up onto the seat. He took the reins in hand, put the team in motion, and wove into traffic. Once he was moving down the street, he looked back at her and waved.

Smiling broadly, Cassandra waved back. She watched him until he passed from view, feeling the excitement of having a date with the young man who was no doubt richer than any other man his age in Central City.

With her heart banging her ribs, she headed down the street, walking briskly. Moments later, as she was just three doors from the general store, she halted in front of a clothing store, and looked through the window. On display were some colorful ready-made dresses. Taking a cursory glance at them, she sighed, threw her hands up in despair, and moved on to the general store.

When she stepped inside, she heard the sound of her aunt's voice. Following the sound, she found her between two long rows of shelves, talking to a tall, thin man in his seventies. He spoke kindly to Mabel and walked away.

Mabel saw her niece coming and noted the frown on her face.

Cassandra drew up and looked in the direction the man had gone. "Who was that man you were talking to, Aunt Mabel?"

"That was Mr. Wells, the owner of the store."

"Oh."

Mabel studied the frown on her niece's face. "What's wrong, dear? Did your talk with Greg not go well?"

"Oh, it couldn't have been better. He's going to take me out to dinner tomorrow evening. The problem is, I have nothing nice to wear for the occasion."

Mabel took hold of her niece's hand. "When we get home, we'll look through your clothes. I'm sure with a little sprucing up of one of your dresses, you'll look just lovely."

Cassandra sighed. "Well, it's going to take a miracle to put something presentable together by tomorrow night."

"Well, let's finish getting what we need and head for home so we can work on that miracle."

The next morning, Dr. Dane Logan stood over a boy of twelve years in a cabin in the mountains. "Johnny, I really think you should heed your mother's warning next time she tells you not to climb that birch tree out there by the front porch."

Johnny lay with his arm in the fresh cast and sling and nodded. He looked at his parents, who stood together on one side of the bed, then at the doctor, who stood on the other side. "Yes, sir. I'm not gonna climb it again."

"Good. I'd advise you not to climb *any* trees. Find some other way to have fun, okay?"

"Yes, sir."

The doctor turned to the small table beside the bed, closed his black medical bag, and picked it up. "Like I told your parents, Johnny, I want to check on your arm in three or four days."

"We'll bring him in to your office, Doctor," said Johnny's father. "Now how much do we owe you?"

"Three dollars will do it."

The man's brow furrowed. "Are you sure? Seems like it ought to be more than that. After all, you came immediately when I entered your office and followed me all the way up here. You've done a beautiful job in setting Johnny's arm and putting a cast and sling on it."

"Right," said Johnny's mother. "We need to pay you more than three dollars. Let's give him ten, Clyde."

"All right," said Clyde, pulling his wallet from his hip pocket.

As Clyde opened his wallet, Dr. Dane said, "You really don't need to pay me that much. Three dollars is fine."

Clyde grinned as he took out a ten-dollar bill and pressed it into the doctor's free hand. "We happen to know that Dr. Fraser was underpaid far too many times, Dr. Logan. And I'm sure it's already happened to you. Let the extra money take the place of some you didn't get when you should have."

Dr. Dane smiled and shook his head. "All right, sir, if you say so."

"I say so, and so does my missus."

"Me too," put in Johnny.

Dr. Dane thanked them, saying he would see them in three or fours days at the office, and moved outside. He mounted his horse, thanked them once again as they stood on the porch, and rode away.

When Dr. Dane arrived in Central City some forty-five minutes later, he found a young woman sitting in the waiting area. "You're Mrs. Dexter, aren't you?"

"Yes, Doctor. I made an appointment a few days ago."

"And you're here because you think you might be expecting a baby, if I remember correctly."

"Yes," she smiled. "Your wife is in the examining room right now with a boy who burned his hand. His father works for the Holton Mine, as does my husband."

"I see. Well, I'll get on back there and see about the boy, and I'll get to you as soon as I can."

"That's fine, Doctor. I understand the boy's problem is an emergency. I'll wait."

When Dr. Dane stepped into the examining room, he found Tharyn standing over one of the examining tables, where a small boy lay. The boy's mother was standing next to Tharyn, trying to comfort him.

Both women looked up as the doctor moved toward them. Tharyn was applying salve to the boy's right hand as he watched, his lips quivering.

"Hello," Tharyn said as he drew up and placed his medical bag on a nearby cart. "This is Belva Matthews, and this is her son, Craig. He's eight years old. He burned his hand earlier this morning."

"Hello, Mrs. Matthews," said Dr. Dane with a smile, then looked down at the boy.

Belva afforded him a thin smile. "Hello, Doctor. We've heard a lot about you lately, and we're glad you're here. Craig tried to help me clean up the kitchen from breakfast after his father left for the mine this morning. He grasped the handle of a skillet on the stove, not realizing that the handle was extremely hot. I tried to take care of the burns, but finally decided I should bring him to you. Mrs. Logan has put salve on them, but you can see that his palm and four fingers have big blisters on them."

Dr. Dane could tell the boy was trying not to cry while Tharyn was applying the salve. He looked closely at Tharyn's work. "Well, Craig, it looks like my wife has you just about fixed up. You'll need a bandage on that hand, and we can let you go home."

Tharyn set her eyes on her husband. "I'll let you take over here, darling, so I can get back to the office. Is Mandy Dexter still out there?"

"Yes, she is."

"All right. I'll tell her it'll only be a few minutes until you can see her."

"Right. I'd say we'll be finished here in about twenty minutes."

When Tharyn entered the office, she noted that Mandy Dexter was still the only person in the waiting area. As she moved behind her desk, she said, "Mandy, Doctor said to tell you he'll be finished with Craig in about twenty minutes."

"That will be fine, Mrs. Logan. Is Craig's hand going to be all right?"

"Oh yes. The burns are serious, but they will heal with no problem, I'm sure."

"That's good."

Suddenly they heard pounding hooves outside, a man's voice calling "Whoa!", and the sound of a wagon rattling to an abrupt halt.

Both women looked out the window and saw a man in his early sixties hop down from the seat and dash toward the office door.

"Looks like another emergency of some kind," said Mandy.

Tharyn fixed her eyes on the door just as the man came in.

He hurried to the desk, a look of surprise on his face. "Nadine isn't here, ma'am?"

As Tharyn was shaking her head, ready to explain, he snapped his fingers and said, "Oh, of course. Dr. Logan told me a few weeks ago that he was getting married and that his wife would be taking over Nadine's job. I'm Eric Cox. You *are* Mrs. Logan?"

"Yes. I'm Tharyn Logan."

"Glad to meet you, ma'am. Dr. Logan has treated my wife, Nelda, twice since taking over the practice from Dr. Fraser. She's fifty-eight years old and has a bad hip. Dr. Logan told us that Nelda was going to need a hip replacement sometime in the next year or so, but I think it'll have to be sooner. Nelda just fell down a flight of stairs and her hip is hurting something awful. We live a few miles out of town. Our daughter is with her at the moment, doing everything she can to help alleviate the pain. How soon could the doctor come and look at her?"

Before Tharyn could reply, Mandy rose from her chair and approached the desk. "Mrs. Logan, I can come back tomorrow. It's best that Dr. Logan get to this man's wife as soon as possible."

"Are you sure you want to wait till tomorrow?" asked Tharyn. "I know you are quite anxious to learn the doctor's opinion of your condition. I could send a messenger to your house when the doctor gets back, and he could still see you today."

Mandy shook her head. "That's not necessary. Another day won't make that much difference. This man's wife needs the doctor, and he may need to stay with her for a while. Can you work me into your schedule tomorrow?"

Tharyn picked up a pencil and opened the appointment book. She set her eyes on the page before her. "I have an opening at nine o'clock in the morning and one at eleven-thirty. Or I could give you an afternoon appointment at two-thirty, three-thirty, or four o'clock."

"Well, I'll take the one at nine o'clock in the morning."

While writing in Mandy's name, Tharyn said, "All right. It's done. We'll see you at nine in the morning."

The silver-haired Eric Cox set appreciative eyes on Mandy. "Thank you, ma'am. You are very kind."

Mandy smiled. "I hope everything turns out all right for your wife, sir."

As Mandy was stepping out on the boardwalk, Tharyn headed for the door of the examining room and said over her shoulder, "I'll see how Doctor is doing with the patient back here, Mr. Cox. Be right back."

Eric nodded and remained standing in front of her desk.

In a few minutes, she returned. "I explained to Doctor about Nelda's fall, Mr. Cox. He said he will be able to go to her aid in about ten minutes."

"Oh, good. Thank you, ma'am. I'll go on back to the house and let Nelda know that the doctor will soon be on his way."

As Eric hurried out the door, Tharyn thought of when she and Dane first met in Manhattan ten years ago, and how desperately the fifteen-year-old Dane wanted to be a physician and surgeon.

"Thank You, Lord," she said in a soft tone. "Thank You that You made it so Dane has been able to realize his dream, and thank You for the great measure of success he has known in his few short years as a doctor."

Just over three quarters of an hour later, Dr. Dane Logan bent over Nelda Cox's bed with her husband and daughter beside him, while he was finishing his examination. He covered her hip and leg with the sheet, and said, "Well, Nelda, the fall definitely has accelerated your need for the hip replacement. It must be done as soon as possible."

Still somewhat in pain though the doctor had given her a strong dose of laudanum upon his arrival, Nelda looked up at him and nodded. "Whatever you say, Dr. Logan. I'm just so thankful I have you to do the surgery."

"For sure," said Eric.

Bonnie Wilcox, the Coxes' daughter, set quizzical eyes on the physician. "Dr. Logan, please help me to understand what it is exactly that you do when you perform a hip replacement. I know you're well-known for this surgery. Mama was trying to explain it, but I want to make sure I understand."

"Certainly," said Dr. Dane.

"I understand you use an ivory ball in the hip socket instead of a steel one, like most doctors do. Why is that? Wouldn't the steel ball last longer?"

"I learned in medical college that the ivory ball is better because the heavy steel ball tends to damage bone tissue in the socket. This means that after so much time, the socket is so damaged that there can never be another hip replacement. The person is then committed to a wheelchair for the rest of his or her life."

Bonnie rubbed her chin and nodded. "I see."

"I can tell you now that almost all surgeons who do hip replacements on both continents have gone to the ivory ball. It's very strong but extremely light in comparison to the steel ball. So far, all the hip replacements I've done in Wyoming, Nebraska, and Colorado have turned out quite successful, and the recipients are still very satisfied with the results."

"So the ivory ball lasts a long time?"

"Yes. It will last as long as the recipient lives. Like I said, it is very strong."

Bonnie smiled and took hold of her mother's hand. "Sounds like it's going to be all right, Mama."

Nelda nodded. "I believe so, honey."

Eric looked at the doctor. "Let me tell you, Dr. Logan, I'm so glad that you are the one who will be doing Nelda's surgery."

"Thank you. Now let me explain about the surgery. It must be done at Mile High Hospital in Denver. My office doesn't have the proper facilities."

"We understand," said Eric. "So we'll make the trip to Denver whenever you say."

Nelda adjusted her position on the bed. "Dr. Logan, you told us when you were treating me several weeks ago that the young lady you were going to marry had been your surgical nurse to help you with the hip replacement surgeries at Mile High Hospital."

"Yes, ma'am."

"Would it be possible for you to take her along when we go to Denver so she can assist you with my surgery?"

"Most certainly. I still have Dr. Fraser to fill in for me when I'm gone, and Nadine has volunteered to fill in for Tharyn whenever she has to be out of town. I'll talk to Tharyn about it, and we'll plan on it."

"Wonderful!" exclaimed Nelda. "That makes me feel even better."

The doctor grinned. "I'll wire Dr. Matthew Carroll at Mile High Hospital right away and set up a time for the surgery."

Arriving back in Central City, Dr. Dane drove his buggy to Main Street and pulled up in front of the Western Union office.

Charlie Holmes, the Western Union agent, was behind the counter when Dr. Dane entered, and looked up at the doctor with a broad smile. "Howdy, Doc! Something I can do for you?"

Drawing up to the counter, Dr. Dane said, "You sure can, Charlie. I want to send a telegram to Dr. Matthew Carroll, the director of Mile High Hospital in Denver."

Charlie lifted his cap and ran splayed fingers through his thinning silver hair. "That can be arranged."

Dr. Dane chuckled. "Good! That's why I came in here."

Charlie picked up pad and pencil. "Shoot!"

While Charlie wrote speedily on the pad, Dr. Dane dictated the message. He told Dr. Carroll what date he would like to do the hip replacement surgery on Nelda Cox and asked if Dr. Carroll would wire him back and let him know if the date would be all right.

Charlie laid the pencil down. "I'll bring the telegram to you when Dr. Carroll sends his reply."

"I appreciate that, Charlie. Well, I've got to get back to the office."

"Before you go, I want to say something."

"Yes?"

"You've treated me twice since you took over Dr. Fraser's practice."

"Mm-hmm."

"Well, I'd just like to tell you how glad I am that it's *you* who took over his practice. I appreciate your medical knowledge, and I also appreciate your professional demeanor. And let me tell you something else. There are a whole lot of people in this town and the surrounding areas who have told me they feel the same way."

"Well, thank you, Charlie. That means a lot to me."

"Just thought you oughtta know. I'll bring that reply to you as soon as I get it, whether it's to your office or to your house."

"Thanks," said Dr. Dane, heading for the door. "And for such good service, your next medical treatment is free."

Charlie laughed. "Really?"

"Really."

"Well, come to think of it, Doctor, I have this pain in my back. Could you—"

Dr. Dane laughed, gave Charlie a wave, and stepped out onto the boardwalk with Charlie's laughter in his ears.

SEVEN

$\mathcal{A}$s Dr. Dane Logan crossed the boardwalk heading for his buggy, he heard a man's loud, angry voice pierce the air. He looked down the street in the direction of the sound. A half-block away he saw Central City's mayor, Mike Anderson, facing the angry man, who was pouring out hot words of rage at him. They were standing in the dusty street in front of the Rusty Lantern Saloon.

Dane had become well-acquainted with the mayor in his short time as Central City's physician and surgeon. Mayor Anderson, who was in his early fifties, was a Christian. He and his wife, Betty, were members of the church where Mark Shane was pastor.

People were gathering at the spot as the man—who was a stranger to Dane—was railing at Anderson about a family feud sometime in the past. Blood was flushing the sides of the man's neck as he spewed out a string of hostile words at Anderson, who was trying to reason with him in a low, controlled voice.

Serious trouble was like a rank smell on Dr. Dane's senses. He stepped into the street and hurried in that direction, noting that the angry man had his hand on the handle of the gun in his holster.

Dane knew that the mayor did not wear a gun.

He was within twenty yards of the two men when he saw the

stranger whip out his revolver and snap back the hammer while taking a few steps backward and swearing loudly at Anderson.

The people in the crowd looked on wide-eyed as they retreated.

Running hard, Dane shouted, "Hey, you! Don't shoot! Don't shoot!"

Before he could get to the spot, the gun roared. Mike Anderson buckled from the impact of the bullet and started to fall.

Holding the smoking gun trained on the mayor as he fell to the ground, the gunman looked at the man running toward him. He swung the muzzle on him and shouted, "Stop right there, mister!"

But Dr. Dane's attention was on the wounded mayor lying in the dust, gripping his bleeding midsection. He gave the gunman a flicking glance, then dropped to Anderson's side to examine the wound. Mike was gritting his teeth and gasping for breath.

The gunman's features were broken into sardonic lines, and his eyes were narrowed as he fixed them on Dane. "Get away from him!"

On his knees beside the wounded mayor, Dane retorted, "I'm a doctor. I've got to take Mike to my office immediately and treat him, or he will die."

The crowd stood with pale faces, eyes wide, mouths gaping.

The angry man's voice was shrill as the scrape of a file. "I told you to get away from him! Do it, or I'll shoot you too!"

Dr. Dane's determination gleamed in his eyes as he lifted the wounded man up into his arms and rose to his feet. Putting a flat emphasis on his words, he said, "Mike was unarmed. If he dies, you'll be up on a murder charge, mister. All these people are witnesses. I've got to take that slug out of his midsection right now, or he'll die for sure."

With that, Dr. Dane pivoted and headed in the direction of his office.

The crowd watched the gunman aim the gun at Dr. Dane's back as he hissed, "Then you die, too!"

A shot rang out, and the gunman went down like a rotted tree in a high wind.

Every eye in the crowd turned to the man with the badge on his chest in the middle of the street.

When Dr. Dane heard the shot, he expected to feel the bullet plow into his back. With the bleeding mayor cradled in his arms, he paused, looked back, and saw Central City's young town marshal, Jake Merrell, standing over the fallen gunman, but looking his way.

"Go on, Doc," Merrell said solemnly. "Take care of Mike. This man's dead."

Dane nodded, then set his gaze on a man in the crowd named Alf Roberts. "Alf, would you do me a favor?"

"Sure, Doc. Name it."

"I need you to bring my horse and buggy to the office for me. They're up there at the Western Union office."

"Will do," said Alf, and headed that direction.

While the doctor was hurrying down the street with Mike Anderson in his arms, people who had heard the shot looked on with bulging eyes.

A man called out, "What happened, Dr. Logan?"

Dr. Dane did not break his stride. "A man shot Mayor Anderson!"

As Dr. Dane neared his office, he saw more people on the street watching him. He was answering another man who had asked what had happened when he caught a glimpse of Tharyn standing on the boardwalk. When she saw him carrying the mayor and heard his reply to the man, she opened the office door and held it for him.

Seeing the shocked look on Tharyn's face, Dr. Dane said, "He's gut shot. I've got to get the slug out quickly or he'll die."

Tharyn fixed her gaze on the mayor's twisted, pallid face as her husband carried him past her, then followed him into the examining and surgical room.

As the doctor laid Mike on the nearest table, he said, "He's still slightly conscious, honey. He'll need some chloroform."

When Dr. Dane finished the surgery on the unconscious Mike Anderson almost two hours later, he turned to Tharyn and sighed. "He's going to make it, sweetheart. He's going to make it!"

"Oh, praise the Lord!" she said.

Three times during the surgery, Tharyn had left her husband's side long enough to go into the office to explain to patients with appointments, and those who had come in without appointments, what was happening. The first time she had gone out, Betty Anderson was there, having been notified of the shooting by some friends who had witnessed it. Upon her return to the operating table, Tharyn had told her husband of Betty's presence in the office.

Dane was putting the finishing touches on Mike's bandage. Tharyn looked up at him with relief showing in her eyes. "I'll stay with Mike, honey, while you go out and tell Betty he's going to live. When I was out there in the office the last time, she was near hysteria. I tried to calm her, but she was still on the edge. Hearing the good news from you will carry more weight."

As she spoke, Tharyn reached down and took hold of Mike's wrist, pressed experienced fingers down to check his pulse, and looked at the watch that was pinned to her white apron. After several seconds had passed, she said, "His pulse is a little weak and thready, but that's to be expected after all the blood loss."

Concentrating on his bandage work, Dane nodded in agreement.

Tharyn put his wrist back at his side. "I'll keep a watchful eye on him, and while you're out there relieving Betty's mind, I'll clean all of this up quickly so you can bring her in to see him. He's still under the chloroform, but I know it'll make her feel better just to see and touch him."

Dane made the final knot in the bandage and set loving eyes on her. "Okay. I'll wash the blood off my hands before I go out."

As he spoke, he walked to a nearby table where a ewer of warm water and a bowl waited for him. He poured the water in the bowl, and while soaping his hands, he looked over his shoulder and watched Tharyn as she began cleaning up the operating table around Mike Anderson. At the same time, she was carefully watching the patient for any sign of distress.

After drying his hands, the doctor took one more look at the mayor and satisfied himself that indeed the man would live. He looked at Tharyn. "Thank you for your excellent help during that touchy surgery, sweetheart. I couldn't have done it without you."

Tharyn's eyes sparkled. "Glad to be of assistance, Dr. Logan," she replied, giving him a tired smile.

Dane put his arms around Tharyn and hugged her. "I'll go talk to Betty now and let her come in for a few minutes. Seeing him breathing will ease her heart and mind. While we were doing the surgery I could literally feel her prayers."

"You too? I sure felt them."

In the office, Betty Anderson was pacing the floor while those who were waiting to see the doctor watched her.

An elderly couple who were also members of the church and knew the Andersons well, looked on her with compassion.

The silver-haired gentleman said, "Betty, I feel in my heart that the Lord is going to spare Mike's life. One thing about it, He certainly has given Mike an excellent surgeon to care for him. We've been to Dr. Logan every week since he's been here, and we have the utmost confidence in him. Putting that with the prayers we just offered to the Lord together, I have peace about it."

"Me too, Betty," said the man's wife. "I really believe Mike is going to make it."

At that instant, the door to the back room opened, and the form of Dr. Dane Logan appeared.

When Betty saw the smile on the doctor's face, she knew he had good news.

The elderly couple and the others who were waiting looked on as the doctor stepped up to Betty. "He's doing fine. I'm sure he is going to live."

Betty leaped for him, wrapped her arms around his neck, and broke into happy tears. "Oh, thank You, Lord! Thank You!" She backed up and released the doctor. "Thank *you* too, Dr. Logan, for doing such a wonderful job on Mike!"

Dr. Dane glanced out the window and noted the large crowd that was gathered outside in front of the office. He looked into Betty's tear-filled eyes. "Mike is under the chloroform right now and won't wake up for a couple of hours, but I know you'd still like to see him."

"Oh yes!"

"Before I take you back, let me explain that it will take several weeks for him to recover, but he'll have to take it easy for much longer than that."

"I understand."

"I wish Central City had a hospital, which would really be best for Mike, but it would be too dangerous to transport him to Denver. We'll keep him here at the office for a couple of days; then he can come home. I'll stay with him at night. When he comes home, you'll just have to keep a sharp eye on him and let me know if you see anything that seems to be wrong. Being shot in the midsection is a very serious thing."

Tears were running down Betty's cheeks. "I'll take good care of him, doctor. Now, I want to say this to you. Thank you for your bravery."

Dr. Dane's eyebrows arched. "Bravery?"

Betty used a hankie to dab at her tears. "Yes. I've been told how that gunman threatened to shoot you if you tried to take Mike away, but, dear doctor, you risked your own life to do just that."

Dr. Dane's face flushed. "Well, I—"

"We all heard about it, Dr. Logan," cut in the elderly man. "That was some deed!"

The other patients joined in.

Dr. Dane cleared his throat just as Tharyn was coming into the office from the back room and said, "Folks, I only did what any other doctor would have done."

One of the men said, "Most doctors would not have jeopardized their own lives in the face of a gun to do what you did, Dr. Logan. You're a brave man."

The others spoke their agreement, and the loudest voice was that of Betty Anderson.

Tharyn said to her husband, "Nadine came in the back door a minute ago, having heard about the shooting incident. She's watching over Mike at the moment so I can do my work here in the office. Darling, what's this about your bravery? Exactly what happened out there?"

Dane's face flushed again. "Honey, I told the man who shot Mike that I had to get him to the office and treat him immediately or he would die. He pointed his gun at me and told me not to do it. I had no choice. I had to carry Mike here in a hurry. I'm not some hero. I just did what had to be done."

Betty moved up close and looked at Tharyn. "Well, he's a hero as far as I'm concerned. He risked his life to save my husband!"

Tharyn smiled. "I agree, Betty. Dane has been my hero since we were orphans together on the streets of New York City."

Dane smiled at his wife, then said, "Let's take Betty back so she can take a look at Mike."

"You go ahead, honey. I'll stay here in the office so I can have these patients ready when you're ready to see them."

Dane nodded and led Betty to the back room.

Tharyn was about to talk to the people who had come into the office without appointments, wanting to know the order they came in, so she could line them up in that order to see the doctor. However her attention was drawn outside when one of the men in the crowd called out, "Mrs. Logan! What's the mayor's condition? We want to know how he is!"

Voices from the crowd pled with her to let them know about Mayor Anderson. She hurried to the door, opened it, and stepped out onto the boardwalk. The crowd went quiet immediately.

Tharyn let a wide smile capture her face. "Folks, I'm happy to tell you that though Mayor Anderson has been seriously wounded, my husband is certain that he is going to live."

There were cheers of elation.

When the cheers faded, Tharyn said, "My husband and Betty are with Mike right now, but if you want to wait, I'll ask the doctor to come out and explain the mayor's condition to you in detail shortly."

At that instant, Dr. Dane came out the door with Betty on his heels and moved up beside Tharyn. "I'll talk to them right now, honey."

Betty moved up beside Tharyn, and Tharyn put an arm around her.

Pastor Mark Shane was in the crowd near the front standing beside Marshal Jake Merrell. All the townspeople knew that Merrell was a Christian, and that Shane was his pastor.

Dr. Dane explained the details of the wound that Mayor Mike Anderson had sustained, but that he was able to get the bullet out and the internal bleeding stopped in time. He assured them that he would keep a close watch on him.

One of the townsmen lifted his voice so all could hear: "Dr. Logan, we all know how you defied that gunman and risked your own life by walkin' away with Mike in your arms!"

Tharyn could tell that her husband was embarrassed, but joined with the crowd, applauding him.

At that moment, Betty Anderson took a step forward and the crowd quickly grew quiet, knowing she wanted to speak to them.

Betty had tears in her eyes as she spoke of Dr. Dane's courage. The crowd broke into applause and cheers again.

When they grew quiet once more, Betty looked at the doctor through her tears, then looked back at the crowd. "This man now has a special place in my heart! From now on, I will call him the beloved physician of Central City!"

Cheers were raised again, and one man shouted, "Yes! Dr. Logan, to all of us you are the beloved physician!"

Pastor Mark Shane and Marshal Jake Merrell wove their way through the press to the boardwalk. Pastor Shane said, "Dr. Logan, I would like to go in and pray over Mayor Anderson."

Dr. Dane smiled. "Mike is still under the chloroform, Pastor, but you're welcome to go in. Nadine Wahl is with him at the moment, but Betty and Tharyn and I will go in with you."

Marshal Merrell stepped up and said, "Dr. Logan, may I speak to Mrs. Anderson just for a moment?"

"Of course."

The crowd began to disperse, but a few people remained, looking on. One of those people was Dr. Robert Fraser.

The marshal turned to Betty. "Mrs. Anderson, the identification I took off the dead gunman's body showed his name to be Vincent Orcutt."

Betty's mouth sagged. "Vincent Orcutt! How in the world—"

"Do you know him, ma'am?"

"I know the name quite well."

"I see. Well, some of the people who saw the whole thing told me that when the argument started between Orcutt and your husband, there was something said about a family feud. Do you know about that?"

"I sure do. My husband has told me all about it. Mike and Vincent are both from Dallam County, Texas, near the town of Dalhart. Both families were country folk, and a feud got started between them when Mike and Vincent were small children. The feud went on for several years, with family members on both sides being wounded or killed by gunfire. Finally, both Mike's and Vincent's fathers were killed in a gun battle between the two sides. After that, things cooled down, but neither side ever got over the hard feelings they had for each other. Mike has told me several times about the last time he saw Vincent when they were teenagers. Vincent told him if he ever saw him again, he would kill him. But that was a long time ago. Both of them moved from Texas and haven't seen each other since."

The marshal frowned. "Do you think Orcutt somehow found out where Mike was and came here to follow up on his threat?"

Betty shook her head. "Marshal, I seriously doubt that. It probably was a chance thing for them to run into each other."

"Mrs. Anderson?" came a man's voice from the small part of the crowd that was left.

Betty turned. "Yes, Bart?"

"You're right. It was a chance situation. I happened to be standing on the boardwalk when Mayor Mike came along. At the same time, that Orcutt fella came out of the Rusty Lantern Saloon. There was a surprised look on his face when he saw and recognized Mayor Mike. Apparently Orcutt was just passing through town. But, oh boy, when he saw Mayor Mike, he lit into him royally!"

The marshal smiled at Bart. "I'm glad you were able to see what happened. Thanks for speaking up."

At that moment, Dr. Robert Fraser stepped up onto the

boardwalk and smiled at Dr. Dane. He patted him on the back. "I'm mighty proud of you, my boy. That was some courageous deed you did."

Dr. Dane was glad that his predecessor was not jealous of the accolades that had been poured out on him by the crowd. "Thank you, sir. I appreciate that."

Pastor Mark Shane heard the elderly doctor's comments and smiled to himself.

Marshal Jake Merrell stepped up to the young physician and said in a joking manner, "Dr. Logan, if you ever decide to give up your medical practice, I sure could use a brave deputy like you."

They both had a good laugh; then Dr. Dane, Tharyn, Betty, and the pastor moved inside to have their time of prayer over Mike Anderson.

EIGHT

*I*t was midafternoon in Denver when Dr. Matthew Carroll's secretary, Hilda Satterlee, entered the Western Union office.

Agent Alex Connor was at his desk behind the counter, tapping out a message on the telegraph key. He smiled at Hilda, holding up the index finger of his left hand to signal that he would be with her shortly. She nodded.

Less than two minutes had passed when Alex finished the message. He arose from the desk and stepped up to the counter.

"Howdy, Miss Hilda. Let me guess. You're here to send another telegram for your boss."

She smiled again. "You guessed correctly, Alex. I seldom ever send a telegram myself, so when you see me come through the door, chances are pretty good that it will be another telegram I'm sending for Dr. Carroll."

Alex picked up a paper pad and a pencil. "All right, who does this one go to?"

"Dr. Dane Logan in Central City."

"That's D-A-N-E L-O-G-A-N?"

"Sure is."

He scribbled it on the pad. "Central City. The *Colorado* Central City, correct?"

"Correct."

When he had scribbled that down, he said, "All right, what's the message? As you know, I can write pretty fast, so just spill it out."

"The message is that Dr. Carroll has agreed on the date for Nelda Cox's hip replacement that Dr. Logan had requested in his wire this morning."

He frowned. "This morning? I don't recall—oh, of course! It came in when I was out of the office earlier."

"Right. Your able assistant, Chet Mullins, brought it over to us."

"Okay." He scribbled some more, then held up the pad for Hilda to see. "Do I have the lady's name spelled right?"

"Sure do."

Putting the pad back down and poising the pencil, he said, "All right. Go ahead."

"The date is next Wednesday, July 20. A week from tomorrow."

Alex wrote it down. "Go ahead."

"Dr. Carroll agrees that this will give Mrs. Cox time to get over her trauma from the fall down the stairs. He also agrees that they should come to Denver on Monday. This will give Mrs. Cox a day to rest before the surgery and will give her husband and the Logans an opportunity to rest up from the trip. Dr. Carroll will make reservations for the Logans and Mr. Cox at the Brown Palace Hotel."

Alex scribbled for a few more seconds, then looked up at her. "Anything else?"

"No, sir. That's it."

"All right. That'll be a dollar twenty-five."

As Hilda was placing a dollar bill and a quarter in his hand, the telegraph key began to sing out. Alex quickly laid the money on his desk and sat down on the chair. "See you next time."

Hilda nodded and walked out the door with the sound of the telegraph key ringing in her ears.

In Central City, when Dr. Dane Logan and Pastor Mark Shane came into the office after having prayer over Mike Anderson, they found Dr. Robert Fraser chatting with the people who were waiting to be seen by Dr. Logan.

Fraser excused himself to them and moved up to Dr. Dane. "I understand you're going to keep Mike here for two days for observation."

Dane nodded. "That's right."

"And you're planning to spend those nights here with him."

"Mm-hmm."

"Well, I know what that's like. I'm sure you've got busy days ahead of you, so I'll come and stay with Mike these next two nights."

Dr. Dane grinned and shook his head. "Dr. Fraser, you're supposed to be retired. You come in here so often already to fill in for me. I can't ask you to come and stay with Mike those two nights."

A sly grin curved the aging physician's lips. "You didn't ask me. I volunteered. Now don't argue with me. I'm staying here the next two nights with Mike."

Pastor Shane laughed. "Well, Dr. Dane, it sounds to me like he's got it all planned, and no matter what you say, it's going to remain that way."

"You got it, Pastor!" said Fraser.

Dr. Dane shrugged. "What can I say?"

Dr. Fraser winked at him. "Just say you're not going to argue with me anymore about it."

"Okay. I'm not going to argue with you anymore about it."

"Good! Then it's settled." The silver-haired physician headed for the door. When he reached it and pulled it open, he looked back at Dr. Dane. "I'll be here just before closing time."

Late in the afternoon, Tharyn Logan was at her desk in the

doctor's office when Charlie Holmes came in with a yellow envelope in his hand.

Tharyn gave a warm smile. "Hello, Charlie. Is that telegram Dr. Matthew Carroll's reply to my husband's wire?"

"Sure is," he said, handing it to her.

Tharyn opened a drawer, took out a dollar bill, and placed it in his hand. "Thank you."

Charlie shook his head. "You don't need to pay me for bringing it over here, ma'am."

"Yes, I do. Nadine told me that's the way Dr. Fraser did it, so that's the way Dr. Logan will do it."

Charlie thanked her. Tharyn opened the envelope and read Dr. Carroll's message. Knowing Dane would want to know what Dr. Carroll had to say on the subject of Nelda Cox's surgery, she headed toward the examining room where he was with a patient.

A few minutes later, Tharyn returned to the office and sat down at her desk. A smile spread over her face. Her husband had read the telegram and told her that after he took her to dinner at one of Central City's restaurants this evening, they would drive out to the Cox home and let them know that they would be going to Denver next Monday and the surgery would be on Wednesday.

That evening, just before six o'clock, Cassandra Wheatley and her aunt were sitting on the front porch of the house in rocking chairs, with Cassandra keeping her eyes on the street, watching for Greg Holton to show up.

Mabel was weary as she sat in the rocking chair, barely moving it back and forth. A deep sigh escaped her as she looked at her young niece. Cassandra did look lovely. Mabel had sewed a good part of the day on the dress Cassandra was wearing. She told herself the girl was difficult to please, but finally she had restored one of her dresses to Cassandra's satisfaction for her date with Greg.

With her eyes still on the girl, Mabel said, "I guess by now word has gotten all over town about how Dr. Dane Logan put himself in jeopardy to save Mayor Anderson's life."

"I would suppose so," replied Cassandra, keeping her eyes fixed on the street.

"Wonderful man, that doctor. His determination to save Mike's life and the courage he displayed to defy that gunman so he could do it was really something."

"I agree, Aunt Mabel. Dr. Logan did a wonderful and marvelous thing."

"This world needs more men like Dr.—"

"Here he comes!" cried Cassandra, moving up to the railing with her gaze fixed on the buggy that was moving down the street.

As the buggy drew near and Greg guided it into the circular driveway, Cassandra waved. He smiled and waved back.

Greg pulled rein in front of the house, hopped out of the buggy, and bounded up the steps.

"Hello, Mrs. Downing," he said with a smile. "How are you?"

"I'm fine, Greg," Mabel replied.

Greg then looked at Cassandra. "Ready to go?"

Eyes flashing with elation, she said, "Yes, I am."

Mabel said, "Greg, I'd like for you to have Cassandra home by nine-thirty."

Cassandra was about to object to such an early hour, but she refrained when Greg assured Mabel he would have her home by then.

He took her by the hand, guided her down the porch steps, and helped her into the buggy.

Mabel released another big sigh, pulled herself up from the chair, and moved to the edge of the steps. "Have a nice time!"

They both waved at her, and Greg put the buggy in motion.

Mabel watched them drive away, then turned and entered the house to prepare her own supper. As she made her way into the kitchen, she couldn't help but wonder why Cassandra was such a self-centered girl and why she had such a love for money. So much of what came from her mouth was about being rich and living luxuriously.

My sister and brother-in-law are not greedy, she thought. *I just hope I can help her in some way. The most important thing is to win her to Jesus. Then He could take care of the rest. But that's not going to be easy. I've never seen someone this young so hardened against the Lord and His Word.*

Weary to the bone after working so long on Cassandra's dress, Mabel tried to think of something quick and easy for her own supper. "I think I'll just have some bread with butter and jam and some milk, and call it good."

She sliced some bread, put butter and jam on it, and poured a cup of milk. Sitting down at the kitchen table, she bowed her head, thanked the Lord for her simple nourishment, and asked for wisdom and grace in dealing with her wayward niece.

As Greg turned the buggy onto Main Street with Cassandra holding onto his arm, he said, "I'm going to take you to Central City's fanciest restaurant, the Golden Eagle."

"Oh, wonderful! I've seen it several times, but I've never been inside. Thank you, Greg, for being so good to me."

"My pleasure, pretty lady."

Soon they drew up to a hitching post near the restaurant and went inside. After they had been seated by the host and had given their orders to their waitress, Greg ran his gaze over the crowded room and spotted Dr. Dane Logan and the lovely redhead a few tables away. He looked across the table. "Cassandra, did you hear about Mayor Mike Anderson being shot today?"

"Yes, and it was a brave thing that the doctor did."

"It sure was." Pointing with his chin, he said, "That's Dr.

Logan right over there. The good-looking man in the dark suit with that pretty red-headed lady."

"Oh, so that's him. I've heard a lot about him in the short time I've been here."

"The lady is a nurse from Denver. They got married recently. He did all right for himself, didn't he? Isn't she beautiful?"

A stab of intense jealousy pierced through Cassandra, but she masked her feelings. She had become quite adept at making people see her as something other than the self-centered person she really was. "Yes, Greg. She is very beautiful."

He smiled, reached across the table, and took hold of her hand. "Of course, she isn't as beautiful as you, Cassandra."

Those words erased the thoughts she was having about Greg. She blushed and batted her eyelids. "Thank you."

"I've been to Dr. Logan twice since he came here to take over Dr. Robert Fraser's practice. Both times it was for minor injuries that I sustained on the job. I like him very much."

The waitress came with their food and placed it on the table.

While they were eating, Cassandra reached deep inside for courage and said, "Greg, I need to have a little talk with you this evening before you take me home."

Greg glanced up at a clock that hung on the wall. "Unless it needs to be a long talk, we should have plenty of time."

"N-no. It shouldn't take but a few minutes."

"Okay. Since we're going for a moonlight ride after dinner, we can talk then."

"All right. That will be fine."

Greg met her gaze. "Is this about something special I can do for you?"

She swallowed her food. "Well, in a way, yes."

"Good. I've been waiting for something like this."

Cassandra wished the "something special" was different than it was, but she hoped it would turn out all right.

They ate silently for a couple of minutes; then Greg said, "It must have been terrible for you to lose both parents. It was hard enough for me to lose my mother, but to lose both parents had to be something awful."

Cassandra felt her stomach cramp. She had her coffee cup to her lips. She took a sip and waved her free hand through the steam that was rising from the cup.

Anything to avoid comment.

Greg grinned. "Really hot, huh?"

She nodded.

Greg was quiet for a few seconds, then said, "I sure am glad I still have Dad. He and I are really close."

Cassandra took another sip of coffee.

Greg sensed that she would rather not discuss her parents, so he dropped the subject.

Time seemed to pass quickly.

Greg and Cassandra were eating their dessert when they noticed the Logans rising from their table in preparation to leave.

At the same instant, Dr. Logan's eyes settled on Greg. He smiled and guided his wife toward their table.

When they drew up, Dr. Dane said, "Hello, Greg. I don't think I've met this young lady."

Because of Mrs. Logan's presence, Greg stood up. "This is Cassandra Wheatley, Doctor. She's Mrs. Mabel Downing's niece."

The doctor smiled at Cassandra. "I had heard that Mabel's niece had come to live with her. Glad to meet you, little lady." Taking hold of Tharyn's hand, Dr. Dane drew her close. "Cassandra, Greg, this is my wife, Tharyn. Honey, this is Greg Holton. His father owns the Holton Coal Mine just west of town. And as you heard, this is Mabel Downing's niece, Cassandra Wheatley."

"Happy to meet both of you," Tharyn said pleasantly.

Greg grinned. "Same here, ma'am."

"Yes," said Cassandra. "I'm happy to meet you, ma'am." She

then looked up at the doctor. "Dr. Logan, you did a very commendable thing in the face of that gunman's threat this morning. I was glad to hear that Mayor Anderson is going to be all right."

"Everybody in town is glad he wasn't killed, and thank you for your kind words, Miss Wheatley. I want to welcome you to Central City. We attend the same church your aunt does, and we really think a lot of her. Hope you can come to church with her sometime soon."

Cassandra felt a hot surge rush through her chest. She was trying to think of what to say when Tharyn said, "I want to welcome you to our town too, Cassandra."

Dr. Dane glanced at the clock on the wall. "We'd better go, sweetheart. We have to visit the Coxes."

"Yes, we do. Well, it's been nice meeting both of you. I hope we meet again soon."

"Me too," said Greg.

Cassandra nodded and this time had to force a smile. "Yes. Me too."

The Logans headed for the cashier's counter.

Moments later, Greg and Cassandra left the restaurant. Greg drove the buggy to the south edge of town, left the road, drove over a hill on a bumpy path, and hauled up beside a small, gurgling brook that flowed through a forest of pine trees.

The three-quarter moon was already high in the sky and was sending down its silver beams on the faces of the couple. The wolves at higher elevations began their haunting, mournful howls. The stars twinkled like lights in a fairy palace and the soft wind moaned through the pines.

Greg turned and set admiring eyes on Cassandra. Her soft, lovely features were framed by hair as black as the wing of a raven. Moonlight was reflected in her beautiful eyes. "There's a fallen tree down there on the bank of the brook. Would you like to go down there and sit?"

Cassandra was already feeling shaky because of what she had to tell Greg, but masking it, she smiled and said, "Yes, that would be nice."

Greg helped her out of the buggy and held her hand while he guided her a few steps down the gentle slope to the fallen tree.

When they were sitting comfortably, he looked into her fathomless eyes. "Now, what was it you wanted to talk to me about?"

Cassandra felt her heart lurch in her chest and decided to put it off a little longer by saying, "I'll get to that in a moment, but I'd like to ask you something."

"Sure. Ask away, pretty lady."

"Do you and your father go to church?"

Greg looked at her blankly. "Well…uh…no, we don't."

Relief washed over her.

Greg's brow furrowed in the moonlight as distant wolves continued to howl higher up in the mountains. "Why do you ask if Dad and I go to church?"

"Well—I—ah—my Aunt Mabel is very religious, and she makes me nervous. Don't misunderstand. I love Aunt Mabel, but she is really a fanatic. She goes to church every time the doors are open. She reads her Bible twice a day and prays over every meal. I—I want to get to know you better, Greg, so I thought it best to find out if you and your father are like her. If you were—well, I guess we just wouldn't become close friends or anything like that."

Greg studied her dark eyes, but did not comment.

Cassandra cleared her throat gently. "Do you believe in God?"

He nodded. "Yes. So does Dad. But we're just not churchgoers. Your aunt's pastor has visited us a few times. Pastor Mark Shane is a nice man, but like your aunt, he's a fanatic. Each time he has come to our house, he has showed us from the Bible about Jesus Christ dying on the cross for sinners and that we must put our faith in Him for salvation and forgiveness of our sins, or we will go to hell when we die."

"I don't believe in hell," Cassandra said.

"Well, I'm not really sure I do either. Dad and I have talked about it each time after Pastor Shane has come to the house, and we've agreed that since we live decent lives, if hell exists, God wouldn't put us there. In spite of what Pastor Shane has preached to us from the Bible, we believe because we're not outlaws or killers, God will take us to heaven."

Cassandra shook her head. "I don't believe in heaven, either. I had a friend back home in Aurora who let me read a book written by Charles Darwin. It was actually a book that compiled letters he had written to people on the subject of God and evolution. Darwin said the Bible is no more to be trusted than the sacred books of the Hindus, or anybody else's sacred books. He said even if God exists, there is no heaven and there is no hell. When we die, that's the end of us. We no longer exist."

Again, Greg studied Cassandra's eyes, but did not comment.

There was a moment of silence with only the babbling of the brook and the howling of wolves in their ears; then Greg said, "So what was it you wanted to talk to me about?"

Cassandra's mouth went dry. For a moment, fear froze her. She could feel her heart pounding and a vein in her forehead pulsing. There was a hot commotion in her chest.

"W-well, I—I have s-something to confess, G-Greg."

He frowned. "What's that?"

"I—I told you a lie that day we first met."

"A lie?"

"Yes."

"About what?"

"About my parents. They're not really dead."

"Oh?"

"No. I also lied to Rosemary about it."

Greg stared at her questioningly.

Cassandra told herself she had no choice but to lie to him

again. She cleared her throat. "You see, Greg, my parents treated me terribly. It's hard to tell you this, but you need to know it. Both Mother and Father beat on me for no sensible reason time and time again. Sometimes they made me go for days without eating as punishment for something I hadn't even done. I took all I could and finally ran away from home."

"Oh, you poor kid."

It was working. Greg was buying it.

She went on. "With what little money I had, I took a train from Chicago to Denver, then took a stagecoach to Central City. Though I knew about Aunt Mabel's religious fanaticism and I didn't like it, I knew she would take me in."

Cassandra then turned on the tears. "Greg, I need your forgiveness. Will you forgive me for lying to you about my parents being dead?"

He took hold of both her hands and looked into her tear-dimmed eyes. "I forgive you, Cassandra. I can understand why you wouldn't want people to know you had parents like that. I'm sorry you've had to have so much sorrow and heartache in your life."

Cassandra was smiling inside. Now that she had Greg in the palm of her hand, she would go on to embellish her poor-me status.

Letting the tears flow down her cheeks, she said with trembling voice, "Wh-when my parents told me to get out of their house, they let me pack a bag with the bare essentials. The bag was small, and I couldn't bring but a few dresses, and most of them were threadbare. It's been so difficult to keep up appearances with my meager wardrobe."

Compassion was showing in Greg's eyes.

Cassandra would do her best to get all the sympathy from him she could, hoping that would cause him to give her money. She slipped her hands from his and rubbed the sleeves of her dress, affording him a sad little smile. "You see, Aunt Mabel worked all day on this old dress, trying to make it suitable for our date this evening."

Greg's brow furrowed. "Why doesn't your aunt buy you some new dresses? Everyone in town knows her husband had a life insurance policy worth enough to comfortably care for her the rest of her life."

Cassandra had come to Central City because she knew her aunt, though not exactly wealthy, was comfortable enough financially to provide for her niece. But she had found that Aunt Mabel was reluctant to give her money or buy her new clothes.

"Greg, Aunt Mabel was kind enough to give me a home with her, and to feed me, but that's about all. I—I'm trying to find some sort of work here in town, but so far, no one seems to be hiring young ladies with no experience."

Greg rubbed his chin. "Cassandra, I—I don't want to embarrass you. Please don't be offended at what I'm about to offer. Would you let me supply you with some money until you can get a job?"

As he spoke, he pulled a money clip out of his pocket, removed several bills of currency, counted them, and extended them to her. "Here's two hundred dollars."

Cassandra blushed, putting on a false face of humility. "Oh, Greg, I…I really shouldn't let you do this."

He took hold of her hand, placed the bills against her palm, and closed her fingers over them. "I want to help you. Please accept it."

She looked down at the bills, then back at him. Tears flowed freely again. "I—I don't know how to thank you."

"No need. It's my pleasure. And when you need more, I want you to let me know, okay?"

"Oh, I could never—"

"Cassandra, promise you will let me know when you need

more. It may take time for you to get a job, so I want your promise."

Her heart was thumping her rib cage. Putting a look of humility in her teary eyes, she nodded. "All right, if you say so."

Greg smiled. "I say so."

"You will never know what this means to me."

"I'm just glad I can do it." He looked up toward the moon. "Well, we'd better go. I don't want your aunt to be upset at me for getting you home late."

Moments later when she was seated comfortably in the buggy and they were headed back toward town, Cassandra gloated within herself at her success in winning Greg over. Soon she would get him to propose.

NINE

Eric Cox stood on the opposite side of his wife's bed from Dr. Dane and Tharyn Logan as Tharyn held Nelda's hand and the doctor gave them the details of their upcoming trip to Denver next Monday, July 18.

Dr. Dane explained the details of the surgery, making sure they both understood the use of the ivory ball.

When the doctor had finished his explanation, Eric said, "Then we'll plan on leaving at seven o'clock on Monday morning as you said, Doctor."

Dr. Dane nodded. "That will get us to Mile High Hospital by about one o'clock in the afternoon. Nelda will be given a nice room and bed so she can rest until surgery time Wednesday morning."

Eric smiled. "It was awfully nice of Dr. Carroll to make reservations for you two and myself at the hotel. I'm going to pay for your room, too."

Dr. Dane shook his head. "You don't need to do that."

"Oh yes, I do. It is part of your expense so you and Tharyn can perform Nelda's surgery. That's the way it's going to be."

"But—"

"No 'buts.' I said I'm paying for your hotel room."

Dr. Dane grinned. "Well, if you insist."

"I insist."

"No sense arguing with my husband, Doctor," said Nelda, her face contorted with pain. "He's stubborn as a mule."

The doctor grinned again. "I just found that out. Well anyway, Nelda, I know this will be a long ride for you, so I'll be renting a special carriage from Central City's stable for the trip. I've rented them before when taking patients to Denver to do surgery on them at the hospital. These carriages have a flat, padded place in the center where you can lie at least reasonably comfortably during the trip. But I'll tell you what I'm going to do."

Nelda looked at her husband and back to the doctor. "Yes, sir?"

"I'm going to give you a good dose of laudanum just before we pull out on Monday morning. It will ease the pain that you most surely will experience on the rough roads. The laudanum will also induce sleep so you can get the rest you need. We don't want you tired and worn out when it's time to do the surgery."

Nelda managed a smile in spite of her pain and discomfort.

She reached up and clasped his hand. "Thank you, Dr. Logan. You think of everything. I really appreciate the kind of care you are giving me."

Tharyn turned her gaze from the patient to her gentle husband. Tears misted her eyes and a smile beamed on her face.

Eric spoke up. "Dr. Logan, I appreciate your planning to rent this specially equipped carriage for Nelda's comfort. I will reimburse you for this expense too, when I pay you the bill for the surgery."

"This isn't necessary, Eric," Dr. Dane said.

"No use arguing, Doctor," said Nelda. "He won't budge, and I don't want him to. It is only right that we pay for the use of the carriage. After all, it's for my benefit."

Dr. Dane looked at his wife and sighed. "I think we have *two* stubborn mules here, sweetheart."

Tharyn smiled. "Looks like it."

Nelda chewed on her lower lip. "Ah…Doctor, something just came to my mind."

"Yes?"

"The attacks that some of the Ute Indians have made on ranchers and travelers in the Rocky Mountains of late. Will we be in any danger?"

Dr. Dane scratched an ear. "I'm not aware of any such Indian attacks."

"There have been a couple of renegade Ute bands who have attacked whites lately, Doctor," said Eric. "All of these attacks have been farther west in the Rockies, on the other side of the Continental Divide."

"That's why I haven't heard about them," the doctor said, running his gaze between Eric and Nelda. "But I'll tell you what. If you're afraid to make the trip because of the Indians, I'll go to Fort Junction and see if Colonel Perry Smith will give us a cavalry escort."

"Oh no," said Nelda. "It isn't necessary. I hadn't thought it through, or I wouldn't have said anything about it. Since the renegade Ute attacks have been on the west side of the Continental Divide and we'll be traveling east, there shouldn't be any danger."

Dr. Dane looked at Eric. "What's your opinion?"

"I agree with Nelda. There shouldn't be anything to worry about since we're already on the east side of the Mountains, and we're heading farther east. I'm not worried."

Dr. Dane nodded. "All right, but I'll bring along a couple repeater rifles just in case."

"That'll be good enough," said Eric. "Say, how about that shooting incident on Main Street this morning? Our neighbors just to the south were there when it happened and stopped to tell us about it when they came home this afternoon. They said they never saw such raw courage as you displayed."

Nelda smiled up at him. "So you are now Central City's beloved physician, Dr. Logan. I like that."

Eric chuckled. "Me, too."

A proud smile played on Tharyn's features as she ran her gaze from Nelda to the man she adored.

Once again embarrassed by Betty Anderson's new title for him, Dr. Dane's face flushed. "I'm not some shining hero. I only did what any doctor would have done. Mayor Anderson's life was in danger, and by the blood coming from his midsection, he would have bled to death shortly. Every minute would count. I had to get him to the office in a hurry."

"But Dr. Logan," said Nelda, "you *are* a shining hero. Since that gunman—what was his name?"

"Vincent Orcutt."

"That Vincent Orcutt warned you not to help Mayor Anderson, but you did it anyway. It was a very brave thing to do. And he's alive because you dared take care of him in spite of that gunman's warning. I sure am glad Mayor Anderson is still alive."

"For sure," put in Eric.

A serious look came over Dr. Dane's countenance. He ran his gaze to Eric, then to Nelda. "Well, I can tell you one thing, if Vincent Orcutt had killed me and Mike Anderson would have died from loss of blood, Mike and I would be in heaven together right now."

Tharyn noticed the faces of both Eric and Nelda pinch.

Dr. Dane ran his gaze between them again. "Remember the last time I came here to examine Nelda's hip? I talked to both of you about salvation, but you weren't interested."

The Coxes looked at each other, then looked another direction, avoiding the eyes of the doctor and his wife.

Dane and Tharyn exchanged glances; then he said, "Eric, Nelda, when I talked to you about opening your hearts to Jesus, you told me that Pastor Mark Shane had visited you on two occasions prior to that and had tried to get you to do the same thing, but you hadn't responded to him, either. Right?"

Eric cleared his throat nervously. "Th-that is correct, Dr. Logan. Nelda and I have discussed the subject several times since the day you talked to us about our need to be saved. We even talked about going to your church, but with Nelda's hip so bad, she didn't think she could do it. We...ah...we both have a problem with what both you and Pastor Shane told us."

"A problem?"

"Yes."

"And that is...?"

"Well, we just can't believe that people can know for sure they are going to heaven. What if they just don't measure up to what God expects in their lives after they have asked Jesus to save them? How would they know this? How would they know they were pleasing God enough in their church life and in their daily deeds?"

Dr. Dane smiled. "Many people have this problem, Eric. You and Nelda still have not clearly seen that salvation does not come from your doing good works and religious deeds, but from repentance of sin and simple faith in the Lord Jesus Christ to save you. Salvation is by grace, not by works. When you get that clear in your minds, you will understand that people who receive Jesus as their personal Saviour can *know* they are going to heaven and not just hope so."

Tears filled Nelda's eyes. "Dr. Logan, would you mind going over how to be saved again? I really do want to *know* I'm going to heaven when my life comes to an end."

Eric nodded, and choking on the words said, "I—I do too, Doctor."

"My Bible is out in the buggy. I'll be right back."

Dr. Dane hurried out the front door to his buggy. He took his Bible out of the medical bag, and as he hurried back into the house, he whispered, "Lord, give me wisdom and power to deal with them and to lead them to You."

When Dr. Dane entered the bedroom, Tharyn was encouraging the Coxes to listen closely to what her husband was going to show them and to feel free to ask him any questions they might have.

He smiled and said, "Yes, please feel free to ask any questions you want."

Both nodded.

Tharyn was praying in her heart as her husband opened his Bible.

Dr. Dane said, "I'm going to show you first of all that Scripture says you can *know* that you are saved, and that you have eternal life, which is to go to heaven when you die. I'm going to read a statement that the Apostle Paul made about his own assurance on this matter. It's in the second half of 2 Timothy 1:12. 'I know whom I have believed, and am persuaded that he is able to keep that which I have committed unto him against that day.'"

"Paul had committed his soul to Jesus, not only to save him, but to keep him saved." He flipped a few pages. "Listen to what Scripture says about it in 1 Peter 4:19. 'Wherefore let them that suffer according to the will of God commit the keeping of their souls to him in well doing, as unto a faithful Creator.' See that? The keeping of their *souls*. It's talking about salvation."

He turned a few more pages. "Listen to this in Ephesians 2:8 and 9. 'For by grace are ye saved through faith; and that not of yourselves: it is the gift of God: not of works, lest any man should boast.' That's plain enough, isn't it? You can't earn salvation by good works. You must accept it as God's *gift*. Romans 6:23 says, 'For the wages of sin is death; but the gift of God is eternal life through Jesus Christ our Lord.'

"Think about that. Eternal life, which is to have salvation, is a *gift*. You can't earn it, then, by your good works or doing religious deeds. Just through Jesus Christ, the one who died for sinners on Calvary's cross, was buried, and three days later arose from the dead. He is the living Saviour. He does all the saving all by Himself from start to finish. Just before He died on the cross, with His precious blood flowing from His wounds, he cried, 'It is finished!'

"His finished work on the cross is all that had to be done to make salvation open to all who will come to Jesus by faith. It is the person who turns from their sin, which includes their religion or humanistic philosophy, that is given eternal life. Jesus said in Luke 13:3, 'Except ye repent, ye shall all likewise perish.'

"Repentance is a change of mind that results in a change of direction. We change our mind about our religion or philosophy, and our sin, and turn a hundred and eighty degrees from the road that leads to hell and put our faith in Jesus. According to Romans 10:13, we call on Him to save us. It says, 'Whosoever shall call upon the name of the Lord shall be saved.' And as I just read to you, the Lord will have mercy on that repentant sinner and abundantly pardon him.

"Ephesians 3:17 says, 'That Christ may dwell in your *hearts* by faith.' So when we call on Him to save us, we receive Him into our *hearts*. When a lost sinner has repented and received Jesus into his or her heart by faith, trusting only Him to save them and keep the saved, they have eternal life. And this brings me back to where we started. We can absolutely *know* without a shadow of a doubt that we have eternal life, which means we are going to heaven when we die.

"First John 5:13." He flipped to it and said, "Listen to this. In this passage, the Apostle John writes under the inspiration of the Holy Spirit, 'These things have I written unto you that believe on the name of the Son of God; that ye may know that ye have eternal life, and that ye may believe on the name of the Son of God.' Did you hear that? 'That ye may KNOW that ye have eternal life.' Not hope so, think so, guess so, or maybe so. God says you can KNOW it. And that's by believing the Scriptures—these things that are written right here on the pages of God's Word."

Eric smiled. "I understand it now, Dr. Logan. This wicked sinner wants to be saved."

In spite of her pain, Nelda's face lit up. "Yes! This wicked sinner wants to be saved, too!"

Tharyn blinked at the tears that had welled up in her eyes.

Dr. Dane asked, "Do either of you have any questions?"

Eric and Nelda looked at each other and shook their heads. "Guess not," said Eric. "All we need is your help in knowing what to say to the Lord as we call on Him."

"Just admit that you are a lost sinner and tell Him you are coming to Him in repentance of your sin, and invite Him to come into your heart, save your soul, and wash your sins away in His blood."

Tharyn wiped tears as her husband led Eric and Nelda to Jesus. When they finished, she hugged both of them, telling them how happy she was to see them come to the Lord.

Dr. Dane then showed them in the Bible that their first step of obedience to the Lord after being saved was to be baptized.

"I realize," he said, "that it will be a while before Nelda can do this, since she is going to have the hip replacement surgery, but, Eric, you can take care of it at church on Sunday. We'll stop at the parsonage on our way to the office and let Pastor Shane know that you both have received Jesus into your hearts. He will come and see you right away."

"Good," said Eric. "He will be most welcome."

Nelda looked up at the doctor with a smile on her lips. "Dr. Logan, I'm not expecting anything to go wrong during my surgery, since I know you are the best, but it is a blessing to know that if something did go wrong and I left this world, I would be in heaven."

Dr. Dane reached down and patted her hand. "Yes, Nelda, you sure would. And as for my being the best, in your eyes at least, any ability that I have comes from the Great Physician. I'm so thankful that I can place my patient in His tender care, and that I can rely on Him to guide me when I perform surgery. He says in Isaiah 41:13, 'For I the LORD thy God will hold thy right hand, saying unto thee, Fear not; I will help thee.' You and I couldn't possibly be in better hands!"

A look of peace filled Nelda's eyes. "I know I can depend on you, and more importantly, on Him."

He patted her hand again. "Amen to that." He turned to Tharyn. "Well, sweetie, we'd better be going. But before we do, I want to pray for these two new children of God."

The four of them bowed their heads, and thankful tears were shed while Dr. Dane prayed for the new converts and praised the Lord for His abundant grace.

On Friday, July 15, Betty Anderson hurried up the front porch steps, opened the door, and held it open while Dr. Dane Logan carried her husband toward the house from his buggy. She smiled at them as they passed her. Then as they headed down the hall, she ran past them and guided the doctor into the master bedroom at the rear of the house.

When Dr. Dane placed the mayor on the bed, Betty bent over him and said, "Oh, darling, it's so good to have you home!" She then turned to the doctor with tears misting her eyes. "Thank you so much for all you've done for Mike and me. I promise I'll take good care of him."

Dr. Dane grinned. "I have no doubt of that. I need to explain that Dr. and Mrs. Fraser left town early this morning to visit friends in Georgetown. You know that's a two-hour drive."

Betty nodded. "Yes."

"They will be back tomorrow evening. If for some reason I should get called away for an emergency today or tomorrow, and

Mike should need medical attention, Tharyn can handle it."

"I'm sure she can," said Betty.

"I need to explain also, that Tharyn and I will be leaving Monday morning to take Nelda Cox to Denver so I can perform a hip replacement surgery on her at Mile High Hospital. If you should need any medical help for Mike while we're gone, you can call on Dr. Fraser, who will be working in the office with Nadine Wahl."

Dr. Logan had already shared the news with the Andersons at the office about Eric and Nelda Cox being saved. Mike said, "Dr. Logan, I've just been rejoicing in my heart over the Coxes' salvation."

"Me, too," put in Betty. "Pastor had told us about visiting them before, and how they paid no heed when he preached them the gospel. Praise the Lord, they finally listened."

"Yes. Well, I must get back to the office. I'll look in on you once more, Mike, before we leave on Monday."

At the office, Tharyn was taking care of a little girl who had cut her hand when Dr. Dane came into the examining room, leading an elderly man. He placed the man on a table in one of the curtained areas, then excused himself for a moment. He looked at the little girl's cut, complimented Tharyn on how well she had stitched it, and told the child and her mother that she would be fine.

Tharyn bandaged the child's hand while her husband was taking care of the elderly man. When she was done, she walked into the office with the mother and the little girl. The mother paid the bill, and they left after thanking Tharyn.

A few minutes later, Dr. Dane came into the office with the elderly man, who paid Tharyn for the treatment, and left.

Dane was about to return to the back room when suddenly they both saw a rider pull his horse to a halt in front of the office and leap from the saddle.

The doctor opened the door for the rider as he rushed up and said breathlessly, "You're Dr. Logan?"

Dr. Dane nodded. "I am."

"I'm Rex Wilson, Doctor. I have a ranch in the mountains twelve miles southwest of town. A band of Ute Indians were stealing some cattle on my neighbor Jack Bates's place about an hour ago, just as Jack and his family were returning home from town in their wagon. The Indians shot Jack and his entire family before riding away with the cattle they had stolen."

"Oh my," gasped Tharyn, moving up beside her husband.

Wilson took a deep breath. "Everyone in the family was killed except Jack, and he is seriously wounded. My wife is with Jack right now, trying to take care of him till I can get back with you, Dr. Logan. Can you come with me right now?"

"Sure. I'll saddle my horse."

Moments later, Tharyn stood at the office door and watched her husband ride away with Rex Wilson. "Dear Lord," she breathed, "please keep Dane safe, and please allow him to keep Mr. Bates from dying."

She kept her eyes on them until they disappeared from view in a cloud of dust. "Well," she sighed, "one thing can be said for being a frontier doctor. Life is never dull."

Just as she was about to turn and reenter the office, she became aware of a man and a woman hurrying along the boardwalk. The man was carrying a boy in his arms, and the lad was crying out in pain.

As they drew up, the man asked, "Are you Mrs. Logan?"

"Yes," she replied.

"Is Dr. Logan in?"

"Not at the moment, but please come in." As she spoke, she stepped back and held the door open for them.

TEN

The pallid-faced parents stepped into the office. Then above the moans and cries of the boy, who was gripping his middle with both hands, the father said to Tharyn, "Ma'am, I'm Scott Thomas, and this is my wife, Susan. This is our son, Bobby. He is eleven years old. As you can see, he is having extreme pain in his midsection. We live over on Elm Street and have been patients of Dr. Fraser's for several years. How soon do you expect Dr. Logan back?"

"My husband was called away just a few minutes ago to see about a rancher who was shot by Indians. It's hard to say when he might return." Tharyn looked down at the boy, whose face was twisted with pain. "The way he's clutching his middle, and the pain he's experiencing makes me think it could be appendicitis. I'll send someone for Dr. Fras—"

Her hands went to her mouth. "Oh no! I forgot. Dr. and Mrs. Fraser are in Georgetown." She swallowed hard. "Mr. and Mrs. Thomas, I'm a certified medical nurse, and my specialty is as a surgical nurse. If this is appendicitis, I must remove the appendix immediately."

A chill slithered down Scott's spine. He studied Tharyn with appraising eyes. "Mrs. Logan, are you sure you can do an appendectomy?"

Tharyn did not bat an eye. "Mr. Thomas, I have assisted doctors in Denver with appendectomies over a hundred times, and if indeed this is what is ailing Bobby, I will have to perform the surgery. I can't wait for my husband to come back."

Scott bit his lower lip. "Mrs. Logan, I don't mean to question your ability as a surgical nurse, but isn't it a lot different to just assist the surgeon doing the operation than being the one holding the scalpel?"

In his father's arms, Bobby ejected an especially loud wail and drew up his knees.

Tharyn looked at Bobby, then at Scott. "Yes, Mr. Thomas, it most certainly is different, but if I weren't confident that I could do it, I wouldn't be offering my services. I say to you and Mrs. Thomas, if I diagnosis this as appendicitis—and I'm already 99 percent sure it is—if you give me permission, I will use all of my medical knowledge to bring Bobby through this. If, indeed, it is appendicitis and something isn't done immediately, your son will die."

Scott and Susan looked at each other, brows furrowed.

Tharyn laid a hand on the father's arm. "With God's help, I can do the surgery, Mr. Thomas. Now will you carry him into the examining room and let me work on him so I can diagnose his problem?"

A sudden surge of anxiety flowed across Susan's mind. "Scott, we've got to let her do it now!"

Unbidden tears sprung up in Scott's eyes. There was a catch in his voice as he said, "I just want our boy to be all right, Mrs. Logan."

Tharyn nodded and headed toward the rear door. "Then let's get him to the examining room. If the appendix has already burst, he's in real trouble."

Both parents followed, and Tharyn directed Scott to the nearest examining and surgical table. "Lay him down here."

Bobby was moaning and throwing his head back and forth. Tharyn took hold of his face, held his head still, and looked into his eyes. "Bobby, please stay as quiet and still as you can so I can examine you."

The boy closed his eyes, gritted his teeth, and nodded.

As she began her examination, Tharyn kept her attention on the patient and said to the parents, "Has he been nauseated or vomited or had diarrhea since the pains started?"

Susan licked her lips with a dry tongue. "He has been quite nauseated and has vomited twice since complaining of the pain. So far, no diarrhea."

Tharyn nodded. "These are positive signs, when accompanied with the pain he's experiencing."

As she pressed her fingers all over the abdominal area, she noted what spots made Bobby wince and cry out the most. She picked up a thermometer from the cart beside the table. "Bobby, I have to take your temperature. Open your mouth. I'm going to put it under your tongue. Please don't move it."

Bobby nodded as she placed it under his tongue.

Tharyn looked at the worried parents as she held a palm on the boy's forehead. "While I'm waiting for his temperature to register, let me explain that a person experiencing an attack of appendicitis feels abdominal pain and tenderness, particularly around the navel and the right lower region of the abdomen, exactly as Bobby is feeling it. They also experience nausea, usually vomit, and sometimes have diarrhea. Other than the latter, Bobby has these exact symptoms."

Tharyn saw fear etched in the faces of the parents.

"Let me explain something else. I'll know if the appendix has already burst as soon as I get a reading on the thermometer. If it has, his fever will be over a hundred degrees."

Susan's heart literally squeezed with pain and her hands went to her mouth.

Fear heaved through Scott's stomach. "M-Mrs. Logan, if the appendix has already burst, B-Bobby will die, won't he?"

Tharyn's lips pulled into a pencil-thin line. "Most likely, sir. But let's see what his temperature is. He doesn't feel that hot to the touch. We'll know in another minute. I—I really don't think it's that high."

Scott took hold of Susan's hand and gave it a reassuring squeeze. "She should know, honey. I imagine she has taken thousands of temperatures."

Susan squeezed back, her heart racing.

When the time was up, Tharyn took the thermometer from Bobby's mouth, studied it, and said with a sigh, "It's all right. His fever is nominal. The appendix hasn't burst. I'll have to remove it quickly. Do I have your permission?"

"Yes!" the relieved parents said simultaneously.

"All right," said Tharyn, heading for a nearby medicine cabinet.

While the parents laid hands on their son and watched the nurse, she took out a bottle of chloroform, lifted a soft cloth from a drawer, and hurried back to the table. The boy was squirming in agony. "Bobby, I have to put this chloroform on the cloth and place it over your nose and mouth. It will put you to sleep so you won't feel any pain while I operate on you. Just hold as still as you can and breathe it in, okay?"

Bobby swallowed hard. "Y-yes, ma'am."

Tharyn set steady eyes on Susan as she poured the liquid onto the cloth, then placed it carefully over the boy's nose and mouth. "Mrs. Thomas, will you hold the cloth for me, please?"

Susan nodded and placed her hand on the cloth after Tharyn had let go of it.

Quickly, Tharyn went to a nearby counter and scrubbed her hands in strong lye soap. She dried them on a clean towel, then took a needle, thread, and a scalpel from a drawer in the medicine cabinet. She placed them on a sterilized cloth in a tray, then approached the table and laid the tray on the cart.

She took a moment to thread the needle and cinch the tiny knot, then leaned over Bobby, whose squirming was easing some. What she could see of his face told her he was getting paler by the second.

"Mrs. Thomas, ordinarily it is best that the parents of a child undergoing surgery not be in the operating room, but I need you to stay and help with the chloroform. The cloth must remain in place, even after Bobby is under, and more chloroform will have to be added."

Worry over Bobby's condition was a constant tugging at Susan's insides. She licked her lips. "Yes, of course."

"Thank you. I will let you know when to add more chloroform to the cloth."

Susan nodded and looked back down at her son.

Tharyn turned to the father. "Mr. Thomas, I need you to go out and wait in the office. There will be patients coming in who have appointments and probably others who don't. Will you explain the situation to them and tell them I will get to them as soon as possible?"

Scott looked worriedly at his son, then at Tharyn. "Yes, ma'am." Even as he spoke, he moved quickly toward the door. When he opened it, he looked back at Susan, then was gone.

Tharyn bared the boy's abdomen and used wood alcohol to clean the area where she was going to make the incision. By the time this was done, Bobby was no longer squirming, and his eyes were closed. She raised his eyelids and noted the condition of the pupils. "He's under now, Mrs. Thomas. Be ready to add more chloroform to the cloth when I tell you."

Susan nodded, biting her lips.

Tharyn picked up the scalpel from the tray and took a deep breath. The muscles across her shoulders were tightening, and she was aware that her hands were trembling slightly. *Mr. Thomas was quite right,* she thought. *It is a world of difference when you alone wield the scalpel and are the one responsible for the patient's life.*

Trying to control her shaking hands, she told herself that her heavenly Father, the greatest of *all* physicians, was right there with her, and a calmness came over her. She closed her eyes. "Dear Lord, please guide my hand and help me to do this exactly right."

When Tharyn opened her eyes, she saw a smile on Susan's face, in spite of her concern for her son. "Ready, Mrs. Thomas?"

"I...I guess so." Susan took a deep breath, looked down at Bobby, then back at Tharyn. "Yes, of course, I'm ready. My boy needs me, and I'm here to do my job with the chloroform."

Tharyn let a thin smile curve her lips. "Good. With God's help, let's make this precious boy well again."

Having said thus, she lowered a now-steady hand and placed the sharp tip of the scalpel against the boy's flesh. As she drew it slowly and carefully across his abdomen, her mind was focused completely on the task before her.

Dr. Dane Logan and rancher Rex Wilson galloped their horses through the gate of the *Diamond B Ranch* and headed down the tree-lined lane toward the house, barn, and outbuildings.

Moments later, they pulled the horses to a halt at the front porch, tied them to the hitching posts, and hurried into the house.

Dora Wilson was in a back bedroom, and hearing the two men enter the house, she stepped into the hall and watched them hurry toward her.

As they drew up, Dora said, "He's still alive."

"Good!" exclaimed Rex. "Honey, this is Dr. Dane Logan. Dr. Logan, this is my wife, Dora."

Dora and the doctor exchanged greetings; then Rex asked, "Honey, has Jack regained consciousness yet?"

"No. He's shown no sign of waking up so far."

With that, Dora pivoted and preceded the men into the bedroom where rancher Jack Bates lay on the bed.

Dr. Dane asked, "Where are the bodies of Mrs. Bates and the children?"

"I laid them in the toolshed out back. When Jack regains consciousness, I'll offer to take care of the funeral arrangements with the undertaker in the nearby town of Lawson."

Dr. Dane removed his hat, laid it on the dresser, and stepped up beside the bed. Rex and Dora were standing on the opposite side of the bed. The doctor opened his medical bag, took out a bottle of chloroform and a piece of soft, white cloth. He opened the bottle, poured the liquid into the cloth, and placed it over the lower part of Jack Bates's face. "I've got to make sure he doesn't come to while I'm removing the slug. Mrs. Wilson, would you hold this cloth over his nose and mouth for me?"

"Of course." She laid her hand over the cloth.

Dr. Dane took a bottle of lye soap from his medical bag and turned to Rex. "Do you know where the washroom is?"

Rex nodded. "Yes."

"I need to wash my hands before I go after that slug."

"Washroom is just across the hall. Come on."

Less than five minutes had passed when the men returned and Dr. Dane reached into his medical bag once more. He took out a bottle of wood alcohol and a special pair of steel forceps designed to remove bullets from human bodies. He opened the bottle and doused the forceps with the alcohol.

While Dora held the wet cloth over the wounded man's nose and mouth, the doctor worked on the bleeding bullet wound, which was in his upper chest on the right side.

Rex stood close to Dora, looking on as Dr. Dane carefully removed the bullet that had come from a Ute rifle, and laid it in Rex's hand. "Would you get rid of this for me?"

Rex looked at the bloody slug in his hand and licked his lips nervously. "Y-yeah. Be back in a minute." He hurried out the bedroom door and ran up the hall.

By this time, the patient began to move a bit.

Dr. Dane looked at Dora. "Pour some more chloroform on the cloth."

She nodded, and Dr. Dane began cleaning the wound. Dora placed the wet cloth back over the patient's nose and mouth, and soon the doctor was suturing up the wound.

Rex returned quietly and moved back up beside his wife.

When Dr. Dane finished bandaging the wound, he sighed and looked at Dora. "Okay. All done. You can remove the cloth now. Jack will probably be under the influence of the chloroform for a couple of hours before he is really awake."

Rex let out a sigh. "So he will live, Doctor?"

"Oh yes. But if the slug had been three inches lower, and about that same distance closer to the center of his chest, it would have killed him." He looked at Dora. "Or if you hadn't done such a good job keeping the blood flow from the wound to a minimum while you were waiting for your husband to ride to town and bring me back with him, Jack would have died."

Dora smiled. "I'm just glad I could be of help." She ran her gaze between the men. "I'm sure we could all use a hot cup of coffee. Wanda always kept coffee on hand. How about if I go to the kitchen, light a fire in the stove, and heat up some coffee?"

"Sounds good to me," said Rex. "How about you, Doctor?"

"Sure. I want to go over this Indian problem with you before I go, anyway. You no doubt know a lot more about it than I do."

"Okay. Go on, sweetheart. We'll talk about the Indians while you make us some coffee."

"All right," said Dora. "I'll be back in a little while."

Dr. Dane took a look at his patient, making sure he was resting comfortably; then both men sat down on wooden chairs next to the bed.

The doctor set steady eyes on Rex. "So you're sure those were Utes, and not some other tribe who shot this family down and took their cattle?"

"Yep. Everyone in these parts knows a Ute warrior when we see one. There are some Arapahoes farther south and east of here, but the Arapahoes and Utes dress differently. They're easy to tell apart."

"I see. Well, what I wanted to discuss with you are the treaties that I've heard about. It has been my understanding that both the Utes and the Arapahoes were supposed to be at peace with the whites here in Colorado."

Rex pulled at an earlobe. "Basically they are, Doctor, but there are some renegades in both tribes who have not really submitted to the treaties signed by their tribal leaders."

"Really?"

"Mm-hmm. It is these renegades who are stealing stock from ranchers and often killing them in the process, and who are attacking wagon trains, stagecoaches, and other travelers. Most of this theft and violence is taking place in the Rocky Mountains of Colorado, especially by the Utes."

Dr. Dane glanced at his patient, then looked back to Rex. "How long has this treaty breaking been going on?"

"Well, back in 1863, when the Utes lived on the east side of the Rockies, they often fought whites side by side with the Arapahoes."

"So they are comrades, I take it."

"You might say that. Anyway, early in 1863, President Abraham Lincoln became concerned about the battles going on out here in Colorado between the whites and the Indians, especially the Utes, who were by far the fiercest. The army was building forts as fast as they could and establishing military outposts, but still, much blood of the white people was being shed. President Lincoln authorized some federal officials to come here immediately and see if they could make peace with the Utes. He felt if peace could be made with the Utes, the Arapahoes would settle down too. Those appointed officials of the United States government called for a council with the Ute leaders to convince them to move their villages west of the Continental Divide."

Dr. Dane snapped his fingers. "Oh yes. That's when they met with the Uncompahgre Ute chief, Ouray. I recall reading about it, now that you bring it up."

"That's it. Chief Ouray was chosen by nearly all the Ute leaders to be their spokesman."

"He's a peaceable man, from what I recall."

"Yes. He saw the picture and realized that white people were moving out West by the thousands and bringing their military with them. He was wise enough to know that the Indians were quickly being outnumbered, and that to make war with them would also get a lot of Indians killed."

"So how did the council with Chief Ouray go?"

"Well, it actually took five years for Ouray to convince the bulk of his Ute brothers to go along with the government officials, but in 1868, the Utes agreed to move to the west side of the Continental Divide, providing that all of Colorado Territory west of the Divide—mountains and flat land—was reserved for them."

Dr. Dane's eyebrows arched. "Hmm. That's a lot of territory."

"Yep. But in order to stop the bloodshed in Colorado, the government officials under President Andrew Johnson's authority agreed, and a treaty was made. However, the treaty was broken by the whites shortly thereafter when gold was discovered in the San Juan Mountains. You know where they are, I presume."

"Yes, in southwest Colorado."

"Right. The white men who discovered the gold weren't supposed to be in the San Juans, nor west of the Divide in Colorado, anyway. But some of them hurried back to their families and friends to let them know of their gold strike, and this brought more greedy miners flooding into the area."

Dr. Dane shook his head. "So they didn't care if they broke the treaty with Chief Ouray and his people."

"Not at all. They wanted the gold bad enough to chance being attacked by the Utes. They ignored the treaty."

"And I'm sure the Utes attacked."

"They sure did. There was a fierce onslaught by the Utes. The army had to come in and fight off the Indians to protect the miners. This brought more bloodshed."

"I can well imagine."

"As you said, Doctor, Ouray is a peaceful man. Still wanting peace, in 1877 he asked to meet with the government officials again. President Rutherford B. Hayes agreed and there was another meeting. The government officials came to an agreement that the Utes could maintain their land in western Colorado *except* for the San Juan Mountains. This infuriated some of the Ute chiefs, and though Chief Ouray pled with them to stay at peace with the whites, a few of them still wanted to shed blood. They still feel that way today and are regarded by the bulk of the Utes as renegades. They are the ones who still attack white travelers and steal stock from ranchers here in the mountains and from farmers on the western side of the state. So often in stealing, there are gun battles, and both white men and Indians are wounded or killed."

Dr. Dane shook his head. "Too bad this has to go on."

"Mm-hmm. When Chief Ouray signed the latest treaty, he was also influential in getting most of the Arapaho leaders to sign a treaty, too. However, there are still renegades in both tribes. The Ute renegades are found mostly among the Weminuche Ute tribe, who call themselves the Ute Mountain Tribe. The most adamant chief among the Ute Mountain Tribe is Tando, who has a large village in the mountains some twenty miles southwest of Central City."

Dr. Dane looked surprised. "That close?"

"Mm-hmm. Chief Tando has been known sometimes to send some of his subchiefs east to communicate with the Arapaho chiefs who have not gone along with the treaties their tribal spokesmen have made with the government."

"I see. So Tando keeps company with the renegade Arapaho chiefs to maintain comradeship with them."

"That's it."

Dr. Dane looked at his patient again. Jack was moving his body a little, but was still under the anesthetic. He set his gaze on Rex once more. "You told me as we rode here that you thought Jack might have shot one of the Indians who were stealing his cattle."

"Yes. I saw fresh blood on the ground near the gate where the Indians were driving the cattle out of the corral. Must have just wounded him, though, because Dora and I saw the bunch of them as they were driving the cattle away, and every Indian horse had a rider."

"How many were there?"

"Eight. I know that Chief Tando has a son who is around twenty years old, and he is especially vicious against white people. His name is Latawga. I figure it might have been Latawga who was leading this bunch of cattle thieves who killed the rest of the Bates family. They all looked quite young to me."

"The incident should be reported to the commandant at Fort Junction."

"Yes, it should."

"What's the commandant's name?"

"Colonel Perry Smith. I saw him one time, but didn't get to meet him."

At that moment, Dora came in carrying a tray bearing three steaming cups of coffee. She let the men pick up their cups from the tray, then set it on the dresser and took her cup in hand. As she headed for a third wooden chair, she glanced at Jack. "Still out, I see."

Dr. Dane nodded. "He was moving his body a little a few minutes ago. That's a good sign, but he's still out."

While the three of them were enjoying their coffee, they discussed the care Jack was going to need.

Dora sipped from her cup and said to Rex, "The best thing would be for us to take Jack home with us so we can watch over him."

Rex nodded. "That's what we'll do, honey. We'll take him in our wagon."

Dr. Dane drained his cup. "I'll give you instructions on how to care for his wound; then I'd better be going. I'll ride to Fort Junction right now and report this horrible incident to Colonel Perry Smith. My wife and I are leaving Monday morning for Denver, but I'll have Dr. Fraser come to your place and check on Jack in a few days."

Dora smiled. "That will be good, Doctor."

Dr. Dane rose from the chair and stood over Jack Bates. The Wilsons moved up beside him, and he gave them instructions on how to care for Jack's wound and the bandage. He gave them a bottle of laudanum, told them how much and how often they should give it to him to take the edge off his pain.

"We'll take care of him, Doctor," said Dora.

"I'm sure you will. Don't move Jack until he's fully awake. Do you have a neighbor who can help you get him in and out of the wagon?"

Rex nodded. "Sure do. I'll go and fetch him after Jack wakes up."

Dr. Dane pulled down the sheet that covered Jack Bates and looked him over again.

Rex said, "So you have no doubt the wound will heal up okay."

"I'm sure the wound in his flesh will heal nicely, Rex. But the wounds in his heart from the loss of his family will not heal so easily."

Dr. Dane's heart was aching over this man's tragedy. *What if it were Tharyn lying before me dead? How would I ever get past the pain of her loss?*

A still, small voice echoed in his mind: "I can do *all* things through Christ which strengtheneth me."

Drawing a ragged breath, the doctor looked at Jack Bates's two kind neighbors. "Are you ready to tell Jack he has lost his entire family? It will be a very difficult task. Are you up to it?"

Rex put an arm around Dora. "It's going to be hard, but we'll handle it all right, Doctor."

"I wish I could stay and help you with it, but I've got to make that ride to Fort Junction then head for my office. Tharyn is alone there, and I need to get back as soon as I can."

Dora reached out and touched his arm. "We understand, Dr. Logan. Rex and I will take care of breaking the news to Jack. We'll help him in every way possible."

"This world needs more friends like you," said the doctor as he drew the sheet back up and took his medical bag in hand. "I'm sure Jack will appreciate everything you do for him."

The Wilsons walked the doctor out to his horse. As he was tying his medical bag to the back of the saddle, he said, "Please don't hesitate to come and get me if you deem it necessary between now and when Tharyn and I leave for Denver. Otherwise, as I said, Dr. Fraser will be by your place to look at him in a few days."

Rex said, "Doctor, we'll pay you for what you've done for Jack. How much do we owe you?"

"Nothing. In this case, my services are free of charge."

Rex and Dora looked at each other as if they had heard wrong.

Dr. Dane saw it and smiled. "Just tell Jack I'm glad I could remove the slug and bandage him up. I'll be out to see him when we return from Denver."

Rex extended his hand and Dr. Dane gripped it. "We're mighty glad you're the one who took over Dr. Fraser's practice. Thank you for everything."

Dr. Dane swung up and settled in the saddle.

Rex said, "Tell Colonel Smith that I am positive it was Utes who shot down the Bates family and stole the cattle, and that I feel sure it was one of Chief Tando's renegade bands who did it."

"I'll tell him."

The Wilsons watched the doctor gallop away. When he passed from view, Dora looked up at her husband. "I very much like this young doctor."

Rex grinned. "I do, too."

ELEVEN

*A*s Dr. Dane Logan rode north along the natural trail that followed a bubbling creek, he let his gaze roam about him and took in the majesty of God's creation in the Rockies. The pines, cedars, aspens, and white-barked birch trees waved in the breeze on every side, pointing to the azure sky overhead.

He gazed up into the brilliant canopy of blue and marveled at how the jagged, lofty mountain peaks off to the west boldly took their sharp uneven bite out of the firmament. He reached down and patted the back of his horse's neck where the long mane tossed in the breeze. "How about this country, Pal? Isn't it gorgeous?"

As if the bay gelding understood his master's words, he bobbed his head and whinnied.

They were on a steep incline. Dr. Dane let his eyes roam. Blinking against the glare, he shifted his line of sight to the north where massive white clouds filled the sky. Great banks of cumulus piled to magnificent heights, dwarfing the mountains in comparative insignificance.

Soon horse and rider topped the rise and began a sharp descent on the trail. Dane let his eyes follow the creek as it rushed southward, sliding in a gleam of foamy white into a vast canyon below.

After going up and down on the natural trail northward, Dane and Pal came upon relatively flat land, surrounded by forests, and before them lay one cattle ranch after another.

Dane soon found himself gazing at a huge grassy fenced-in field behind a large red barn, where four cowboys were branding cattle. He smiled at the sound of bawling and bellowing that came to him on the breeze, along with the crackling of horns and pounding of hooves.

The young doctor fastened his gaze on one cowboy who rode a black horse and was chasing a frisky steer. He whirled a lasso around his head and gave it a toss. The rope shot out and the loop caught the right rear leg of the steer. The black horse stopped with marvelous suddenness, and the steer slid to a halt on the grass.

Quick as a flash, the lanky cowboy was out of the saddle with a length of rope in his hand. Grasping the legs of the steer before it could rise, he tied them with the rope. Another cowhand came running with a smoking branding iron in hand and applied it to the flank of the steer. Instantly the steer was released, and with a bawl, jumped up and bolted away, kicking his heels up in reaction to the burning on his flank.

For a moment, the smell of burning hide and hair wafted on the breeze and met Dane's nostrils.

Within a few minutes, Dane and his horse entered a dense forest and wound among the trees. Squirrels ran up and down the trunks, and birds twittered in the high branches. At the sound of Pal's pounding hooves, a pair of buck deer bounded from the shadows just ahead, dashed over a rise, and quickly disappeared. Dane smiled at their speed.

Some twenty minutes later, he emerged from the forest and about half a mile ahead, Dane saw Fort Junction standing where the Boulder and St. Vrain Rivers joined.

He put Pal to a trot and aimed for the front gate, which was visible in the twelve-foot-tall stockade fence. To one side of the gate was a guard tower, the floor of which stood some three or four feet above the fence. Next to the tower rose the flagpole with Old Glory at its top, waving proudly in the breeze.

The two guards in the tower watched the lone rider draw up, and one of them smiled down at him. "Good afternoon, sir. May we help you?"

Dane smiled back. "I'm Dr. Dane Logan, Central City's physician and surgeon, gentlemen. Is Colonel Smith here?"

"Yes, Doctor."

"I need to see him if possible. I want to report to him about a ranch family south of town being attacked by Indians. I did surgery on the rancher and saved his life by removing a bullet from his chest, but the Indians killed his wife and children."

The guard motioned for the other one to go down and open the gate.

"The colonel will want to hear about that, Doctor, I assure you. My partner will escort you to Colonel Smith's office."

When the gate swung open, the guard on the ground said, "I'm Corporal Laird Cotter, Dr. Logan. Please dismount. I'll tie your horse right here by the gate; then we'll go to the colonel's office."

Pal whinnied as his master walked away with the corporal. As Cotter led him farther into the fort, Dr. Dane noted the deep ruts worn into the hard ground; ruts cut by the iron-shod wheels of the military wagons.

He saw the line of the log barracks with the stables beyond them. The officers' quarters were across the grounds, facing them, and the offices were just ahead, to the right. On the same side were the commissary and the sutler's store, sided by the mess hall.

When they reached the offices, the commandant's was in the middle. Corporal Cotter stepped up and knocked on the door, and almost immediately, a husky voice from inside said, "Yes?"

"Colonel Smith, it's Corporal Laird Cotter. I have someone

here who needs to see you. It *is* very important, sir."

"Well, come on in, Corporal."

Cotter introduced the doctor to Colonel Perry Smith, and the colonel shook his hand, welcoming him. He dismissed Cotter, gestured for the doctor to sit down in one of the pair of chairs facing the desk, then moved behind the desk and eased onto his chair.

Perry, a mustachioed man of forty, said, "Now what is it you wish to see me about, Dr. Logan?"

"Indian trouble, sir."

Smith's face took on a stony look. "Something I never like to hear, Doctor, but it exists. Tell me about it."

Dr. Dane told the colonel the story of the Ute attack on the Jack Bates ranch as it was related to him by rancher Rex Wilson, emphasizing that Wilson wanted the colonel to know that the Indians were indeed Utes. He advised Smith of the theft of the *Diamond B* cattle, of the violent deaths of Mrs. Bates and their three children, and of his removing the bullet from Jack's chest to save his life.

As Dr. Dane was telling the story, he saw the glitter of anger gathering in the colonel's eyes.

When he finished by saying that Rex Wilson felt sure the band of Utes were from Chief Tando's village, there was smoldering indignation in his stiff-set cheeks. "I don't doubt it. Tando is the most vicious of the renegade Ute chiefs. I'm going to take my troops to his village, but I know when I confront him with it, he will deny any knowledge of the cattle theft from the Bates ranch and, of course, the killing of the man's wife and children."

He paused. "Knowing Tando and his bloody warriors as I do, I'm positive they thought they had killed Mr. Bates too, or they'd have made sure of it. Dr. Logan, I very much appreciate your coming here to report this to me. Although Tando will deny the whole thing, I am going to go there and at least let that blood-hungry beast know that he is on the edge of disaster. I'm going to make it plain and clear to him that his village will be under tighter scrutiny from now on. There will be patrols from this fort moving about the area of the village like never before."

Dr. Dane nodded. "Good. I hope it serves to put some fear into him."

"We'll do our best. For the past six months, there has been less trouble from the Utes than we had experienced before that time. There still have been some raids on ranches on the west side of the Continental Divide, but not nearly as many as before. However, I received wires from the commandants at Fort Uncompahgre and Fort Lewis on the west side of the mountains just last week, advising me that the Ute renegades were killing ranchers again and stealing their cattle.

"I had hoped they were getting the renegade blood out of their system, but it looks like they're starting again, and it's quite obvious after hearing your report that the stealing and killing is going to include the east side of the Divide once more. Most of the Ute thefts and attacks on the east side of the Divide have been done by Tando and his bunch."

Dr. Dane shook his head. "Well, sir, I hope your show of force will discourage Tando and his warriors from continuing these raids altogether."

Smith sighed and ran fingers through his mustache. "Knowing Tando, I really wonder, but it's worth a try. Tomorrow morning, I'll take a large number of men, plus two Gatling guns."

Dr. Dane's eyebrows arched. "Gatling guns, hmm? That ought to make them sit up and take notice."

"Let's hope so."

The doctor rose from his chair. "Well, Colonel, I need to be going. My wife's having to run the office by herself. She's a certified medical nurse, but she can't do it all."

Smith stood up and extended his hand. "Thank you for bringing this information to me."

At the same time Dr. Dane Logan was riding south toward home, at the Ute village some twenty miles southwest of Central City, Chief Tando and his warrior son, Latawga, were sitting cross-legged on the ground in front of their buffalo hide tepee, discussing the young subchief, Danpo, and the seven warriors whom Tando had sent out to steal cattle from some white man's ranch in the area.

The muscular, dark-skinned chief was in his early forties. He was clad, as was Latawga, in a robe of buffalo hide. Latawga, like all Ute braves, wore a cloth band around his head with a single eagle feather protruding up at the back of his head. Tando was wearing an unusual headdress, which was the scalp of a wolf, mounted with all the terrible grinning teeth. Beneath that gear there showed a thoughtful, meditative face.

Tando frowned and ran his gaze toward the north end of the village. In the Ute language, he said, "I am becoming concerned for Danpo and his men, Latawga. The sun is halfway down the afternoon sky, and yet they have not returned."

Latawga, who strongly resembled his father, replied in Ute, "Possibly they ran into an army patrol, Father."

At that moment, Tando's squaw, Leela, came out of the tepee carrying a metal bucket Latawga had stolen during a raid on a white man's ranch over a year ago. The long shower of black hair fell glistening over her shoulders. She paused and looked down at her husband and son with her brow furrowed. "Should not Danpo and his warriors be back by now?"

Tando nodded slowly. "Latawga and I were just talking about that very thing. Indeed, they should have returned some time ago."

Suddenly, one of the braves on lookout duty high up in a pine tree called loudly, "Chief Tando! Danpo and his band are returning and have a good number of cattle!"

The sentry's voice carried over the entire village, and the sound of bawling cattle could be heard. Almost everyone in the village was out of their tepees and looked in the direction of the cattle. Along with the chief, his squaw, and his son, they noticed that one of the band's pintos had a blood-smeared back and was riderless. Then they saw that Danpo had a bloodied warrior named Yamda on his horse with him. Yamda was slumped over, but as they drew nearer, it was evident that he was breathing.

Rising to his feet, the chief set his eyes on the unconscious, wounded brave, and his crooked, yellowed teeth were bared in the black, shapeless slit of his mouth as he hurried toward Yamda's horse. Latawga followed on his father's heels.

Danpo halted his horse as the chief drew up and gave orders to one group of braves who were gathering around to take the cattle and slaughter them immediately. He reminded them that he wanted the hides destroyed so if the soldier coats should come, there would be no evidence that they had stolen cattle in the village with brands on their hides.

The braves rushed to do as their chief had commanded.

While the eighteen head of cattle were being driven to the place of slaughter, Tando motioned to two young braves in the mounted band, Katasho and Pawaga. They slid from their pintos' backs and drew up to him.

"Yes, Chief Tando?" said Katasho.

"You and Pawaga take Yamda from Danpo's arms. Carry him hastily to Makota!"

The two braves responded quickly. Danpo eased Yamda down into their uplifted arms, and cradling him carefully, they hurried across the open area that was surrounded by tepees to that of the silver-haired village medicine man. Makota's tepee was extra large in circumference. As Katasho and Pawaga drew up, the tepee's flap was back. They saw Makota on his knees inside, beside a young white woman who lay motionless on the grassy floor, her eyes closed.

They knew that Joyce was ill.

Makota was patting Joyce's forehead with a wet cloth. He stopped and looked up at the braves who held the bleeding young warrior in their arms. "What happened to Yamda?"

Katasho said, "Danpo's band was stealing cattle from a rancher. The white man began shooting. We fired back. Before we could kill the rancher and his family, Yamda was shot. It looks bad, Makota."

The old man pointed to a spot on the tepee floor close to the white woman. "Put him down here."

While Katasho and Pawaga were easing their wounded comrade onto the floor, Makota gave the white woman's pallid face a lingering look, then felt for a pulse at the side of her neck. He shook his head and dropped the cloth into the bucket of water beside her and turned his attention to the unconscious Yamda.

Both braves noticed that the white woman had stopped breathing.

"Joyce is dead?" said Pawaga.

Makota nodded solemnly. "She is dead."

Pawaga had been part of Chief Tando's village for only a few days. Alone, he had fled the village of Chief Ouray some ninety miles to the southwest in the state to join the renegade Utes under Chief Tando's leadership.

Makota went to work on Yamda.

Katasho looked at Makota, his eyes wide. "Chief Tando and his squaw are going to be very upset when they learn that Joyce has died."

Makota glanced up and nodded. "Yes. Very upset." He then put his attention back on the wounded warrior.

"I can see that Joyce is white," said Pawaga, "so why will Chief Tando and Leela be upset?"

Katasho drew a deep breath through his nostrils and let it out slowly. "This white woman was captured by Danpo's warrior band many moons ago when we attacked a small wagon train in a valley on the west side of the mountains. We were killing the last of the white people in the wagon train when one of our warriors suddenly caught sight of this woman running into the nearby woods. The warrior's name was Omosso. He was killed shortly after that when we attacked another wagon train.

"Somehow, this woman had managed to slip away during the massacre of the other whites. Omosso called to me when he spotted her entering the woods and motioned for me to go after her with him. We caught her quickly and brought her to the village. Chief Tando asked her name. She told him it was Joyce something. I do not remember the last name. Chief Tando made her a servant to the women in the village, especially Leela. Three moons ago, she came down with a fever. And now she is dead."

Pawaga nodded. "I understand now."

Makota was working furiously to remove the bullet from Yamda's back. He paused and set his dark eyes on the two braves. "You will go now and tell Chief Tando that Joyce is dead."

Katasho and Pawaga looked at each other nervously.

Makota glanced up. "*Both* of you take the unpleasant message to Chief Tando."

They nodded, exchanged glances again, and made their way hesitantly toward the spot where the chief was talking to the people of the village, who were gathered around him.

While other warriors, older men, women, and children gathered around the chief and Danpo, they heard the subchief tell Tando of the rancher whose cattle they were stealing arriving home with his family in their wagon.

Danpo said, "The rancher started shooting at us. My braves and I began shooting back. One of the rancher's bullets hit Yamda, but within minutes, we had shot and killed the rancher, his wife and children."

Chief Tando laid a steady hand on Danpo's muscular shoulder. A thin smile graced the chief's lips. "The gates of the heart of Tando are opened to Danpo and his braves. Those white people you killed have invaded our land. They have paid for it now. Danpo and his braves have done well in bringing the cattle. This will provide meat for our people for many moons."

At that moment, the chief saw Katasho and Pawaga drawing up and weaving their way through the crowd toward him. He knew by the way they had their dark eyes fixed on him that they wanted to speak to him. Motioning for those who were in their path to move, he waited until they stopped in front of him. "You want to speak to Chief Tando?"

The pair exchanged nervous glances, then Katasho met the chief's probing gaze. "Pawaga and Katasho have sad message for Chief Tando."

Every eye in the crowd was fixed on the pair of braves.

Tando frowned. "What is the sad message?"

It was Pawaga's turn to speak. "Chief Tando, the white woman, Joyce, has died."

Leela was standing close to her husband. She gasped at Pawaga's words. "But Makota said she would be all right."

Katasho looked into her shocked eyes. "Makota must have told you this because he *thought* she would be all right. Because he is working hard to save Yamda's life, he told us to come and announce that Joyce is dead."

Suddenly Leela's eyes fell on Makota, who was coming toward the crowd from his tepee, his face a solemn mask. She pointed to him. "Tando, I fear that Yamda has also died."

Everyone turned and watched as the elderly medicine man motioned for people to get out of his way. They made a path for him and he moved up to the chief, his dark, wrinkled features drawn.

Tando waited for him to speak.

Makota swallowed with difficulty. "Chief Tando, this is painful, but I must tell you that Makota could not save Yamda's life. His wound was very deep, and he had lost too much blood. I am sorry."

There were mournful sounds from the women as the men shook their heads in sorrow.

Tando laid a hand on the medicine man's arm. "Makota need not be sorry. Tando knows he did everything he could to keep Yamda alive. Yamda will be given a hero's burial."

Makota nodded. "Katasho and Pawaga have informed the chief that Joyce has died?"

Tando closed his eyes and opened them again. "They did."

Leela still had a shocked look in her eyes. The other women appeared to be in the same state.

Makota licked his lips. "For this, Chief Tando, Makota is also sorry. I could not bring her fever under control."

Tando was noticing the grave looks on the faces of his squaw and the other women. He raised a hand and said, "Do not despair. One day we will find a way to capture another young white woman to be servant to Leela and the other squaws."

The sun was setting over the mountains as Tharyn Logan was tidying up the office after closing time, while wondering what was taking Dane so long at the Bates ranch.

When she had the office ready for the new day tomorrow, she thought back over the day. The appendectomy she had performed on Bobby Thomas, of course, had been the most difficult thing she had done. She had been forced to send two patients back home who had appointments. Their ailments were more than she could handle. Six others had come in, and fortunately, their problems were minor and she had been able to take care of them. She had made new appointments for the two who needed to be seen by her husband.

Tharyn was getting a little nervous about Dane's not having

returned yet. She stepped out onto the boardwalk and looked southward for any sign of him riding in, but there was none. *Must have run into complications with Jack Bates's wound.*

As she turned to reenter the office, the magnificent sunset caught her eye. She paused to take it in. Only the top rim of the fiery sun could be seen as it lowered behind the towering mountains. The western sky shone like a halo over the craggy peaks. Shafts of red-gold light fell with a long slant among the tall pines behind the town and cast long, uneven shadows on Main Street from the rooftops of the buildings.

She took a step toward the door and stopped when she heard a feminine voice call her name. Looking northward where the voice came from, she saw Betty Anderson hurrying toward her.

Smiling as she drew up, Betty said, "Hello, Tharyn. You look a bit weary. Hard day?"

Tharyn returned the smile. "You might say that. My husband has been gone since early this morning, caring for a rancher who was shot by Indians who were stealing his cattle. I even had to do an appendectomy on Bobby Thomas. You probably know the Thomases."

"Of course," said Betty, her eyes wide. *"You* did the surgery?"

"Uh-huh. Had to. The appendix was about to rupture."

"How did it go?"

"Fine. Bobby's home now with his parents."

"Well, that's good. Seems to me we have *two* beloved physicians in Central City."

Tharyn shook her head vigorously. "No, no! You gave my husband that title, and we'll just leave it at that."

Betty laughed. "Oh, all right. If you say so. Well, sweet girl, I'd better keep moving. Got to get home and fix supper for Mike."

"He feeling okay?"

"Oh yes. Dr. Dane is doing a good job helping him to get healed up. See you later."

Tharyn smiled as Betty walked away. "See you later."

She was about to turn and enter the office when she caught sight of a rider on a bay horse trotting down the street from the north.

The horse strongly resembled Pal. She squinted. "It *is* Pal! What's Dane doing coming in from the north?"

Dane saw her standing on the boardwalk and waved. She waved back.

As Dane drew up and pulled rein, Tharyn said, "I was getting worried, darling. And now, I'm puzzled. Why are you coming into town from the north?"

Dismounting, he wrapped the reins around the hitch rail and folded her into his arms. "Long story, sweetheart. And quite a story too. I'll tell you the whole thing over supper at whatever café you choose, okay?"

"Of course."

Since people were moving by, he kissed her forehead, then the tip of her nose. "I need to replenish some supplies in my medical bag. Then we can close up shop and go to supper."

Quickly, he untied the medical bag from the saddle, and they entered the office with their arms around each other's waists. Tharyn asked, "How about Mr. Bates?"

"Had to remove a bullet from his chest. He was still unconscious when I left, but he'll be all right. I'll explain it in detail at supper."

They went into the examining room. Dane set the medical bag down on the counter at the medicine cabinet and began replenishing his supply of medicine. "So how'd it go here today?"

"Well, I saw quite a few patients. Couple of them who had appointments will be back tomorrow. Guess I'd better tell you right now about Bobby Thomas."

Keeping his attention on what he was doing, Dane asked, "Who's Bobby Thomas?"

"You remember when we went over the long list of all of Dr. Fraser's patients?"

"Mm-hmm."

"Remember the names Scott and Susan Thomas, right here in town?"

"Oh. Sure."

"Well, Bobby is their eleven-year-old son."

"I recall now that they have a son."

"Shortly after you rode away this morning, the Thomases brought Bobby in. He had appendicitis and the appendix was close to rupturing."

Dane paused, turned, and looked at her. "Dr. Fraser was in Georgetown."

"Uh-huh."

"What did you do?"

"I had no choice. I did the appendectomy myself."

Dane jumped. Eyes wide, he stammered, "Y-you did?"

"Yes."

"And he's all right?"

"Yes."

A slow smile spread across Dane's face. Pride was shining in his eyes. "Sweetheart, that was a courageous thing for you to do."

"I don't know if I'd call it courage or not, honey, but it was either make an attempt at the surgery or watch that boy die. I—I was pretty confident that I could do it successfully."

"Well, of course. I'm sure you've assisted doctors at Mile High Hospital on a great number of appendectomies. You certainly knew what to do."

She smiled. "Knowing what to do and actually *doing* it are two different things, but I had no idea when you would be back, so when I had explained my surgical nurse's experience to the parents, and they gave their consent for me to do the surgery, I prayed for the Lord's help. Dane, it was as if His hand was guiding mine while He clearly brought to remembrance the details of the countless times I had assisted surgeons through this same procedure."

Dane could tell Tharyn was weary and knew that performing the appendectomy had taken its toll on her. "When a person's life is in your hands, it is a huge responsibility, love, and I'm sure you did a beautiful job."

Tharyn smiled. "'Beautiful' might not be the word for it, but Bobby's home with his parents, alive and breathing. I did promise them that when you got back, I would bring you to the house so you could check on him."

Dane wrapped his arms around her and drew her close. "All right. I'll be happy to go and see *your* patient."

Tears filled Tharyn's eyes and trickled down her cheeks as the weight of responsibility now fell from her shoulders.

Dane eased her back in his arms. "Why the tears, love?"

She sniffled. "I guess it's just such a relief to have you take over. It was one of those things that I knew I must do, so I did it. But now that you're here to take over, it's such a relief. I guess the tears are just a sign of my relief."

"I know a little about that, honey. I so well remember my first surgery in medical school. It wasn't as serious as an appendectomy, but I was sure scared. At least I had other doctors right there beside me to move in if I needed help. I remember my relief when they said I had done a perfect job."

Dane kissed the tip of her nose again. "You are a very brave little gal, and I'm so proud of you. Let's go see Bobby right now. I'll hitch Pal to the buggy. After I check on Bobby, you can relax at the café, and we'll have a nice supper. Like I said, I'll tell you the story of this long day while we eat."

They locked up the office, and Dane helped Tharyn into the buggy. As they drove away, Dr. Dane Logan sent a thankful prayer to his heavenly Father for the young woman with whom he had been blessed.

TWELVE

When Scott and Susan Thomas were just finishing their supper, they heard the sound of a buggy pulling into the front yard.

Scott smiled, pushed back from the table, and rose to his feet. "Must be Mrs. Logan with the doctor."

"I hope so," said Susan, rising from her chair. "I want to meet him, of course, but mostly I'll feel better when he examines Bobby. I very much appreciate what she did for Bobby, but since she isn't a doctor, I'll just feel better when her husband checks him over."

"I understand, honey. I will, too."

The pair left the kitchen and walked to the front door together. Just as Scott was pulling the door open, they both saw Tharyn being escorted up the porch steps by a man who carried a black medical bag.

Scott chuckled. "Well, Mrs. Logan, I see you brought your assistant with you!"

Dr. Dane laughed. "There's more truth than fiction to that statement, Mr. Thomas."

Tharyn laughed along with the Thomases. "I guess an introduction really isn't necessary, but I'll do it anyhow. Mr. and Mrs. Thomas, this is my husband—" she grinned at Dane—"and my assistant, Dr. Dane Logan."

Dr. Dane and Scott laughed while they shook hands, and then Susan offered her hand. The doctor took it gently and bowed. "I'm very happy to meet you, ma'am."

"And I'm happy to meet you, Dr. Logan. Please come in. I think Bobby's awake."

As they were walking down the hall toward the rear of the house, Susan and Tharyn were side by side, with the men behind them. Susan said, "Mrs. Logan, I want to thank you again for saving Bobby's life. You are truly a gallant lady."

"You're right about that, ma'am," said Dr. Dane from behind. "The Lord gave me the exact lady I needed."

When the foursome entered Bobby's bedroom, the boy was awake and clear-eyed. He smiled up at Tharyn. "Hello, Mrs. Logan. You saved my life. Mama and Papa said I would have died if you hadn't done the operation."

Tharyn smiled, leaned over, and hugged his neck. "I'm just glad to see you doing so well, Bobby." Letting go of him, she stood up and pointed at Dr. Dane with her graceful chin. "Bobby, this is my husband, Dr. Dane Logan."

Gingerly, the boy raised his right hand toward the doctor. "I'm very glad to meet you, sir."

Dr. Dane set his medical bag on the small table next to the bed and closed his hand over Bobby's. "And I'm very glad to meet you, Bobby. I have to say that I'm quite proud of my wife. She certainly did save your life. She wants me to look at the incision and make sure she did it correctly. Okay?"

"Yes, sir. I think she did."

"Me, too. But she still wants me to check it."

Bobby waited patiently while the doctor carefully removed the bandage and studied the incision and the stitches while Tharyn and the Thomases looked on.

After a thorough examination, Dr. Dane smiled at Tharyn. "You did a perfect job, sweetheart."

Tharyn let out a tiny sigh. "Thank you, Dr. Logan."

Scott and Susan exchanged glances and chuckled.

Dr. Dane opened his medical bag. "I'll go ahead and put on a new bandage. Once I've removed a bandage to look underneath, I'd rather put on a fresh one."

Moments later, with a fresh bandage over the incision, Dr. Dane said, "Bobby, I'll have Dr. Fraser check on you while Mrs. Logan and I are in Denver for the surgery we must do there."

Bobby let his lips curve in a slight smile. "That'll be all right. I really like Dr. Fraser. Since both of my grandfathers live back East and I don't get to see them much, Dr. Fraser has me call him Grandpa."

Dr. Dane nodded. "That's him all right. He is a fine man. I've never met one of his patients who didn't like him and respect him."

Bobby smiled again. "Thank you, Dr. Logan, for coming to check on me." He swung his gaze to Tharyn. "And thank you, Mrs. Logan, for doing such a good job on me." As he spoke, he slowly lifted his arms up to embrace her.

Tharyn bent down and kissed his cheek. "I'll come back with my husband to see you when we return from Denver." She kissed his cheek again, then looked at Dane. "Well, darling, we'd best be going."

Scott and Susan thanked both the Logans as they walked them outside to the buggy.

When Dane and Tharyn were eating supper at the café, he thoroughly explained about the Ute attack on the Bates family. He went on to describe Jack's wound and because as a nurse she would be interested in the removal of the slug from Jack's chest, he described it in detail.

Tharyn took a sip of hot tea and placed the cup back in its

saucer. "So what do you think? Will Jack be all right?"

"I believe so. He'll be a long time healing, but once the wound is healed, he should be able to do ranch work again. The Wilsons are going to keep him at their house, expecting Dr. Fraser to come and check on him while you and I are in Denver. They are also going to take care of the burial arrangements for the rest of the Bates family."

"Good neighbors."

"That they are."

"Were you able to discern if either the Wilsons or Jack Bates are Christians?"

"There was no indication of it. Nice people, the Wilsons, but there was nothing said that would lead me to believe they know the Lord. That's something to pray about and work on in the future."

"Yes. We certainly want to witness to them when the circumstances are better and bring them to Jesus if we can." She took another sip of tea. "What a horrible thing to happen to that poor Bates family. I know the Indians were here in the West first and that when white men came, they were usurpers, but we're here now. Oh, how I wish this Indian problem didn't exist."

"Me, too. Let me tell you some things I learned from Rex Wilson on the history of the Utes and the Arapahoes in the recent past."

Tharyn listened intently as Dane gave her the details of the recent history of the Utes and Arapahoes, and how the Utes' spokesman, Chief Ouray had tried to keep the peace between the Utes and the whites in Colorado.

She nodded. "I've heard enough from residents of Central City about Chief Ouray since I've been here to understand that he is very unhappy with the renegade chiefs and their warriors. They have told me that Chief Ouray has tried hard to keep the peace between his people and the white man."

She sighed and shook her head. "Honey, something's got to be done about these renegades. I hate to think of more ranchers facing the theft of their livestock and the guns of the renegade Indians."

Dane was buttering his third bread roll. "Well, that brings up the second part of my story, and why I was riding into town from the north and was so late in getting home."

He went on to tell her about riding to Fort Junction and informing Colonel Perry Smith about the incident at the Bates ranch. He also explained that Rex Wilson felt sure the band of hostile Utes who stole the Bates cattle and shot the family down were from the village run by the bloody Chief Tando, which was located some twenty miles southwest of Central City.

"And what was his reaction?"

"He was quite angry. Tomorrow morning he is taking a large unit of men with him to Chief Tando's village. He told me that he knows Tando will deny any knowledge of the Bates incident, but that he is going to warn him that things are going to get real bad between Tando and the army if this kind of thing happens again."

"I'm glad to hear this."

The waitress came with their dessert, which was apple pie. When that had been devoured, Dane paid the bill and they left the café.

Dane helped Tharyn into the buggy by the glow of a nearby street lamp, then climbed in beside her, took up the reins, and put Pal in motion.

As Dane drove the buggy down Main Street in the direction of their home, he said, "Well, sweetheart, I guess you've got a taste of the medical business in Central City by now. We're staying quite busy, wouldn't you say?"

She giggled. "Yes, Dr. Logan, I would say so. But, of course, that's what we want."

"Sure is. It gets pretty hectic for both of us sometimes, with me having to make house calls outside of town while you're running the office, but I love it."

She patted his arm. "I'm sure you don't love having to ride to the nearest fort and having to deal with renegade Indian problems."

He nodded. "No, I don't love that. When I was a boy, dreaming of becoming a doctor, I didn't have Indian trouble in mind at all."

"I can't really say I enjoyed doing that appendectomy today. That's really for a man with an M.D., not a woman with a C.M.N."

At that moment, Tharyn noticed that Dane had just driven past the intersection of Main and Walnut Street, which would lead them to Spruce Street, then home. She squeezed his arm. "Ah…darling, are you aware that you just passed Walnut Street?"

Dane chuckled. "Yes, ma'am."

A frown puckered her brow. "Where are we going? Do you have another house call this evening that I don't know about?"

He glanced at her and smiled. "No more house calls tonight."

"Then where are we going?"

"We've had very little time for romance these past several days, so we're going to take a little moonlight drive."

Tharyn's eyes widened. "Well, you don't have to twist my arm to get my positive vote on that!"

He laughed. "Good! I'm not in an arm-twisting frame of mind right now."

Tharyn cuddled up closer to him and slipped her arm around his neck. "Drive on, O husband of mine!"

Dane drove out of town to the south for a couple of miles, then veered off the road and pulled rein on a slight rise above a gurgling creek.

The full moon was clear edged and bright above them in the starlit sky. Its silver reflection was dancing on the surface of the rippling water.

Tharyn looked around at the pines in the moonlight, casting their dark shadows on the ground and the creek. "Oh, Dane, isn't it beautiful? I just marvel at the handiwork of our wonderful God."

Dane hopped to the ground, rounded the back side of the buggy, and lifted her down. He folded her in his strong arms and kissed her soundly. Then he held her and gazed into her eyes. "All of this around us is God's handiwork, all right, and it is indeed beautiful. But His most beautiful handiwork is right here in my arms."

Tears misted Tharyn's blue eyes.

At the same moment, the howl of a wolf in the higher country to the west pierced the night.

Dane smiled. "See there? That wolf heard what I said and he agrees."

Blinking at her tears, Tharyn placed a tender palm on his cheek. "Oh, darling, how can I ever thank the Lord for bringing us together when it looked like we would never see each other again?"

"Well, I can never thank Him enough for that, but now that we're together again, I want to make up for those ten years we were apart." He glanced down at the gurgling creek. "Let's go down there."

"Okay."

Dane took hold of her hand and together, they made their way down to the bank of the creek. Looking around, he said, "Come over here, honey. There's a fallen log right on the edge of the water."

Dane looked at his lovely wife in the silvery light of the moon. "I was just thinking on my ride home from Fort Junction this afternoon about the very first time we met. You were thirteen, and I was a mature man of the world at fifteen."

Tharyn chuckled. "Mature man of the world, eh? Well, if you say so." Abruptly, a lump came to her throat and she frowned.

"Honey, what's the matter?"

"I—I can't help but think about my parents being killed when that frightened team of horses hitched to that wagon loaded with building materials charged into them. And—and—"

"What, sweetheart?"

"Dane, I would have been killed, too, if you hadn't been there and so courageously risked your own life to remove me from the path of those same charging horses."

There was a loving expression on his handsome face as he seemed to catalogue each of her features.

He reached out and with a forefinger, tipped up her chin. He kissed her tenderly. "I would do it again if called upon to do so."

They held on to each other for a long moment; then Tharyn said, "You not only saved my life, but with Mama and Papa gone, you took me to the alley where you lived with all those other orphans and so willingly gave me a home with you."

Dane grinned. "Mm-hmm. I just had this feeling toward you like a big brother has about his little sister. My own little sister, Diane, was dead like the rest of my family, and you filled an emptiness in my heart."

She reached up and stroked his cheek. "And it didn't take you long to show it."

He chuckled. "No, it didn't. And it didn't take you long to respond to it. We hadn't known each other but a matter of weeks when we were calling each other 'brother' and 'sister.'"

"Uh-huh. I really loved having a big brother."

"We indeed had a brother-sister love between us."

She smiled. "We sure did. And I owe you so much."

"What do you mean?"

"Well, you—who had only been saved a short time yourself—began witnessing to me about Jesus. You were already doing that with the other orphans in the colony, and it was because of your testimony that the others and I turned to Jesus when you had Dr.

Lee Harris come to the alley and show the rest of us from the Bible how to be saved."

Dane nodded. "It was my pleasure and joy."

They both looked down at the bubbling creek with the white foam floating on its rippling surface.

After a moment, Tharyn lifted her head and put her soft gaze on him. "You know what?"

As he looked at her, he saw the reflection of the moonlight in her eyes. "What?"

"Even though you're my husband now, I still have a feeling about you as my protective brother. Do you understand what I'm saying? You were such a protector back in those days when I called you my brother, and that particular relationship still lives in my heart. I believe it always will. That's not wrong, is it?"

Dane chuckled and tweaked her nose lovingly. "Of course it's not wrong, sweetie. In fact, it is quite scriptural."

A surprised expression flitted across her features. "Really?"

"Mm-hmm. Just a few days ago in my devotions, I was reading in the Song of Solomon about the love between King Solomon and his wife, the Shulamite. This took me back to one time in Manhattan just before you came into my life, when Pastor Alan Wheeler preached a sermon from the Song of Solomon and pointed out that Jewish history said her name was Solyma."

Tharyn nodded and waited for him to go on.

"The Jewish historians had no way of knowing if she changed her name to Solyma after she married Solomon, or if it was the name given her by her parents. Anyway, when I was reading in chapter 4 a few days ago, it struck me that Solomon called her 'my sister, my spouse'; and I thought of how I still had brotherly love for you, in addition to the love that I have for you as your spouse—your husband."

She moved her head slowly back and forth. "Hmm. I recall

reading that term in the Song of Solomon not so long ago, but I didn't give it much thought."

"Well, sweetheart, I *have* given it some thought since reading it recently, and I realized that Solomon called Solyma 'my sister, my spouse' as if he could not express his near and dear relationship to her by any one term. He called her his sister because they were partakers of the same natural love for each other, and he called her his spouse because in one shared love, they were joined by sacred ties of passion that only a husband and wife can know."

Tharyn's eyes were swimming in tears. "Darling, I agree with your assessment of that Scripture passage. It's wonderful!"

They were in each other's arms again.

Dane held her close and whispered into her ear, "I love you, my sweetheart, with a powerful, undying love that only the Lord Himself could put there."

She looked at him dreamily and lifted her lips toward him. When they had kissed, she said, "Oh, darling, I love you so much! And my love for you is equally as powerful and undying."

The gurgling stream, the soft mountain breeze, and the beautiful moonlight seemed to embrace the young couple and to draw them closer together than they had ever been. They relished it wholeheartedly while falling deeper in love.

They kissed again, and Dane said, "Tharyn, my sweet, I didn't know it was possible to love someone as much as I love you."

"I was about to say the same thing, darling. I love you so very, very much!"

Periodically the sound of one wolf calling to another in the nearby mountains filled the air.

Dane squeezed his wife's hand and met her soft gaze. "Sweetheart, this is such a marvelous way to close a day like I've had. The terrible tragedy I saw this morning at the Bates ranch so struck my heart that I almost became sick to my stomach."

"I can well imagine. What a dreadful thing to happen to that poor man. I can't even pretend to grasp his grief over losing his entire family. If he isn't a Christian, he doesn't have the peace and comfort that the Lord can give to one of His own children. We must go and see him as soon as we return from Denver."

"We'll do it, honey. But at least right now, Jack is in good earthly hands with Rex and Dora Wilson. I'm sure they'll be as much a comfort and strength to him as human beings can."

"I'm glad for that, but I know the sadness must be overwhelming. I know we need to head for home, but how about we pray for him right now?"

"Yes. Let's do that."

The Logans bowed their heads and prayed for Jack Bates, asking the Lord to help him in his hour of need and to allow them to show him the gospel when they returned from Denver.

When they had finished, Dane stood up and offered his hand to Tharyn. As she took it and rose to a standing position, he said, "Feel better about Jack, sweetheart?"

"Yes, indeed. The Lord has really burdened my heart for Jack, and there is nothing as precious as giving our burdens to Him. 'Casting all your care upon him; for he careth for you.' We serve a wonderful God, don't we?"

"Indeed we do, my love. Indeed we do."

"We'll keep praying for Jack till we can see him in person."

"We sure will. Well, sweet stuff, you ready to head for home?"

"Sure am."

Dane surprised her by sweeping her off her feet and cradling her in his arms. He kissed her again and said, "All right, my sister, my spouse; this brother, your spouse will now drive you home."

THIRTEEN

On the west edge of Chief Tando's village in the mountains, a bright fire burned at the burial ground beneath the star-filled sky.

While six warriors beat softly and rhythmically on drums, the dark figures of all the village people, who were gathered around Yamda's grave, moaned and wailed as four warriors began filling in the grave from the mound of dirt they had piled up earlier.

Next to Yamda's grave was that of Joyce, the young white woman who had been their servant. Though Leela and the other women were unhappy that Joyce had died, there had been no crying or moaning when her body had been placed in the yawning hole in the ground, then covered over with shovels that had been stolen from various ranches where the Indians had plundered the white men's cattle and goods after massacring them.

Chief Tando had given a speech, marking Yamda as a hero because he had gallantly fought the whites since the day he had been commissioned by Tando as a warrior some five grasses previously. And now, the chief stood with Latawga and Danpo flanking him. His angular face was a mask of sorrow beneath the wolf's scalp headdress with the white teeth showing in their strange grin.

The fire was dying down and a soft wind fanned the embers,

blowing sparks, ashes, and coils of smoke away into the enshrouding blackness.

When the last of the dirt was now a mound directly over the body of Yamda, Chief Tando lifted his hand. Instantly, the drummers stopped their haunting beat, and the moans and wails of the Utes died out.

The leader ran his dark eyes over the faces that reflected the dancing flames of the fire. "We have paid our respect to the brave Yamda, who is now in the presence of the Sky People. Let us treasure his memory, but grieve no more. Return to your tepees now and get your rest."

As the Ute people began moving back into the village, two braves shoveled dirt on the fire to extinguish it, and Chief Tando moved toward his tepee with Leela and Latawga at his side.

The gray gloom on the eastern horizon was beginning to lighten the sky as Colonel Perry Smith and some two hundred mounted cavalrymen moved through the moderately dense forest and drew near Chief Tando's Ute village in rugged mountain country.

There was a dull thump of hooves on the grassy floor of the forest, plus the creak of the wheels on the two flatbed wagons that carried the deadly fifty-caliber Gatling guns. The ranks were broken and uneven because of the tall pines, birches, and cottonwoods that made up the forest. Riders and wagons alike had to constantly weave around the trees.

The soldiers who manned the Gatlings were ready for action, as were the mounted men who held their rifles in hand as the unit moved ever closer to the south edge of the forest.

Through the trees, they could now see the long rows of tepees across an open area a hundred yards beyond the edge of the forest.

The grayness was vanishing as the morning sun—not yet above the eastern elevations—sent its rosy and golden shafts between the towering mountain peaks to tip the lofty pines.

As the troops moved out of the forest onto the grassy open land, they closed ranks.

Colonel Perry Smith rode in the lead with Major Colin Harper on one side of him, Captain Ron Craddock on the other, and a wagon bearing a Gatling gun on either side of them. Sergeant Clint Burke rode on the far side of the wagon on the right, holding a long stick with a white flag at its tip, flapping in the breeze. The other mounted men were now spreading out behind them in a show of force.

As they drew nearer to the village, suddenly two Ute warriors assigned as lookouts sprang to their feet from a low spot in the terrain and dashed toward the gathering of tepees.

Sergeant Clint Burke watched the Indians as they ran toward the village, then said, "Colonel, I hope they saw this white flag."

"I don't know how they could have missed it," replied Smith. "They've had time to look us over real good since we came out of the woods." He ran his gaze around to the rest of the men. "Just keep your pace as is."

They were within forty yards of the village when Major Colin Harper pointed to the west side of it. "The burial ground, Colonel. See it? There are two fresh graves."

Smith fixed his gaze on the two mounds. "I wonder if one of them is the grave of the warrior Dr. Logan told me had been shot in the raid on the Bates ranch."

"Could very well be, sir."

Captain Ron Craddock said, "Look over there, Colonel!"

Smith saw him pointing to several beef carcasses that had been skinned and dressed out, hanging from trees in a small patch of woods off to the east side of the village. "Yeah. Probably Bates cattle."

The two warriors were now in the village and there was a stirring among the people who were milling about.

The day brightened, and a long bank of high, fleecy clouds

was turning a bright rosy color. The sun would soon put in its appearance.

By the time the army unit was drawing up to the edge of the village, the scene had changed. The only Indians in sight now were warriors who were scurrying about, rifles in hand. Chief Tando was moving toward the oncoming army unit with several warriors collected around him. A few women could be seen peering out of the tepee openings, but no children were in sight.

"Looks like we've got Tando's attention, Colonel," said the major. "That's his son, Latawga, beside him."

Smith nodded. He said loudly, "Everybody stay alert. Be ready for anything."

"We are, Colonel," said one of the men in the wagon with a Gatling gun.

The mounted men remained in their saddles as previously instructed by their commandant. When the chief and the group with him drew up and halted, Colonel Smith raised his hand in a sign of peace.

Tando's dark features were like stone as he eyed the white flag held by Sergeant Clint Burke and the formidable Gatling guns. Then set his icy glare on the colonel. "You are from Fort Junction?" he grunted in English.

"Yes. I am the commandant, Colonel Perry Smith. You have been in conversations with some of my officers before, including Major Colin Harper."

Tando fixed his gaze on the major, but made no comment. He looked back at Smith. "Why are you here?"

Latawga glanced at his father. The tension in the chief's jaw and the pinched wariness at the corners of his dark eyes told Latawga that his father was very uneasy.

Feeling the pressure of Tando's glare, Colonel Smith replied, "There was a Ute band that stole cattle yesterday morning from a rancher named Jack Bates near Central City. Bates caught them in the act. A gun battle followed. Bates and his family were gunned down. Neighbors saw it, and reported that it was definitely Utes. There were eight of them."

The seven surviving young warriors who had stolen the cattle and gunned down the Bates family were clustered together within the group who stood with the chief. Each of the seven felt tension rise within him at the colonel's words.

The stony look remained on Tando's dark face, but he did not comment.

The weight of the colonel's gaze was as heavy as a hand against Tando's forehead as Smith said levelly, "Chief, I want to know if it was one of your warrior bands who did this."

Tando's mouth pulled down at the corners. His voice was as cold as his eyes. "It was not one of my warrior bands."

Smith had expected him to deny it. He then pointed to the carcasses of the cattle that were hanging from the trees. "Where did you get those cattle you just butchered?"

"There are Utes who raise cattle on the plains west of the mountains. They often give me and my people some of their cattle for food."

"I want to see the hides. Where are they?"

The chief bristled. "I know you want to see if there are brands on the hides. There are no brands. Indians do not brand their cattle. The Utes who brought us the cattle had need of the hides for making winter coats for their people. They waited here until the cattle were slaughtered, then took the hides with them."

The colonel felt confident that Tando was lying and knew he would not give him the true names nor the location of the Ute cattle raisers who were supposed to have given them cattle and left with the hides. He adjusted himself in the saddle. "Chief Tando, the Bates's neighbors reported that one of the warriors among those who stole the cattle and shot down the Bates family was shot by Jack Bates."

He looked toward the burial ground, then back at Tando. "I see two fresh graves. Who is buried in them?"

The chief's wrath was rising in him at the colonel's brazen question, but he suppressed it. "Two of our women died yesterday. We buried them before sundown."

"I'm having a hard time believing you, Chief. I am going to have my men open the graves so we can see if two of your women are buried there."

Tando stiffened and his voice jumped at Smith. "You cannot do this! The graves of our people are sacred to us!"

"I do not order this with pleasure, Chief Tando, but my government needs to know who killed the Bates family and stole their cattle."

The warriors around Tando were showing their anger. The chief's face was a mask of fury. "Do not give the order, Colonel Perry Smith! If you do, blood will be shed!"

Smith turned and nodded at his men.

Rifles were brought to bear, and the men at the Gatling guns released the safety switches loudly and aimed them into the group.

The Ute warriors tensed.

Smith cleared his throat. "Chief Tando, we will open only one grave. If we find one of your women in the grave, we will believe that there is a Ute woman in the other one."

In his mind, Smith knew if there was a dead warrior in the second grave, he would possibly have made the Indians and their chief nervous enough to bring their thefts and attacks on white ranchers to a halt.

The colonel pointed toward the burial ground. "Men, there are shovels leaning against that cottonwood tree right there. Corporal Baxter, Trooper Walvord, use the shovels to open the grave closest to us."

"Yes sir!" The two cavalrymen trotted their horses toward the burial ground.

Tension ruled over both Utes and cavalrymen, but nobody moved. The Indians gripped their weapons, but their fear of the deadly Gatling guns held them in check.

Latawga leaned close to his father and whispered in the Ute language so only he could hear. "Father! The grave they are going to open is that of Yamda! There are more of them than of us, and they have those death-spitting guns on the wagons. What will we do when they find Yamda with the bullet in him?"

Keeping his eyes on the cavalrymen and the two threatening Gatling guns, Chief Tando whispered back, "Your father will handle it. Do not worry."

Latawga swallowed hard. "But what if they decide to open the other grave in spite of what the colonel just said? If they find the white woman—"

"Your father will decide what to do if that happens," Tando cut in.

"Say no more! The colonel is watching us."

Latawga glanced at Smith from the corner of his eye and could tell he was looking their direction. When the whispering ceased, Smith set his line of sight on the two men who were now digging into the designated grave.

The tension remained while Baxter and Walvord continued digging. The rest of the warriors and the village people looked on, their own nerves taut.

Finding the grave relatively shallow, the two men in blue soon discovered the stiff corpse of Yamda, wrapped in a dirt-caked blanket. They lifted the body onto the ground beside the grave, flung aside the blanket, and quickly found the bullet hole. Corporal Baxter looked back toward his commanding officer. "Colonel Smith, come and look at this!"

Turning to Harper, the colonel said, "You stay here and keep a sharp eye on those warriors." Then to Craddock he said, "Captain, you come with me."

Chief Tando spoke up. "My son and I are coming with you."

Smith nodded. "Captain Craddock and I will dismount, and we will walk together."

Tando and Latawga waited for the officers to dismount. Then without speaking, all four made their way across the grassy land on the edge of the village to the burial ground where Corporal Baxter and Trooper Walvord were standing over the lifeless form of the young Ute warrior. As they drew up, Baxter knelt down and pointed to the bullet wound. "As you can see, sir, he was shot right here."

Smith knelt down beside him, examined the wound, and shook his head. He rose to his feet and set steady eyes on the chief. "Your warrior has a bullet in him. It's evident to me that he is the one who was shot by Mr. Bates."

There was rank anger in Tando's eyes. "Can you prove he is the one who was shot by the rancher Bates?"

Smith sighed and rubbed a hand over his mustache. "No. I can't prove it. So tell me how he got shot then."

"This is private business of Tando and his people. We are not obligated to give Colonel Perry Smith this information."

Smith and Craddock noticed that all the village's warriors were now making their way toward the scene at the burial ground. The cavalrymen were following on their horses, rifles ready, and the two wagons bearing the Gatling guns were among them. The warriors were already less than twenty yards away.

Smith put his attention back on Tando. "Like I said, Chief, I can't prove the dead brave is the one who was shot by Jack Bates, but I will say this. I know that you and your people are not in sympathy with the majority of the Utes here in Colorado. Their spokesman is Chief Ouray, who is a man of peace. He is a sensible man. He has asked all of the Ute Tribe to live in peace with the white men. Am I speaking the truth?"

Tando stared at the colonel, his stomach tightening. His lips pulled into a thin, shapeless line. It was obvious that no answer was forthcoming.

The warriors—with the cavalrymen on their heels—were drawing up. They could all tell that Chief Tando was angry, and they all fixed their attention on the colonel, who was about to speak.

Smith put some gravel in his voice. "I'm warning you, Chief Tando. You and your warriors are on the edge of disaster. Understand this. Your village will be under the eagle eye of the United States Army from now on. There will be army patrols from Fort Junction moving about this area like never before. If other ranchers or white men of any other occupation are killed or wounded by your warriors, you and they will suffer severe consequences."

The observers, Ute and men in blue, stared at the scene, eyes wide.

The colonel paused and scrutinized the chief's stone-like face. "I'm not aware of how much English you understand, Chief. Do you understand what I just said?"

Tando's stony features seemed somehow to droop, hanging heavy on the sharp angles of his bones. Something was burning in his eyes. Behind the glimmer of his irises something was white hot. Something with a life all its own.

Anger showed in the faces of Tando's one hundred and fifty warriors.

The chief said stiffly, "I understand your words, Colonel Perry Smith. Do you have anything else to say?"

"No. I've told you how it is going to be, and I mean what I said."

The colonel turned to his men. "Captain Craddock and I will go get our horses, and we'll be heading back to the fort. My edict has been pronounced to Chief Tando."

"We'll go with you, sir," said Major Harper.

The mounted men rode behind Smith and Craddock as they walked back to their horses. The wagons bearing the Gatling guns brought up the rear with the guns pointing in the direction of the chief and his warriors, who stood looking on with hatred in their eyes.

The colonel and the captain swung aboard their mounts and trotted them up beside Major Harper, who was already positioned in the lead. As they moved southward away from the village, the flatbed wagons took up a position in the rear. Sergeant Clint Burke took the white flag from the stick, stuffed it into a pocket, and dropped the stick on the ground.

The two officers were flanking their leader as before. Captain Ron Craddock said, "Colonel, sir, I noticed that in all of the conversation with Chief Tando, you never told him that Jack Bates is still alive."

Smith chuckled. "I figured since his warriors weren't the ones who stole Bates's cattle and shot him and his family down, they didn't need to know that Mr. Bates is still living."

Both Craddock and Harper laughed.

"Sure," said Craddock, still laughing. "That lying renegade chief never sent that band of warriors out to steal Bates's cattle, did he?"

At the village, as the Indians watched the army unit ride away, Latawga turned to the chief. "I am proud of my father for standing firm before the soldier coats. White men are intruders in this land, which once belonged only to the Indians. They must pay for coming here uninvited and stealing Indian land."

Emotions warred in Tando's heart. "You are correct, my son. The white men still owe us, and we will continue stealing their cattle, in spite of what Colonel Perry Smith says. And when the opportunities are offered to us by our gods, we will also attack stagecoaches and wagon trains as we have been doing for many grasses."

After seeing patients who had early appointments on Saturday morning, Dr. Dane Logan stepped out of the office and climbed into his buggy to make house calls on patients that he needed to check on before leaving for Denver.

When he arrived at the home of the foreman of the Holton Coal Mine, Wilma Frye responded to his knock on the front door. "Hello, Dr. Logan. Nice to see you. Please come in."

As he stepped in, the doctor asked, "So, is Ben doing all right?"

"I believe you will be quite satisfied with his progress," she replied, closing the door behind him. "His boss is with him at the moment."

Dr. Dane halted. "Oh? Well, I'd better come back later."

Wilma waved him off. "No need for that. He'll be glad to see you. C'mon."

When Wilma led the doctor into the room where Ben lay in bed, the mine owner was seated on a chair beside the bed, and quickly rose to his feet.

"Dr. Logan!" Ben said warmly. "Nice to see you."

Kirby Holton shook the doctor's hand, with a big smile on his face. "Dr. Logan, I very much appreciate the good care you've given my foreman. He's looking worlds better."

"I'm glad for that, Mr. Holton. How's everything at the mine?"

"Doing almost 100 percent, Doctor. I say 'almost' because without Ben, it's not quite running smoothly."

The doctor chuckled, placed his medical bag on the small table beside the bed, and said, "Well, we're going to get him back on the job for you just as soon as possible."

While Wilma and the mine owner looked on, Dr. Dane checked his patient over, replaced the bandages on his temple and neck, then looked down at him, smiling. "You really are doing well, Ben. I've got to go to Denver on Monday to do a hip replacement on Nelda Cox at Mile High Hospital. Do you know the Coxes?"

"Oh, sure. I've known Eric and Nelda for years. I'd heard that this hip replacement surgery was going to be done on her."

"I'm taking my wife with me to be my surgical nurse for the surgery, so she won't be here, either. But Dr. Fraser and Nadine Wahl will be filling in for us at the office. I will have Dr. Fraser come and check on you while we're gone."

Ben nodded. "Thank you, Dr. Logan."

Wilma smiled. "I'm so glad Dr. Fraser is still able to fill in for you when you have to be away."

"Me, too. Bless his heart, he won't be able to do it much longer. His age is showing on him."

"What will you do when he no longer can do it?" she asked.

"Well, I've got some plans taking form in the back of my mind, but I don't have time to explain them right now. I've got to keep moving."

Kirby Holton said, "Before you go, Doctor, I'd like to ask you: Have you ever been down in a mine?"

"No, sir. Never have. But as far back as I can remember, I've wanted to see what it was like."

"Well, how about letting me take you down in the Holton Coal Mine sometime soon?"

"I'd love it."

"All right. I'd be glad to take you down and give you the grand tour when you get back from Denver."

"I hereby accept the invitation, Mr. Holton. When I get back, I'll let you know when I can work it into my schedule."

"Good! I'll look forward to it."

Esther Fraser was on the front porch of her house, watering her flower pots, when she saw Dr. Dane Logan pull up in his buggy. Holding the watering can in one hand, she waved with the other. "Hello, Dr. Dane. Come in. Bob will be glad to see you."

From inside the house, Dr. Robert Fraser overheard his wife speak to Dr. Dane, and came out the door. The physicians greeted one another; then Dr. Dane entered the house, and they sat down in the parlor.

Dr. Fraser adjusted his spectacles and set scrutinizing eyes on Dr. Dane. "You look pretty tired, son. Are you working too hard?"

Dr. Dane smiled. "Well, this has been an arduous week, Doctor, I'll say that. I thought of you today, wondering how you've held up so good the past few years with the pace this practice demands. No wonder you're ready to completely retire. You always seem so full of energy whenever I ask you to cover for me."

Fraser chuckled. "Well, sometimes I put on a show of energy I really don't have."

Dr. Dane shook his head. "Then I shouldn't be putting all this work on you when I have to be out of town."

Fraser chuckled again. "I said *sometimes,* son. I love filling in for you. I know the day is approaching when I will have to retire completely. But not yet, thank the Lord. Even though you're young, you're a genuine physician and surgeon, so I know you understand that the need to heal people is born in us. I'm glad I can still do some of it."

Dane sighed, reached inside his coat pocket, produced a folded piece of paper, and handed it to the elderly man. "I'm sure glad you still want to fill in for me. I've made up a list of the patients I'll need you to check on while Tharyn and I are in Denver. I've written down what I'm treating them for, and how to find those out there in the mountains who are first-time patients."

Dr. Fraser unfolded the paper, and while scanning it, said, "I'll take care of them, son. You just center your thoughts on performing that hip replacement." His head bobbed. "Jack Bates?"

Dr. Dane cleared his throat gently. "Yes, sir. As you see there, he'll be at the Wilson ranch with Rex and Dora."

Esther leaned closer to the young doctor. "I can tell by the look on your face that something bad has happened to Jack, and if he's staying with Rex and Dora, something bad has happened to Wanda and the children."

Dr. Dane took a deep breath. "Yes. Something really bad. Let me tell you the story…"

Dr. Dane had been at the Fraser home almost an hour, and as he drove toward his office, he ran his gaze to the mountains that surrounded Central City, marveling at the magnificent grandeur of it all.

What a perfect place to live, he thought. *I'm doing what God put in my heart to do so many years ago. There were times that it looked impossible that I would ever become a doctor. Like those terrible months I spent in that Manhattan prison for a crime I didn't commit. It certainly looked like my dream of a medical career would never be realized.*

Yet my wonderful heavenly Father is always faithful, and He has given me the desires of my heart. I'm able to practice medicine to my heart's content, which is wonderful. But even more wonderful than that is the way my Father—in His wisdom and grace—brought Tharyn and me back together. In this great big world, the Lord let us find each other, joined us again in the love we had for each other, and joined us in marriage. Jesus is the head of our home, the very center and core of our lives.

Lifting his eyes to the vast canopy of blue above him, Dane

Logan said, "Thank You, Lord, for giving me more than I could ever ask for or deserve. Truly, You are such a generous and wonderful Father."

FOURTEEN

*I*t was almost noon when Cassandra Wheatley and Rosemary Snyder were in Central City's newest clothing store, known as Wortman's, which had a large selection of ladies' ready-made dresses.

Rosemary had money in her purse to purchase a new dress, and with eager anticipation, was taking dresses from the racks and trying them on in the dressing room. Cassandra was moving along the racks, admiring the large selection of dresses. With each dress, Rosemary appeared from the dressing room to ask Cassandra how she looked in it. Cassandra was consistent, telling her she looked perfect in each one.

Rosemary came out of the dressing room in the seventh dress she had tried on, which was light green cotton with white daisies that had yellow centers. It had white pique trim around a square neck, elbow-length sleeves, and a full sweeping skirt. She found Cassandra holding a yellow dress up to herself in front of a floor-length mirror.

Rosemary smiled. "Hey, honey, that dress really goes with your black hair."

The beautiful brunette smiled back, got a dreamy look in her eyes, and said in a silky voice, "Greg would like me in this one, don't you think?"

Rosemary chuckled. "Actually, I think Greg would even like you in a burlap sack, but yes, I'm sure if he saw you in that dress, it would take his breath away."

Cassandra giggled. "You really think so?"

"I don't think so. I *know* so. I've watched the love light glow in his eyes when he looks at you. And the same kind of light also glows in *your* eyes when you look at him."

"Oh, it does, does it?"

"Mm-hmm. I think my friend Miss Cassandra Wheatley is falling in love with Mr. Greg Holton, and it sure appears that Mr. Greg Holton is falling in love with Miss Cassandra Wheatley."

A bright smile spread over the brunette's face, reaching from ear to ear.

Suddenly there was a deep rumbling sound from somewhere outside.

Cassandra's eyes widened. "Th-that c-can't be thunder, can it? The sky was clear when we came in here."

"No, honey. It isn't thunder. What you heard came from the Holton Coal Mine. Periodically, they set off dynamite sticks down in the mine to open up new sections where they can dig more coal."

"Hmm. That's interesting. I do recall that I heard somewhere once that they use dynamite in gold mines to do that. Guess they have to do it the same way with coal."

"That's right. Well, I'm going to buy this dress, Cassandra. I'll change back into my old dress, buy this one, and we'll be going."

At the same time Rosemary and Cassandra were in Wortman's, Marshal Jake Merrell was walking along Main Street, keeping an eye on the business district, when he saw Dr. Dane Logan coming down the street in his buggy.

Merrell was almost in front of the doctor's office as Dr. Dane swung the buggy to the hitch rail. "Hello, Marshal!"

"Howdy, Doc."

Dr. Dane hopped out of the buggy and chuckled when Pal whinnied. "Okay, Pal, you can rest a while now."

The bay gelding blew and bobbed his head.

The marshal laughed. "You know, Doc, sometimes I think this horse of yours knows every word in the English language."

"I've thought the same thing. You walking the beat by yourself?"

"Mm-hmm. I sent my esteemed deputy out of town to deliver a court summons."

"I see. Len seems like a good lawman."

"That he is. Len's daddy, George Kurtz, was marshal of Raton, New Mexico, until he was killed in a gun battle about fifteen years ago with outlaws who had held up one of the town's banks."

"Oh. I didn't know about that."

"Len had already announced that he was going to be a lawman like his father when he was six years old. He was only eight when his father was killed, but he stuck to his goal, and I think he's better than the average lawman his age because of what happened to his father. He's sensible about it, but he has a special grudge against outlaws. I'm quite pleased to have him as my deputy."

Dr. Dane grinned. "That's obvious. The two of you make a great team."

"Thank you."

Both men smiled and nodded at people who were passing by on the boardwalk.

Dr. Dane said, "It helps, both of you being Christians, doesn't it?"

"Sure does. And speaking of great teams, you and Tharyn make a great team, too."

Dr. Dane grinned again. "I thank the Lord every day for giving her to me."

"You're staying pretty busy in your practice, aren't you? I'm noticing a greater number of people going and coming from your office all the time."

"Yes, I'm staying quite busy. And that's the way I like it."

"You're still doing a lot of hip replacements, I understand."

"Yes. About 80 percent of the time I'm out of town, it's to do another hip replacement either at Mile High Hospital in Denver or some other town that has a hospital."

"Any chance that Central City will have a hospital someday?"

"Well, maybe someday. It'll have to at least double in size before that can happen, but I'm already thinking about trying to buy one of the vacant lots on Main Street here in the business district and putting up a building large enough to have a clinic with some beds so we can keep patients here instead of having to transport them to the hospital in Denver. It would depend on just what was wrong with them, but I'd say about half the patients we take to Denver could stay right here if we had the proper facilities for certain kinds of surgery and other medical treatment."

"That would be great, Doc. I hope you're able to do it soon."

"Me, too. And speaking of hip replacements, Tharyn and I will be taking Eric and Nelda Cox to Denver on Monday so I can perform a hip replacement on Nelda."

"I'd heard that was going to happen. I just didn't know when."

Suddenly a sharp male voice from behind the marshal cut the air. "Hey! Jake Merrell!"

The marshal turned around and Dr. Dane followed his line of sight to see a man in his late twenties standing in the street some forty feet away, just off the boardwalk. He was in a gunfighter's stance with his right hand hovering over the gun in his holster. There was a dangerous glitter in his narrowed eyes and a wicked sneer on his face. "I'm challengin' you, Merrell! Go for your gun!"

People on the boardwalk looked on, eyes wide.

Dr. Dane observed the scene with his heart pounding as Jake Merrell stepped off the boardwalk, his hands dangling at his sides.

Merrell fixed the stranger with a steady gaze. "Do you see this badge on my chest, mister whoever-you-are? You're challenging a lawman."

More townspeople were appearing on the boardwalk and on the street, coming out of stores and shops. When they realized what was happening, they moved closer to the scene, whispering among themselves.

Noting the gathering crowd, the challenger snapped loudly, "I know you're a lawman, Merrell! My name's Waco Belton." He ran his gaze to the gathering crowd. "You hear that, everybody? I'm Waco Belton! You'll have good reason to remember my name after I show this tin star what a *real* fast draw is!"

A man in the crowd shouted, "Do you know who you're challenging, Belton? Marshal Jake Merrell is known for his fast gun!"

Without taking his eyes off the marshal, Belton muttered brazenly, "Yeah, I know who I'm challengin'. And I know about his reputation for bein' fast on the draw. Your marshal used to be one of Chief U.S. Marshal John Brockman's deputies over in Denver."

Dr. Dane's mouth fell open. He had not been aware of this. He was wishing for a way to stop the impending bloodshed, but knew he was helpless to do so. At that instant, he saw Tharyn come out of the office with a female patient she had just taken care of. Their eyes locked, and he motioned for her to stay right where she was. She nodded her agreement.

Merrell pinned Belton with arctic eyes. "So I used to be a deputy U.S. marshal. Why does that make you want to challenge me?"

Belton sneered and his hand eased down closer to the handle of his revolver. "I know Brockman taught you the fast draw, Merrell. I'm workin' my way up to challengin' Brockman, but I wanna do it slowlike. In the past week, I challenged and killed two of Brockman's former deputies in Wyomin'. One in Laramie and one in Rock Springs." His lips whipped back in an evil grin, showing his crooked teeth. "I decided you're next."

Anger was rising red in Merrell's face. "You're under arrest, Belton! It's against the law to challenge an officer of the law to a shootout. Move your hands down slowly, unbuckle that gun belt, let it drop to the ground, and lift your hands above your head. Don't make me have to draw my gun. Just do as I tell you."

Belton laughed. "I won't do it! You're gonna draw against me, Merrell. I'm gonna outdraw you, and I'm gonna kill you!"

Tension on the street grew tighter.

Merrell's gun hand lowered closer to the handle of his holstered Colt .45 Peacemaker. "I don't want to shed your blood, Belton. Do as I told you and you'll only spend a year or so in jail for defying the law and challenging me. Like I said, you're under arrest. If you resist, you'll suffer the consequences."

The gunfighter guffawed. "Tryin' to scare me won't work, Merrell. You're gonna draw against me right now."

"Belton!" rasped the marshal. "You can't outdraw me. Do as I tell you! I'm giving you one last chance to drop that gun belt!"

Waco Belton set his jaw and leered menacingly at the lawman. "You ain't in control, here, Marshal."

Merrell's face crimsoned. "You're about to find out who's in control."

Belton grinned menacingly. "No, *you* are." Keeping his eyes on Merrell, he threw the thumb of his left hand over his shoulder. "Maybe you'd better take a look down there in front of Wortman's clothin' store."

Merrell's line of sight quickly focused on Cassandra Wheatley down the boardwalk, who was being held by another stranger, with the muzzle of his revolver pressed against her temple. Her neck was locked in the crook of his free arm. Merrell could tell she was terrified.

The crowd stood in shock as they beheld the sight.

Rosemary Snyder was leaning against the wall of the store, her face devoid of color.

Cassandra's eyes were widened and filled with fear. There was a circle of white around her mouth and two blotches of white on her cheeks. She stood perfectly still, hardly daring to breathe, fearful that the man holding the gun to her head would kill her if the marshal didn't take Waco Belton's challenge and draw against him.

Cassandra looked at Rosemary, who leaned weakly against the storefront for support, her hand covering her mouth.

Cassandra drew a shaky breath. "P-please, Rosemary. Help m-me."

"Ain't nobody gonna help you, girlie," said the man who had her in his grasp, "unless that there marshal meets Waco's challenge."

Cassandra's heart was pounding so hard, she was sure it would soon burst through her rib cage. She had thought nothing exciting would ever happen in quiet Central City. And now that it was indeed happening, she certainly never expected to be in the middle of it. It had seemed like an ordinary peaceful Saturday only moments before, and now it was almost certain that someone was going to die. *Just don't let it be me!*

No one had noticed Greg Holton, who had been on his way into town in one of the mine's wagons. He had seen the crowd gathered on the boardwalk and in the street, then caught sight of Cassandra in the gunman's grip and heard the man who identified himself as Waco Belton challenging Marshal Jake Merrell to a shootout.

Greg had stopped the wagon on the side of the street, picked up a crowbar from the wagon bed, and was now moving up behind the man who was holding Cassandra.

Unaware of what was taking place behind her, Cassandra watched Marshal Jake Merrell run his gaze toward her as had been suggested by Waco Belton.

A wicked smile curved his lips as Waco Belton saw the marshal taking in the scene in front of Wortman's clothing store. Belton's gun hand hovered eagerly over his revolver. "Looks like we've got us a Mexican standoff here, Merrell. My pal will put a bullet in that girl's head if you don't draw on me. If you'll do as I say and draw on me in front of all these nice people, I promise you, the girl will not be harmed."

The marshal was bracing himself for what he must do, when he caught sight of Greg Holton with a crowbar in his hand, easing stealthily up behind the man who was holding his gun to Cassandra's head.

Since Belton was facing the marshal, he did not see Greg Holton.

As he was silently moving up behind the man who had Cassandra in his grasp, Greg noted that the hammer of the man's gun was not cocked. This would make things easier.

Still unaware of what was taking place behind her, Cassandra jerked when she heard the sudden sound of the crowbar savagely striking her captor's head. Instantly, the man's hold on her slackened; then his arm fell away. His gun clattered on the wooden floor. She was aware of a loud *thump* on the boardwalk behind her.

She spun around and saw the man motionless on the wooden floor. Suddenly, she was aware of Greg standing there with the crowbar in his hand, grinning at her.

Eyes wide with surprise, Cassandra threw herself into Greg's arms, releasing a wail of relief. Greg grabbed her tightly, realizing her knees were giving way. She slumped into the safety of his arms, but the trauma was too much for her. She fainted.

Down on the street, Waco Belton heard the feminine wail of relief and gripped his gun handle as he looked over his shoulder and saw his accomplice lying on the boardwalk and the girl in the young man's arms.

Everybody in the crowd knew blood was about to be spilled. They began edging their way toward the walls of the stores and shops.

Wrath swept through Waco Belton like lava flowing from an erupting volcano and brought stinging blood into his cheeks. Still gripping his gun, he turned back to face Merrell, drawing as he turned.

Merrell saw it and his gun came out of its holster with lightning speed.

Thunder from the Colt .45 Peacemaker rocked the street, and in ear-stabbing reverberations, racketed through the town.

Waco Belton's eyes bulged in unbelief as he dropped his gun and staggered backward a few steps, throwing both hands to the wound where the .45 slug had plowed into his chest. His face seemed to pull apart as his eyes glazed. With a strangling sound, he fell flat on his back.

Dr. Dane Logan moved up beside the marshal. "I think he's dead, Jake."

"Let's see."

The crowd looked on wide-eyed and silent as the marshal and the doctor knelt down beside Waco Belton. There was no rise and fall of his chest and no part of his body was moving.

Dr. Dane placed experienced fingers to the side of Belton's neck and shook his head. "He's dead."

Merrell nodded solemnly. "I tried to keep from killing him, Doc. He flat wouldn't let me."

"Anybody could see that," said Dr. Dane, rising to his feet. "I'd better see to Cassandra and the accomplice. Greg hit him pretty hard. But he had it coming."

"I'll be with you in a minute. Manfred Wiggins is in the crowd. I'll turn Belton's body over to him. If the other guy is dead too, he'll have two to bury."

Dr. Dane hurried to the spot on the boardwalk where Greg was sitting on a bench, holding the unconscious Cassandra cradled in his arms while Tharyn was bending over her with Rosemary at her side. Others were standing around, looking down at Cassandra.

Tharyn looked up at her husband. "She'll come to in a minute, I'm sure."

Dane smiled at his wife. "Thanks for seeing to her." He laid a palm on Cassandra's cheek, raised an eyelid, and examined the eye. "You're right, honey. She'll come around shortly."

The doctor then looked to the spot where Waco Belton's accomplice lay facedown on the boardwalk. Two townsmen were standing over him. One of them held the accomplice's gun in his hand. The other one said, "He took a pretty good whack on the head by Greg, Doctor. He's bleeding some, but he's still breathing."

Dr. Dane knelt beside the unconscious man, examined the bloody gash on the back of his head, and looked at Greg. "You really did whack him a good one."

Cassandra was stirring now.

Greg met the doctor's gaze and nodded. "I wanted to make sure I eliminated him as a threat."

Dr. Dane grinned. "You did that, all right."

On the street, Marshal Jake Merrell motioned to undertaker Manfred Wiggins, who was in the forefront of the crowd. Wiggins hurried to him.

"Manfred," said the marshal, "take Belton's body and bury it. The town will pick up the bill. This other guy who was with him may be dead, too. If he is, the town will also pick up the bill on him."

The undertaker nodded. "Be back in a few minutes, Marshal." He stepped up to a man in the crowd and asked him for help in carrying the body to the undertaking parlor.

Merrell watched them carrying the body away, then hurried toward the boardwalk where Dr. Dane had gone to see about Cassandra and Belton's accomplice. While he was threading his way through the crowd, people were shouting their congratulations to him for the way he took out Waco Belton.

The marshal drew up to the boardwalk in front of Wortman's clothing store to hear Greg Holton saying that Cassandra had fainted just before Marshal Merrell gunned down Waco Belton.

At that moment, Cassandra began moaning in Greg's arms and rolling her head back and forth.

Greg looked up at the doctor and nurse. "She's waking up."

Dr. Dane and Tharyn both smiled as they looked at her.

Tharyn began rubbing Cassandra's hands with her own as Dr. Dane stood over them looking on. She smiled at Greg. "You'd better prepare yourself. Since you saved this girl's life, she's going to look at you as her hero."

Greg grinned. "I can handle it, Mrs. Logan."

Tharyn winked at Rosemary, then looked back at Greg. "I think you probably can."

Cassandra was moaning and rolling her head back and forth.

Greg said, "Cassandra, it's okay. You're safe now. Come on. Open your eyes. Dr. and Mrs. Logan are here. No one is going to hurt you."

Ever so slowly, Cassandra opened her eyes, blinking rapidly at the brightness of the early afternoon sun. Licking her dry lips, she tried to speak, but the words came out in a croak. She swallowed and tried once more, but could only make a gasping sound. Her eyes went shut again.

Greg looked at the doctor. "Would you hold her, Dr. Logan, while I run down to the general store and get her some water?"

"I'll get her some," spoke up a middle-aged man on the front edge of the crowd. "Be right back."

Greg called out a word of thanks as the man hurried away.

Dr. Dane leaned down and laid a hand on Cassandra's brow. "It's Dr. Logan, Cassandra. Water is on the way."

Greg looked down at her with adoration. "Cassandra, try again to open your eyes."

She forced her glassy eyes open, trying with difficulty to focus them on Greg's face.

He smiled. "Did you hear what I said before? No one is going to hurt you now."

She nodded. Her words came out shakily and with a croaking sound. "Yes, Greg. I heard you."

At that moment, the man who had gone after the water drew up, puffing, holding a cup of water in his hand.

Rosemary smiled at him and took the cup from his hand. "Thank you, sir."

He grinned and took a couple of steps back.

Greg raised Cassandra's head slightly. "Rosemary's got water for you."

"Just take small sips, Cassandra," said Dr. Dane.

After Cassandra had drained the cup sip by sip, she set her eyes on Greg. Her voice was still a bit raspy. "Y-you hit that vile man on the head with something, didn't you?"

Greg nodded. "Mm-hmm. A crowbar."

She smiled. "You're my hero."

Greg looked at Tharyn and blushed.

Dr. Dane bent down and said, "Cassandra, you're going to be fine. Mrs. Logan will stay with you a little longer and make sure you can walk all right. I've got to see to this man who was holding his gun to your head."

She blinked. "Is he going to jail?"

"He sure is. It's my duty as a doctor to do what I can to stop the bleeding on his head where Greg popped him, but after that, I'm turning him over to Marshal Merrell for arrest and prosecution. There were plenty of witnesses, that's for sure."

Merrell said, "I'll get someone to help me, Doctor, and we'll carry this guy to your office so you can look him over and stitch up that gash in his head. When you're finished, he's going into a cell. I'll bring him up before one of the county judges as soon as he's able to stand before him."

As Dr. Dane was about to comment, Deputy Len Kurtz rode up and dismounted. Immediately, people in the crowd began telling Kurtz what happened. He stepped up to the spot where his boss and the doctor were standing over the unconscious man. "Need help, Marshal? Doctor?"

"Yes," said Merrell. "Help me carry this guy over to the doctor's office."

Dr. Dane led the two lawmen as they carried Waco Belton's accomplice toward the office.

The crowd was still cheering Marshal Jake Merrell for taking out the gunslinger.

FIFTEEN

$\mathcal{A}$s the two lawmen were carrying the unconscious accomplice of Waco Belton down the street with Dr. Dane Logan beside them, Tharyn kept her eyes on them.

Greg Holton noticed it. "Mrs. Logan, if you need to be there to help Dr. Logan work on that man, I'll stay right here with Cassandra until she's doing better. You go on."

"When Cassandra is feeling up to it," said Rosemary, "Greg and I will take her home. If Dr. Logan wants to check on her later, I'm sure her Aunt Mabel would welcome it."

Tharyn smiled at both of them. "All right. There are patients waiting to see my husband, too. I'll go help him."

Stepping off the boardwalk into the dust of the street, Tharyn lifted her skirt just above her ankles and ran after her husband and the other men as fast as she could go.

She drew up beside her husband, who was surprised to see her. They were almost to the office, where the patients who had appointments were waiting on the boardwalk and looking on.

Tharyn looked up at Dane. "I thought I'd better come and help you. Greg and Rosemary are going to take Cassandra home as soon as she feels like it. You can check on her later, if you wish."

"I'll do that…and yes, I really do need you."

As they drew up to the front of the office, Dr. Dane hurried ahead of Marshal Jake Merrell and Deputy Len Kurtz as they carried the man who had put the gun to Cassandra Wheatley's head.

He was now moaning, moving his head back and forth, and blinking his eyes.

Dr. Dane hopped up onto the boardwalk and opened the door. As the lawmen carried the man past him into the office, Tharyn was on their heels. Just as he was about to follow her inside, he heard the voice of Western Union Agent Charlie Holmes call his name.

Holmes stepped up with a yellow envelope in his hand. "Telegram for you, Doctor. It's from Chief U.S. Marshal John Brockman in Denver."

"Thanks, Charlie."

"You're welcome, Doctor. I'm sure glad Marshal Merrell took out that gunslinger and Greg whacked his accomplice on the noggin. See you later."

Dr. Dane turned to his patients, who were standing on the boardwalk. "Come on in and sit down, folks. I'll get to you as soon as I can."

One of the male patients took hold of the door, freeing the doctor to hurry after the two lawmen and his wife. As he passed Tharyn's desk, he dropped the yellow envelope on top and dashed into the examining room, where the lawmen were placing the groggy man on a table.

The marshal looked at the doctor. "We'll stay right here till you've patched him up. Then we'll take him and put him in a cell."

Dr. Dane nodded. "Right." He then reached into the man's hip pocket, took out his wallet, and handed it to Merrell. "Maybe there's something in here that'll tell you who this guy is."

The marshal grinned and took the wallet. "We'll soon find out."

Tharyn was at the medicine cabinet, picking up needle, thread, bandage material, and a bottle of wood alcohol. She hurried to the cart beside the table and laid them in place, while her husband went to the nearby basin to wash his hands.

When the doctor drew up to the table, the foggy-eyed man gave him a hard look. "What about Waco?"

"He's dead. He lost when he drew against Marshal Jake Merrell here."

The patient mumbled something indistinguishable under his breath, clenched his teeth, and looked up at the marshal.

"So your name's Claude Yardley," Merrell said levelly.

The patient frowned and started to speak, but Dr. Dane cut him off by saying, "Mr. Yardley, relax. I've got to stitch up this gash in your head."

Greg Holton was still holding Cassandra Wheatley in his arms when her eyes finally came clear. Rosemary Snyder sat beside them on the bench, and smiled down at her friend when she saw her looking at her.

Cassandra blinked. "Rosemary, are you all right?"

"Just a little shaky down deep inside, but now that you're doing better, I'll be okay."

Cassandra nodded, focused on Greg's face, then threw her arms around his neck. "Thank you, Greg, for saving my life! That beast would have killed me for sure if you hadn't hit him with the crowbar."

Many townspeople had gathered around them and were commending Greg for what he had done.

Rosemary set appreciative eyes on Greg. "I want to thank you too, Greg, for having the courage to bash that guy on the cranium. He's looking at jail time, for sure."

"He deserves it."

Rosemary glanced at Cassandra again, then looked at Greg. "I think she's ready to be taken home now, where she can lie down and rest."

Greg found Cassandra looking at him in a loving manner. He felt a tingle slither down his backbone. "I'll take you and Rosemary both home in the wagon I was driving."

She flashed him a warm smile. "All right. We both really appreciate it."

Greg rose to his feet with Cassandra in his arms, thanked the people who were still gathered around for their kind words, then headed for his wagon. Carrying the package that contained her new dress, Rosemary followed.

At the doctor's office, Dr. Dane finished stitching up the gash in Claude Yardley's head, and he and Tharyn wrapped his head with gauze. He was lying on his right side on the table.

Dr. Dane looked at Marshal Jake Merrell. "Okay, you can take him now."

Yardley glared up at the marshal. "Take me where?"

"You're under arrest for putting Cassandra Wheatley's life in danger, Yardley. Deputy Len Kurtz and I are taking you to the town jail for now, and within a day or two, you'll face one of the Gilpin County judges for your deed."

Yardley's beefy face twisted in fury. "What're you talkin' about? I never hurt that girl!"

Merrell scowled at him. "No, but you put a gun to her head. And if the man who bashed you on the skull hadn't done so, you might have killed her. You're going to spend some time behind bars, mister. It'll be up to the judge just how long."

Yardley's features reddened. Before he could make the angry retort that was forming on his lips, Merrell interrupted. "You give me any trouble, mister, and you'll be plenty sorry. The judge will add length to your sentence in the county jail if I tell him you resisted arrest."

Deputy Kurtz said, "Better cool down, Yardley. Believe me, you don't want Marshal Merrell getting any more put out with you than he is already."

Merrell said, "Might as well tell you this too, pal. I extracted ten dollars from your wallet to pay Dr. Logan for stitching you up and bandaging your head."

Yardley gave the marshal a hateful look but did not reply. A plan was forming in his mind. It would take some things falling into place for him, but he was devising a way to get away from the lawmen when they were taking him to Central City's jail.

Dr. Dane looked at Merrell with a smile. "I didn't know you had been a deputy marshal under Chief U.S. Marshal John Brockman. He and I are good friends."

Merrell smiled back. "Well, I'm glad to hear that. I was with Chief Brockman for over five years, then decided to take a lawman's job that would not require the traveling that being a federal deputy does."

"Mm-hmm. I can understand that. And I'll say this, Jake. The way you drew your gun and beat Belton to the draw when he already had his hand on his gun, tells me that you were trained by the man who used to be known as the Stranger. There's never been a man who was able to match his speed and accuracy, whether it was just a friendly fast-draw contest, or some hotshot gunslinger like Waco Belton who challenged him because he wanted to make a name for himself."

Deputy Len Kurtz chuckled. "Yeah, every one of those hotshots who challenged John Brockman made a name for themselves, all right—on a grave marker or a tombstone."

Claude Yardley scowled up at Kurtz. When Marshal Merrell's tight gaze fell on him, the scowl disappeared.

The marshal turned to the doctor and grinned. "Doc, I'm

mighty proud to say that it was Chief Brockman who taught me how to fast-draw."

"When Tharyn and I take Nelda and Eric Cox over to Denver to do Nelda's surgery, we'll no doubt see John and Breanna. I'll tell the chief that he taught you well."

Jake smiled. "Please tell the chief and Mrs. Brockman hello for me."

"We both will, Marshal," spoke up Tharyn.

The marshal said, "Well, Doc, we can take our prisoner and go, can't we?"

"Sure can. We've got a bunch of people out there in the waiting room to see."

Kurtz frowned. "Yardley can walk, can't he, Doctor?"

Dr. Dane nodded. "Should be able to. I don't think you'll have to carry him now that he's awake."

Tharyn said, "I'll go out and bring in whoever's first on the list, darling."

"Okay."

Yardley looked up from the table. "I—I ain't near ready to walk by myself. You two guys will have to help me."

"We can do that," said Merrell.

"Should we put him in cuffs, Marshal?" asked Kurtz.

"Don't think we need to, Len. He'll be hanging onto us as much as we'll be hanging onto him. Let's go."

Yardley smiled secretly to himself. So far his scheme for making his escape was working perfectly.

As the lawmen were half-carrying a shuffling Yardley through the examining room door, Dr. Dane said to her, "Honey, Charlie Holmes handed me a telegram just before I followed the rest of you in here. It's from John Brockman, but I laid it on your desk. I've got to wash this blood off my hands. Will you bring it to me, please?"

"John Brockman, hmm? Sure will. Wonder what it's about."

"Don't know, but it's got to be important."

"I'll get it right now, then go back for the first patient."

Dr. Dane was drying his hands at the washbasin when Tharyn returned with the yellow envelope. "Three of the patients left, darling. They told the other two to let us know that they had things they had to do, but they will be back later. We still have two women out there to see. Here's the telegram. Be back in about three minutes."

Dane took the envelope and started opening it. "Okay. See you in three minutes."

In exactly three minutes, Tharyn returned alone. "Sarah Bradley will be first, honey. I checked the burn on her hand, and it's looking much better."

Dane was placing the telegram back in its envelope. "Good."

"I thought I'd see what the telegram is about before I bring her back."

"Chief Brockman learned from Breanna's brother-in-law, Dr. Matt Carroll, that you and I are coming to Denver on Monday in preparation to do the hip replacement surgery on Nelda Cox on Wednesday. He and Breanna want us to stay with them at their place in the country while we're in Denver, instead of the Brown Palace Hotel."

"Well, that's nice of them."

"Sure is. And John says Eric is welcome to stay with them, as well. They have a second spare bedroom he can stay in."

"I'd love to stay with John and Breanna."

"Me, too. We'll tell Eric what John said in the telegram and encourage him to stay with the Brockmans."

"I'm sure he will take John up on the offer," said Tharyn. "Well, I'll go bring Sarah in."

As Marshal Jake Merrell and Deputy Len Kurtz were half-carrying Claude Yardley along the boardwalk toward the marshal's office and jail, people stared at Yardley with acrimonious eyes. One man focused on the bandage that was wrapped around Yardley's head and commented to the man next to him, "He deserved that clout on the head. Too bad Greg didn't hit him harder."

Yardley heard it, but his mind was fixed on creating a way to escape. He acted as if he were weaker than he really was and leaned heavily on the lawmen as he shuffled along the boardwalk.

As they crossed the street, Yardley looked up into the next block and saw the sign at the far end that read: *Marshal's Office and Jail*. He knew he had to think fast.

Suddenly, Yardley saw the chance he had been hoping for. Just ahead, in front of the hardware store, a small group of people were collected and looking toward him and the lawmen as they moved slowly down the boardwalk. One man was bending over to help a little boy tie a shoestring. On the man's hip was a holstered revolver. The handle seemed to be inviting Yardley to grab it and make his escape. If he timed it right, he could grab the gun, then snatch up the child, and put the gun to his head like he had that brunette girl. His horse was too far down the street, so he would take one that was tied at the hitch rail close by, and ride out of town with the boy as his hostage.

As they drew up to the spot, Yardley purposely stumbled, made it appear that he was falling, and caused the lawmen to lose their hold on his arms. He adeptly got his legs under him, quickly grabbed the gun from the man's holster, then sank the fingers of his free hand into the boy's shirt and yanked him close.

The boy's father reacted quickly. He snatched his son from Yardley's grasp and swung a fist at his face. The blow glanced off Yardley's jaw and at the same time, Yardley angrily snapped back the hammer, meaning to shoot the man.

Suddenly a shot rang out and Claude Yardley collapsed, dropping the gun. The little boy was wailing in terror and his mother quickly folded him into her arms.

Everyone on the boardwalk looked on in shock as Marshal

Jake Merrell moved toward the fallen man, his gun smoking. Len Kurtz was instantly beside the marshal. As Merrell picked up the revolver Yardley had dropped, he said so all could hear, "He's dead."

Merrell handed the gun to its owner and holstered his own weapon. "Ralph, I'm sorry about this. The guy made Len and me think he was almost totally immobile. He just surprised us."

Ralph put an arm around his wife, who was consoling the frightened child. "It's all right, Marshal. You handled the situation quite well. This guy won't be putting anyone else in danger…ever."

At the doctor's office, Dr. Dane and Tharyn were working on their second patient in the examining room when the sound of the gunshot echoed down the street. The heads of all three came up, and the woman said, "Oh no. More trouble."

Dr. Dane had just lanced a boil on the woman's arm and was squeezing it to make it drain. "Can't stop to go see what happened. We'll just have to wait a few minutes till I get this done."

Ten minutes later, the bandage was on the woman's arm as Dr. Dane and Tharyn were walking her to the office. When they stepped into the office, they saw people moving by on the street from the direction of the gunshot. Dr. Dane stepped out the door and called to a man who was drawing near. "Albert, do you know what that gunshot was all about?"

Tharyn and the woman moved to the door so they could hear what was being said.

The man hauled up and nodded. "Yes, Doctor. That no-good who put the gun to Mabel's niece's head just tried to get away from Marshal Merrell and Len as they were taking him to the jail. He grabbed a gun from Ralph Stanley's holster and tried to nab little Joey and take him as a hostage. Ralph punched him, and just before the guy could shoot Ralph, the marshal shot and killed him."

Dr. Dane breathed a sigh of relief. "So nobody else is hurt?"

"Right."

"Okay, Albert. Thanks."

When Albert was gone, the woman with the bandage on her arm paid Tharyn and left. Dane had already gone to the back room.

Since there was no one else in the office, Tharyn hurried to the back room, where her husband was cleaning up the table.

Tharyn rushed up and threw her arms around him.

Dane pulled her close. "Mm-mmm! I love the hug, but is it for something special?"

"Yes! I haven't had a moment alone with you since we came back from the first shooting incident. When I heard that Waco Belton trying to get Jake to draw on him and saw you standing close to Jake, my heart almost stopped. I'm just so relieved that nothing happened to you. I couldn't very well hug you like this with people looking on, so now you're getting your hug!"

He squeezed her tight. "Good! I'll take all the hugs I can get." He held her tight for a moment, then released her. He kissed her tenderly. "I'll leave the rest of the cleaning up to you, sweetie. I've got to look in on Mike Anderson right now."

Mabel Downing was on her front porch, watching for her niece and Rosemary to come down the street with Greg Holton. She was wondering what the second gunshot from over on Main Street meant when her eye caught sight of the Holton Coal Mine wagon coming around the far corner.

As the wagon came closer, Mabel saw Cassandra sitting on the seat between Greg and Rosemary. She left her chair, moved down the porch steps, and made her way toward the wagon as Greg pulled it to a halt.

"Did you children hear that gunshot just a minute ago?" asked Mabel.

Greg jumped down from the seat. "We did, Mrs. Downing. We don't know any more than you do about it."

Greg lifted Cassandra from the seat carefully and set her down. Mabel wrapped her arms around Cassandra and started weeping. Rosemary was holding on to her package while Greg helped her down.

As Greg and Rosemary moved up to Mabel and Cassandra, Mabel let go of her niece and wiped tears with both hands. "Walt and Myra Stockton came home a few minutes ago and told me about the shooting that took place in front of Wortman's store. They saw the whole thing. They told me about the gunslinger who challenged Marshal Merrell and about his accomplice who grabbed Cassandra and put a gun to her head. They also told me what you did, Greg. What a brave thing to do. The Stocktons wanted to let me know that Cassandra was unhurt. They also told me that you two were bringing her home."

Mabel sniffed and looked at her niece. "Are you all right, my dear?"

In a feigned, shaky voice, Cassandra replied, "Oh, Auntie Mabel, it was just awful. I've never been so frightened in all my life."

Greg moved up and put an arm around Cassandra's shoulder.

She took hold of his hand for effect. "Greg is my hero, Auntie Mabel."

Mabel smiled at Greg. "Yes. I can understand why. He might very well have saved your life. I commend you, Greg, for your courage and quick thinking." She looked at her niece. "Cassandra, you look a bit peaked. Let's get you in the house so you can lie down."

Greg put loving eyes on Cassandra. "Do you feel like walking up the porch steps, or should I carry you?"

Cassandra would take full advantage of his attention. She gave him a weak smile. "Maybe you'd better carry me."

Greg chuckled and picked her up, cradling her in his arms.

Rosemary said, "Cassandra, I need to go on home. I'll check on you later."

Cassandra smiled at her. "Okay. Come on over whenever you can."

Mabel said, "Greg, take Cassandra on in the house and put her on the sofa in the parlor. I'll bring something in to refresh her in a few minutes."

"Yes, ma'am," said Greg and headed for the porch.

While Greg was climbing the porch steps with Cassandra in his arms, Mabel smiled at Rosemary. "I want to thank you, honey, for being a friend to Cassandra. You really have come to mean a lot to her."

"I'm glad, Mrs. Downing. See you later."

Inside the house, when Greg carried Cassandra into the parlor, she kissed him on the lips. "Thank you again for saving my life."

Thrilled by the kiss, Greg smiled from ear to ear and placed her down on the sofa. "I'm glad I was there to take Waco Belton's accomplice out. And I'm glad you were not harmed."

At that moment, they heard Aunt Mabel come through the front door and make her way into the foyer.

Both of them glanced toward the hall and heard Mabel's footsteps pass the parlor door, then fade in sound as she neared the kitchen. Cassandra raised her arms to him. He leaned down, and she wrapped her arms around his neck, looking deeply into his eyes.

He lowered his lips to hers, and after the brief kiss, she said, "Greg, there is something I want to tell you."

"Mm-hmm?"

"I—I have fallen in love with you."

Greg's eyes widened. Overwhelmed to hear these words from

the beautiful young woman, he said softly, "Cassandra, I want to tell you something, too."

Her eyes danced. "What?"

"I'm in love with you, too."

They were about to kiss again when they heard Aunt Mabel coming down the hall.

Greg stood up straight.

Mabel entered the parlor, carrying a pan full of cool water and a soft cloth. "Here, dear," she said, placing the pan on the small table at one end of the sofa. "I want to bathe your forehead with this water. It'll make you feel better."

"Tell you what," said Greg. "I need to be going. I must complete the errand I was on when I drove into town. Cassandra, I'll be by to see you again as soon as I can."

She put on a mock frown. "Don't let it be too long."

He grinned. "If not today then tomorrow."

"All right."

Mabel said, "Greg, how can I ever thank you for going to Cassandra's rescue?"

"No need, ma'am. I'm just glad I was there to do it."

"May I walk you to the door?"

"Sure." He looked down at Cassandra. "See you soon."

She smiled and nodded. "Soon."

While her aunt was walking Greg to the front door, Cassandra smiled to herself. *The day will come when I'll have lots of dresses. Expensive ones, too!*

Mabel returned, dipped the cloth into the water, and bent over her niece. "Are you sure you're all right, Cassandra?"

"I'll be fine once I get over that awful episode. I'm still a little shaken up by what that horrible man did to me."

Mabel placed the cool, wet cloth on Cassandra's forehead. "This will make you feel better, dear."

Cassandra closed her eyes.

Holding the cloth in place, Mabel said, "Honey, you should thank God that Greg was there to knock that man out. He might well have shot you."

Cassandra's eyes came open. She fixed them on her aunt. "I can't thank somebody who doesn't exist," she said levelly. "There is no God. I *did* thank the person who rescued me—Greg Holton."

Mabel sighed. "I've told you before, and I'm telling you again, Cassandra, the Bible says two times, 'The fool hath said in his heart, There is no God.' If you refuse to believe God's Word, refuse to believe the gospel of Jesus Christ, and refuse to repent of your sin and receive Him as your Saviour, you will die lost and go to a fool's hell."

Cassandra reached up and patted her aunt's hand. "You can believe all that if you want, Aunt Mabel, but since there is no God to produce a Bible, it is only the words of some man to say that I am a fool for being an atheist."

SIXTEEN

Since Mayor Mike Anderson's home was only a short distance from the doctor's office, Dr. Dane Logan chose to walk. Carrying his black medical bag, he made his way along the boardwalk, greeting people with a smile and a friendly word. The sun was shining down from a clear sky, and it was obvious by the heat of the day that it was mid-July.

As he turned off Main Street onto a side street, Dr. Dane came upon a group of a dozen or so boys who were from ten to twelve years of age. Three of them had toy guns in holsters on their hips while facing one boy who stood alone, also in a gunfighter's stance. The lone boy was one of his patients. The other boys in the group looked on excitedly.

Dr. Dane slowed as he heard the lone boy with his hand hovering over his gun while facing the trio say, "All right, you guys, I'm Marshal Jake Merrell. Unbuckle those gun belts, drop 'em on the ground, and put your hands up. I took care of that Waco Belton and his pal, and if you resist me, I'll take care of you in the same way!"

Dr. Dane stopped, noting that the boy who was pretending to be Central City's marshal had a toy badge pinned to his shirt.

One of the trio said, "Hah! I don't care who you are, tin star! I'm Billy the Kid, and I'm challengin' you to a fast-draw. Go for your gun!"

"Wait a minute!" said the boy next to him. "I'm John Wesley Hardin, the world's greatest gunfighter, and you're gonna draw against me, Merrell!"

"No, he ain't!" blurted the third boy. "I'm Wild Bill Longley, and I'm *really* the world's greatest gunfighter. Go for your gun, lawman, and I'll show you!"

Suddenly, the boy playing the part of Marshal Jake Merrell noticed Dr. Dane Logan standing there. "Oh! Hello, Dr. Logan."

The doctor quickly had the other boys' attention.

Dr. Dane nodded. "Hello, Donnie." He turned to the trio, and said, "Boys, I know you're just playing, but why don't you all be good guys?"

The boy who was pretending to be Billy the Kid said, "Just because a guy's a gunfighter don't mean he's bad. I wanna be a real gunfighter when I grow up and make men tremble when they see me comin'."

"Me, too," said the boy who was pretending to be John Wesley Hardin.

"Me, too," said the other one.

Dr. Dane spoke to the latter boy. "Do you realize, son, that Wild Bill Longley was hanged in Texas three years ago?"

The boy's jaw sagged. "Really?"

"Really."

Dr. Dane set his gaze on the one who was pretending to be John Wesley Hardin. "Do you know where the real John Wesley Hardin is?"

The boy shook his head. "No, sir."

"He's in prison at Huntsville, Texas, with a twenty-five-year sentence. He'll be an old man when he gets out."

The boy swallowed hard.

Dr. Dane turned to the third boy. "Do you know that Billy the Kid is dead?"

The boy blinked. "No, sir."

"He was shot and killed two days ago in Fort Sumner, New Mexico, by a sheriff named Pat Garrett. I saw it in a newspaper this morning."

The trio exchanged glances, eyes wide.

"When you're playing with toy guns, boys," said the doctor, "why don't you all be good guys? Donnie's being a good guy, pretending to be Marshal Jake Merrell. The rest of you pretend to be lawmen like Sheriff Bat Masterson, Chief U.S. Marshal John Brockman, or Sheriff Pat Garrett. Don't aspire to be grown up and be gunfighters. They're not heroes. And they end up dead or in prison as very young men."

"But how can we play with our guns and all be lawmen?" asked the boy who had been pretending to be John Wesley Hardin. "There won't be any bad guys to shoot it out with."

Dr. Dane chuckled. "Just let the bad guys be imaginary. It'll work."

Donnie said, "That's a good idea, Dr. Logan. That's what we'll do. Okay, guys?"

The other three smiled and agreed. The boys who had been looking on also agreed. Each of the trio told the doctor they would plan to be lawmen.

Feeling better about the aspirations of the trio, Dr. Dane started down the street.

He stopped when he heard Donnie call after him, "Dr. Logan?"

"Yes, Donnie?"

"I just changed my mind. Instead of bein' a lawman, I want to be a doctor like you. You sure did fix up my foot when Pa ran over it with the carriage."

Dr. Dane smiled. "Okay, Donnie, you just set your mind to be a doctor. We need lots more here in the West."

Feeling even better, Dr. Dane moved on down the street.

A few minutes later, Betty Anderson opened the front door of the house in response to Dr. Dane's knock. "Hello, Dr. Logan. Mike and I figured you'd be coming by today since you and Tharyn are going to Denver on Monday. Please come in."

Dr. Dane stepped in, removed his hat, hung it on a peg by the door, and used his handkerchief to mop the perspiration from his brow. "It's a mite warm out there today."

Betty grinned. "I think the proper word is *hot*. How about while you're checking Mike over I fix you a nice tall glass of cool tea? Our well is deep, and even in the summer the water comes up almost cold."

"Sounds good to me."

As they were walking down the hall toward the bedroom where the mayor was resting, Dr. Dane asked, "Mike's doing okay, isn't he?"

"Yes. He's doing quite well, thanks to the Lord and Dr. Dane Logan."

Dr. Dane chuckled. "At least you got it in the right order."

As he followed Betty into the bedroom where Mike Anderson lay in the bed, she said with a smile, "Look, honey, it's Central City's beloved physician here to see you!"

Mike grinned. "Hello, beloved physician! It's nice to see you."

Dr. Dane's face tinted. "You two embarrass me with such a title. I'm just plain Dane Logan, M.D."

Betty touched his arm. "Well, because of what you did for my husband, in my heart you will always be Central City's beloved physician."

The mayor was still grinning and nodded.

Dr. Dane shook his head slowly. "You two could give a fella a big head. Well, let's get down to business."

"I'll go fix you that glass of tea I promised," said Betty.

He smiled and nodded.

The doctor checked his patient thoroughly and removed the old bandage. As he was finishing with the new bandage, Betty came in with the glass of tea in her hand.

"Here you are, Doctor."

Dr. Dane thanked her, took the glass, and drank half of it immediately. "Your husband is showing signs of healing well, Betty. I have Dr. Fraser planning to look in on him while Tharyn and I are in Denver."

Betty smiled. "Thank you, Doctor. And I sure hope Nelda Cox's surgery goes well."

"Me, too."

"Mike and I sure were thrilled when you told us on your last visit that Eric and Nelda both opened their hearts to the Lord."

"Amen," said Mike.

Dr. Dane nodded. "They have a sparkle in their eyes that wasn't there before. Eric is going to be baptized at church in the morning. Nelda will have to wait till after she heals up from the surgery."

Dr. Dane tipped up the glass and finished his tea.

"Wish I could be there to see Eric baptized," said Mike. "But at least Betty can tell me about it when she gets home."

Dr. Dane chuckled. "Sure enough. Well, I've got to move on." He handed Betty the empty glass, thanked her, then looked down at the mayor. "See you when we get back, Mike."

"Okay."

"Hopefully, you'll be able to return to your office in a few more weeks and start running this town again."

Mike's face lit up. "Boy, will I ever be glad when that day comes, Doc!"

Betty turned her head away so neither man could see that she was smiling with anxious anticipation for that day.

In the preaching service the next morning, Eric Cox was sitting with the Logans. At announcement and offering time, Pastor Mark Shane said to his congregation, "I'm asking that all of you hold Dr. Dane Logan and Tharyn up in prayer as they travel to Denver tomorrow. Most of you know that Dr. Logan is going to do a hip replacement at Mile High Hospital on Mrs. Nelda Cox, with Tharyn's able assistance. Mrs. Cox's husband, Eric, is going with them."

Some of the people in the pews were smiling.

The pastor smiled. "A few of you already know what hap-- pened at the Cox home this past week. But for the rest of you, let me tell it. Last Tuesday evening, a wonderful thing happened. Dr. Logan and his wife were in the Cox home, making plans for Nelda's upcoming surgery. While they were there, they witnessed to the Coxes about the Lord Jesus Christ and had the joy of leading them to the Lord."

There were amens all over the congregation.

"I visited the Coxes after Dr. Logan had said that they had become Christians and both of them plan to be baptized. They want to become faithful members of our church."

There were amens again.

Pastor Shane explained that Eric was going to be baptized after the morning service and that Nelda would be baptized as soon as possible after her surgery.

After two ladies from the choir sang a duet, it was time to preach his sermon. Pastor Shane stepped to the pulpit and opened his Bible. "Turn in your Bibles to 2 Timothy 4."

When the sound of fluttering pages faded, Shane pointed out that the Apostle Paul was in prison in Rome when this epistle was written and would soon be executed for his faith in Jesus Christ. He then read Paul's inspired words in verses 6 through 8, showing that Paul knew his martyrdom was imminent.

"Now, look at verse 9. Paul says to Timothy, 'Do thy diligence to come shortly unto me.' We can see that Paul desperately wanted to see his spiritual son Timothy once more before he was martyred."

People were nodding all over the audience.

"Now, look what Paul said in verse 10. 'For Demas hath forsaken me, having loved this present world, and is departed unto Thessalonica; Crescens to Galatia, Titus unto Dalmatia.' Let me point out that there is nothing said about Crescens and Titus forsaking him. They had simply gone on errands of usefulness to various other places. But Demas had forsaken Paul, having loved this present world. He was not interested in spiritual things. Now look at verse 11.

"Paul says, 'Only Luke is with me.'"

At this point, the pastor spoke of the friendship between Luke, the physician, and Paul, the apostle. Then he said, "You see, brethren, while others left Paul, and Demas forsook him—in the face of being persecuted or even martyred for remaining outside Paul's cell door, Luke stayed with him! Can you imagine what it must have meant to Paul to have his faithful friend Dr. Luke stay with him? Now, turn to Colossians 4."

The preacher said, "Look at verse 14. 'Luke, the beloved physician, and Demas, greet you.' This, of course, was before Demas forsook Paul when he was in the Roman prison. What I want you to note is Paul's description of his faithful doctor friend. In an endearing manner, he calls him 'the beloved physician.'"

The preacher ran his gaze over the congregation. "All of you know of the incident that happened here in our town this past Tuesday, when Dr. Dane Logan risked his own life to save that of Mayor Mike Anderson."

People were nodding and looking at Dr. Dane Logan.

"Dr. Logan," said Shane, "lift your hand, please, so if there are people here who don't know you, they will see who I'm talking about."

Dr. Dane's features flushed as he lifted his hand, keeping his eyes on the pastor.

Pastor Shane then looked down at Betty Anderson, who sat a couple of pews in front of the Logans and Eric Cox. "Mayor Anderson's dear wife, Betty, is seated right down here in front of me. Betty, raise your hand, in case there is someone here who doesn't know you."

Betty released a warm smile and lifted her hand.

"Well, folks," said the preacher, "this dear lady has dubbed Dr. Dane Logan as Central City's beloved physician."

There were loud amens from the crowd, and a red-faced Dr. Dane smiled at Betty as she turned around where she sat in her pew and smiled warmly at him and Tharyn.

The pastor set his appreciative gaze on the young doctor. "Indeed you *are* our beloved physician, Dr. Dane Logan."

Dr. Robert Fraser and his wife, Esther, who were sitting just across the aisle from Dr. Dane and Tharyn both nodded, smiling. Dr. Fraser said a loud, "Amen!"

With tears misting her eyes, Tharyn squeezed her husband's hand.

The pastor then returned to his sermon. Once more, he brought up the friendship between Paul and Dr. Luke, then preached about true friends. He pointed out that speaking of a true friend, God says in Proverbs 17:17 that "A friend loveth at all times."

He spent some time encouraging each Christian to always be a true friend to others. "If you want friends, you must *be* a friend. Look over here in the very next chapter. Proverbs 18:24. 'A man that hath friends must shew himself friendly.' I say again, if you want friends, you must *be* a friend. Now look at the second half of this verse: 'And there is a friend that sticketh closer than a brother.' Who is this speaking about, folks?"

From all over the congregation came the name: "Jesus."

The pastor smiled. "Right. The dear Lord Jesus is indeed a Friend that will stick by you closer than a brother."

Pastor Shane then took them in their mind's eye to Calvary and brought in the gospel, showing them Jesus' bloodshedding death on the cross, His burial, and His glorious resurrection. He showed that Jesus is not only a Friend to those who know Him, but He is also the Friend of sinners. The invitation was given and many Christians came forward, dedicating themselves to be better friends to others, and two people came to open their hearts to Jesus.

At the close of the invitation, Eric Cox was baptized, as well as the two people who had come and received Jesus as their Saviour.

At the same time the baptisms were taking place at the church, Kirby Holton and his son were sitting on the front porch of the Holton mansion.

Kirby was talking to Greg about the courage he had displayed by knocking out the man who was holding his gun to Cassandra's head while Waco Belton was trying to force Marshal Jake Merrell to draw against him.

Kirby smiled. "Sure wish I had been there to see you crack him over the head with that crowbar, son."

Greg chuckled dryly. "It wasn't anything spectacular, Dad. I just had to keep him from hurting Cassandra."

Kirby grinned. "I'm proud of you for doing it, son, and I imagine Cassandra must have a very special spot for you in her heart."

Greg sighed. "Yes, she does, Dad. In fact, she told me that she is in love with me."

Kirby's eyes widened. "Really?"

"Mm-hmm."

"And how do you feel about her?"

"I'm in love with her too, Dad. And I told her so."

Kirby rubbed his chin. "Well, whattya know? This is very interesting."

At that moment, the cook and housekeeper came out onto the porch and said, "Mr. Holton, dinner is ready."

"That's good news, Edith!" said Kirby, rising from his chair. "Let's go get some more of that good cooking, Greg."

As father and son were walking toward the door, Greg said, "Speaking of Cassandra, Dad, I want to talk to you about something while we're eating."

"Sure, son. As soon as I'm stuffing myself, I'll be ready to listen."

When Mabel Downing arrived home from church and opened the front door of the house, a tantalizing aroma met her nostrils. She smiled and hurried down the hall. When she stepped into the kitchen, the succulent aroma was stronger and her stomach growled with hunger.

At the stove, Cassandra turned, wiped her hands on the apron she was wearing, and a broad smile graced her features. "Hello, Auntie Mabel."

Mabel moved toward her. "My, my, you've been a busy girl, haven't you? It smells so good!"

Cassandra patted her aunt's arm. "Take off your bonnet and wash up, Auntie Mabel. I'll have everything ready in just a few minutes."

"Okay, dear. I'll be right back."

Mabel climbed the stairs to the second floor. She went into her bedroom, removed her bonnet and her gloves, then went to the washroom down the hall.

Moments later, when Mabel entered the kitchen, all was ready.

Cassandra had covered the kitchen table with a flowered table-cloth, and the blue willow dishes she had placed on the table looked almost festive.

The early afternoon sun was brightening the kitchen and a gentle breeze was blowing through the open windows, fluttering the lace curtains. The breeze brought comfort into the warm room.

When they sat down to eat, Mabel prayed as usual, with her head bowed and her eyes closed. While she was praying, she knew Cassandra was just sitting there looking at her.

As they began eating, Mabel brought up Dr. Dane Logan's show of courage last Tuesday when he risked getting shot in order to assist the wounded Mayor Mike Anderson to his office.

Cassandra swallowed a mouthful of mashed potatoes. "It was quite a demonstration of Dr. Logan's love for people, Auntie Mabel, and his dedication to his profession. I liked the label put on him by Betty Anderson."

Mabel smiled. "That's why I brought up what he did for Mayor Anderson, dear. This morning, Pastor Shane preached on how Paul called his friend Dr. Luke the beloved physician in the Bible. Then he paused in the sermon to pay tribute to Dr. Logan for what he had done for Mayor Anderson, and to point out that Betty had dubbed him Central City's beloved physician."

"That's nice. I believe the preacher did the right thing."

When they were almost finished with their meal, Mabel said, "Cassandra, how about if we take our pie and coffee and sit on the front porch? It's well-shaded out there by now, and the breeze will make us even cooler."

"Sure, Auntie Mabel. You go on out, and I'll bring our dessert and coffee out on a tray."

Mabel was a bit stunned by how her niece had been pampering her the past couple of days, but she was also very much pleased. "All right, dear. I'll just do that."

A few minutes later, Mabel stepped out onto the front porch and sat down on her favorite rocker with a sigh. She ran an admiring look toward her flower beds that adorned the yard. "I just love flowers. And just think, when I get to my mansion in heaven, I can grow as many as I want and there won't be any weeds to dig up!"

Mabel's thoughts drifted back to the days when she and her beloved husband would sit on the porch together and spin their daydreams. This was the house they purchased when they were first married. Many precious memories filled her mind.

Cassandra came out with the tray in her hands and set it down on the table beside her aunt's rocker.

They had just finished their pie and coffee when Cassandra saw Greg Holton walking down the street toward the house.

"Oh, Auntie! Look who's coming!"

Mabel followed her niece's line of sight. "Well, lookee there! Greg's coming to see me."

Cassandra laughed. "Maybe so, Auntie Mabel, but I'll dominate his time, anyhow!"

Mabel laughed. "Okay, honey, you dominate his time!"

When Greg reached the Downing yard, he waved, ran to the porch, and bounded up the steps. "Hello, Mrs. Downing," he said warmly. "How are you doing?"

"Just fine, Greg. Just fine. I was just kidding Cassandra, telling her you were coming to see me."

"Well, ma'am, it's always nice to see you, but—"

"I know, I know. Go ahead and speak to the young, beautiful one."

Greg chuckled at Mabel's humor, then set his adoring gaze on Cassandra. "Hello. I—I came over to invite you to dinner at the Holton house tomorrow evening."

Cassandra's expression showed her delight. "Why, I'd be honored, Greg. You're sure this is all right with your father?"

"Oh yes. Dad just hired a new cook and housekeeper a few days ago. Her name is Edith Linden. She's from Colorado Springs. And believe me, her cooking is excellent. I asked Dad if I could invite you for dinner tomorrow evening so you could enjoy it. I've made it clear to Dad that I'm in love with you, and that you feel the same about me. He seemed pleased by the news, and said you are most welcome to come."

Cassandra's countenance showed the joy she was feeling. She glanced at her aunt, who was smiling. Cassandra knew she didn't have to ask Aunt Mabel for permission to go, but she said, "Do you mind eating dinner tomorrow night alone, Auntie Mabel?"

"Of course not, dear. I wasn't aware that you two had shared that you have fallen in love with each other, but I'm happy for both of you. Don't pass up this invitation because of me."

Cassandra was breathing hard from excitement. "Oh, Greg, I'm honored that your father wants me to come to your mans—er, your house! I would really love to get to know your father."

"All right, then. I'll be by at about six-thirty tomorrow evening to walk you to my house."

Cassandra stood at the porch railing and watched Greg as he hurried away. When he passed from view and she sat down again, Mabel said, "I'm really glad to learn that you and Greg have fallen in love. He is such a nice young man."

"Yes, he is, Auntie," she said with a lilt in her voice. In her mind, she thought, *And he's rich, too!*

Having her own private thoughts, Mabel wished Greg was a Christian so he could influence Cassandra toward the things of God.

Well, at least, she thought, *he is of good stock, and he is a gentleman. And he certainly showed what he is made of when he rescued Cassandra from that bad man.*

SEVENTEEN

*T*hat evening while her aunt was at church, Cassandra Wheatley stood before the dresser mirror in her room, touching up her hair. When she had it like she wanted it, she laid the comb down, looked at her reflection, and smiled at herself.

"Everything's going well, Cassandra. Just think, you've now been invited to the Holton mansion by Greg, with his father's approval. I think it's so marvelous that Greg wants to bring you to his father right away." She giggled. "One day soon, Cassandra, Greg will ask you to marry him."

A tingling ran through her body. Looking at herself in the mirror, she said, "Won't that be some moment when Greg proposes?" She popped her hands together. "Oh, I can only imagine what it's going to be like to be married to a very wealthy young man, who will one day be even wealthier by the time his father grows old and dies! And it will be mine, as well!"

She smiled at her reflection again.

When she stepped out of the front door onto the porch, the chilly mountain breeze greeted her. She ran her gaze toward the high peaks to the west and marveled that they were still covered with snow. Aunt Mabel had told her that when it was raining down here in Central City it was snowing above thirteen thousand feet, so the highest peaks never lost their snow, even in the middle of the summer. When the breezes came down from the snow-capped peaks in the evening or at night, they were quite cool, even after a very hot day.

She sat down in her aunt's rocker, laid her head back, and closed her eyes. "And just think, Cassandra, you're going to live in this beautiful mountain country for the rest of your life as the wife of wealthy Mr. Greg Holton, who will one day own that rich coal mine!"

Early on Monday morning July 18, Dr. Dane and Tharyn Logan drove away from the stable in Central City in the special carriage the doctor had rented to carry Nelda Cox as comfortably as possible to Denver.

They drove to the Cox home, and when Eric and Dr. Dane had carefully laid Nelda on the flat, padded place in the center of the carriage, Tharyn sat on the seat beside her to watch over her on the trip.

Dr. Dane and Eric climbed onto the carriage seat and with the reins in hand, Dr. Dane put the team of horses in motion.

As they were heading east, winding through canyons and gradually lowering in altitude toward the Mile High City, Eric said, "Dr. Logan, it sure was nice of Chief Brockman and his wife to invite me to stay at their house along with you and Tharyn."

"They're nice people, Eric. I'm sure when they received my telegram confirming that you will be their guest, it made them very happy."

Eric nodded. "I'm really looking forward to meeting them. Especially the chief. I remember years ago of hearing about the mysterious man they called the Stranger who roamed the West helping people in trouble and catching outlaws and turning them over to the law. And then to learn from you on the way to church yesterday that he was also a gospel preacher, that was really something."

Dr. Dane chuckled. "He's quite a man, Eric."

"I believe that."

The carriage hit a bump that Dr. Dane hadn't noticed in the road. He looked over his shoulder. "Are you all right, Nelda?"

"Yes, Doctor. This padded section I'm on absorbed most of the bump."

"Good. I'm sorry. I just didn't see it in time to slow down or avoid it."

"It's all right. I barely felt it."

They rode on in silence for a few minutes; then Eric said, "Back to this man who is now known as Chief United States Marshal John Brockman, Doctor…"

"Yes?"

"I remember hearing about the medallions the size of a silver dollar that he used to give to people he helped. The medallions had something inscribed on them about a stranger from a far land. Do you know anything about them?"

"Yes. He and Breanna told me about them one time when I was staying in their home. Each medallion had a portion of a verse of Scripture on it. It was centered with a five-point star and around the circular edge, it said in large capital letters, THE STRANGER THAT SHALL COME FROM A FAR LAND. Then in small letters it gave the Scripture reference: Deuteronomy 29:22."

"Hmm. So Chief Brockman apparently came to America from some distant country."

"Yes."

"Do you know what country it was?"

"No. I understand that Breanna is the only person besides the chief who knows, and she keeps it to herself. Even their children don't know."

"I see. I also remember that when the Stranger helped people who were in trouble, he often gave them large sums of money."

"Yes."

"Do you know where he got his money? Why he had a seemingly unlimited supply of it?"

"No. People in Denver told me that the Stranger never revealed anything about where he got his money. That and the far country he's from remain mysteries. But I'll tell you this: You've never met a man like him."

"I can believe that, all right. Like I said, I'm really looking forward to meeting him."

It was almost three o'clock in the afternoon when Dr. Dane pulled the carriage up to the front entrance of Mile High Hospital in Denver.

Dr. Dane hopped out of the carriage so he could go inside and find a wheelchair for Nelda. Eric climbed in the rear of the carriage, and with Tharyn's help, soon had Nelda in a sitting position.

Dr. Dane returned with a hospital attendant who was pushing a wheelchair. Eric and the attendant picked Nelda up and eased her into the wheelchair, and they entered the lobby.

Dr. Dane hurried ahead of the others to the receptionist's desk. Rosie O'Brien saw him coming and smiled at him as he drew up. "Hello, Dr. Logan. Nice to see you again."

"You too, Rosie. I have a patient, Mrs.—"

"Nelda Cox," Rosie finished for him, picking up a sheet of paper. "Dr. Carroll already brought the information to me this morning. You're doing a hip replacement on her Wednesday morning. We have a private room waiting for her on the second floor just a little ways down the hall from the surgical unit. Room 224."

Dr. Dane chuckled. "I just love the efficiency around here."

Rosie saw the redhead move up beside him and smiled at her. "Hello, Tharyn. How are you?"

"Just fine, Rosie. And you?"

"Doing fine." She looked past the Logans as the attendant brought the wheelchair to a stop. "And this has to be Mr. and Mrs. Cox."

Dr. Dane quickly introduced the Coxes to Rosie, and then she went to work getting further information beyond what she had on the paper from Dr. Carroll.

When the paperwork was done, Rosie said, "Dr. Logan, I'll advise Dr. Carroll that you're here. I'll just send him up to room 224."

"All right. Thank you, Rosie." Dr. Dane turned to the others. "Let's go."

As the group moved from the lobby into the hall that led toward the stairs, Eric held on to one of Nelda's hands and Tharyn held on to the other. When they reached the stairs, the attendant turned the wheelchair around and carefully pulled it up the stairs backwards, one step at a time. Soon they were on the second floor. The attendant stopped at the nurses' station to inform them that he was taking Mrs. Cox to her assigned room, and a nurse joined the group as they proceeded down the hall.

When they entered room 224, they saw that the covers were already turned down on the bed. The attendant lifted Nelda from the wheelchair and placed her gently on the bed, and the nurse covered her up, doing what she could to make her comfortable.

After the long, bumpy ride from Central City, Nelda was more than happy to settle into her soft hospital bed.

The nurse gave Nelda a drink of cool water, told her to ring the little bell that was on the nightstand if she needed anything, and left the room, saying she would check on her later.

Eric, Tharyn, and Dr. Dane were just gathering around the bed when they heard footsteps in the hall and turned to see Dr. Matt Carroll enter the room.

A smile broke over Dr. Carroll's face as he focused on the

Logans. "Dr. Dane! Tharyn! It's so good to see you again!"

"Good to see you again, too," said Dr. Dane, shaking hands with him.

Tharyn then greeted him and offered her hand. As Dr. Carroll took the small hand into his own, he said, "I sure do miss you around this hospital, Tharyn. It just isn't the same place without you."

Dr. Dane chuckled. "Well, you can't have her back."

Carroll shook his head. "I was afraid you would say that."

Dr. Dane then introduced Dr. Carroll to Eric and Nelda Cox.

After Eric and the doctor shook hands, Carroll looked down at Nelda. "Mrs. Cox, I don't know if you and your husband realize it, but Dr. Logan is the hip replacement expert of the West. I am confident that you will be very happy with his work."

Eric smiled. "Dr. Logan hasn't told us that he is the hip replacement expert of the West, Dr. Carroll, but Nelda and I have the utmost confidence in him. We know Nelda is in good hands."

Dr. Carroll nodded, then turned and winked at Tharyn. "Actually, Mr. and Mrs. Cox, Dr. Logan wouldn't be so good if he didn't have the all-time expert surgical nurse of the West to assist him."

Tharyn blushed as the Coxes and Dr. Dane laughed.

When the laughter subsided, Dr. Dane said to Dr. Carroll, "I have some very good news about Eric and Nelda."

"Oh?"

"Mm-hmm. Last Tuesday, Tharyn and I had the joy of leading this precious couple to Jesus."

The eyes of Mile High Hospital's superintendent widened. "Well, wonderful! I'm always glad to hear of souls being saved and added to the family of God."

Both Coxes smiled and nodded.

"Eric was baptized in our church on Sunday," said Dr. Dane, "and Nelda is going to be baptized when she has sufficiently healed from her surgery."

"Indeed, this *is* good news. I've heard much about Pastor Mark Shane, and I know he will be a real blessing to you."

"He already has been," said Nelda, "and Eric and I know he will be a greater blessing in the days to come."

Eric grinned. "For sure. We have so much to learn. And Dr. Logan and his dear wife have been such blessings, too. Not only did they lead us to the Lord, but they have taught us a lot about the Bible."

"I have no doubt of that." Dr. Carroll patted Nelda's hand. "Well, I have to get back to my office. We'll see that you get the best of care while you're at Mile High Hospital."

Nelda smiled up at him. "Thank you, Dr. Carroll, and God bless you."

When Dr. Carroll was gone, Eric and the Logans sat down in chairs beside Nelda's bed, and they talked about the Coxes' new-found salvation. Both Eric and Nelda spoke of the peace they had in their hearts, knowing that their sins had been forgiven and washed away in the blood of God's Lamb.

Eric said, "Nelda and I have been reading the Bibles you gave us, and we're learning so much. We've been reading through the Gospel of John, as you suggested, and we have a question about what Jesus said about Himself and the Father in the tenth chapter. What did He mean when He said, 'I and my Father are one'?"

Dr. Dane and Tharyn looked at each other, smiling, then Dr. Dane went to a small table against the wall, where a Bible lay. He picked it up. "You will recall that in our conversation last Tuesday, we made it clear to you that Jesus is eternal, as is the Father and the Holy Spirit. The three make up what the Bible calls the Godhead."

Eric and Nelda both nodded. "And we believe that," said Eric, "but what did Jesus mean that He and the Father are one? Does that mean one in purpose or one in agreement?"

"They are that, all right. But much more. Let me say first, that we human beings will never understand the great and almighty God, who wonderfully, yet mysteriously, is in three persons. He is too far above our finite minds. We believe that the Father is God, the Son is God, and the Spirit is God, yet there is only *one* God. We don't believe it because we understand it. We believe it because God's Word says so. He wouldn't be much of a God if His creation could understand Him. Let me show you some Scriptures that declare that God is one in three."

As Dr. Dane opened his Bible, he said, "I'm going to read you a couple of prophetic verses in the book of Isaiah about Jesus Christ. First, a verse prophesying His virgin birth. Isaiah 7:14. 'Therefore the Lord himself shall give you a sign; Behold, a virgin shall conceive, and bear a son, and shall call his name Immanuel.' Do you know what the name Immanuel means?"

Both shook their heads, indicating they did not.

Dr. Dane looked at Tharyn. "Tell them, honey."

Tharyn smiled. "The name Immanuel means 'God with us.'"

"Right. So, Eric, Nelda, who would this virgin-born child be?"

"He would be God," said Eric.

"Yes," said Nelda. "So Jesus is God."

Dr. Dane nodded. "Right." He turned a page. "Now, let me read you Isaiah 9:6. 'For unto us a child is born, unto us a son is given: and the government shall be upon his shoulder: and his name shall be called Wonderful, Counsellor, the mighty God, the everlasting Father, the Prince of Peace.' This is the same virgin-born son that is spoken of in Isaiah 7:14."

"Jesus," breathed Nelda reverently.

"Correct. Did you notice that this Child, this Son, is the Mighty God?"

"Yes," said Eric. "Jesus is God."

"Yes. Did you also notice that in this verse He is said to be the everlasting Father? It's like He said in John 10:30, 'I and my Father are one.' Don't try to understand it. You can't. But believe it because the Word says so. Jesus *is* the Father, yet He is the Son."

Eric and Nelda looked at each other, marveling.

Dr. Dane flipped back to the New Testament. "Listen to what it says in Hebrews 1. Verse 6 tells us what God the Father said when He brought Jesus into the world. 'And again, when he bringeth in the firstbegotten into the world, he saith, And let all the angels of God worship him.' I'm sure you know that to worship anyone other than the true God is idolatry."

"We know that," said Eric.

Nelda nodded.

"Good," said Dr. Dane. "Then you will realize that the Father in heaven is saying His only begotten Son is to be worshiped. That means Jesus is God then. Now listen to verse 8, where the Father calls Jesus *God*. 'But unto the Son, he saith, Thy throne, O God, is for ever and ever: a sceptre of righteousness is the sceptre of thy kingdom.' The Father flat calls His Son God."

"This is wonderful to hear," said Nelda.

Dr. Dane's brow furrowed as he looked at Nelda, then glanced at the clock on the wall. "You're looking pretty tired, Nelda. It's almost four-thirty. I'll show you one Scripture, which deals with the Holy Spirit being God; then we'll get out of here and let you rest."

While Dr. Dane was flipping to the book of Romans, Eric set loving eyes on Nelda and said, "You really do look tired, dear."

Dr. Dane found his passage. "Listen to Romans 8:9. Paul is writing to born-again people, who used to have a carnal, fleshly mind before they were saved. 'But ye are not in the flesh, but in the Spirit, if so be that the Spirit of God dwell in you. Now if any man have not the Spirit of Christ, he is none of his.' Did you catch that? The Holy Spirit, here, is not only called the Spirit of God, but He is also called the Spirit of Christ. We have here, the three in one. The Father is God, the Son is God, the Spirit is God. There is plenty more on this subject in God's Word, but that's all for today."

"Thank you, Doctor," said Eric. "Now we know what Jesus meant when he said, 'I and my Father are one.'"

Nelda's eyes were droopy. "It's just beautiful," she said. "What a wonderful God we have!"

Dr. Dane suggested they have prayer, and as the four of them joined hands, he prayed about the surgery that would be performed on Wednesday and asked the Lord that all would go well.

When he had finished, Dr. Dane looked down at Nelda. "You get some sleep now. Soon it will be time for them to bring your supper. We need to get to the Brockman place so we can let Breanna know we're here and can get settled in our rooms. We'll be back to see you this evening."

Eric kissed his wife's cheek, Tharyn squeezed Nelda's hand, and the three of them left the room.

As the trio was heading for the stairs, Dr. Dane and Tharyn saw Dr. Tim Braden coming toward them. He greeted them; then Dr. Dane introduced him to Eric, explaining that he was the husband of Nelda Cox, who would be having a hip replacement on Wednesday.

When the two men had shaken hands, Dr. Tim said to all three, "Dr. Carroll had advised me that the Logans would be bringing one of Dr. Dane's patients in for a hip replacement."

Tharyn quickly told Dr. Tim that the Coxes had received the Lord Jesus as their Saviour just this past Tuesday, and Dr. Tim rejoiced to hear it.

Dr. Dane said to Eric, "Dr. Tim is doing his internship here at the hospital, and will finish up next May. He's engaged to marry Tharyn's best friend, Melinda Kenyon, who lives here in Denver."

Eric smiled. "Well, congratulations. When's the wedding?"

"Next May, right after I finish my internship."

Eric patted his shoulder. "I know you will both be very happy."

"It wasn't so long ago, Mr. Cox," said Tharyn, "that Melinda and Dr. Tim met at church and fell in love. Dr. Tim's plan is to have his own practice or become a partner in a practice somewhere here in the West."

"Well, he looks like an energetic young man to me. I'm sure he will do well in the medical profession."

Tim looked at Tharyn. "Melinda talks about you every day, saying how much she loves you."

Dane grinned. "Well, I can testify that Tharyn does the same thing about Melinda."

"I'm not surprised. And I should tell you that the Brockmans have invited Melinda and me to dinner tonight so we can have some time with you two."

"Hey, that'll be great!" said Dr. Dane. "We'll look forward to it."

Tharyn's features lit up. "We sure will!"

Dr. Tim glanced down the hall. "Well, I've got a patient to look in on, so I'd better get going."

Moments later, while Dr. Dane was driving the carriage out of town toward the Brockman place to the west, Tharyn told Eric that she and Melinda Scott had become good friends when they both lived as orphans in an alley in Manhattan, New York. She went on to explain that they were on the same orphan train together, and that Melinda was chosen by George and Hattie Kenyon at Topeka, Kansas. She and Melinda kept contact by mail for many years. Then to her pleasant surprise, George Kenyon was sent to Denver by the Denning Hardware Company to manage their Denver store.

"It was so good to be reunited with Melinda, Mr. Cox. We are still very close friends. In fact, we are best friends. The Kenyons live out here in the country, near the Brockmans."

Soon the carriage pulled into the yard of the Brockman place, and Tharyn pointed toward the house. "Oh, look, Dane! Melinda is here already! I see Abe!"

Dane focused on the bay gelding with the white blaze on his

face and the white stockings on all four legs. "Sure enough!"

Eric frowned. "Who's Abe?"

"That bay horse that's tied at one of the hitching posts in front of the house. Melinda named him Abe in honor of her favorite United States president of all time, Abraham Lincoln."

"Oh. Well, that's nice."

"Aren't those flower gardens beautiful? Breanna sure knows how to grow flowers!"

"She does. But you're just as good at it. You just don't have as much area around your house in which to plant flowers."

She smiled. "Aren't you sweet?"

Just as Dr. Dane pulled the carriage to a halt in front of the house, two blondes came out the front door, smiling at them. Melinda said something to Breanna and dashed off the porch as Dane was helping Tharyn out of the carriage. The best friends were quickly in each other's arms.

Dr. Dane introduced Breanna and Melinda to Eric Cox. Eric was welcomed warmly; then Dr. Dane told them about Eric and Nelda being saved last Tuesday. Breanna and Melinda were over-joyed.

Breanna asked about Nelda, and Dr. Dane told her that she was in a private room at the hospital and resting well.

Eric said, "Miss Melinda, Mrs. Logan told me this is your horse over here."

A proud look came over Melinda's face. "Yes, sir."

"Mrs. Logan also told me that his name is Abe."

"That's right, Mr. Cox. Would you like to pet him?"

"I sure would."

The others followed as Melinda led Eric to her horse. While Eric was stroking Abe's white-blazed face, he asked, "How long have you been riding horses, Miss Melinda?"

"Just about ten years. When I was first adopted off the orphan train, we lived on a small farm just outside of Topeka. I was given a horse shortly after that, and I've been an avid horsewoman ever since. Daddy bought Abe for me shortly after we moved here. We live just about a mile southwest from here."

"I see. So you ride him a lot, do you?"

"Oh yes, sir. Almost every day I take Abe out for a good fast ride all the way over to the South Platte River, which is two miles west of our place. There is plenty of open, level ground between our place and the river, and Abe and I enjoy being together. In fact, we just got back from a good ride, and I decided to come on over to the Brockmans' place so I could be here to see Tharyn and Dr. Dane when they arrived."

Breanna said, "Well, now that Mr. Cox has met Abe, I'd better take my guests inside so they can get settled in their rooms."

Eric was led to his room and began unpacking his suitcase.

Tharyn and Dane's room was the same one they had stayed in on several occasions before, but the beauty of it always struck Tharyn anew each time. The wide windows were open to a breathtaking view of the snowcapped Rockies. The room was decorated in lovely cool green colors and was a refreshing sight on such a warm day.

A bouquet of fresh-cut flowers sat on a small table and sent off a wonderful fragrance. Tharyn was amazed at how well-kept the Brockman house always appeared. She appreciated the loving effort that Breanna put into it.

After the guests had unpacked their suitcases and were settled into their rooms, Breanna took them into the parlor. Melinda and Tharyn sat down side by side.

Moments later, the Brockman children—nine-year-old Paul and seven-year-old Ginny—arrived home from school. They were glad to see Tharyn and Dr. Dane and to meet Eric Cox.

Shortly thereafter, Dr. Tim Braden arrived, eager to spend some time with Dr. Dane and Tharyn.

After a little while, Breanna took Tharyn, Melinda, and Ginny to the kitchen so they could help her finish preparing supper. They were busy at their task when the tall, broad-shouldered chief U.S. marshal came through the back door. Melinda had just stepped into the hallway and called to the men in the parlor, telling them supper was ready in the dining room.

Ginny rushed into her father's arms, and after he had kissed her cheek and that of Breanna, he welcomed Tharyn, saying it was good to see her again. Breanna then led everyone in the kitchen to the dining room.

At that moment, Dr. Dane, Dr. Tim, Eric, and Paul entered the dining room from the hallway. Paul dashed to his father and hugged him.

John then shook hands with Dr. Dane, welcoming him, and did the same when he was introduced to Eric Cox.

John was pleased to learn that the Coxes had received Christ as Saviour six days ago. He then said, "Now, Mr. Cox, let me tell you something I know to be a fact."

Eric looked up at the towering figure. "Yes, sir?"

"The Lord has provided your wife the best surgeon this side of the Mississippi River to do her hip replacement. He's good at what he does. She's in the best of hands."

Dr. Dane laughed softly. "I appreciate your kind words, John, but let me add that even more important, Nelda is in God's hands."

The chief nodded. "Can't argue with that."

Breanna said, "All right, folks, let's sit down here at the table. Supper is ready. I'll show you where to sit."

Breanna's lovely features beamed as she seated the group around the large table. They all looked the food over and made comments on how tasty it looked. She had made a huge chicken pot pie, filled with succulent carrots and peas that she had grown in her garden. She had placed it in the middle of the table, which was covered with a snowy white, embroidered cloth.

Small bouquets of flowers had been placed at both ends of the table, sided by candles that sent off a soft glow.

Breanna had also made a large bowl of freshly picked lettuce, tomatoes, cucumbers, and radishes, mixed into a cool, inviting salad. A pink glass dish was piled high with warm applesauce, and bowls of pickled beets and green beans rounded off the meal.

John stood at the head of the table and prayed over the food, asking the Lord to guide Dr. Dane's hands when he performed the surgery on Nelda Cox.

While they were eating, Melinda asked how long the Logans were going to stay in Denver. Dr. Dane replied that they were planning on heading back to Central City on Thursday. They would leave Nelda in Dr. Matt Carroll's capable hands until she was feeling well enough to go home. Eric would be staying until that time also.

Dr. Dane continued, "When Dr. Carroll wires me that Nelda can travel, I'll come back over and pick up her and Eric. I'll probably be alone, since Tharyn will need to stay at the office."

Dr. Tim set his coffee cup in its saucer and looked at Dr. Dane.

"Tell you what. I'm pretty sure I can talk Dr. Carroll into giving me a couple days off if I tell him I want to drive Mr. and Mrs. Cox back home. I'd like to do this for you, Dr. Dane, so you can carry on your work in and around Central City without interruption. I know you're awfully busy. Yes, I also know that Dr. Fraser fills in for you when you're gone, but I'm sure you would like to stay there and do your own work."

Dr. Dane swallowed a mouthful of chicken pot pie. "It really would help me if you could do this, Dr. Tim. Could Melinda come with you?"

"I sure can!" Melinda said.

"Oh, wonderful!" exclaimed Tharyn. "I would love for you to see our house."

"Well, that settles it," said Dr. Tim. "I'll talk to Dr. Carroll about it in the morning, and then we'll know. I am quite sure he will go along with it."

There was a moment of silence while everyone was enjoying the meal; then Dr. Dane looked at the chief U.S. marshal. "Oh, John, there's something I want to tell you."

"Mm-hmm?"

"Jake Merrell sends his greetings to you and your family. I need to tell you what he did."

Everyone listened intently as Dr. Dane told John Brockman of his former deputy having to draw against Waco Belton and how he took him out.

John smiled. "I know about this guy Belton. He recently forced two lawmen up in Wyoming who used to be my deputies to draw against him and killed them. One in Laramie and the other in Rock Springs. Jake was one of the best deputy U.S. marshals I ever had. It doesn't surprise me that Jake outdrew Belton."

EIGHTEEN

*L*ate in the afternoon on the same day Dr. Dane and Tharyn Logan had arrived in Denver, Cassandra Wheatley was in her room, preparing herself for dinner with Greg Holton and his father.

She had washed her luxuriant black hair earlier in the afternoon and now stood before her dresser mirror in her white petticoat, brushing it carefully while continually adjusting herself so she could see the sides and back in the mirror. It was a shining cascade of curls falling down her back, almost to her waist.

She smiled at her reflection. "Yes! Greg will like this style."

It was now time to put on the dress she had chosen for the occasion. Not wanting to appear too formal, yet limited by the number of dresses to choose from, she had selected a pale yellow dress printed with light green leaves. It had a high neck with a round white collar and elbow-length sleeves that were also trimmed in white.

She picked up the dress from the bed where she had laid it out, slipped into it, and buttoned it up. When her eye caught the yellow ribbon that still lay on the bed, she wondered if she should put it in her hair as she had at other times when wearing the dress, or leave it as it was.

"Let's try it," she said, picking up the ribbon and moving to the dresser mirror.

She wrapped the yellow ribbon around her hair just behind her head, pulled the hair back from each side, and tied the ribbon in a bow.

She studied herself for a moment. "Yes! Greg will like this style even better."

She sat down on the bed, put on her black shoes with the straps over her insteps, moved across the room and examined herself in the full-length mirror that hung on the backside of the door.

A sly smile formed on her lips. "Mm-hmm! This will do nicely. Not too showy but still eye-catching. I must remember to mind my *P*s and *Q*s. I want Greg's dad to like me. That will be to my benefit in my scheme of things."

Taking one last look in the dresser mirror, she was pleased with the reflection staring back at her. Cassandra gave her image a wink and walked out the door.

Mabel Downing was busy in the kitchen, preparing supper for herself when she saw her niece come in. She looked the girl up and down. "Well, you look mighty spiffy, Miss Wheatley!"

Cassandra spun all the way around. "Do you think Greg will like the way I look, Auntie?"

"If he doesn't, it'll be because he's gone blind."

The brunette giggled. She started to say something else when there was a knock at the front door.

Cassandra glanced at the kitchen clock. "Oh my! It *is* almost six-thirty! That has to be Greg."

At the Kirby Holton mansion, Cassandra thoroughly enjoyed Edith Linden's meal while getting acquainted with Greg's father, whom she felt was as handsome and charming as his son. She was fascinated by the expensive china and eating utensils that were used by the Holtons.

Greg had seated himself beside Cassandra, and all during the meal he kept looking at her. It seemed to him that she became more beautiful every day.

When the three of them were finishing the dessert that Edith had prepared, Kirby looked at Cassandra and smiled. "Well, little lady, Greg and I promised you a tour of the house. You ready?"

Cassandra swallowed her last bite of apple pie. "Yes, sir. I sure am!"

Leaving the spacious dining room, Kirby and Greg guided Cassandra on her own private tour of the mansion. They started by taking her up the elegant winding staircase to the second floor. As they passed from one beautifully furnished room to another, Cassandra's mouth hung open at times as she took in the luxury all around her.

Never had she seen such tapestries, carpets, furniture, and decorations. She was amazed at the exquisite paintings that hung on the walls both upstairs and downstairs. The whole tour had Cassandra almost speechless with pleasure. She told herself she could get used to living in a place like this real fast, but she was careful in expressing herself to Kirby and Greg. She did not want to go overboard with her praise of the place. She knew she must show a great deal of decorum so as not to be pushy in Greg's eyes. Good manners were very important, and she wanted both father and son to be pleased with her comport-ment.

However, on the inside, her heart was quaking with joy. Just imagine, she thought, one day this kind of luxury will be mine. I'm sure it won't be long before Greg proposes to me, and I'm more than ready with my answer. "Yes!"

Later that evening, as Greg was walking Cassandra back to the Downing home in the glow of the street lamps, she looked up at him and said softly, "Greg, darling, I have fallen more in love with you tonight."

Greg stopped and squeezed her hand gently. "Cassandra, my sweet, I'm falling deeper in love with you every minute."

The sound of his voice and the words that came from him played through her like a warm breeze. Her graceful chin tilted upward as she looked deep into his eyes. Fragrance rose from her hair and somehow the soft curves of her throat sent the same kind of warmth through his veins. He lowered his face toward hers and kissed her.

They looked into each other's eyes for a long moment; then Greg took her hand again and proceeded along the street.

Greg glanced down at her. "Well, I could sure tell that Dad likes you."

"He seemed to. And I'm glad."

Cassandra was wishing Greg would bring up marriage, but she knew she would just have to wait until he was ready to do so. Then and there, she secretly made plans to turn on more charm and do her best to make him want to propose.

Soon they reached the Downing house. Greg walked Cassandra up onto the porch, and looked into her eyes by the yellow glow of the lanterns shining from inside the parlor window. "Cassandra, darling, I love you with all of my heart."

This thrilled her. She rose up on her tiptoes and kissed him tenderly. "And I love you with all of *my* heart."

Later, when Cassandra was lying in her bed in the darkness, she looked at the starry sky through the window and whispered,

"Cassandra, dear, you've got that rich young man wrapped around your little finger. I just know it won't be very long until he will put a golden ring on your finger in a wedding ceremony. You'll be married to a multimillionaire. Greg will build you a mansion like his father's and decorate it and furnish it like his father's too. Oh, Cassandra…you're going to be one rich woman!"

In the foothills of the Rocky Mountains some ten miles southwest of Denver early on Tuesday morning July 19, Chief Tando led his mounted band of twenty warriors across the South Platte River into a dense forest. Soon they were approaching the spot where Arapaho Chief Red Arrow had agreed to meet when Tando had sent a messenger to him a few days previously.

Dark clouds were gathering in the sky and the air smelled like rain.

Riding on one side of Chief Tando was his son, Latawga. On his other side was one of his subchiefs, Nandano.

Soon, Tando spotted the band of Arapaho Indians and their horses in a small clearing just ahead. There were twelve braves flanking Red Arrow, who set his dark gaze on the approaching riders, then stepped forward and made the Indian sign for *welcome* to the Utes.

The Utes dismounted, and after the chiefs had greeted one another, they sat down on a fallen tree to talk. Latawga and Nandano stood very close to where the chiefs were sitting, as did two of Red Arrow's men. The other Utes and Arapahoes collected within earshot of where the chiefs were sitting. They greeted each other, talked for a moment about the rain that no doubt was coming, then put their attention on the chiefs.

Red Arrow, who was some twenty years older than Tando, looked at him with his dark, shaggy-browed eyes. Since neither chief spoke the other's language, but both spoke English, Red

Arrow asked in English, "What is it Tando wishes to speak to Red Arrow about?"

Tando's dark features were wooden as he looked Red Arrow in the eye. "Tando would like for Red Arrow and his people to join forces and work together to shed white men's blood and make them pay for invading Indian land."

Red Arrow shook his head slowly. "Red Arrow cannot lead his people to do this. There is no reason to continue making war against the whites. They are building more forts and bringing troops in great numbers from back East. To continue fighting them would only result in more Indians being killed."

Sitting like a carved figure, Tando pulled his lips back, flared his nostrils, and scowled. "Tando does not like to hear this kind of talk."

Red Arrow made his own scowl. "Need I remind you that Chief Ouray, your tribe's official spokesman, has called upon all Utes to cease making war against the white men, and to make peace with them instead?"

The storm signals were up in Tando as the braves of both tribes looked on. His anger showed in the down-angled lines of his mouth and in the steely way he looked at Red Arrow.

The Arapaho chief felt the daggers in Tando's eyes. "Red Arrow agrees with Chief Ouray, and I feel that Chief Tando and his people will live longer and be happier if they face the fact that they are vastly outnumbered by the white man's army and make peace with them."

Tando's countenance was becoming as cloudy black as the sky overhead. The wind was picking up and fluffing the feathers of his wolf's headdress.

Red Arrow went on. "Chief Tando must understand that the entire Arapaho tribe no longer has any renegade leaders who want to make war against the white men. The Arapaho all want to live in peace."

The disgust Tando felt rippled his flushed cheeks. "White men must pay for what they have done to Indians!"

"It is fact, Chief Tando. Even if Red Arrow would join Chief Tando in killing whites, it would only bring the soldier coats with their Gatling guns and repeater rifles. In a short time, they would wipe out the renegades. Red Arrow chooses to live in peace with the whites. I am leading my people in this way."

Tando pictured himself whipping out the knife he wore on his waist and driving it into Red Arrow's heart. But he maintained his self-control, drawing a deep breath. Letting it out slowly, he rose to his feet and set icy eyes on Red Arrow as the Arapaho chief also stood up. "It is Red Arrow's choice to live in peace with the whites who have come and stolen Indian land, but it is Tando's choice to make them pay for what they have done!"

With that, Chief Tando turned toward his men, who were fully aware that he was very angry. "Mount up! We go!"

Under the stern eyes of Red Arrow and his braves, the Utes mounted their horses, and without another word to the Arapaho chief, Tando led his men as they trotted into the forest.

While moving among the trees, Latawga, Nandano, and the other eighteen warriors thought they could almost see smoke coming from Chief Tando's ears. His entire body shook with wrath.

Riding beside his father, Latawga looked at him and said with a shaky voice, "We will still make war with the white men, my father. They will pay."

Tando set his fiery eyes on him. "My son must allow his father's blood to cool. Then we talk."

At the Kenyon place—not far from the forest where the angry Chief Tando was riding with his warriors—George, Hattie, and Melinda sat down at the breakfast table. Outside, the wind was blowing steadily and unrelentingly across a heavily clouded sky.

George led them in prayer as they thanked the Lord for the food. As they began eating, George glanced out the kitchen window. "Tell you what, ladies, it looks like I might get wet while riding into town to work this morning."

Hattie nodded. "It really does look like it's going to rain. You need to take your slicker along, that's for sure."

"I will," said George, then looked across the table at his daughter. "Melinda, I know you and Abe have a date every morning except Sunday to take a good ride right after breakfast. With those clouds hanging low like they are, it would be best that you don't go riding today. Or at least till it clears up."

"Daddy, I'm planning to spend some time with Tharyn today," said Melinda. "She will be at the hospital with her husband this morning to be with the lady they are going to operate on tomorrow morning. The lady's name is Nelda Cox. Dr. Dane and Tharyn led Mrs. Cox and her husband to the Lord a week ago today, so they not only want to be with both of them this morning to talk about tomorrow's hip replacement, but also to pray with them and read the Scripture with them."

Hattie smiled. "That's wonderful, Melinda. Dr. Dane and Tharyn are such precious people. They must be having a marvelous time with their practice in Central City."

"They sure are, Mama. From what Tharyn has been telling me in her letters, the practice is growing by leaps and bounds. People are traveling greater distances than ever to be treated by Dr. Dane."

George shook his head in wonderment. "The Logans indeed are amazing people. It's great to see God blessing them like He is."

"For sure, Daddy. It's such a blessing to see that young man I first met in the alley in New York City realizing his dream. His greatest desire way back then was to become a doctor."

Hattie set her gaze on Melinda. "So you and Tharyn have set a time to be together today?"

"Well, sort of. She and Dr. Dane will be back at the Brockman place this afternoon. We didn't set an exact time, but Tharyn is expecting me to show up sometime in early afternoon."

Melinda looked out the window again. "Daddy, I really want to get my ride in. I already have my riding skirt and boots on. You know that sometimes when the sky looks like it does at this moment, it will be hours before it actually starts to rain. I'll take my ride immediately after I help Mama do the dishes and clean up the kitchen. I sure don't want to disappoint Abe. He knows it's not Sunday."

George snickered and shook his head. "You are really quite the horsewoman. Okay, okay, I give in. I sure wouldn't want Abe to be disappointed. But you take your slicker along just in case it should start raining before you and Abe get back."

Melinda scooted her chair back and stood up. She moved to her father, bent down, and kissed his cheek. "I'll do that, Daddy. And I'll not ride as far as usual. I'll just ride to the river and back."

"All right, honey. I hope Abe doesn't object to your shortening your time with him today."

Melinda laughed and kissed her father's cheek again.

When breakfast was over, George went to the barn and saddled his horse. He took another few minutes to saddle Abe, then noting that it was not yet raining, he led both horses to the front porch of the house.

Hattie and Melinda came out the door, and Melinda said with a smile, "Thank you for saddling Abe for me, Daddy."

"My pleasure," he said as he tied Abe's reins to one of the hitching posts.

He then kissed his wife and daughter and mounted up. With the wind plucking at his wide-brimmed hat and the sky growing darker overhead, he rode toward Denver for his day's work at Denning Hardware.

Hattie and Melinda returned to the kitchen and began cleaning up and doing the dishes.

Rain had still not started to fall from the sky when the breakfast chores were done, but the wind was blowing harder. Hattie followed her daughter to the closet at the front of the house and watched as she put on her denim jacket and her bright yellow bonnet. She took her black slicker off its hook in the closet and closed the closet door. "Okay, Mama. I'm off."

They stepped out on to the front porch and Hattie followed as Melinda moved down the steps with the wind plucking at her bonnet and her long blond hair.

Hattie stopped at the bottom of the steps, her eyes following her daughter.

As Melinda approached the gelding, he began to whinny excitedly and toss his head. Melinda looked at her mother and smiled. "See? He's been waiting with great anticipation. I sure wouldn't want him disappointed."

Hattie laughed. "That's for sure, honey."

Melinda stepped up to Abe, stroked his long neck. "Good morning, boy. You ready for our ride?"

Again, Abe tossed his head and whinnied.

Melinda tucked her slicker under the back side of the saddle and mounted up.

Hattie looked up at the dark sky, then at her daughter. "Hurry, honey. And please do as you told your daddy. Just ride to the river and back."

The pretty blonde smiled. "I won't do any more than that, Mama." With that, she put Abe to a gallop and rode in the direction of the South Platte River.

Hattie watched her go, and Melinda was no more than a half-mile away when Hattie felt small drops of rain hit her face. She turned and moved up onto the porch where she was sheltered from the fine mist of rain, but did not take her eyes off Melinda and Abe.

Hattie bit her lower lip, willing Melinda to turn around and head for home and refuge from the storm that was about to break.

She watched until horse and rider vanished from sight. Her voice quivered as she said, "Hurry, honey. I don't want you out there in a bad storm."

Hattie waited a few more seconds in the wind and the cool air, then turned and reluctantly entered the house with a prayer on her lips for the safety of her only child.

When she stepped inside and closed the door, a slight chill slithered down her spine and a deep sense of foreboding filled her heart.

NINETEEN

*M*elinda Scott Kenyon wiped tiny raindrops from her face as the wind lifted her bonnet, making it flap on her head.

Feeling the thrill of riding, Melinda smiled as she looked up at the swirling, dark clouds. "We'll be back before it gets bad, Abe! Hah-h-h-h! Faster, boy! Faster!"

Cattle in the fields lifted their heads and stared at the galloping bay gelding as he raced past them in the direction of the South Platte River with Melinda bent forward on his back. Exhilarated with the wind and the rain in her face and the feel of the big muscular body beneath her, Melinda kept Abe at a full gallop.

Within a few minutes, she blinked against the rain in her eyes and saw the South Platte ahead and the trees on the other side bending with the wind.

Across the river, Chief Tando and his twenty mounted warriors had just crossed through the swift four- to five-foot depth of the South Platte on their way back home.

They were now stopped for a moment some fifty or sixty feet from the riverbank in the dark timber, and under Chief Tando's directions, had formed a circle with their horses. They were deep enough in the shadows to be out of Melinda's view as she galloped their direction.

There was a white flash of lightning farther toward the mountains and the clap of thunder.

Tando looked at the subchief next to him. "All right, Nandano, what is it that you wanted to say to us?"

Nandano's dark features were streaked with rain. "I want to speak to *you* first, Chief Tando."

"Yes?"

"I want to tell you that I am in full agreement with your words to Red Arrow. We must make the whites pay for stealing our land!"

A thin, ominous smile crept onto Tando's lips.

Nandano ran his gaze over the faces of the warriors in the circle. He raised his rifle over his head. "To you, my brothers, I say we must shed white men's blood! Kill! Kill! Kill!"

Lightning flashed overhead and thunder rolled as the other nineteen warriors raised their rifles and shouted their agreement, loudly chorusing the word "Kill!"

Tando's smile broadened at the strong show of agreement from those particular warriors. He knew the adamant attitude they displayed regarding their war against the whites would fire up the greater amount of his warriors, who were back at the village. They must continue their war against the white intruders.

Just as the chorusing of the warriors faded away, Latawga, who was facing the river, noticed a horse galloping their direction in the open field just beyond it, carrying a rider with a bright yellow bonnet and hair of about the same color.

Melinda tugged back on the rein as Abe drew near the river on the ground already made muddy by the falling rain. She had not allowed for the condition of the ground beneath the horse's hooves, and realized they were drawing up on the bank of the river much too fast.

She leaned back in the saddle, pushed her feet hard into the stirrups, and yanked back on the rein. "Whoa! Whoa!"

Abe stiffened his forelegs at her command, but found himself sliding swiftly as he skidded toward the edge of the steep path that rose from the riverbank.

Melinda was anxiously trying to turn him parallel with the river just as a bolt of lightning lashed out of the sky directly overhead with a loud cracking sound.

Frightened by the sudden noise, Abe jumped, whinnied, and helplessly slid closer to the edge of the steep path that led between the grasses down to the swift current of the river.

At the same instant, Melinda saw that she must get out of the saddle before Abe plunged down the path. Suddenly there was a tension pounding behind her temples. Desperation seized her. She slipped her feet from the stirrups, ready to slide out of the saddle to the ground, when Abe's forelegs buckled and he hit the ground on his knees with bone-shuddering force, coming to a sudden stop at the very edge of the path.

Melinda sailed off his back. Her bonnet came loose and was carried by the wind into some tall grass right next to the path. She splashed into the swift, churning current of the river.

The bay gelding whinnied in pain, rose up on his legs, and wheeled about. The slicker that had been tucked underneath the back part of the saddle fell to the ground.

Abe limped on his right foreleg, moving slowly in a circle. When he looked down at the river, he saw no sign of Melinda, for at the moment, she was holding her breath and struggling beneath the surface, trying to lift her head above the water.

The horse looked to the right, and to the left, then back to the river. His mistress was nowhere to be seen, so he turned around and began limping in the direction of home.

In the churning water, Melinda was being carried downstream.

Finally, after struggling for what seemed an eternity, she was able to lift her face out of the water and take a deep breath. With her heart thudding wildly in her chest, she gasped as she splashed about, trying to paddle her way toward the bank. But the swift-moving water was too strong, and it carried her farther out toward the middle of the river.

On the other side of the river, Latawga, his father, and the other warriors were all on their horses at the edge of the west bank, watching the young white woman being carried helplessly downstream. She kept plunging beneath the surface, then splashing desperately up.

One of the warriors said, "White woman will be drained of strength soon and drown."

"She is getting what she deserves for being on Indian land like all other white invaders."

"Good," Nandano said. "She drowns, and we have one less white person to antagonize us."

Others were speaking their agreement when Latawga turned and looked at his father. "It is not the white *women* who shoot at us with repeater rifles and Gatling guns, Father. It is the white *men*. Should we let her drown?"

This caught the attention of the other warriors.

Chief Tando said, "We have been needing another white slave girl to take Joyce's place as servant to your mother and the other squaws, my son."

Latwaga's eyes lit up. "Does my father want me to dive in and save the white girl's life?"

Tando motioned toward the struggling figure in the river. "Go, Latawga!"

As Latawga slid off his horse's back, the warriors exchanged glances. Latawga's desire to save the girl from drowning had been a weight on their minds. The chief's reason for saving the young white woman's life made them feel better.

The chief and his warriors watched as Latawga ran as fast as he could along the riverbank, stumbling at times on the rocks that lined the bank. When he had passed the white girl by several yards, he dived in.

The swift current battled Latawga as if to keep him from reaching the girl. But he battled back fiercely, swimming for all he was worth. Just ahead, there were large rocks sticking up out of the water in the middle of the stream. The current struck the rocks with a drenching spray.

Latawga knew he must reach the girl before the rapid stream would slam her into the rocks.

Chief Tando and his warriors watched the scene downstream as Latawga swam even harder to reach the girl. He was getting close when they saw her finally run out of strength and lose her battle with the river. She flung her arms in desperation, then sank limply beneath the surface.

The Indians saw Latawga plunge beneath the surface and come up quickly with the girl in his arms.

Holding her head out of the water with one arm, he paddled vigorously toward the west bank with the other.

Tando put his horse to a trot, hurrying to meet his son on the bank. The others followed, with one of them leading Latawga's horse.

Lightning lashed out of the dark sky in a jagged bolt of fire, and seconds later, thunder rocked the air with its loud, explosive roar.

Tando and his warriors reached the spot on the bank where Latawga was headed just seconds before he reached the shoreline. Nandano and another warrior slid off their horses, and were there, waiting for Latawga as he came closer to the bank. They stepped into the river and took hold of him to help him out of the water with the weight of the unconscious girl in his arms.

Just as they laid her down on the bank to try to revive her, the falling rain became a heavy downpour.

By this time, all the Indians were off their horses, and Tando moved up and stood over Latawga and the other two, who were bent over the girl.

Nandano pumped on Melinda's chest with the heels of his hands, driving water from her lungs while the rain splashed in her face. Latawga and the other warrior watched closely for some sign of life. Concerned that it might be too late to revive her, Tando kept his gaze riveted on her. After about two minutes, Melinda began rolling her head back and forth while coughing and gasping as Nandano continued pumping.

Tando's taut features relaxed.

Nandano removed his hands when Melinda opened her eyes, blinking against the hard rain. When she focused on the dark, copper-skinned men around her in the downpour, a look of horror etched itself on her face. Shock registered clear to the marrow of her bones, and terror riffled through her. A strangled moan escaped her lips as if someone was choking her from the inside. Her breath was coming fast now, irregular, rasping.

Her face was a mask of anguish, and her mouth shaped into the open curl of a sounded cry, but nothing came out. Eyes wild, she threw her head back and forth and finally let out a wild scream. She was making an attempt to scramble to her feet, when Tando knelt down beside her, laid a hand on her shoulder, and prevented her from getting up. She looked at him with fearful eyes and let out one scream after another.

When she ran out of breath and the screaming stopped, Tando said, "Listen to me, young woman."

Melinda blinked, and feeling weak from all the exertion she had made in the river, she relaxed.

Tando patted her shoulder. "I am Chief Tando of the Ute

tribe. We are not going to harm you. It was my son, Latawga, who dived into the river and pulled you out."

She worked her lips, trying to form words, and finally was able to say, "Chief Tando?"

"Yes."

Melinda had heard of Chief Tando, that he and his people were renegade Utes, and that they continued to prey on white people and kill them in spite of Chief Ouray's pleas to the contrary.

Horror came over her afresh, but she had no strength to resist him.

Tando patted her shoulder again. "We will take you to our village."

With that, he slid his arms beneath her, hoisted her into a cradled position, then stood up. A feeling of panic ran through Melinda.

The chief spoke to the others. "Mount up. Even though it is raining hard, we must go home." He carried Melinda to his horse, hoisted her up on the animal's back, then swung up behind her.

Melinda prayed as she rode with the chief on his horse. *O dear Lord, I beg of You! Please deliver me from the hands of these Indians. I don't believe they will not harm me, in spite of what Tando says. They hate white people. Why wouldn't they harm me? Or even kill me?*

The thought of her plight tightened her nerves and sent her heart pounding.

There was no conversation between Chief Tando and Melinda as they rode west and climbed into the towering Rocky Mountains beneath the dark sky with the wind slapping against them. They, as well as the twenty warriors, bowed their heads against the drive of the rain.

Melinda noticed a herd of deer dash across the path in front of them some fifty yards away. They quickly disappeared in the dense forest that led up to higher ground.

For the next hour the trail grew steeper and the rain whirled down from the clouds overhead. Then it began to dissipate, and after another twenty minutes, the rain stopped completely. The clouds were breaking up and soon the sun was shining down from a clear blue sky.

Nandano rode on one side of the chief and Latawga rode on the other side. Latawga ventured a glance at the blond white woman sitting in front of his father and saw a strained, somber expression. He started to say something that might ease her fear, but decided to remain silent.

For Melinda, the time seemed to drag by, but finally, as they reached the village, the sun had set and only its glow from the western sky showed Melinda the long rows of tepees. Many cook fires were in front of them, with wisps of smoke lifting skyward. There was a gathering group of Indians who were looking at her with curiosity written on their faces.

Melinda looked them over with a candid eye. There were many young men, whom she decided were more of Tando's warriors. There were also a good number of young women, whom she thought might be the squaws of the warriors. Some of them carried papooses on their backs and in their arms. She also saw several children that she guessed ran from two and three years old up into their teens. There were many men and women in middle age and a good number were silver-haired, deeply wrinkled, and moved with a shuffling walk.

Tando rode his horse up to his tepee, where Leela stood, looking questioningly at the blond white woman sitting in front of her husband. Two older squaws stood beside her.

The other warriors drew their horses to a halt just behind the chief. Latawga dismounted, glanced at his puzzled mother, and stepped up beside his father's horse. He looked up at the young white woman, whose eyes were wide with fear in the ashen pallor of her skin.

Raising his hands toward her, Latawga said, "I do not know your name. What is your name?"

Her lips quivered and her voice trembled. "M-Melinda."

Latawga almost smiled. "I will help you down, Melinda."

Feeling very weak, Melinda leaned toward him, and felt Tando firmly grip her arms. Tando eased her into his son's grasp. Latawga lowered Melinda into his arms, then stood her on her feet.

A crowd had gathered by this time and from his horse's back, Chief Tando ran his gaze over the curious faces and said, "After we met with Chief Red Arrow, we crossed the South Platte River to come home. We stopped for a short time in the forest to talk about Red Arrow's refusal to join us in making war with the whites." A scowl formed on his face for a moment.

The people exchanged glances.

Tando went on. "While we were talking about Red Arrow, we saw this young white woman fall from her horse into the river from the opposite bank. She was alone and was being carried swiftly and helplessly downstream. I ordered Latawga to dive in and rescue her, which as you can see…he did."

At this point, the chief slipped off his horse's back and stood beside Latawga and the young woman. "Since our other white woman servant, Joyce, is dead from the fever, I will have this young white woman take her place."

Melinda's heart was pounding at those words, and it only got worse when Tando turned to her with a deep frown on his brow. "I heard you tell my son your name is Melinda. Did I understand correctly?"

"Yes," she said timidly.

"Melinda, you will now be servant, first to my squaw, Leela, then to other squaws as Leela directs you." He pointed to Leela as he spoke and stepped back.

Leela took a couple of steps toward her.

Melinda flinched and moved back a pace, only to run into Tando. He gripped both of her upper arms, not grasping them hard, just letting her know there was no place to run.

Suddenly, Melinda's eyes filled with tears. She turned and looked at the chief. "Please, sir. Please let me go home! I beg of you to let me go home! Please!"

The tears began to spill down her cheeks.

Leela stepped up to her, laid a hand on her shoulder, and said in a soft tone, "If Melinda obeys Chief Tando and Leela she will not be mistreated, but the chief has spoken. She will not be allowed to go home. But Melinda should be glad that our son saved her from drowning."

Through her tears, Melinda gazed at Leela. Even in her distraught state, she noted that the chief's squaw was quite lovely. She was petite, and there was a grace in her shoulders and shining beauty in her tender eyes. Her copper skin glowed from the reflected light of the cook fire, and two long, lustrous braids hung down her back.

Tando moved up beside Leela and set his dark eyes on Melinda. "You must dry your tears. As my squaw has said, if you obey us, you will not be harmed. But you are now Leela's servant and will serve other squaws as she directs you. You will live in the tepee next to ours with two widows of our warriors. Please do not try to escape. We will only catch you, and you will be punished."

Melinda lifted a hand and wiped away her tears. Whiteness covered her face, turning her lips scarlet against such pallor.

Leela said in a soft voice, "Perhaps in time, Melinda, you will learn to like it here and learn our ways."

Melinda felt horror at that awful prospect. Her head started spinning and her knees buckled. She fell to the ground.

Leela bent over her, saw that she was unconscious, and looked up at her husband. "Carry her into our tepee, and I will take care of her."

Tando picked up the limp Melinda and Leela followed Tando into the tepee. He laid her on a sleeping pallet on the floor and moved outside.

Leela knelt down and with a soft cloth, dabbed the tears from the girl's face. Then taking the white hands into her own dark-skinned hands, she rubbed them briskly.

Melinda started to become aware of what Leela was doing and her eyes fluttered open. The two women stared at each other for a moment; then Melinda sucked in a deep breath, preparing to let out a scream. Leela let go of one of Melinda's hands and clamped her own over the girl's mouth, stifling the scream.

As Melinda looked at her wide-eyed, Leela said, "You must learn now that to scream will only get you into trouble. You will be given work to do, but none of it will be unreasonable. I know you will miss your people, wherever they are, but you are now the property of Chief Tando and Leela."

Melinda blinked and swallowed hard, looking at the squaw with tear-filled eyes. She knew she dare not try again to scream. It would not help, anyhow, she told herself. There was no one to hear her scream and come to her rescue.

"Stand up now," Leela said, "and let's get you out of this stained dress. You and I are near the same size. You can wear something of mine."

When Melinda was on her feet, Leela handed the trembling girl a dark brown deerskin dress. While Leela looked on, Melinda slowly slipped out of her soiled dress and put on the one Leela had given her. She was surprised at how soft it felt against her skin and looked at Leela with astonishment.

Leela smiled. "It is nice, isn't it? I will teach you how to make your own."

Melinda's eyes were full of shadow. Her voice quivered across the tepee. "Ma'am, I have a young man who loves me, and I have promised to marry him. I also have parents who love me. If I do not go back to all three of them, it will break their hearts. They will think I am dead. Please, ma'am, please ask your husband to let me go home."

Leela shook her head. "It would do no good. It would also make him very angry at me. You must accept being our servant and not complain. Our son saved your life, and we will feed and clothe you."

At that moment, the dreadful fear of being with these savage people strangely began to dissipate. Melinda thought about her heavenly Father and knew He was always with her. Hebrews 13:5 came to mind. "I will never leave thee, nor forsake thee."

A gentle peace filled her heart.

Melinda looked at Leela. "Thank—thank you for the dress."

Leela smiled. "You are welcome." She bent down, took a pair of beaded moccasins from a basket, and handed them to her. "These doeskin moccasins will feel good on your feet, too."

Melinda sat down on the pallet, removed her sodden boots and stockings, and slipped her feet into the moccasins. She stood up and took a walk around the inside of the tepee. Indeed, they felt good to her feet. A tiny smile crossed her pale features. "Thank you, ma'am."

Leela said, "You can call me by my name."

Melinda let the smile grow a little. "All right. Thank you, Leela."

Still feeling the gentle peace from God, Melinda thought, *Tim and my parents will no doubt have the army scouring the plains and the mountains for me. Surely in a few days the soldiers will come to my rescue. In the meantime, I will be much better off if I do as I'm told and obey these people. At least the chief's squaw is kind to me.*

Suddenly another thought popped into her mind. *Maybe the Lord has allowed me to be captured by these Indians for a short time so I can be a witness to them! Lord, You know how difficult this situation is for me, and You know how terribly frightened I am. But the Indians need Jesus. They need salvation. Please give me the wisdom and courage to talk to Leela and these people, and help me to recall enough Scripture to plant the seed of the Word into their hearts.*

Even more peace seemed to invade her inner being. She looked at Leela and said, "Since there is work to be done, what would you like me to do?"

Leela frowned slightly. She was perplexed over the sudden transformation that had come over the white girl.

Melinda saw the puzzlement in Leela's dark eyes and resolved with God's help to tell her of Jesus and His love.

TWENTY

At the Kenyon house, Hattie was standing on the front porch, looking in the direction of the South Platte River. Melinda should have been back an hour ago. Even if she had taken refuge somewhere when the rain came down hard, it wasn't raining any longer. She should be home by now. If all was well, she *would* be.

Hattie let out an uneasy sigh and began imagining all kinds of things that could have happened to her. With each thought, what she imagined became worse. Panic was beginning to squeeze her chest.

"Oh, dear Lord," she said with a quivering voice. "Where is she? Is she hurt? Has someone kidnapped her? Or—or did something happen that took her life? Is—is she dead?"

With the latter thought, a floodgate opened in her mind, washing old memories to the surface. She recalled the very first time she laid eyes on the pretty blond girl at the railroad station in Topeka ten years ago, where the orphan train was and the orphans were lined up to be inspected by the prospective foster parents. At first sight of her, she and George both knew they wanted to take Melinda home.

Hattie thought of the day shortly thereafter, that they went before the judge in Topeka and went beyond the status of foster parents. They adopted her and changed her name from Melinda Scott to Melinda Kenyon.

Sweet memories of how the girl had endeared herself to both parents ran through Hattie's mind.

She drew a shaky breath and fixed her eyes toward the field where she should have seen Melinda riding home on Abe when she first came out on the porch. No sign of her. "Oh, please, Lord. Don't let anything be wrong. Please bring her home to me right n—"

Suddenly Hattie spotted movement on the wet, grassy field some three hundred yards away. She blinked and squinted to bring the moving figure into focus. Was it a horse?

She watched intently as the dark figure came closer. After a few more minutes, she saw that it was definitely a horse, moving slowly toward her.

It was a bay horse!

Her hand went to her mouth. "Is that Abe?" she whispered.

Hattie's heart pounded while she kept her eyes glued to the horse. As he drew closer, she was able to make out the white blaze on the animal's long face, and the four white stockings.

"Yes! It's Abe and—"

Abe was limping on his right foreleg. *He was not carrying a rider.*

Hattie Kenyon's skin tingled with consternation. Her pulse pounded. Her forehead dampened with perspiration. With a hot lump in her throat, she bounded off the porch and ran toward Abe, holding the skirt of her dress above her ankles.

The gelding saw her coming, lifted his head, whinnied, and kept limping toward her.

Hattie was panting as she drew up to Abe. He whinnied again and halted. Efforts to calm herself by a series of deep breaths proved fruitless. "Abe!" she cried. "Where's Melinda? What happened?"

She stroked his long face and looked down at his injured leg. It was coated with a thin layer of mud. She could not see any torn flesh, but the leg was swollen considerably between the knee and the hoof.

Filled with alarm, Hattie took hold of the rein and led the limping horse to the barn. As she led him inside, she said, "Lord, what should I do? Abe can't carry me. He's hurt bad. George has our only other horse in town with him."

Suddenly, Breanna Brockman came to mind. "Yes! Breanna!"

Quickly, Hattie removed the saddle and bridle from Abe and hung them on the pegs where they belonged. Leaving him inside the barn, she lifted her skirt ankle-high again and ran down the road. Ten minutes later, when she reached the gate of the Brockman place, she ran as hard as she could down the tree-lined lane and headed for the front porch.

Panting and gasping for breath, she bounded up the porch steps and pounded loudly on the door. "Oh, please, please be home, Breanna!"

All was quiet.

Hattie leaned against the door jamb and sucked hard for breath. "Please, Breanna. Open the door!" She pounded on it again repeatedly.

Just then, the door swung open and Breanna frowned as she saw the gasping, panting Hattie, whose features were plainly distraught. Before Breanna could speak, Hattie stumbled toward her and fell into her arms.

Breanna held her up, running her gaze to the yard to see if anyone was with her and noted that there wasn't even a horse. Hattie broke into uncontrollable sobs. Supporting Hattie's weight, Breanna said, "Honey, what is wrong?"

Hattie could only gasp and sob.

Breanna guided her down the hall. "Come on, Hattie, dear, let's go into the parlor and sit down."

When they entered the parlor, Breanna sat Hattie on the sofa and settled down next to her. She took the woman's hands into her own.

Hattie set her tear-filled eyes on Breanna, gasped, and finally was able to say, "Melinda! Melinda! Abe—Abe came home—" She choked.

Breanna looked her in the eye. "Honey, slow down now. Tell me very slowly what has happened."

Still trying to catch her breath, Hattie inhaled sharply, then let the air out in an attempt to calm her rattled nerves.

"That's better," said Breanna, rising to her feet. "Just sit here and get control of yourself. I'll be right back with a bracing cup of hot tea. I was just drinking some myself."

Breanna was gone less than two minutes when she came in and handed Hattie a cup of tea. "Take a few sips. It will help you. Then you can tell me about Melinda and Abe."

Fifteen minutes later, having hitched one of the Brockman horses to a buggy, Breanna repeatedly snapped the reins and raced across the fields in a straight line toward the South Platte River with Hattie on the seat beside her.

As they were drawing near the river in the bouncing, fish-tailing buggy, Hattie pointed to a wide spot between the trees that lined the bank. "There! Pull up there, so we can see both ways up and down the riverbank!"

Breanna guided the horse directly to the spot and drew the buggy to a halt on the wet ground near the bank of the river. Rainwater was puddled all around.

Both women sat on the seat, craning their necks, looking up and down the bank and all around them when Hattie gasped and pointed at the yellow bonnet that lay in the grass near the river's edge. "Breanna! It's Melinda's bonnet!"

Even as she spoke, Hattie jumped down from the seat and ran toward the bonnet.

Breanna followed, and just as Hattie was picking up the bonnet and wailing that something terrible had happened to Melinda, Breanna spotted the black slicker lying on the steep slope that led down to the water's edge. She rushed to it and picked it up. "I'm sure this is Melinda's slicker!"

Hattie burst into tears. "It is! It is!"

When Breanna reached her, Hattie grasped the slicker, held it close to her bosom along with the bonnet, and wept. Then she said, "Oh, Breanna, with both of these lying this close to the river, there's only one thing that could have happened. I told you about the mud on Abe's right leg and how swollen it is. For some reason, he must have gone down on that knee at a gallop, or at least at a fast trot, and Melinda must have been thrown into the river."

With that, she burst once again into uncontrollable sobs, wailing, "She's dead! My Melinda is dead, Breanna! She drowned in the river! She's dead! She's dead!"

Breanna wrapped her in her arms. "Honey, she might not be dead. Maybe she didn't fall into the river. Maybe somehow, she's stumbling up or down the riverbank, dazed and confused. She might have hit her head on the ground as she went out of the saddle when Abe went down."

Hattie blinked and looked at her. "Do you really think so?"

"It's possible. Let's hurry into town. We'll let George know about this, then advise John of it, so he or the sheriff can put a search party together and look for Melinda."

A tiny ray of hope flickered in Hattie's eyes. "All right, maybe she is still alive and somewhere along the river. We'll have to let Tim know, too."

"Of course. Come on. Let's put the bonnet and the slicker in the buggy and head for town."

When George Kenyon had been advised by Breanna and Hattie at the hardware store of Melinda's disappearance, he went with them to the Chief U.S. Marshal's office in the federal building, riding his horse. Together, they told Chief U.S. Marshal John Brockman the story. John said he would rather put together a search party than to have the sheriff do it. Some of his deputies were in town at the moment. He would gather them together and have them ready to go in about an hour.

George told the chief he wanted to be in on the search for his daughter. He felt that Dr. Tim would also want to be in on it, and because of Tharyn's close friendship to Melinda, Dr. Dane would no doubt want to take part in the search also. They would be back to the chief's office shortly with Dr. Tim and Dr. Dane.

Chief Brockman agreed and told them that he knew his pastor well enough that he would want to be in on the search too. He would send one of his deputies to the parsonage to inform the pastor what had happened and offer to let him be part of the search party.

As George, Hattie, and Breanna headed for the hospital, the chief went to work to gather his deputies.

When the trio entered the hospital, Breanna told George and Hattie that Dr. Dane was probably in Nelda Cox's room with Eric and Nelda. She led them to the room on the second floor, and they waited in the hall while Breanna entered the room.

There she found Nelda lying in her bed, with Eric on one side and Dr. Dane and Tharyn on the other. Tharyn moved to Breanna and embraced her. "I didn't expect you to be at the hospital today."

Breanna shook her head gently. "I wouldn't be, but I have something to tell you and your husband that you need to know."

Dr. Dane frowned and looked at Breanna. "What is it?"

Breanna invited the Kenyons into the room. When she had finished telling the story to the Logans and the Coxes, Tharyn's eyes were filled with tears as Dr. Dane said, "I have Nelda's surgery to do first thing in the morning, but I sure can be in on the search for the rest of today."

George said, "We're going to find our future son-in-law and let him know about Melinda. I know he will want to be in the search party, too."

"For sure," said Dr. Dane. "He's observing a cesarean section down the hall right now, but I'll go in, call him aside, and tell him what has happened."

Tharyn took hold of her husband's hand. "Honey, I'll be praying that the search party will find Melinda alive and well, and that you will find her quickly."

"We'll all be praying that way," said Breanna. "Tharyn, Hattie is going to stay at my house while the men go on the search. Can you go with us?"

Tharyn nodded. "Yes. Nelda is in good hands with the nurses here. I'd like to be with you."

Dr. Dane took time to pray once again with Nelda and Eric about the surgery that he would perform in the morning; then he and Tharyn left the room with Breanna and the Kenyons. Together, they went down the hall to the doors of the surgical unit. Saying he would be right back, Dr. Dane left the others in the hall and hurried inside.

Moments later, Dr. Dane came out with Dr. Tim Braden at his side. Tim's pallid face showed the jolt the news had put on him.

The Kenyons clasped him in a three-way embrace, and after they talked about the situation, Dr. Tim told them he was going with the search party. He would go by Dr. Matt Carroll's office, explain it to him, and they would head for the federal building.

When the small group arrived at the federal building, they found Chief U.S. Marshal John Brockman at the hitch rail with five of his deputies and Pastor Nathan Blandford. They were tying kerosene lanterns to the saddlebags. Chief Brockman and the pastor were glad to see that Dr. Tim and Dr. Dane were both going with them. Pastor Blandford spoke words of encouragement to the Kenyons and to Dr. Tim. John explained that they were taking the lanterns so that if necessary they could keep up the search after dark.

Dr. Dane told the chief he would need to go by the closest stable and rent a horse. John told him they had an extra horse in the federal building barn out back. They would saddle him up.

A short time later, the Brockman buggy hauled up to the bank of the South Platte River at the place where Hattie and Breanna had found Melinda's bonnet and slicker, which were still in the buggy. Tharyn was on the front seat between Hattie and Breanna.

As the men in the search party dismounted, Breanna left the buggy and guided her husband to the spots where the bonnet and slicker had been found.

John ran his gaze up and down the riverbanks and said, "All right, men. We've got to split up. Half of this group will cross the river and work the bank both ways, while we do the same thing on this side."

Breanna told her husband that she, Hattie, and Tharyn would wait right there in the buggy until it was almost dark. If none of the search party had returned by then, the three of them would go and wait at the Brockman house.

John assured her that if they hadn't found Melinda by midnight, they would give up the search until morning. He told his men if they found Melinda, they were to fire three shots into the air in succession, and everybody would collect at the spot on the bank where they were at the moment. They would also meet back at this spot at midnight if she hadn't been found by then. He quickly named the deputies he wanted to work the other side of the river, and they guided their horses into the stream and headed for the other bank.

The chief U.S. marshal divided his half of the search party up, and the women watched from the buggy as the search began.

Hours later, when the searchers had not returned to the buggy and darkness was falling, the women headed for the Brockman place.

It was just after midnight and the silver moon was shining down out of a clear sky when the women heard the sound of horses blowing at the front of the house.

Having already put her two children to bed, Breanna led Hattie and Tharyn to the front door. They stepped out on to the porch and saw George, John, Dr. Dane, Dr. Tim, and Pastor Blandford dismounting in the moonlight.

As the men stepped up on the porch, it was obvious by the dejected look on their faces that they had found no sign of Melinda.

"No sign of her?" said Breanna.

George took Hattie into his arms as John sighed and said, "None at all. If there had been any tracks on either side of the river, Melinda's, or even hoofprints of somebody's horse who might have picked her up, the heavy rain obliterated them. We could see no tracks at all of any kind. My deputies went on home to get to bed so we can start again early in the morning. Dr. Dane has to perform the hip replacement for Mrs. Cox in the morning, so he won't be going with us." He looked around. "Is Eric here?"

Breanna nodded and smiled thinly. "Mm-hmm. He was pretty tired, and since he's got the strain of the surgery in the morning, I encouraged him to go to bed." She ran her gaze over the faces of the others. "I know you want to get to your beds, but come inside for a moment; and we'll have Pastor Blandford lead us in prayer."

As they moved inside, Hattie looked at Dr. Tim. "Will you be going on the search in the morning?"

His face drawn, Tim nodded. "Yes, I will. Dr. Carroll told me to stay with it as long as necessary."

As the group entered the parlor, which was well lighted with lanterns, Dr. Tim noticed the bonnet and slicker lying on a small table beside the sofa. He bit his lips. The fresh reminders of Melinda's disappearance wounded him like a physical pain.

Tharyn set her concerned gaze on the chief. "Will you do anything different tomorrow, John?"

"Yes. We'll all work downstream this time. We'll cover several miles and check both sides of the river, just in case she somehow might have been able to crawl out of the water, and is lying on or near the bank, needing help. In addition to this, we'll talk to residents of the area, both upstream and downstream, and ask if they have seen anything that would lead us to believe Melinda is still alive."

George's throat was very dry. He spoke in a husky, low-pitched voice. "Chief Brockman, if it should turn out after another day's searching that there is no sign of Melinda at all, what then?"

John shook his head and sighed. "Then we'll have to face it, George. It will give strong indication that she fell into the river and drowned. Her body may never be found."

Dr. Tim made a moaning sound, and with tears in his eyes, he went to the small table beside the sofa and picked up the bonnet and the slicker. Pressing them against his face, he sobbed, "No, dear God! It can't be! My darling Melinda can't be dead! You know where she is. Bring her back to me!"

Pastor Blandford put an arm around the young doctor. "Don't give up, Tim. It is still possible that she is alive." He looked around at the others. "Let's pray right now."

The pastor kept his arm around Dr. Tim and led the group in prayer. He asked the Lord if Melinda was still alive to let them find her quickly, but if He had taken her home to heaven, to let her parents and Dr. Tim and the rest of them know, so they could have peace and closure about it.

When he had finished praying and he and the others were about to leave for their homes, the pastor told them he was going to contact all the members of the church in the morning so they could be praying also.

On Wednesday morning, Dr. Dane Logan did the hip replacement surgery on Nelda Cox with Tharyn at his side. When it was done, Dr. Dane left Tharyn with Nelda and went to the waiting room to tell Eric that the surgery was successful, and that in a few months, Nelda would be walking as well as before her hip problem began. Eric was elated and poured out his thanks to the doctor for his skilled work.

Late in the afternoon, the Logans and Eric Cox went to the Brockman place where they found Hattie Kenyon with Breanna and her children. The chief U.S. marshal and his search team had not yet returned.

When darkness fell, Breanna and Tharyn prepared a light meal. No one had much of an appetite, but they sat at the table, picking at their food and talking about Melinda. After a while, the subject went to Nelda, and Eric had nothing but praise to the Lord and to Dr. Dane for how well the surgery had gone.

That night, Paul and Ginny were sent to bed at ten o'clock, and the adults had barely settled down in the parlor when they heard pounding hooves outside.

"They're back!" said Dr. Dane and jumped out of his over-stuffed chair.

He helped Tharyn to her feet, and they all headed into the foyer. Before they reached the front door, it came open. John, George, Dr. Tim, and Pastor Blandford came in with weary and sad faces.

"Nothing?" asked Hattie, her voice cracking.

George put his arms around her and looked to John, who said, "We found no evidence that Melinda is alive. The search party talked to dozens of people in the areas up and down the river, but they had seen nothing. We have to assume that she fell into the river and drowned. We went much farther downriver than we had planned, but I wanted to make sure." He paused and choked a bit. "Her—her body may well have caught on some of the under-growth in the river and will never surface."

Tim Braden joined the Kenyons as they held on to each other and wept. The others tried to comfort them but were having a difficult time, especially Tharyn, who was in the arms of her husband.

When emotions had subsided some, Pastor Blandford said to the group, "Chief Brockman and I are in agreement that there is nowhere else to search and no one else to talk to." He turned to the Kenyons. "Would you feel it premature if we have a memorial service for Melinda tomorrow morning at the church?"

George and Hattie looked into each other's swollen, bloodshot eyes.

When they had not answered after several seconds, the pastor said, "I—I just wanted Dr. Dane and Tharyn to be able to attend the memorial service. I know they have to head back to Central City tomorrow. I thought if we had the service at ten o'clock, they would still have time to make it home before it gets too late in the day."

Hattie nodded. "I certainly want Dr. Dane and Tharyn to be at the memorial service."

"Me, too," said George. "Since the search has been exhausted, I don't think having the service tomorrow is premature. How about you, Tim?"

Dr. Tim swallowed hard. "No—no, sir. I don't think it's too soon. I certainly want Dr. and Mrs. Logan to be able to attend it."

"We sure want to be there for the service when you have it," said Dr. Dane.

Tharyn wiped away a tear and nodded. "Tomorrow morning would be fine, Pastor."

The pastor let a weak smile curve his lips. "Then tomorrow morning it is. Ten o'clock. I'll see that all the church members are notified, and I will ask them to advise as many townspeople as possible, too."

Dr. Dane said, "Since I have now turned Nelda over to Dr. Matt Carroll, Tharyn and I will leave for Central City right after the memorial service. We need to get back so Dr. Robert Fraser and Nurse Nadine Wahl can get some rest."

Dr. Tim Braden said, "Dr. Dane, I will still drive the Coxes back to Central City when Nelda is able to travel, as planned."

Dr. Dane laid a hand on his shoulder. "I really appreciate that, my friend."

Dr. Tim managed a smile, then turned to the Kenyons. "You need to get home now. Both of you are completely exhausted."

John said, "Since George and Dr. Tim are riding horses, I'll drive Hattie home in our buggy."

At the Kenyon home, when Hattie, George, and Tim entered the quiet house, Tim said, "I'll light some lanterns."

While he was doing so, Hattie clung to her husband and began sobbing once again.

George guided her into the parlor and sat her down on the couch. By the time Tim had fired a sufficient number of lanterns in the house and had returned to the parlor, Hattie began drying her eyes with an already soggy handkerchief.

She sighed deeply as Tim sat down in a chair, facing them. "We—we only had Melinda for a few short years, but she was such a blessing. The Lord knew how desperately we wanted a child, and when we first saw her standing on the depot platform that day with all the other orphan children, we knew immediately that she was the one God had chosen for us."

Sitting next to her on the couch, George said with a catch in his voice, "Yes, we did, dear. And she has been such a wonderful joy in our lives. We will always be grateful to the Lord for letting us be her adoptive parents."

Tim wiped tears. "And I'll always be grateful that I had her love and had her for the short time the Lord allowed us to be together."

Both parents nodded silently.

After staying with the grieving parents for a little longer, Tim felt his own need to be alone to mourn his loss. He explained this to the Kenyons, and they both told him they understood. They walked him to the front porch. When he and the horse were swallowed by the night, they walked back into the house arm in arm.

Aboard the horse, Tim guided the horse toward town in the moonlight with tears coursing down his cheeks. "Lord," he said with a tight throat, "I love Melinda more than life itself. I don't know what to do. Please help me. We were so close to being married. Just a few months. Come May, she would have been my wife. How—how will I ever live without her?"

Ever so gently the Saviour's words came to him: "I will never leave thee, nor forsake thee."

A measure of peace filled his wounded heart. Tim knew that the Lord was with him as promised and would heal his heart in His own time.

TWENTY-ONE

*D*r. Dane and Tharyn Logan arrived back in Central City late Thursday afternoon in the special carriage they had used to carry Nelda Cox to Denver, and as they entered the office, Dr. Robert Fraser and Nadine Wahl were talking to the last patient of the day. He was a middle-aged man named Harry Miles, whom Dr. Dane had been treating for arthritis in his hands.

Dr. Fraser explained that Harry had come in to have him examine his hands and to get more salicylic acid powders. Harry welcomed the Logans back, then left the office.

Nadine rose from the desk chair. "So how did Nelda's surgery go, Dr. Logan?"

"Just fine. She'll be walking well in a few months."

"I'm glad to hear that."

"Me, too," said the elderly physician with a grin. "But then she had the West's greatest hip replacement surgeon perform the operation."

"Amen!" said Nadine.

"You two may be just a bit prejudiced."

"Oh no," said Fraser, chuckling. "We speak the truth."

Nadine set her eyes on Tharyn and frowned. "Honey, are you all right? You seem a bit melancholy."

Dane looked at Tharyn as she bit her lips and blinked at the tears that suddenly filmed her eyes. He put his arm around her shoulders. "Nadine, you've heard Tharyn talk a lot about her best friend, Melinda Kenyon."

Nadine frowned again. "Yes."

"Let me tell you why Tharyn is sad."

Dr. Dane explained to Nadine and Dr. Fraser about Melinda's disappearance at the South Platte River, of the extensive but fruitless search led by Chief U.S. Marshal John Brockman, and of the memorial service that was conducted that morning by Pastor Nathan Blandford.

Nadine moved to Tharyn and embraced her, saying how sorry she was. Dr. Fraser did the same.

Tharyn dabbed at her eyes with a hankie, and Dane put his arm around her again. She sniffed and said, "I know I'll meet Melinda in heaven, and that is what sustains me."

"Of course," said Dr. Fraser. He took a deep breath. "I...ah...have some good news."

Dr. Dane smiled. "Tell us."

"Well, you remember that you sent me to check on Jack Bates?"

"Yes. How's he doing?"

"Very well. Both ways."

"Both ways? What do you mean?"

"Physically and spiritually."

Dane and Tharyn looked at each other quizzically; then he said, "All right, Dr. Fraser, explain it."

"When you made the note for me to go check on Jack, you said you were going to take time to deal with him about salvation next time you saw him, since he would be feeling better."

Dr. Dane nodded. "Mm-hmm. Both Jack *and* his neighbors, Rex and Dora Wilson. The opportunity just wasn't there the day I took that slug out of him."

"Well, I figured it ought to be done as soon as possible, so when I went up there to the Wilson place to see Jack, I took Pastor Shane with me. He preached to them and led all three of them to the Lord!"

Dr. Dane's face beamed. "Wonderful!"

"Yes!" said Tharyn. "That's wonderful!"

"And as soon as Jack is healed up so he can be baptized, all three of them are coming to church to take care of that matter," put in Nadine.

"That indeed is good news," said Dr. Dane. "I'll get up there to check on Jack in a few days. I want to congratulate all three of them."

Nadine noticed three people standing at the large window on the boardwalk. Greg Holton was smiling through the window at them, then turned and said something to his father. Kirby nodded. The third person was Cassandra Wheatley. Greg took her by the hand, and all three entered the office.

"We were just passing by," said Kirby, "and Greg noticed that the Logans were back. Nice to see you."

"You, too," said Dr. Dane.

"Yes," said Tharyn, smiling.

"How did Mrs. Cox's surgery go?"

"Just fine, Kirby. She'll be walking like normal again in a few months."

"Great! Ah…we talked before you left for Denver about your letting me take you on a tour of the mine."

"Mm-hmm."

"How soon can you come to the mine and take the tour?"

"Well, let's see…"

Dr. Fraser spoke up. "If you'd like to do it tomorrow, I can fill in for you here in the office. I've taken the tour. It's really interesting. I know you'll enjoy it."

Tharyn laid a hand on her husband's arm. "Why don't you take the tour tomorrow, honey? You could use a little diversion from your work."

Dane smiled at her, then turned to Kirby. "How about right after lunch tomorrow? Say one o'clock?"

"That'll be a good time. I'll meet you at my office at the mine at one o'clock. I'd suggest, Doctor, that you come in clothing you don't mind having stained with coal dust."

Dr. Dane chuckled. "Okay."

Greg's eyes sparkled. He was still holding Cassandra's hand. "Dr. and Mrs. Logan, something wonderful happened while you were in Denver."

"What was it?" asked Tharyn.

The young couple looked at each other and smiled. Then Greg said, "On Tuesday evening I asked Cassandra to marry me, and she said yes!"

Cassandra's face was beaming.

"Well, congratulations," Dr. Dane responded warmly.

There was a silent moment; then Tharyn said, "Yes. Congratulations. Have you set a date?"

Greg shook his head. "Not yet, but it will probably be in November. Before I asked her to marry me, I discussed it with Dad. He advised me to let the engagement period be at least three months. He felt this would give Cassandra and me time to make preparation for the wedding. I agreed, and after Cassandra had said she would marry me, I told her about Dad's suggestion and she agreed."

Cassandra was smiling, but in her heart she wished the wedding could be sooner than November. She knew if she had disagreed with Greg, it would only cause trouble between him and his father.

"I'm excited about it," Kirby said jubilantly. "I'm going to give the entire third floor of the mansion over to Greg and Cassandra when they marry; then next spring I'll have a mansion much like it built for them on a piece of ground I already own on the north side of town."

The thought of having her own mansion made Cassandra's heart skip a beat. She took hold of her future father-in-law's arm and flashed a smile at the Logans. "Isn't he just wonderful?"

"Sounds like you're going to be happy as Mrs. Greg Holton, Cassandra," said Dr. Dane.

"Oh, I most certainly am!"

Tharyn did not comment. Again there was a silent few seconds before she said, "Well, husband of mine, we'd better be heading to the house."

While the Logans were driving home, Dane turned to her with a questioning look in his eyes. "Honey, I could tell you weren't overjoyed with the news of the engagement."

She looked surprised. "Was I that obvious?"

"To me you were."

"I just feel so uncomfortable around Cassandra. Mabel has told me at church how the girl is so blatant with her atheism and how greedy she is. And I can see it for myself that the only reason she wants to marry Greg is because he's rich."

Dane nodded. "I think you're right, sweetheart, but Greg is a grown man and makes his own decisions."

"I know, but I just hate to see him so taken by her. I know he's not a Christian, but I still don't want to see him marry a woman who's after his money."

As they turned off Main Street to head for their house, Tharyn took hold of his upper arm and squeezed it. "I wish everyone could have a perfect marriage like ours. Centered on Jesus, with all this love between us."

At one o'clock the next afternoon, Kirby Holton opened his office door in response to Dr. Dane Logan's knock.

"Welcome, Doctor! Come on in. I need to put a helmet on you."

Wearing old clothes, Dr. Dane stepped in and noted two metal helmets lying on Kirby's desk. Each had a lamp in the front.

Picking up one of the helmets, Kirby struck a match and lit the lamp. "This is so you can see where you're going anywhere down in the mine. The grease in the lamp that I just lit is called 'sunshine.' All the miners wear them so they will have light to work by when they leave the torchlit main passageways and can see to make their way in the darkness of the narrow tunnels."

Dr. Dane grinned as Kirby placed the helmet on his head. "Well, I'm glad somebody invented that 'sunshine' stuff."

Kirby chuckled as he picked up the other helmet and lit the lamp. "Me, too. Sure makes things a lot easier down there in all that darkness."

As Kirby placed the lamp on his own head, Dr. Dane said, "I just went by the Frye home. Ben is doing quite well."

The mine owner smiled. "You did a good job on Ben, Doctor. He's the best foreman I've ever had. Well, let's go."

They stepped outside and Kirby Holton led the doctor down toward two large open shafts.

"See those shafts in the ground, Doctor?"

"Mm-hmm."

"They are operated with cages. You will notice that only one cage is visible at the top of a shaft at this moment."

"I see it."

"The other one is down in the mine. Those two cages are on pulleys and are used to lower miners into the depths of the mine and raise them out, and to raise coal out of the mine in the small rail cars that are pulled through the mine tunnels by the mules that live and work down there. Up here on the surface, the coal is weighed, then placed in those large wagons over there."

"I see."

Kirby pointed to the two harnessed mules at each shaft. Each pair was hitched to a large horizontal wheel beside the shafts. "See how those mules are hitched to those big wheels?"

"Uh-huh."

At that instant, a mine worker stepped up to the pair of mules at the shaft where no cage was visible. He put the mules in motion, leading them by short lengths of rope.

Kirby went on. "The wheels control the cages' pulley ropes. As you can see, the mules walk in a circle, turning the wheels, lowering and raising the cages."

Dr. Dane nodded. "Well, those wheels are large enough to give plenty of leverage for the mules, I'll say that."

"Yes, sir." Kirby pointed to the large wagons close by. "Those wagons are used to carry the coal to our customers in other mountain towns, as well as carrying it all the way to Denver to be marketed to customers on that side of the Rockies. They also load coal into railroad cars and carry it to distributors north, south, east, and west in the country."

"Sounds like you've got the coal mining business working good for you, Kirby."

They were drawing up to the two shafts. Dr. Dane noticed small piles of shale and rock in the area.

The cage that had been down in the mine moments ago was coming up with a loaded coal car and four men. As the mine owner and his guest came to a halt, the car was rolled onto stationary ground tracks by the four men. Then Kirby Holton walked up to the man who was in charge of the mules and told him to lower Dr. Logan and himself down into the mine.

Kirby ushered his guest into the cage, and the mules were put in motion at the large wheel.

While they were being lowered slowly into the dark shaft, Dr. Dane said, "I've read a little about black lung disease. What percentage of your coal miners get it?"

"I can't really give you an accurate percentage, but many men come down with it after they've worked in the mine for a few years. Eight or nine years, I'd say. For others it takes maybe a dozen years or so. And still others never get it."

"Oh. Guess I haven't read enough on the subject. I thought all of them eventually get it if they stay at it very long."

As they dropped into the mine's depths and the darkness enveloped them, Dr. Dane was glad for the lamp on his helmet. The thought of being so deep in the earth sent a shudder through him. The damp chill in the air seemed to trickle into the marrow of his bones.

Soon they reached the bottom of the shaft. Dr. Dane noted the flaming kerosene torches that were fixed on the rough walls of the passageway where they stood.

"Well," said Holton, "we're now almost three hundred feet below the surface."

The thought of it brushed Dane like a cold finger, raising a chill on the surface of his skin.

Holton looked at his guest, noting his uneasiness. "Just so you'll know, Doctor, throughout the mine there are air shafts some twelve inches in diameter to let gases out and clean air in."

Dr. Dane nodded. "That's good to know."

Kirby then pointed to eight-by-ten-foot structures on each side of the two shafts. "Those are called 'powder houses.' They contain dynamite sticks, which as you probably know, are used in the mine to open up new tunnels. We also use it to blast away stubborn sections of coal from the walls of existing tunnels. All the loose coal is loaded into the small coal cars on the tracks that you see at your feet. These tracks are on the floor of every tunnel and passageway. My men also use picks to break loose coal that is embedded shallowly in the tunnel walls, which of course, have been opened with the dynamite."

Dr. Dane ran his gaze over the wooden structures. "Interesting."

Moving a few steps with his guest following, Kirby pointed to the other side of the passageway. "Over here, Doctor, you see feeding troughs and bins along the wall. As you can see, the bins are stuffed with hay bales. This hay feeds the mules I mentioned, that live down here and pull the coal cars. You will notice that next to the troughs are these open tanks of water. We keep our beasts of burden well supplied with water."

"I can see that they are well-fed and well-watered."

"Let's go on down the passageway."

As they moved slowly between the rugged stone walls, Kirby pointed upward. "See those twelve-by-twelve-inch wooden beams that rest on those vertical beams?"

Looking up, Dr. Dane nodded. "Uh-huh. They form a protective ceiling, don't they?"

"Yes. They are in every tunnel and passageway."

Soon they came to a pair of mules that were pulling a loaded coal car on the track in the center of the passageway.

Dr. Dane recognized the man driving the mules. He had treated Russ Mooney for a burned hand the first week he had owned the practice.

"Hello, Russ!"

Mooney smiled broadly. "Howdy, Doc!" He chuckled. "You lookin' for a job down here?"

Dr. Dane laughed. "Not exactly. I'm just taking the tour."

Mooney looked at Holton. "Well, give him a good one, boss!"

"He's doing that, all right," said Dr. Dane.

Mooney moved on.

Moments later, they left the wide, torchlit passageway, and Dr.

Dane found himself more than glad he was wearing the helmet with the sunshine lamp.

They visited miners who were busy chipping coal from the walls of the tunnels and filling coal cars to which mules were harnessed.

At one point, they came upon assistant foreman Art Berman, who was teaching a new young miner how to dig the coal from the walls. Kirby and Dr. Dane heard him giving the young man instructions on how to hold the pick he was using.

Art looked up and recognized his boss first.

"Howdy, Kirby. Who you got with—Well, I'll be! Howdy, Dr. Logan!"

Dr. Dane grinned. "Howdy, yourself, Art." A tiny light twinkled in his eyes. "This young man teaching you anything?"

The young miner chuckled. "I'm trying, sir, but he's so old, he's havin' a hard time getting it. Can't teach an old dog new tricks, you know!"

Art playfully cuffed the young miner on the chin. "Back to work, buster, or I'll cut your pay!"

Kirby and Dr. Dane were laughing together as they moved on.

They came to a spot where the tunnel was a bit narrow and the combination of walls and darkness seemed to envelope Kirby's guest.

Dr. Dane took a deep breath. "Whew!"

Kirby stopped and looked at him. "You all right?"

Dr. Dane took another deep breath. "Having a little claustrophobia."

"Oh. I had that problem the first time I went down into a mine. Lots of new miners have it, but in time, it goes away."

The tour was over after an hour and a half, and Dr. Dane was glad that he and the mine owner were riding upward in the cage where there was more air and lots of sunshine.

When they reached the top and the cage came to a halt, they

saw Greg Holton and three other miners climbing into the cage of the other shaft, about to descend into the mine.

Greg smiled at his father and the doctor. "Hi, Dad. So how'd it go, Doctor?"

"Well, I had a little touch of claustrophobia, but I made it through the tour all right."

"What do you think of the mine?"

Dr. Dane smiled. "It's awesome, Greg. Awesome."

The cage started down, and Greg gave his father and the doctor a wave.

Kirby climbed out of the cage with Dr. Dane right behind him. As they moved toward the office building, Dr. Dane said, "Thanks for the tour."

"You're welcome. I hope you enjoyed it."

"Oh, I did, even though I felt a little apprehension at times, being so far down into the mountain's bowels, but I really did enjoy it."

When Dr. Dane returned to his office, Dr. Fraser was alone. He was seated at the desk, making notes in a patient's file. He looked up with a smile. "Tharyn's in the back room, stocking the medicine cabinet. A new shipment just came in on the stagecoach from Denver. She should be just about finished."

Dr. Dane nodded. "Good."

Fraser rose from the desk, placed the file in the cabinet, then turned and cocked his head sideways. "So did you have a good time?"

At the same moment, Tharyn came into the office.

Dane smiled at her, then looked at the elderly doctor as he replied, "I had a very good time. That mine is awesome."

Fraser nodded. "I knew you'd enjoy it."

Moving up to him, Tharyn asked, "How about all that darkness? Did it get to you at all?"

"Well, I did experience some claustrophobia in those tunnels and passageways. Those rock walls seemed to be closing in on me at times. Add the darkness to that, and I did feel a little apprehension once in a while."

"I thought you might. I'm told that most new miners experience that kind of thing for a while." She reached down and picked up a yellow envelope off the desk. "Charlie Holmes delivered this about an hour ago. He said it's from Dr. Carroll."

"Okay." Taking the envelope in hand, Dr. Dane opened it, took out the telegram, and read it while Tharyn and Dr. Fraser looked on. He set his gaze on Tharyn. "Dr. Carroll wanted to let me know that Nelda is doing well, but he asked us to pray for Dr. Tim Braden. He says Tim is having a very difficult time over Melinda's death."

"Bless his heart," said Tharyn, her eyes growing misty.

"Esther and I will pray for him," said Dr. Fraser. "Well, I guess I'd better go home. See you later."

When Dr. Fraser was gone, Dane said, "Honey, I'll go over to the telegraph office and send two telegrams; one to Dr. Carroll and the other to Tim. I'll tell Dr. Carroll that I will have Pastor Shane tell the church about Melinda's death and ask everyone to pray for their brother in Christ, Dr. Tim Braden. In my wire to Tim, I'll tell him that you and I are holding him up in prayer."

Tharyn sniffed and wiped the mist from her eyes. "All right, darling. If anyone comes in needing you, I'll tell them you'll be back shortly."

Nearly a half hour had passed when Dr. Dane returned to his office. When he stepped in, there were no patients in the waiting area, and Tharyn was not at her desk.

He moved across the office, opened the door to the back

room, and saw Tharyn standing by the medicine cabinet, her head bent low. She was weeping.

She looked up through her tears as he headed toward her and wept harder.

Dane folded her in his arms. "Honey, what's wrong?"

Tharyn clung to him and laid her head against his chest. She sobbed hard for a moment, then took a deep breath and sniffed. "Like Tim, I'm having a hard time over Melinda's death. I'm not questioning the Lord, darling. I know He has a plan for all of His children, but some things are just hard to understand."

She had a hankie in her hand. She used it to wipe tears from her eyes and sniffed again. Her head was still laid against his chest.

Dane's chin was resting on top of her head. His strong arms held her tight. "I know, love. But we don't have to understand God's reasoning. We only need to accept His will, and to remember that in all things, He is sovereign. Let me show you a couple of verses that have meant a lot to me. I'm sure they will help you."

A Bible lay on a small table nearby. Dane let go of her, stepped to the table, and picked up the Bible. She stepped up close as he flipped pages.

"Here, honey. This one's in Nahum 1:7. 'The LORD is good, a strong hold in the day of trouble; and he knoweth them that trust in him.'"

Tharyn wiped more tears and looked up at him. "That's good, honey. Really good."

Dane flipped back to the Psalms. "Here's another one that has meant so much to me. Psalm 61:2. 'From the end of the earth will I cry unto thee, when my heart is overwhelmed: lead me to the rock that is higher than I.' Claim it as your own, sweetheart. Jesus is the Rock. Take this burden over Melinda's death to Him. He alone will sustain you as no one else can."

Tharyn wiped away more tears and looked at the verse as Dane held the Bible in his hands. She read it silently, then looked up at him again. "Thank you, darling. What a beautiful verse. My heart is indeed overwhelmed. I surely will let the Rock that is higher than I comfort me and give me peace."

She rose up on her tiptoes and kissed him tenderly. "Thank you. Both verses have already given me a measure of peace and strength."

TWENTY-TWO

*O*n Sunday morning Greg Holton felt he had never been happier as he guided the buggy off of Main Street and headed for the street where the Downing house was located. The sun was shining brightly in a clear blue sky, and he was excited about the picnic he and Cassandra had planned in the mountains.

Greg was so in love with the beautiful brunette, he could hardly think of anything else but the upcoming day in November when the two of them would stand before the Gilpin County judge and take their marriage vows.

As he turned the corner onto the street where the Downing house stood, he caught sight of Cassandra standing on the front porch, holding the picnic basket. She saw him coming and waved to him. The sight of her fanned the flame in his heart.

He waved back and put the horse to a faster trot. When he pulled up into the yard, his pulse quickened. She was in a blue and yellow dress and had a matching ribbon in her long, black hair. He loved the smoothness of her skin and the way she carried herself. To him, what he saw in her eyes was a knowledge of what life was all about. He felt it in her, and as he hopped out of the buggy while she was coming down the porch steps with the picnic basket in her hand, that profound knowledge was a quality that came across the space between them and touched him.

Smiling, Cassandra drew up to him. "Good morning, my darling. I'm so excited about our having this day together."

"Me, too," he said, taking the basket from her.

She lifted her lips up to him. He looked around to see if anyone in the area was watching them.

She giggled. "Don't worry about the neighbors. You can kiss me. We're engaged. Aunt Mabel has already gone to church. And even if she was still here, you could still kiss me."

Greg kissed her tenderly, then put his arm around her and guided her to the buggy. He placed the picnic basket on the floor behind the front seat, then helped her in. Quickly, he rounded the buggy, climbed in, and sat down beside her. Taking the reins in hand, he put the horse in motion.

Moments later, they turned onto Main Street and headed out of town. Soon they were driving past the church. The windows were open, and they could hear the people singing inside.

Cassandra made a snorting sound and sneered as she looked at the steepled building with the cross on top. "What a waste of time—going to church and singing hymns."

Greg shrugged. "Oh, I don't know. I've thought of visiting a service sometime, just to see what it's like. Pastor Shane has visited Dad and me at our house a few times and showed us things from the Bible that make good sense."

The muscles of Cassandra's face tightened at such words, and she felt a hot ball form in her stomach. She told herself she must keep Greg from ever getting interested in church and all that went with it.

She was glad she had already convinced him that when they got married, it would be before the county judge. She didn't want to get married in a church building before some fanatical Bible preacher.

On Monday morning, Deputy Marshal Len Kurtz was standing on the boardwalk in front of the marshal's office just as the sun was rising over the eastern peaks. Marshal Jake Merrell handed his deputy a white envelope. "You know where the Jamison ranch is, don't you?"

Len nodded. "Mm-hmm. 'Bout five miles southwest of the Holton Mine. Big red barn with white trim, just like the ranch house."

Jake grinned. "That's the place. Since Fred Jamison was a witness to that drunken brawl at the saloon on Saturday when that drifter got himself killed, Judge Cook wants him to get this court summons this morning. I figure by sending you right now, you'll catch him at home, probably doing his chores."

Sticking the envelope in his vest pocket, Len said, "I'll see that he gets it right away, Marshal." With that, he stepped off the boardwalk, mounted his horse, and rode away at a gallop.

Some ten minutes later, Kurtz slowed his horse as he drew near the Holton Coal Mine. The tall rock formations to the rear of the mine were rosy in the golden sunlight. He saw a large group of miners gathered at the two large shafts where the cages glistened in the early sunlight. Kirby Holton was addressing his men, apparently giving them instructions.

Greg Holton was in the group and happened to look toward the road and see the deputy riding by. Kirby had just finished his instructions, and Greg waved and called out, "Hey, Len! Where you going?"

Kurtz told himself he could spare a few minutes to talk to Greg. As he trotted his horse toward Greg, some of the miners climbed in the cages. The mules at the large wheels were put in motion, and the cages began to descend into the shafts while the other miners waited for them to return.

Greg stepped up to Len as he dismounted. "The lawman business starts early, I see. On your way to arrest somebody?"

Len shook his head. "No. Not today, anyway. I just have a court summons to deliver to a rancher who witnessed that brawl at the saloon on Saturday when that drifter got killed."

"Oh. Well, I won't keep you. Just wanted to say hi."

"'Preciate that. So you got a hard day's work ahead of you?"

"You might say that, Len. I'll be working with a small group of men, drilling holes in the walls of a tunnel so we can place dynamite sticks in them in preparation to blast more coal out of the walls."

"I see. We'll be hearing some more of those muffled explosions then, won't we?"

"Sure will."

Len ran his gaze over the miners who were waiting for the cages to return so they could go down into the mine. "I think you've hired more miners in the past few weeks, haven't you? I see faces in that group I've never seen before."

"We've been hiring new men now for about a month."

"So how many men do you have working for you?"

"Exactly two hundred and fifty."

Len started to comment, but was interrupted as Kirby Holton stepped up, spoke to him in a friendly manner, then said to his son, "Greg, I'll be in my office if you need to talk to me before you go down."

Greg smiled. "Don't think I need to, Dad. I'll see you when we come up for lunch."

Kirby walked away, and the deputy said, "Well, Greg, I'd better go get this summons delivered. See you later." As he mounted, he grinned at Greg. "Oh yes. And congratulations. I hear you're now engaged to that gorgeous brunette."

"Sure am. And thanks. See you later, Len."

The deputy trotted away, and Greg headed for the closest shaft where the cage was just surfacing. He joined some sixteen men who were going down in the cage.

When they reached the bottom, most of the group in the cage headed their respective directions to carry on their routine work. With Greg in the lead, he and six other men in his group moved down the tunnel to the powder houses by the light of carbide lamps that hung along the walls. There they picked up a full box of dynamite sticks, placed it on a small cart along with an unlit kerosene torch affixed to a wrought-iron stand, and with one man pushing the cart, made their way deep into the tunnel where they would set up the dynamite for blasting. The carbide lamps created spooky illuminated pockets in the enveloping darkness.

Each man was carrying a heavy hammer and a steel rod with a sharp point that he would use to drill holes in the walls of the tunnel in which to insert the dynamite sticks.

While they were making their way down the main passageway toward the tunnel where they would work, two of the men began arguing with each other. Greg looked back to see that it was Wayne Lewis and Earl Selby, who he thought were good friends. Facing forward once again, he kept up the pace he had begun. Lewis and Selby kept snapping at each other, and Greg soon picked up that Lewis had loaned Selby some money a few weeks ago, and because Selby had not paid him back as promised, Lewis was calling him some bad names.

One of the other men spoke up and told them to stop their arguing.

Lewis rasped, "Mind your own business!"

In the lead, Greg felt irritation rise in his blood.

The group turned into their dark tunnel. Their helmet lamps cast a tiny trembling glow, throwing scant light and wavering shadows in their path as Lewis lit into Selby once more. Selby bit back at him angrily.

Greg's irritation peaked at that moment. He stopped. "All

right, you two. That's enough! No more arguing! Earl, if you owe Wayne money and are late paying him back, you need to meet your obligation."

Selby's glance swiveled from Greg to Lewis, then back to Greg. "There wasn't any time set for when I was to pay him back."

Wayne Lewis bristled. "You rotten liar! You agreed to pay me back when you got your next paycheck! That was three weeks ago! I want my money!"

Greg stepped between them and ran his gaze back and forth. "No more! You two settle this some other time and some other place. Now let's get to work!"

The other men were staring icily at the two combatants as they followed Greg deeper into the tunnel. Lewis and Selby gave each other angry glares, then followed. Some five minutes later, Greg stopped the group and ordered the man who was pushing the cart to place it at a certain spot next to the tunnel wall on the right side.

The men had helmet lamps, but also appreciated the kerosene torch when Greg took it from the cart in its wrought-iron stand, and moved along the same wall a few steps, struck a match, and lit it.

Under Greg's directions the men went to work, using their hammers and sharp-pointed steel rods to drill holes in the walls of the tunnel. However, Wayne Lewis and Earl Selby were still arguing as they worked side by side.

Greg was considering taking both of them to the office and telling his father about their dispute when suddenly Lewis punched Selby hard, causing him to stumble backward into the wrought-iron stand that held the flaming kerosene torch. The impact flipped the torch loose. It sailed through the air and landed in the box of dynamite sticks that sat on the cart.

Instantly, the fuses on the sticks caught fire and began to hiss.

Greg stared at the hissing fuses. "Run, men! Run!"

Deputy Marshal Len Kurtz was heading back toward town from the Fred Jamison ranch at a mild gallop. Just as he was passing the Holton Coal Mine, his horse did a quick jump and almost dislodged him from the saddle as a deafening roar came from inside the mine. As Len was working to gain control of his horse, he saw smoke and flames spew from three of the twelve-inch air shafts like a volcanic eruption.

In Central City, people heard the thunderous explosion coming from the direction of the mine. They were used to small explosions periodically when a few dynamite sticks were set off to loosen more coal in the tunnels, but this was a much larger explosion than they had ever heard before.

At his office, Dr. Dane Logan was at the medicine cabinet in the back room when he heard the loud rumble. He dashed into the office to find Tharyn standing wide-eyed at the open door. Shouts could be heard on the street as she cried, "Oh, Dane! It must be the mine!"

Just as the Logans rushed out onto the boardwalk, they saw Deputy Len Kurtz galloping down the street, angling toward them. He skidded the horse to a halt. "Dr. Logan! It's the mine! There was a horrible explosion up there! They'll need you, for sure!"

"I'm going right now," said the doctor. He dashed back into the office, grabbed his medical bag, and as he rushed to his buggy, he told Thayrn he would be back as soon as possible. He jumped into the buggy and put Pal to a gallop. Frightened people were hurrying toward the mine on the street as he raced past them.

Moments later, when he arrived at the mine, Dr. Dane saw black smoke rising from some of the air shafts on the side of the mountain and tiny tendrils of smoke rising from the large shafts that held the cages.

Kirby Holton was at the cage shafts with his assistant foreman, Art Berman, talking to a small group of half-crazed miners who had just surfaced. The larger crowd of miners had already surfaced and stood around in a half circle, looking on.

Shock showed in Kirby's eyes and his face was covered with a cold sheen of sweat when he noticed Dr. Dane halting the buggy a few feet away.

Dr. Dane bounded out of the buggy and ran to Kirby, who seemed frozen in his tracks. Kirby stammered, "Dr. Logan! Th-these men just surfaced. Th-they were in the area of the explosion and told me that the explosion was in the t-tunnel where Greg and s-six other men were working! Some of them are buried under rock and coal, and are no doubt dead. The others, including Greg, are partially b-buried beneath the huge support timbers that have collapsed, as well as rock and coal. When these men last saw Greg and the others, s-some were still alive, including Greg."

Dr. Dane frowned. "Nobody stayed with them? Nobody's trying to get them out?"

While Kirby was trying to find his voice again, Art Berman spoke for him. "Doctor, we have a rule here, as do all mines. When there is an explosion or a cave-in, every man is to get out as fast as possible. You never know when more of the mine will cave in."

Dr. Dane took a deep breath. "Those who are buried beneath the timbers and still alive will need my help. I'll need somebody to take me down there."

One of the men in the group that had just surfaced stepped up and said, "Dr. Logan, you can't go down there. It's too dangerous. That section of the mine could totally collapse at any moment. We were working in that same general area. That's why we caught sight of them as we were trying to get out. It would be insane to go down there!"

Dr. Dane turned to the white-faced Kirby Holton. "I want

your permission to go down there. If I can save lives, I must go."

Kirby shook his head. "Hal is right, Doctor. It could collapse any minute."

Dr. Dane gripped Kirby's upper arm. "But it might *not* collapse, right?"

Kirby scrubbed a shaky hand over his eyes. "There is no way to know for sure."

"I must go to those men who are still alive, and I'm going to need men to help get them out if I can save their lives. One of them is Greg, remember?"

"Yes. I sure do," Kirby replied. "I'll take you down there myself. I know where Greg and the others were working. Let's not endanger any more men at the moment. I *do* want to be with my son." He turned to his assistant foreman. "Art, if any of them are still alive, I'll send Dr. Logan back up to ask for volunteers to go down and help get them out."

Art nodded. "All right, boss. And I will definitely be one of those volunteers."

Kirby patted his shoulder in appreciation, then turned and said, "Let's go, Doctor."

Kirby Holton carried a lighted lantern as he and Dr. Dane were lowered in a cage. By then there was not enough smoke to bother them. When they touched bottom, Kirby led the way. Soon they reached the spot of the explosion. By the light of Kirby's lantern, Dr. Dane hurriedly checked on Greg with Kirby at his side. They found Greg alive and conscious, though he was in extreme pain. The large beam that had collapsed on him had severely crushed his chest and there was a lot of coal and rock piled on his lower body.

Greg's eyes were clear and he was alert.

Kirby set his lantern down, laid a hand on Greg's cheek, and looked at the doctor. "What do you think?"

Dr. Dane's face was grim. "He's critical. I'll be back to him after I check on the other men. You stay with him."

Kirby squared his jaw and nodded.

Dr. Dane hurried to the other six men who lay in the shadows cast by Kirby's lantern. They were partially buried by the large wooden beams, rock, and coal.

Kirby was talking to his son, trying to encourage him, and every few seconds, he cast a glance toward the shadows where the doctor was moving from man to man.

In less than two minutes, Dr. Dane returned to Kirby and Greg, his face drawn and somber. "They're all dead, Kirby. It's better that I stay with Greg while you go bring some volunteers to get this beam off him."

Kirby could feel something cold surging up in him like a giant ocean wave. Suddenly it stuck between his stomach and his throat. He shook his head intently. "No! I can't leave him! You said he's critical. What if—"

"I understand how you feel, but I'm the doctor here, Kirby. I need to stay with him."

Kirby wiped a palm over his face and sighed. "Of course. I'll go after help." He patted Greg's cheek. "I'll be back as soon as I can, son."

Greg licked his lips and nodded. "Okay, Dad," he said weakly.

When Kirby was gone, Dr. Dane pulled the lantern closer and examined Greg more thoroughly. His chest was crushed even worse than he had thought. He was amazed that Greg's heart was still beating. Dr. Dane felt sick all over.

He opened his medical bag and took out a bottle of clear liquid. "Greg, I know you're hurting bad. I'll give you a dose of laudanum to ease your pain."

When the doctor had administered the laudanum and was putting the bottle back in the medical bag, Greg looked up at him gravely. "I'm going to die, aren't I, Dr. Logan?"

Dr. Dane swallowed hard. "I can't lie to you, Greg. It is quite likely. I want to talk to you about your need to be saved. Listen closely now, and—"

"Doctor, I'm afraid to die. I do want to be saved. Pastor Mark Shane visited our home a few times and showed Dad and me from the Bible about heaven and hell. Please help me."

Glad to know the seed of the Word had been sown in Greg's heart, Dr. Dane quoted several salvation verses to him, asking if he understood them.

Greg grimaced from the pain the weight of the huge beam was putting on his chest, sucked in a shallow breath, and said, "Yes, sir. I understand. I want to ask Jesus to save me."

Dr. Dane led the dying young man in his prayer to the Lord, and after Greg had prayed, he looked up at the doctor, gasped, and said, "Th-thank you. I—I—"

"Yes, Greg?"

Greg Holton breathed out his last breath. His eyes closed and his head went limp.

Dr. Dane took a shuddering breath and looked at the dead young man by the light of the lantern. His face had become a soft mask, unblemished, and colorless. There was a slight smile on his lips.

The doctor whispered, "Thank You, Lord, that You let me get to him before he died. He's with You now."

At that moment, he heard the volunteers coming and saw light from their lanterns in the tunnel. When they drew up, there were eight of them—including Kirby Holton and Art Berman, who led the others. Dr. Dane also recognized Willie Dunbar among them, who was a member of the church.

Kirby stood over him, looking down at Greg, his face whitening.

Dr. Dane rose to his feet and said solemnly, "He's dead, Kirby. There was nothing I could do for him. That beam had done more damage than I realized."

Kirby felt as if his stomach were pulled hard against his backbone. He worked his jaw as his face screwed up, but no words would come. Suddenly he burst into heartrending sobs. His knees buckled, and Art grasped him to keep him from falling. Talking to Kirby softly, Art guided him a few steps away from where Greg's body lay and helped him to sit down on the floor of the tunnel, placing his back against the wall.

Kirby continued to sob.

Dr. Dane turned and looked at the other men. "Let's get this beam off Greg's body and those other bodies over there. I'll help you."

Just then there was a loud rumble, accompanied by the walls and floor of the tunnel trembling. Terror showed in their eyes as they started to turn with escape in mind. Suddenly the tunnel collapsed with a thundering roar in the direction from which the men had just come.

When the roaring and trembling of the tunnel walls and floor stopped, most of the lanterns were still burning. Kirby was groping against the wall, trying to get to his feet. Art was helping him.

One of the men wailed, "We're tra-a-apped!"

Kirby staggered to the forefront and stood trembling, with his legs bent. "With this many of us breathing in this small space, we'll run out of oxygen in a hurry. We're—we're doomed."

Dr. Dane knew Kirby was right. His thoughts ran to Tharyn and the life they had thought they would have together. He prayed in his heart, asking the Lord to take care of her, then stepped up beside Kirby. "Men, we haven't much time. I want to talk to you about going into eternity. Willie knows what I mean. Listen to me. I—"

"Look!" cried one of the miners, pointing at the remaining lanterns that were burning. Their flames were flickering weakly, obviously about to go out. "The oxygen is about gone!"

The men began gasping and choking, trying to breathe.

Dr. Dane said, "Let's all lie down on the floor, right now! We'll be able to get air a little longer down there!"

The lanterns were going out one by one as the men were dropping to the floor, mustering every ounce of energy to fight off the viselike suffocation and overwhelming weakness caused by the lack of oxygen.

Suddenly, above the sounds of their gasps and moans, they heard the sounds of picks striking dirt, coal, and rocks in the direction of the main passageway. The last lantern flickered out just as a muffled voice cried, "Hey! Anybody alive in there? We're here to dig you out!"

All of them began shouting back, letting their would-be rescuers know that they were still alive.

Kirby Holton sucked in a breath. "There's hope here, men. Apparently there's not that much rubble between us and them. Stay low and try using as little air as possible when you breathe. It will still take some time to get us out of here."

In front of the mine office and around the cage shafts, most of Central City's citizens were gathered.

Women wept and wailed. Terrified children cried, clinging to their mothers' skirts, and wanting to know if their fathers would be rescued from where they were trapped below.

Cassandra Wheatley and her Aunt Mabel were at the forefront of the crowd, near the cage shafts. A horrified Tharyn Logan was standing near them with Pastor Mark and Peggy Shane beside her.

The people had been told that there were volunteers down in the mine who had gone down to attempt rescuing the men trapped in the last collapse of the tunnel where the dynamite had exploded. They had also been told that Dr. Dane Logan was among those who were trapped. No announcement had been made naming any men who were known to be dead.

Pastor Mark and Peggy flanked Tharyn.

Soon, Art Berman was brought up in a cage. People began shouting, asking about their loved ones. Art raised his hands to quiet them. "Mr. Holton sent me up to tell you that all of the men who went down to help rescue those men trapped in the tunnel where the dynamite exploded are all right. As the owner of the mine, he will be up soon to give you word about the others."

Moans and cries swept across the crowd.

Cassandra Wheatley left her aunt's side and ran up to Berman. Her voice showed the horror she felt. "Mr. Berman, I have to know! Is Greg alive?"

Everyone in the crowd watched and listened.

Art said, "Little lady, Mr. Holton wants to be the one to tell everybody here who is dead and who is alive."

Cassandra grasped his shirt and shook him. "I want to know right now if Greg is alive!"

Art's features sagged. "All right. I may get into trouble with the boss for this, but I'll tell you. Dr. Logan went down with us to try to save the lives of as many men as possible, but he couldn't save Greg."

Horror settled over Cassandra like a dark veil. Her flesh went cold. She felt as though her body had turned to stone. With a strangled cry, she pivoted and ran back to her aunt, screaming, "He's dead, Aunt Mabel! Greg's dead!"

Mabel gathered Cassandra in her arms as the girl broke down and sobbed.

Art Berman climbed back into the cage and told the man who led the mules at the wheel to lower him back down into the mine.

Tharyn wanted to cry out and ask Berman if Dr. Dane was still alive, but refrained. Other wives wanted to know about their husbands, too. Like them, she would have to wait.

At this point, Pastor Mark Shane stepped away from the crowd to an open spot, then turned to face them. Peggy and

Tharyn, holding hands, joined him.

Above the moans and cries in the crowd, the pastor said, "I want all the members of our church who are here, and anyone else who wants to join with us, to gather around for prayer."

Most of the citizens—men, women, and children—began gathering around Pastor Shane, his wife, and Tharyn Logan.

At the spot where Mabel Downing stood with her arms around her niece, she eased back so she could look into Cassandra's tear-filled eyes. "I'm going to join them. Will you come with me?"

Cassandra shook her head and wiped tears from her cheeks. "There's no sense praying to a God who doesn't exist. But if you want to, go ahead."

Mabel sighed, let go of Cassandra, and headed for the crowd that was gathering before the pastor, Peggy, and Tharyn.

Pastor Shane called for everyone to bow their heads and prayed for those who were still alive down in the mine to be brought out safely. He also prayed for strength and comfort for those in the crowd who would soon learn that their loved ones had not survived the disaster.

Many tears were shed as he was praying.

Cassandra stood with eyes open and looked at the crowd with disdain, her eyes filled with contempt.

TWENTY-THREE

*S*hortly after the time of prayer, the men who handled the mules at the cage shafts heard voices down below, calling for the cages to be lifted.

The crowd gathered close and waited breathlessly to see who was still alive.

The Shanes stayed with Tharyn Logan, wanting to be close so they could help her if it turned out that Dr. Dane had been killed.

When the cages reached the top, all three spotted Dr. Dane at the same time, and the Shanes let her run ahead of them so she could reach her husband first. Dr. Dane stepped out of the cage, saw her coming, and hurried to meet her.

Bursting into tears as she dashed into his arms, Tharyn sobbed, "Oh, darling, I'm so glad you're alive! Thank You, Lord! Thank You!"

Other family members were hurrying to those men who were getting out of the cages, while others, who did not see their loved ones, began weeping.

Kirby Holton was answering questions being put to him by people whose loved ones had not been in the cages. He was telling them how sorry he was that their sons, husbands, and fathers had been killed in the mine disaster, adding that his own son had been killed.

Cassandra Wheatley dashed up to Dr. Dane, weeping. "What happened? Why couldn't you save Greg?"

Dr. Dane swallowed hard. "Cassandra, Greg's chest was crushed by the heavy beam that fell on him when the dynamite exploded. There was nothing I could do to keep him from dying."

Cassandra ejected a heavy sob, wheeled and ran away.

Mabel followed her, asking God to give her wisdom in dealing with her niece.

At that moment, Kirby Holton—having talked with each family who had lost a loved one in the disaster—stepped up beside Dr. Dane, laid a hand on his shoulder, and ran his gaze over the teary-eyed crowd. "Folks, I want all of you to know that Dr. Logan came to me and volunteered to go down into the mine. He knew the danger he would face, but he was willing to risk his own life in order to save any lives that he could."

Though broken-hearted over the disaster, everyone in the crowd applauded the young physician.

During the next few days, the bodies of all the miners who had been killed in the explosion were found and brought up. Funerals were held for each one.

Though short-handed due to the loss of those men, Kirby Holton paid his miners extra to work overtime each day, and soon had the mine producing coal on a regular basis once again. Though there was a huge hole in Kirby's heart over the loss of his son, he knew that so many of Central City's citizens depended heavily on the work at the mine. Laying his own sorrow aside, he concentrated on keeping the mine in full operation.

During that week, Pastor Mark Shane and Dr. Dane Logan

went to the Holton mansion and talked with Kirby about salvation, making it clear that Greg had become a child of God just before he died and was now in heaven. Kirby told them he wanted to see his son again in eternity, but that he didn't want to make this momentous decision while in such a state of grief. They could understand that to press him further would turn him completely the other way, so they backed off.

On Sunday morning, Mabel Downing was in her kitchen preparing breakfast for Cassandra and herself, expecting the girl to appear at any moment. When breakfast was ready and Cassandra still had not shown up, Mabel went upstairs to her niece's room and tapped on the door.

There was a five-second delay, then Mabel heard: "Yes, Aunt Mabel?"

Mabel opened the door and saw her niece still in the bed. "Breakfast is ready, honey. I thought you'd be up by now."

Tears misted the girl's eyes. "I don't feel like getting up. Greg is gone. My life is so empty."

Mabel moved in, sat down on the side of the bed, and took Cassandra's hand in her own. "I'm sorry for what has happened, dear, but may I remind you that Dr. Logan came here to see us last Monday night and told us he had been able to lead Greg to the Lord down in the mine just before he died. Greg is in heaven now. That should give you some measure of comfort."

Cassandra clamped her mouth shut and made her lips a thin line.

Mabel was unaware that her niece's grief was not in the loss of Greg, but in the loss of the wealth she would have gained as Greg's wife.

Cassandra opened her mouth and said, "I don't want to get up yet."

Mabel squeezed her hand. "Honey, I want you to get up, eat breakfast with me, and go to church with me."

Cassandra jutted her jaw and shook her head. "I don't want to go to church. Even if there was a God, like you claim, why would He be so cruel? Why would He take Greg from me?"

"Honey, I—"

"There is no God, Aunt Mabel! I'm sure there isn't! Please leave me alone!"

Mabel let go of her hand and headed for the door. Her voice cracked as she paused, looked over her shoulder, and said, "I'll see you when I get back from church."

Cassandra lay in the bed, thinking about her loss. She had come so close to being wealthy. Now the opportunity was gone.

She contemplated her situation. She had to do something. Living with her fanatical aunt was becoming more difficult every day. Suddenly an idea came to her. Maybe the opportunity wasn't gone, after all. Kirby Holton had to be grieving heavily over Greg's death. His heart was tender. Now was the time to go to him and ask him to set her up financially as if she had been married to his son when he was killed.

After all, they *were* engaged. Maybe, just maybe, he would feel sorry for her as if she were his widowed daughter-in-law.

Cassandra hopped out of bed. She would go to the Holton mansion and talk to Kirby this morning.

It was just after ten o'clock when Cassandra knocked on the front door of the Holton mansion. When Kirby opened the door, she was surprised. His features were drawn and weary-looking. It was obvious that he was still shaken by Greg's death.

"H-hello, Cassandra."

"Good morning, Dad—uh, I mean, Mr. Holton. Excuse me. I—ah—had already thought of you as my father-in-law."

He formed a thin smile. "Nothing to be excused for. What can I do for you?"

"I—ah, I need to talk to you about something very important."

"Of course. Please come in."

As Cassandra stepped inside, she looked around. "I expected Edith Linden to answer my knock."

"Well, I gave Edith the day off. Some friends of hers from Georgetown picked her up a few minutes ago. She's spending the day with them."

"Oh. I see."

Kirby guided Cassandra down the hall to the library, where the two of them sat down on overstuffed chairs.

"Now," he said, widening his smile. "What was it you wanted to talk to me about?"

Cassandra presented her request as planned.

Her hopes were dashed when Kirby ran his fingers through his hair and said, "Cassandra, I don't mean to be unkind, but since you and Greg were not actually married, I am not obligated to treat you as an heir. There is nothing further to discuss on this matter."

Cassandra slid hopelessly into panic. All the blood seeped out of her face, leaving a colorless mask. Inside a fiery rage was welling up. Though her anger was just below skin level, ready to explode, she turned on the tears, "Please, Mr. Holton! I'm desperate! I need to get away from my aunt, who is a religious fanatic. She makes my life miserable, and I'm living in near poverty." She let her tears stream down her cheeks. "Please! Please help me!"

Kirby shook his head. "I'm sorry about your misery, Cassandra, but I have no obligation to you. Like I said, there's nothing further to discuss on this matter."

With that, Kirby rose from his chair. Cassandra stood up, wiped tears, and nodded. She wanted to claw his eyes out, but walked silently beside him as he accompanied her to the front door.

As she was walking home, the anger inside her turned to wrath. The farther she walked, the hotter her wrath became. Shaking her fists, she said with a throbbing passion, "I'll get even with you, Mr. Kirby Holton! You're gonna be sorry for this!"

When Mabel Downing arrived home from church and there was no sign of her niece on the first floor, she went upstairs and knocked on Cassandra's door.

A pitiful, shaky voice called, "Come in."

Mabel opened the door and stepped in. She was shocked when she saw Cassandra lying facedown on her bed with her bare back exposed. The girl's white flesh was crisscrossed with glaring reddish purple welts from her shoulders all the way down to her waist.

Mabel gasped and dashed to her. "Cassandra! What happened to you?"

Without moving, Cassandra looked up at her aunt, tears flowing. "Auntie Mabel, I've been needing money of my own. I felt guilty with you spending your money to feed me and keep me in your home, so I went to see Kirby Holton. I thought that because I was engaged to marry Greg, he might treat me as if I was Greg's widow and share some of the Holton money with me."

Mabel looked down at her welts. "He did this to you?"

Cassandra swallowed hard and squeaked, "Yes." She drew a shuddering breath. "When I presented my case to him in his library, he became angry and told me that I wasn't getting a penny from him. I—I began to cry and begged him for just a little money. This infuriated him. His face was beet red when he ordered me to get out of his house. This frightened me, Auntie Mabel."

Mabel's body was trembling as she wrung her hands.

Cassandra went on. "I was so scared, Auntie Mabel. When I started to leave, my knees gave way, and I fell. He stood over me like a madman, screaming at me to get up and get out. Afraid he was going to hurt me, I cried out for help to his housekeeper, Edith Linden. By this time, Kirby was breathing heavily. He laughed and told me Edith wasn't home.

"I was trying to get up when he went absolutely insane, Auntie Mabel! He took off his belt and pushed me flat on the floor, face-down. He lashed me repeatedly with the belt across my back, calling me a greedy money monger! Still acting like a madman, he began pacing the floor, muttering to himself. While he was doing this, I managed to get to my feet and run out of the house."

Mabel was stunned. "I—I can't even imagine what you were going through, Cassandra."

Pointing to her blouse on a nearby chair, Cassandra said, "Take a look at that."

Mabel saw that the back of the blouse was in shreds. She picked it up, looked at it, then set her eyes on the girl. "Oh, honey, if it weren't for this blouse, the belt would have cut your skin. You would be bleeding profusely. I'm going to Marshal Jake Merrell and have him arrest that beast! Then I'll go to Dr. Logan's house and bring him here so he can treat those horrible welts."

Mabel dropped the blouse back on the chair and dashed out of the room.

When Cassandra heard the front door slam downstairs, she smiled to herself. She would stay on the bed just as she was so when the doctor came, he would get the impact of seeing the horrible welts when Aunt Mabel brought him into the room.

Less than an hour had passed when Mabel returned with Dr. Dane Logan at her side, medical bag in hand. When he saw the welts he frowned. "My, oh my, girl." He turned to Mabel. "You described these stripes perfectly. I'll have to take a close look."

While the doctor was examining the crisscrossed wales on Cassandra's back, Mabel said, "Honey, I went to Marshal Merrell first. He's on his way to talk to Kirby Holton."

Cassandra nodded.

Mabel then picked up the blouse from the chair and dangled it in front of the doctor. "Take a look at this."

Dr. Dane glanced up momentarily, ran his gaze over the shredded blouse, then went back to his examination. A minute later, he stared at the welts and rubbed his chin as if perplexed.

Mabel's brow furrowed. "What's wrong, Doctor?"

"I'm thinking about treatment. I have some salve at the office that should go on these stripes. I won't be long. I know Cassandra can't lie on her back, but I suggest that you cover her back with a clean sheet while I'm gone."

Cassandra gave the doctor a wary glance as he left the room, carrying his medical bag. Mabel did not notice the look in her niece's eyes as she walked to the linen closet and took out a clean white sheet.

While Mabel was covering her, Cassandra said, "Auntie Mabel, I'm going to take that beast Kirby Holton to court and sue him for assault and battery."

"Well, we have a good attorney here in town, honey. His name is Lawrence Pettit. He has done legal work for me on a few occasions. With Dr. Logan's testimony in court of what that vile brute did to you, and Mr. Pettit presenting your case, the judge will no doubt sentence him to prison for a long time."

Cassandra smiled, feeling a great sense of satisfaction. "Mm-hmm. And maybe the judge will give me a healthy settlement too."

Mabel did not comment. It bothered her that money was the most important thing in her niece's life. She was absolutely obsessed with being wealthy. Mabel drew a short breath. "You want something to eat?"

Cassandra shook her head. "No, thanks. I am thirsty, though. How about some water?"

Saying she would be right back, Mabel made her way down the hall. As she neared the staircase, she told herself it was no wonder that Cassandra's parents gave up on her. In her whole life she had never known anyone as greedy as Cassandra.

Moving down the stairs, Mabel said aloud, "That girl has such an evil spirit about her. Nothing I say seems to penetrate it. Lord, You know I want so desperately to lead her to You, but I'm not getting anywhere."

As she reached the bottom of the stairs and headed down the hall toward the kitchen, a heaviness seemed to press against her chest.

Moments later, Mabel entered Cassandra's room with a pitcher of water and a tablespoon. Since Cassandra had to lie on her stomach, Mabel used the tablespoon to drop the water in her mouth. When Cassandra had taken her fill of the water, she put her head down on the pillow and sighed. "Shouldn't Dr. Logan be back by now?"

"I'm sure he'll be here soon," said Mabel, setting the pitcher and spoon on the dresser. She then moved to a chair that stood close to the bed and sat down.

When another fifteen minutes had passed, Cassandra looked at her aunt. "What do you suppose is keeping him?"

Mabel was becoming concerned. "I don't know." She rose from the chair and walked to the window that overlooked the front yard.

While she peered through the window, Cassandra said, "Any sign of him?"

"No." With that, she turned from the window and began pacing the floor, wringing her hands.

Time seemed to drag.

When three hours had passed since the doctor had left,

Cassandra looked at her aunt, who was now back in the chair. "Auntie Mabel, I've had it with that doctor. I don't want him treating me. And I sure don't want him putting that salve on me that he supposedly went to get."

"But, honey, you need that salve."

"No. I'll be all right without it. Whenever he comes back, just tell him he is not needed."

At that moment, there was a knock at the front door downstairs. Mabel stood up and sighed. "That has to be the doctor. I want him to put that salve on you. I'll bring him right up."

As soon as her aunt left the room, Cassandra threw the sheet back and jumped off the bed. Her breath was tight in her lungs, and she was down to the bone in panic. Still having her skirt on, she quickly put on another blouse, slipped into her shoes, and hurried to a window that overlooked the yard at the side of the house.

She opened the window as quietly as possible, climbed out, and began inching her way along a narrow ledge toward the rear of the house, where she planned to drop onto the back porch, then swing down onto the ground and run away where nobody would find her.

Downstairs, Mabel opened the front door to discover Dr. Dane Logan there with Marshal Jake Merrell. The doctor had his medical bag in hand.

When they stepped in at Mabel's invitation, the marshal said, "Mrs. Downing, I had a long talk with Kirby Holton. He acknowledged that Cassandra had come to his house asking for money, but he swears he did not touch her in any way, and that he absolutely did her no harm."

Dr. Dane spoke up. "Mabel, I believe Kirby. I am quite sure Cassandra inflicted those welts on herself."

Mabel's jaw dropped. Her body went rigid, and her eyes widened in shock. "*What?* Why do you believe him instead of my niece?"

"Let me explain. When I first laid eyes on those welts, I knew they were not like a belt laid to her back would leave if it had hit her hard enough to shred her blouse. There would definitely be blood flowing from the welts, and there would be blood on the blouse. The more I examined the welts, the more convinced I was that she had done this to herself."

Mabel shook her head in disbelief. "Doctor, I—I can't believe she would do that kind of damage to herself just to try to get even with Kirby Holton for not giving her any money!"

"Well, I'm quite sure she did. I used the salve I mentioned as a reason to leave the house and be gone for at least three hours. If somehow I'm wrong, I have the salve here in my bag. But I don't believe there will be any welts on her back at all by now."

"What? I looked at those welts and I felt of them! They are real!"

"I'll explain why I was gone for three hours in a moment, ma'am. But let me tell you first that during that time, I talked to Kirby in the marshal's presence. I'm telling you, he is innocent of these charges Cassandra is leveling at him."

Mabel was dumbfounded. Hardly able to breathe, she said, "Tell me why you were gone for those three hours."

"This is going to surprise you, Mrs. Downing," interjected the marshal.

Dr. Dane grinned at him, then said to Mabel, "I think Cassandra has a rare skin condition called in the medical world *dermatographia*. I explained it to Marshal Merrell on the way over here. A person with this condition can actually draw anything they want on their skin with the blunt end of a pencil or something like it. This will appear to be a reddish purple welt, but whatever is drawn on the skin will completely disappear within three to four hours. I first learned of this skin condition when a circus came to town when I was a boy, and they had a man in a sideshow who could draw on his arms with a small stick while people watched.

He would let them examine the welts to see that they were real, then challenge them to come back in three hours and look at them again. When the people came back, the welts had disappeared."

Mabel thought of how it had been three hours since the doctor had left and Cassandra didn't want him to see her again. Her mouth sagged open. "Let's go up to her room. I want to look at her back right now."

The two men mounted the stairs with Mabel, walked down the hall, and followed her as she entered Cassandra's room.

All three of them saw at once that Cassandra was not in the bed, but the side window was open, with the breeze flapping the lace curtains. They rushed to the window, and Marshal Merrell gasped as he pointed down at Cassandra, who was lying on the ground below, near the back side of the house.

"Oh no!" cried Mabel.

Dr. Dane whirled and ran toward the door, saying over his shoulder, "Help Mabel, Jake. I've got to get down there!"

Moments later, Jake Merrell and Mabel Downing came off the back porch and rushed around the corner of the house to the spot where Dr. Dane was kneeling beside Cassandra, who lay on her back, her neck twisted awkwardly. The doctor's features were gray as he looked up at Mabel. "I'm sorry. Her neck is broken. She's dead."

Mabel's knees gave way, and the marshal had to catch her to keep her from falling.

While Mabel wept loudly, Dr. Dane rolled the body face-down, stood up, then waited for Mabel to gain control of her emotions. This came within a minute or so, and then she said in a shaky voice, "You must be right about her self-infliction, Doctor. She was trying to run away."

Dr. Dane nodded. "It appears that she was."

Mabel swallowed. "She must have jumped off the bed the instant I started downstairs to answer your knock."

"Mm-hmm. When she fell from that second-story ledge up there, she landed on her head. That's what broke her neck. Let's see if those welts are gone."

Mabel and the marshal looked on intently as Dr. Dane knelt down, pulled the blouse loose from under the waist of Cassandra's skirt, and exposed her bare back.

There were no welts.

Mabel gasped. "Doctor, you were right!"

"You sure were," said Marshal Merrell in a low voice.

Mabel looked at the doctor. "I wonder why we didn't hear her scream when she fell."

Dr. Dane rubbed his chin. "She was probably so frightened when she slipped that it took her breath away. She must have let out a gasp, rather than a scream."

Mabel nodded. "I should tell you that Cassandra got nervous when you hadn't shown up in three hours and said she didn't want you to see her again. I was to tell you that you were not needed and to send you away. Now I know why."

Dr. Dane stood up.

Mabel said, "Doctor, Marshal, the only thing that girl loved was money. I'm so glad to know that Kirby Holton is innocent." She frowned and added, "I think I know what she used to draw those welts on her back."

"What was it?" asked Dr. Dane.

"I want to know, too," said Merrell.

"I'll show you. Would you gentlemen carry her body into the house for me?"

Trying not to do any more damage to the body, the two men carried it carefully into the house and placed it on the sofa in the parlor. Mabel covered it with a blanket. "I'll have the undertaker come and get the body."

Mabel then led them upstairs to Cassandra's room, opened one of the drawers in the armoire, and took out the Chinese backscratcher. "Here. This is what she used, I'm sure."

When Dr. Dane looked closely at it, he noted the small spaces between the prongs. "Mm-hmm. This is indeed what she used to make the crisscrossed welts on her back."

The marshal shook his head in wonderment. "I'm sure glad I didn't arrest Kirby Holton."

Dr. Dane grinned. "Me too. Well, I've got to get home. Mabel, I'm sorry for your loss."

Merrell said, "Me too, ma'am. You have my condolences."

She thanked both of them. Then the marshal said, "How about I stop by the undertaking parlor and tell Mr. Baldwin you need him to come and pick up the body?"

Mabel nodded. "I would appreciate that."

When Mabel closed the front door as the two men were leaving, she wept silently as she returned to the parlor. She went to the sofa, pulled the blanket back from her niece's lifeless face, and drew a shuddering breath. Her voice quivered as she said, "Well, Cassandra, now you know there is a God."

TWENTY-FOUR

A few weeks later

On Thursday, September 15, Dr. Dane Logan walked an elderly couple to the front door of his office after treating the woman for a skin rash. He told her to apply the salve he had given her regularly, and as they went out the door, he turned around and walked back in to the examining room at the rear of the building. Tharyn was doing some cleanup work at one of the examining tables, and Dane noticed that there were tears in her eyes.

He stepped up to her with concern showing on his face. "Sweetheart, are you all right?"

She looked up at him, brushed at her tears, and nodded. "I'm all right, It's— it's—"

"Melinda?"

"Uh-huh. I'm just having a tough time over her death. I know she's in a far better place than we are, but it's still hard to let her go."

"Hello-o-o!" came a familiar voice from the office out front.

"Charlie Holmes," said Dane. "Must have a telegram for us. I'll go see what it is."

"All right, honey. I'm almost through here."

Dane hurried through the door, and Tharyn hurried to finish her cleaning job. "Help me, Lord," she said, her voice quivering. "I just miss Melinda so much."

A few minutes later she completed the job and went into the office to find her husband holding a telegram in his hand and talking to the Western Union agent.

Charlie Holmes greeted her with a warm smile. Dane turned to her and said, "Telegram's from Dr. Tim Braden, honey. He says that Dr. Carroll has pronounced Nelda Cox able to travel. He will be bringing the Coxes home on Saturday. They will arrive sometime in late afternoon."

When Charlie was gone, Dane and Tharyn talked excitedly about Nelda being able to come home and about getting to see Tim again.

Tharyn looked up at her husband. "I sure hope Tim has adjusted better to Melinda's death than I have."

Suddenly a rider halted out front, slid from the saddle, and headed for the door.

Tharyn said, "Sherrie must be about to give birth."

"I'd say so," said Dr. Dane, reaching for his medical bag on a nearby shelf.

Sam Drummond's wife was due to give birth to their first child. Sam's parents, Chet and Alice Drummond, owned a cattle ranch in the mountains a few miles southwest of Central City. Sam and Sherrie lived in a small house on the Drummond ranch, which was not far from the Jack Bates ranch.

When Sam came through the door, he grinned when he saw the medical bag in Dr. Dane's hand. "Saw me coming, didn't you?"

"Sure did. When did her labor pains start?"

"About three hours ago. Sherrie wouldn't let me come after you till the pains got closer together."

"Let's go. I've got my horse today, instead of the buggy."

"Yeah. I noticed him out there at the hitch rail. We can get there faster with you in the saddle."

"You go ahead and mount up, Sam. I'll kiss my wife and be right with you."

At the Drummond ranch, Dr. Dane had just delivered Sherrie's new baby boy when the grandfather looked out the window of the bedroom window in the small house and growled, "Indians! They're stealing some of our cattle!"

Dr. Dane looked out and immediately saw that they were Utes.

Alice gasped and moved close to Sherrie where she lay in the bed, holding the baby.

Chet and Sam dashed into the kitchen where Sam had a pair of rifles standing in the corner by the back door. They grabbed the rifles, dashed out the door, jumped off the porch, shouldered the weapons, and opened fire on the small band of Utes.

The Indians turned around on their horses' backs and fired in return, but when bullets kept coming from the ranchers' rifles, they put their mounts to a gallop, leaving the stolen cattle behind.

One of the Indians was hit, and though he tried to stay on his horse's back while the rest of the band was galloping away, he finally fell to the ground. His horse followed the others at a full gallop.

At this point, Dr. Dane had joined Chet and Sam, and all three saw the wounded Indian fall from the horse.

The other Indians suddenly realized their companion was not with them, and when they looked back and saw him on the ground, they began pulling rein to turn around. At the same time, a cavalry patrol from Fort Junction had heard the gunfire and was charging at them speedily from off to their right. They wheeled their mounts and galloped away with the patrol after them.

Burning with anger, Chet Drummond grumbled, "I hope they kill every one of those thieving savages! I'm gonna kill that one on the ground!"

Even as he spoke those last words, he charged across the yard, gripping the rifle.

Dr. Dane bolted after Chet, and Sam was on the doctor's heels.

The wounded Ute was lying on the ground in the field some sixty or seventy yards away with a bullet in the upper thigh of his left leg. When he saw Chet running toward him, rifle in hand, he painfully crawled toward his rifle, which lay in the grass a few feet away.

Chet beat him to it, kicked the Indian's rifle out of his reach, and took aim at his head.

The Indian's eyes bulged.

Dr. Dane came running up, shouting, "No! Chet, don't shoot him!"

Chet held the rifle pointed at the Indian's head and looked at the doctor. "Why not?"

"Because he's wounded and unarmed."

Chet's temper gave his tanned cheeks a wicked, honed-down tautness. "So what?"

"If you shoot him, it will be murder!"

Chet's teeth showed in a grimace of wrath. "Indians ain't human! They're nothing but wild beasts that need to be exterminated!"

Dr. Dane hastily placed himself between the rancher and the fallen Ute. "Listen to me, Chet! This Indian is a human being. He will bleed to death if he isn't treated immediately."

The wounded Indian looked on in thankful amazement at the white man.

Dr. Dane bent down and picked the warrior up, cradling him in his arms. "Do you speak English?"

The Indian nodded.

"Good. I'm Dr. Dane Logan from Central City. I'm going to take the bullet out of your leg and stitch you up quickly so you don't bleed to death." He turned to Chet. "I'll need a table to lay him on while I work on the wound."

Chet's features were like stone. The look in his eyes told the doctor he was going to refuse just as Sam said, "Dad, Dr. Logan's right. This Indian is a human being. We can't stand in the way of his life being saved."

The older Drummond wiped a hand over his mouth, then looked at the doctor. "All right. There's a table on the front porch of the big house."

"Fine. Sam, would you go get my medical bag for me?"

Sam nodded and ran toward his house.

Moments later, Dr. Dane laid the young warrior on the table while Chet and Sam looked on.

Dr. Dane opened his medical bag, and quickly gave the Indian a dose of laudanum. As he was capping the bottle, the Indian said in a strained voice, "Thank you, Dr. Dane Logan, for keeping the rancher from killing me. I am Latawga, son of Chief Tando."

The Drummond men looked at each other, eyes wide.

Dr. Dane nodded. "I have heard much about your father, Latawga."

When the surgery was completed, and the wound had been bandaged, Latawga looked up at the doctor with slightly clouded eyes. "Thank you for saving my life a second time, Dr. Dane Logan. I would have soon bled to death if you had not taken care of me. I—I need to ask you to do something else for me."

Dr. Dane smiled down at him. "Yes?"

"Would you take me home to my village?"

"Don't do it, Doctor!" blurted Chet Drummond. "Those savages will kill you!"

Latawga rolled his head back and forth, setting his gaze on the rancher. "No. When my father and the others in the village see Dr. Dane Logan bringing me into the village, they will not harm him." He looked up at the doctor. "I will tell my father what you did to save my life. Both times. You will not be harmed, I promise."

Dr. Dane said, "I will put you on my horse with me and take you home."

Chet shook his head. "Doc, I hope this savage is telling you the truth."

"He is. I am sure of it."

"Me, too," said Sam. "And, Doctor, thank you for delivering our new son. I'll stop by your office tomorrow and pay the bill."

At Chief Tando's village, he and his people were wondering why subchief Nandano and his band—including Latawga—had not returned with stolen cattle.

Tando and a group of his warriors were discussing the fact that the band should have been back some time ago when one of the Ute sentries at the northeast side of the village called out loudly, "Chief Tando! A white man is riding in with a wounded warrior on his horse!"

The sentry's voice carried throughout the village. Melinda Scott Kenyon was standing in front of the chief's tepee, braiding Leela's long black hair. Leela was sitting on a wooden chair that had been stolen from some white man's ranch. Melinda looked up to catch sight of the white man who was bringing in the wounded Ute.

Leela stood up and ran her gaze in the same direction.

As Tando and some of his warriors hurried toward the edge of the village, one of them cried, "Chief Tando! The wounded warrior is Latawga!"

Hearing the name of her son, Leela left Melinda at the tepee and hurried in that direction.

Melinda stood looking on as many of the villagers began moving that way.

When Dr. Dane and Latawga were met at the edge of the village, Latawga was lowered into the arms of two warriors by the doctor. As Latawga was being held in the warriors' arms, his parents moved up to him and he told them that the white man was Dr. Dane Logan from Central City, who had saved his life.

Chief Tando invited the doctor to dismount.

Dr. Dane stood at the edge of the group who had gathered as Latawga told the story to his father and mother of how he was shot in the leg while he and the others in the band were stealing cattle from a ranch. He explained how the others in the band were being chased by an army patrol the last time he saw them.

Latawga then told how this good man, Dr. Dane Logan— who happened to be at the ranch delivering a baby—kept the rancher from killing him and saved his life a second time by removing the bullet from his leg and stitching it up so he would not bleed to death.

Chief Tando looked at the doctor with appreciative eyes. "I want to thank you, Dr. Dane Logan, for saving my son's life."

Dr. Dane smiled. "Chief, I'm just glad I was there so I could save Latawga's life. The ranchers wouldn't——" Dr. Dane's attention was drawn to a blond woman running toward him, calling his name.

Suddenly he recognized her and while his heart was hammering his ribs and she was drawing near, he gasped. "Melinda! Melinda! You're alive!"

The publisher and author would love to hear your comments about this book. *Please contact us at:* www.allacy.com

Visit

www.letstalkfiction.com

today!

Fiction Readers Unite!

Y ou've just found a new way to feed your fiction addiction. Letstalkfiction.com is a place where fiction readers can come together to learn about new fiction releases from Multnomah. You can read about the latest book releases, catch a behind-the-scenes look at your favorite authors, sign up to receive the most current book information, and much more. Everything you need to make the most out of your fictional world can be found at www.letstalkfiction.com. Come and join the network!

Frontier Doctor Trilogy

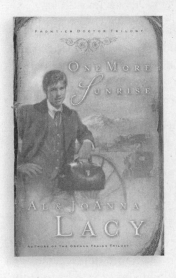

ONE MORE SUNRISE
Frontier Doctor trilogy, book one

Countless perils menaced the early settlers of the Wild West—and not the least of them was the lack of medical care. Dr. Dane Logan, a former street waif puts his lifelong dream to work filling this need. His renown as a surgeon spreads throughout the frontier, even while his love grows for the beautiful Tharyn, an orphan he lost contact with when he left New York City as a child. Will happiness in love ever come to Dane—or will the roving Tag Moran gang bring his hopes to a dark end?

ISBN 1-59052-308-3

BELOVED PHYSICIAN
Frontier Doctor trilogy, book two

Dane and Tharyn Logan, back from their honeymoon, take over a medical practice in Central City and join the church there. It's not long before Dane establishes a name for himself. After he risks his life to rescue the mayor, the townspeople officially dub Dane the "beloved physician of Central City." Nurse Tharyn faces a challenge of her own when her dear friend Melinda is captured by the local band of renegade Utes. Melinda's friends and fiancé don't know any better than to give her up for dead...

ISBN 1-59052-313-X

Orphan Trains Trilogy

The Little Sparrows
#1 The Orphan Trains Trilogy

Follow the orphan train out West as children's hearts are mended and God's hand restores laughter to grieving families…in a marvelous story of His perfect providence.

ISBN 1-59052-063-7

All My Tomorrows
#2 The Orphan Trains Trilogy

Sixty-two abandoned children leave New York on a train headed west, oblivious of what's in store. But their paths are being watched by someone who carefully plans all their tomorrows.

ISBN 1-59052-130-7

Whispers in the Wind
#3 The Orphan Trains Trilogy

Dane Weston's dream is to become a doctor. Then his family is murdered and he ends up in a colony of street waifs begging for food…

ISBN 1-57673-880-9